Justin stood and began to unbuckle his belt. "Are you coming out?" he asked.

"I am not. And I doubt that you're going to take off your pants either," she retorted confidently.

"Well, you're wrong, so you'd better turn your back."

To her surprise he started undoing the buttons. About two seconds later he faced her naked, and he was magnificent. She simply stood in the creek, the water swirling around her, and stared. His thighs and calves were corded with muscle, beautifully formed, the result of years in the saddle she supposed.

"Damn it, Anne, I don't know a woman in the world who'd want to stare at a naked man." He sounded furious, and she raised her eyes to his, smiling a little.

"Why, Justin," she said, laughter overcoming her, "I believe you're flustered."

Widow's Fire

ELIZABETH CHADWICK

LEISURE BOOKS   NEW YORK CITY

*For Joann, good friend and fellow writer,
who read this book in manuscript form
almost as many times as I did.*

A LEISURE BOOK ®

July 1990

Published by

Dorchester Publishing Co., Inc.
276 Fifth Avenue
New York, NY 10001

Printed in the United States of America.

CHAPTER
One

"**Y**ou ain't gonna believe what I just seen," said Rollo Tandy, his voice barely audible above the din of the milling tangle of riders and cattle spread out on the prairie below.

Justin Harte squinted into the dust cloud and asked himself why he hadn't elected to start the roundup at home in Palo Pinto County instead of miles to the east in Tarrant County. At least in the cedar brakes and hills of his home range, the noise would have been muted by broken country. Here, even before the cattle were driven together for cutting and branding, the uproar made it almost impossible to pass on orders. It was noisier than a trail drive.

"You hearin' me, Justin?" Rollo demanded. "I said I just seen somethin' you ain't gonna believe."

If Rollo's news was bad, which it probably was, Justin didn't want to hear it. They had yet to clear the first range, and there had already been enough trouble.

"A woman! I seen a woman back there by the creek."

Justin turned to stare at his foreman, a short, broad-faced man who couldn't have looked more indignant had he discovered a hundred Comanche warriors driving off the remuda.

"Think she was in Morehead's camp."

Justin swore under his breath. Colonel Morehead had been a problem from the first day. Evidently the colonel had expected to be chosen roundup boss, for he had turned sullen and uncooperative after Justin's election by the other ranchers. "Are you telling me he brought along that brainless, young flirt—"

"'Twarn't his daughter," Rollo interrupted. "'Peared to be some widder woman. I asked her real polite what was she doin' there, an' she like to bit my head off."

"Keep an eye on things," Justin instructed, wheeling his horse toward the creek along which the twelve participating outfits had scattered their camps.

A woman at spring roundup? He hoped that Rollo was mistaken. Maybe she was just passing through, stopping to water and rest her horses, but if so, what the hell was she doing way out here? The camp wasn't that close to the Fort Worth-Weatherford road. And if she had actually come with one of the outfits, God grant that she was wrinkled, weather-beaten and seventy years old. The last thing he needed was some young female distracting the men.

Anne dipped the second bucket into the creek and set off toward the fire, her black skirts swishing over trampled grass. She'd been up since dawn and, under the pressure of preparing one meal and starting another, still hadn't finished washing the tin plates from breakfast. Tomorrow the men would have to wash their own, she decided. She could put out buckets of hot water and. . . .

"Ma'am, would you mind telling me what you're doing here?"

She was so startled to find her way blocked by a very

grim-looking rider mounted on a large blood bay that she dropped the buckets, causing the water to splash her skirt and shoes, turn the patch of churned dirt around her to mud, and to set off her already smoldering temper. "Do you always sneak up on defenseless women?" she demanded, her anger aimed at herself as much as at the stranger because she had so thoughtlessly left her rifle inside the chuck wagon where she couldn't use it to chase off this glowering cowboy.

"Riding a horse into a camp can't rightly be called sneaking up," muttered Justin, who was thinking, with a good deal of irritation, that this particular female sounded more like a confounded shrew than a defenseless woman. "And my question still stands unanswered, ma'am. This is a roundup camp and no place for a woman. You'd best go back to wherever you came from."

"I'd be delighted to," snapped Anne, who had protested vigorously when the colonel added chuck-wagon cook to the already extensive list of her responsibilities. "Why don't you take it up with my stepfather, Colonel Bates Morehead?"

"I've met Miss Sissie Morehead, ma'am, and you are not—"

"Sissie," Anne finished for him. "That's right; I'm not. I'm Anne McAuliffe. Colonel Morehead is my stepfather, although why I should have to explain that to you, I don't know."

"Look, Miss McAuliffe—"

"Mrs. McAuliffe."

"Mrs. McAuliffe." Justin glared at her, increasingly impatient because he should be back at the roundup, not in camp arguing with a woman who wore the ugliest black bonnet he'd ever seen in his life. "If you're married, why doesn't your husband—"

"My husband is dead, Mr. . . . What is *your* name, if I may ask?"

"Harte. Justin Harte."

"I might have known," muttered Anne, who had endured a surfeit of complaints from her stepfather about the arrogant frontier cattleman who had been elected captain of the roundup over men of more experience like himself.

"You might have known what?" demanded Harte.

Anne returned his glare. For once, she agreed with her stepfather. Mr. Justin Harte seemed a very rude and unpleasant person.

"Oh, it's Mr. Harte come to call! Hello, Mr. Harte."

The two combatants looked away from each other toward the chuck wagon from which seventeen-year-old Sissie Morehead emerged, clad in a fashionable, if unsuitable, pink dress with a flounced and pleated bustle and matching ruffled parasol. Anne's mouth fell open. Her half sister had slept through the entire morning's work. So how had she managed to wake up and get herself, unaided, into that outfit in the brief time since Mr. Harte's arrival? It was obvious to Anne that Sissie had dressed because of the rancher, for Sissie was taking dead aim at Justin Harte with her blond curls aflutter and her parasol tilted fetchingly.

"Miss Sissie." Harte removed his hat, something he hadn't seen fit to do for Anne. She was about to take offense when she got her first good look at the man and her heart and breath froze while an unexpected flash of heat suffused her body. She hadn't felt that lightning-struck reaction to a man since she had walked into the arms of David McAuliffe on their wedding night. Drawing an unsteady breath, she watched helplessly as Sissie began to test her newly realized femininity on yet another target.

"Could I prevail upon you, Mr. Harte, to help me down from this wagon?" Sissie asked, smiling prettily from beneath her parasol.

Justin Harte replaced his hat, covering a head of dark, curly hair. His beard and mustache, close cut and thick, emphasized a stubborn jaw and unsmiling lips whose sensuality drew Anne's fascinated attention. What color had his eyes been? Dark as well, she thought, and shadowed by heavy brows. He had a powerful face, as powerful as the hard-muscled body now swinging down from the saddle. Suppressing a sigh, Anne backed away as he reached for her sister's tiny, tightly-corseted waist.

Sissie gave him a demure smile and leaned forward provocatively as he lifted her off the wagon, but all her come-hither maneuvers were wasted. Harte did not return Sissie's smile; instead, he frowned and deposited the girl in the patch of mud created by the spilled water buckets. Anne had to swallow a sudden, unseemly bubble of laughter as pink ruffles met brown mud.

Sissie gave a shriek, then, her mouth trembling, said reproachfully, "You've set me down in the mud, Mr. Harte. I'm standing in this nasty mud in my new kid boots."

"Like as not you'll be standing in a sea of mud if you stick with this roundup," said Justin Harte, obviously not the least regretful over his cavalier treatment of a new gown, a gown which Anne herself had made on her much-prized sewing machine.

"I'll never get the stains off," Sissie wailed.

"Wear brown from now on," suggested Harte.

"Brown!" exclaimed Sissie, horrified.

"Under the circumstances, it's more sensible than pink," he replied solemnly. "I'm wearing brown myself."

Anne could have sworn there was a twinkle in his eye. Could he have dumped Sissie into that puddle deliberately?

"Now maybe you ladies could tell me just what you're doing here?" he continued humorlessly, destroying Anne's brief conviction that he might be more personable than he seemed.

"I'm here to cook," said Anne. "As for my sister, I'm

not sure what she's doing here, other than ruining a perfectly good dress."

Sissie sniffed.

"The smaller ranchers don't bring their own cooks. Your stepfather's men should be eating at my camp or at any of the larger outfits'."

"Tell him that!" snapped Anne.

"I intend to," Harte replied. Then he tipped his hat to the two women, murmuring, "Ladies," and, mounting, rode away.

"Beastly man," muttered Sissie, who had stuck her foot out and was staring in anguish at one muddy, but fashionable, buttoned kid boot.

Anne watched him ride away. If he was beastly, he was a magnificent beast. She turned back to her sister, who still pouted tearfully.

"What am I going to do?" Sissie wailed, shaking the muddy hem of her skirt as if Anne could make the offending stains disappear by magic.

"You could do some dishes," Anne suggested.

"I meant about my dress."

Anne sighed. How had her sister managed to get so self-absorbed in just six years? Sissie had been a sweet little girl of eleven when Anne left New Orleans. Now, she was selfish and couldn't be persuaded to raise her hand to anything but the changing of her own clothes.

Justin had put off seeing the colonel all day only to be reminded of it by Homer Teasdale, a Parker County rancher whose outfit was eating at Justin's chuck wagon. After lamenting about how many cattle he was losing to rustlers—a problem common to all the ranchers—Homer had asked what Justin knew about the two women reputed to be in Colonel Morehead's camp.

"Damn," muttered Justin, rising from the campfire and stretching. "Gotta do something about that right now."

"You mean run 'em off?" asked Homer, alarmed. "Say, that'd be too bad. Why, I wouldn't mind visitin' over there myself of an evenin'. 'Cept for the colonel, acourse. Never recall meetin' a man more ornery. Not likely you'll get too far with him, Justin. No sir. . . ."

So it had proved as Justin watched Bates Morehead stalk away after refusing to send his women home. Tradition be damned, he had said when Justin pointed out that the smaller outfits always shared meals at the chuck wagons of the larger outfits. Morehead intended to take care of his own men and didn't want to be beholden to anyone; furthermore, his stepdaughter did the cooking and would continue to do so. As for his daughter Sissie, he wanted her there where he could keep an eye on her, and there she would stay, and no ex-traildriver from the frontier was going to tell Colonel Bates Morehead how to handle his womenfolk, his hired hands, or anything else.

Justin shook his head in disgust and considered his options, one of which was to expel Morehead and his daughters from the roundup. As captain he had that right if his orders were ignored. And if Homer's reaction to the presence of women in camp was any indication, those two, or at least Sissie, would prove to be a pack of trouble as working hours grew longer and tempers shorter. Narrow-eyed, Justin watched the stiff, retreating back of the colonel.

"Ain't exactly cooperative, is he?"

Justin turned to Last Cauley, Morehead's foreman.

"You wouldn't be the first fella to wish the colonel had chose somewheres else to retire an' take up ranchin' once he quit the cavalry," Cauley said.

"It's hard to believe he was much of a cavalry officer," Justin muttered, "not if he was as poor a hand with horses and men as he seems to be with cattle and men."

"Well, I've heard him say as how any good cavalry officer makes a good rancher an' that's why he took it up, so I'd have to agree it ain't likely he was a good horse soldier. Like as not the Army couldn't wait to git rid of him." Last glanced around his camp at the lounging riders and grumbled quietly, "Fact is, we ain't been able to keep hardly any good hands since '73 when he bought out Gilchrist.

"But his stepdaughter Miz Annie, she's a whole different breed," continued Cauley more cheerfully. "That little lady ain't gonna cause no trouble. Why, anyone can tell you that the first decent food we had at the Bar M's been since the colonel brought her home after her husband died." Cauley's grin widened appreciatively. "An' she's pretty too."

Justin looked at the man with astonishment. Pretty? The woman in the hideous bonnet? "And Sissie Morehead?" he asked. "You think she'll make no trouble?"

"We–l–l–l." Last considered the matter as he rolled himself a cigarette, his long, weathered face thoughtful. "Maybe Miz Annie, she'll keep the young 'un in line. I hear she sorta raised Miz Sissie afore. . . ."

Justin had stopped listening. Across the clearing a woman had just stepped into the circle of light from the campfire, a woman in black whose hair glowed with a firelight of its own and whose skin was so fair and delicate that Justin was amazed to find that he couldn't see right through it.

"Mr. Harte," she said, nodding to him before she crossed to the wagon.

Justin's eyes were drawn irresistibly after her.

"Sure would hate to see Miz Annie go home," said the foreman.

"Then make sure she and her sister stay by their own fire," said Justin brusquely, and he turned to leave, but the memory of Anne McAuliffe's wide brown eyes and flaming hair pursued him as he rode back to his own camp.

* * *

The roundup had moved west into Parker County and the Cross Timbers. Each night at the campfire the exasperated cowboys complained of having to chase cattle out of the woods. Anne, however, was missing all the excitement. She had seen nothing but the back end of the chuck wagon since Justin Harte's visit to their camp. Within minutes of his departure, their foreman had convinced the colonel, who didn't take contradiction lightly, that his daughters would have to stay with the wagon or risk getting themselves and the colonel expelled from the roundup.

As a result, the colonel was more irascible than ever; Sissie was pouting by day and practicing her flirtation techniques in the evening on her only available targets, several young cowboys in her father's outfit; and Anne was bored to the point of screaming and determined to see some of the roundup no matter what Justin Harte or her stepfather wanted. If she got sent home, fine. She hadn't wanted to come in the first place. In fact, she should be back at the ranch house starting her garden, not tied to a chuck wagon dishing up beans, biscuits and fresh-killed beef to dusty cowhands.

That morning by nine o'clock she had tossed the last scrubbed pot from breakfast into the crude cabinet in the back of the chuck wagon, put enough flour, salt, and water into her sourdough keg to replace what she had used for the breakfast biscuits, and closed up the tailgate that served as her working surface. Anne was going riding while the stew simmered in a huge iron kettle. Stew and biscuits would be what they got for their midday and evening meals.

She clambered into the wagon, changed into her one black riding habit, and dragged her sidesaddle out over the tongue. Sissie hardly stirred except for a mumbled question about breakfast, which made Anne chuckle. This was one morning when young Miss Sissie was going to have to get her own breakfast or go hungry till midday. After tossing her saddle onto the horse she had talked their wrangler into roping for her, she used a turned-over pot as a mounting block, and off she went toward the sounds of the roundup.

Transportation hadn't been easy to obtain. "What if Indians raid the camp?" she had asked the reluctant young wrangler, who was sure the colonel or the foreman would fire him if they found out he'd brought her a horse. "I'd have no way to escape," she'd told him.

"You could shoot 'em, Miss Annie," he'd suggested hopefully. "I seen you shoot, ma'am. Why, you're almost as good a shot as me."

"No such thing," Anne had said flatteringly, although she was actually a better marksman than he and had, in fact, shot several Indians during those years at frontier posts with David.

"Ain't no Indians anyway these days, ma'am. Not around here. Not since Colonel Mackenzie done drove 'em off back in '74."

No one knew that better than Anne, whose husband had taken an arrow in his lung and a bullet in his thigh at Palo Duro Canyon in September of '74. "Can you promise me they won't come riding off the reservation, catching me without a horse?"

"The Indian Territories are miles from here, Miss Annie."

"What if there's a stampede?"

"Cain't no cattle stampede through the trees."

"A bull might come wandering into camp. The men are always talking about flushing cattle out of the woods. What am I supposed to do? Climb a tree? Could you climb a tree in a dress?" She'd worn him down, but it hadn't been easy.

Still, it felt glorious to be riding again. She'd hardly had the time since coming to her stepfather's ranch. There was so much to be done and no one to do it but her. How had they managed before? she wondered. She couldn't believe that Sissie had handled all the household chores.

Guiding the horse carefully toward the sounds of men and animals, she finally emerged from the post oak grove onto a ledge overlooking the valley where they were driving the scattered herds in. And there was Justin Harte. She hadn't seen him, except at a distance, since his confrontation with her stepfather. He visited other camps but not theirs. Why? she wondered. Who was he avoiding?

Anne was overcome with a spirit of perversity that was one-third sheer boredom, one-third anger at herself for finding him attractive—she hadn't forgotten that unsettling first reaction—and one-third pique because he'd stared at her so pointedly across the campfire and then never returned for a second look. For these reasons, she headed straight toward him, then turned her horse so close to his that her long riding skirt brushed his stirrup. "Good morning, Mr. Harte," she said as coolly as if they'd met on the street in Weatherford.

He turned such hot, hard eyes on her that she felt a fiery tingle down her spine. And his eyes were blue—deep, dark blue. "Mrs. McAuliffe. Have you lost your way?" he asked with a forbidding frown. "If so, I believe your camp is northwesterly. Through those trees." He raised his hand to point the direction, but his eyes were on her hair.

Anne had seen men look at her that way. David had stared at her in the same way when she was seventeen and attending her first officers' ball. Then she froze, for Justin Harte's hand was moving tentatively, not to command the direction of her departure, but to touch a bright, curling strand that had escaped her high chignon.

"Where's your bonnet?" he demanded, pulling his fingers back abruptly from the curl.

Anne drew a belated breath. Her bonnet? She couldn't believe that he had liked that bonnet. It had been a gift, secondhand, from another officer's wife when she needed a black bonnet for her husband's funeral—an ugly thing that puffed out and up in back and had a deep brim, stiffened with hickory splits, that thrust out around her face even further because of the double row of ruffles. Her face practically disappeared from view in that bonnet.

But then, of course, Justin Harte hadn't been taken with her bonnet. He just wanted her hair covered. It was her hair he was taken with. Anne smiled mischievously and watched his frown deepen. What a grim man he was. That twinkle she had thought she had detected in his eye after he dumped Sissie into the mud must have been a gleam of ill temper instead.

"My bonnet, which you have so kindly asked after, Mr. Harte, is back in the wagon. Since I am riding, I'm wearing my riding hat." She gestured to the small brimmed confection trimmed with black ribbons and feathers that tilted forward over her forehead and wasn't a riding hat at all. "Do you like it?" she asked gaily, as if she expected a compliment, which was, of course, the last thing she expected from Justin Harte.

"If you expect to stay with the roundup, Mrs. McAuliffe, you'd best head right back to camp where you belong."

"I have no intention of heading back to camp, Mr. Harte, and, for that matter, no interest in staying with the roundup, as I believe I've already told you. I've more pressing things to do than cook makeshift meals for dusty cowhands."

"I'm sure you have, Mrs. McAuliffe. No doubt, like your sister, you're looking for some eligible rancher to entice, or perhaps you're in the market for a second husband."

"On the contrary," said Anne angrily, "my plans for

spring do not include marriage, which would hardly be a proper goal for any woman so recently widowed. I have a garden that needs planting, and I had hoped to purchase several pigs, among other—"

"Pigs?" He looked almost comically astonished.

"Pigs, Mr. Harte. Did you think the bacon in your beans appeared magically on some butcher's shelf in Weatherford or wherever you go for supplies? Pigs must be raised, and I'm told this is prime pig country."

"This is cattle country," Justin sputtered.

"Be that as it may . . ." Anne shrugged and dropped the subject of pigs. "Then," she continued, "I've several good books I plan to read and a quilt pattern that needs trying. No, Mr. Harte, I'm not much of a coquette, so if you're looking for a flirtation, you'd best try Sissie. She likes to practice and might be willing to accommodate you, although you're a bit on the old side, to be sure." Then with a bright smile, Anne nudged her horse into motion. "Good day, Mr. Harte."

Before she indicated her intention of leaving, Justin had been staring at her with an expression more bemused than angry. When she wished him good day, he resumed frowning and snapped, "Just be sure you ride straight back to your camp, Mrs. McAuliffe."

"Indeed I won't, Mr. Harte," she called over her shoulder, "but you can certainly go complaining to my stepfather again if it pleases you."

"Say, Miss Annie, when you gonna make us some son-of-a-gun stew?"

Smiling, Anne looked up from the batch of biscuits she had just put into a heavy, covered iron pot she used as an oven. "Since I don't know what son-of-a-gun stew is," she said to Bennie Schultz, "I won't be making any unless you have the recipe." All the other hands were doubled over laughing, convincing her that some joke must be attached to son-of-a-gun stew.

"You planning to tell Mrs. McAuliffe what's in it, Schultz?" asked a voice from beyond the circle of firelight.

Bennie turned bright red and backed away from the fire.

"Well, I do believe it's Mr. Harte," Anne drawled. "Have you to come to tattle on me? Or maybe you've come to supplement my knowledge of roundup recipes? Well, Mr. Harte, what *is* in it?" she asked. If anyone had to be put on the spot, she'd choose Justin Harte, who was undoubtedly visiting their encampment to make trouble for her.

"I can list the ingredients, if you like," he replied.

"Ah, now, Harte, you ain't gonna—" one of the cowboys started to say.

"Please do." Anne gave her own stew a judicious twirl with the ladle.

The cowboys, having backed off sufficiently to distance themselves from any responsibility should the roundup boss really give her the recipe, were watching the unfolding scene with avid interest.

"Well?" prompted Anne.

"Son-of-a-gun stew's a trail-drive favorite," said Harte, who was once again staring at her. "It generally contains tongue, liver, melt, and either sweetbreads or prairie oysters. Since we've been castrating calves all day, Schultz here likely meant for you to use prairie oysters."

"I see." Anne willed herself not to blush, for she was sure that's what he intended her to do.

The cowboys were gaping, obviously surprised that Harte had actually mentioned calves' testicles in front of a lady, but then maybe he didn't consider her a lady.

"The accepted procedure is to roll the various ingredients in meal, fry them a little, then boil them with onions and—"

"Oh, you needn't bother to trouble yourself with the details, Mr. Harte," she interrupted, brushing the escaping curls away from her forehead and cheeks. "Since you're here to see me expelled from my cooking duties, our hands will have to share your son-of-a-gun stew in the future."

Bennie groaned and said to the roundup boss, "Sure, you're never gonna send Miss Annie home. She makes the best biscuits this side of the Red River."

Harte glanced at him, then at Anne. "Is that a fact?" he murmured. "And am I invited to sample your stew and your famous biscuits, Mrs. McAuliffe?"

Anne suppressed a tight smile and replied, "I'm afraid the stew has no prairie oysters in it, Mr. Harte, but you're welcome to join us if you don't mind the lack."

"Harte," boomed Colonel Morehead, who had just marched into the camp. "What's your business here?"

"I believe I've been invited to supper," said Harte, smiling at Anne. She blinked, astonished—well, actually, enchanted. He had a wonderful smile. She'd never have guessed. Feeling a bit dazed and clumsy, she dished up his supper. "However, I do have business with you, Colonel," he added.

Anne stiffened as he looked over at her, but she continued to pass plates to the men while she waited for him to complain to her stepfather about her. Harte took a spoonful of his stew and savored it. Then putting the spoon back on the tin plate, he said, "We'll be moving on to your range next, Morehead, which means you'll have the first cut. I need to know whether you want your calves branded or if you want to do it yourself later."

"Later," said Morehead. "We'll do our own."

"Hell, Colonel," Last Cauley interrupted, "it's a lot easier if—"

"I make the decisions here!" snapped the colonel, ignoring the resentful looks he was getting from the men in his outfit.

Anne sighed and wondered how many more hands

they were about to lose. It was becoming clear to her that her stepfather's stiff-necked discipline, which might have been acceptable in the Army, was anathema among the more democratic and easygoing ranch hands.

"Mighty good stew, Mrs. McAuliffe," Justin said, handing her his plate. "My thanks for your kind invitation." He turned to her stepfather. "We break camp tomorrow for the move west," he said brusquely. Morehead didn't bother to reply.

"Rumor has it you're worried about an Indian attack, Mrs. McAuliffe," said Justin, looking amused as he turned back to Anne. "I don't think you need be alarmed."

Anne watched him leave camp with a feeling of wistful surprise, both because it now seemed that he wasn't going to tell her stepfather she had been out riding that morning and because she wished that he would stay a bit longer.

Sighing, she bent to dish up her own meal. And where was Sissie? she wondered. Was the girl avoiding Justin Harte or had she lured some blushing cowboy into the woods?

Anne worried about her half sister. Sissie was going to get herself into trouble if she didn't watch out. And had anyone bothered to tell her just how girls *got* in trouble? Or was that another of the responsibilities the colonel expected Anne to assume in return for being taken into the bosom of his family, such as it was, after her husband's death?

CHAPTER

Two

Justin marveled that a woman in widow's weeds could look so tempting. Anne McAuliffe was kneeling in the spring grass by the creek, scrubbing clothes, with her black skirts fanned out around her, and her glowing hair tumbling from its pinnings. It also worried him that she could be so absorbed in her task as to miss the approach of a horse and rider. He cleared his throat to get her attention, and Anne, glancing sideways, sat back on her heels and brushed the straggling curls away from her face.

"You do choose the worst times to come visiting, Mr. Harte," she muttered as she pulled two chemises from the water and tossed them carelessly onto a flat rock to dry, evidently too tired even to consider that she had just displayed her intimate garments to a man she hardly knew.

"Why don't you turn the washing over to your sister?" he suggested. "From what I hear, you have your hands full cooking for all those admirers."

"That's certainly the truth," said Anne wearily. "I sometimes think every cowboy in Texas has dropped by our chuck wagon to get acquainted with Sissie and eat my food."

It irritated him to admit it, but Justin knew that Sissie Morehead was not the only attraction in the Bar M camp. Every unmarried cattleman on roundup had managed to take a look at Anne McAuliffe, and most stayed to eat. He found it hard to believe that she was unaware of the interest she created. Homer Teasdale, for instance, had been absent from Justin's mess three nights running.

"I don't know what the colonel's thinking of," she grumbled. "I don't have the supplies to feed all those people, and I'm running out of the energy as well."

"In that case, as you're so overworked, the report that you want to watch the branding must have been mistaken."

"No, it wasn't," said Anne hastily. "I do want to, not that you'll let me, I suppose." Because Harte had not told her stepfather of her last outbreak of defiance, she had tried to be cooperative by staying at the camp.

"Come along then," Justin said brusquely. "Since I can't afford to send you with someone who would find you a distraction, I've come to escort you myself."

"Well, that's a gracious invitation if ever I heard one!" snapped Anne. "However, I accept." She rose from the grass with the last of the clothes dripping in her hands and started back toward the wagon, then halted briefly as a thought occurred to her. "What about Sissie?"

"I'm sure your sister can continue to sleep without your assistance," he replied.

"I suppose she can at that." Smiling, Anne set out again, calling over her shoulder, "I'll only be a minute," as she climbed into the wagon.

"See that you are," Justin muttered and was astonished to find her as good as her word. He had brought a horse for her from his own remuda and saddled it when she produced her sidesaddle, although he muttered that a sidesaddle was more dangerous than riding bareback.

"Well, it's that or wear pants," said Anne cheerfully, "and I'm sure you're much too conservative to approve of a woman in pants."

Justin grunted noncommitally and boosted her onto the horse's back. As she settled her skirts to cover both ankles and boots as modestly as a lady should, Justin swung astride.

"Besides," she added, "I do well enough in a sidesaddle. We used to have hunting parties out at Fort Richardson, for wolves and such."

He glanced at her in surprise. "Fort Richardson?"

"Yes, my husband was posted there with Ranald Mackenzie from the end of 1870 till September of '74."

Justin remarked soberly that the frontier ranchers, who had suffered for years from Indian depredations, owed Mackenzie and his Fourth Cavalry a great debt for driving the Kiowas and Comanches back onto the reservations. Then he asked sympathetically if her husband had been killed at Palo Duro Canyon.

"No," Anne replied, "but he was wounded severely. We were posted to Fort Griffin after that."

"A rowdy town," Justin commented as he held a branch aside for her.

"No more than Jacksboro," said Anne of the nearest town to Fort Richardson, "but David asked for frontier duty. We'd been several years in New Orleans, and he was tired of it."

"No doubt you were opposed," Justin remarked. "Women invariably prefer comfortable city life to the frontier."

"What nonsense!" Anne snapped. "Can you imagine trying to bring up Sissie in a place as corrupt as New Orleans? And besides that, the locals hated us. We were Yankees—the same bluecoats who'd occupied the city under General Butler during the war and later backed a carpetbag government they despised. I've never lived in a more hostile, less comfortable place in my life."

Justin's brows rose sardonically. "Less comfortable than Jacksboro or Fort Griffin?"

"I'm not talking about physical comfort," Anne said. "At least, nobody hated us on the frontier. Well, the Indians. But no matter how crude and rough the men in those towns were, they were respectful in their way, and my husband was devoted to Mackenzie."

"And you were evidently devoted to your husband's interests," mused Justin, looking rather surprised. "He was a lucky man."

"Perhaps, but his luck ran out," she said sadly.

"He died of his wounds?"

"He was shot to death by one of his own men in a drunken quarrel at a gambling table," Anne muttered.

Justin's heavy brows rose.

"It was no reflection on David. He was a good officer," she added defensively. "It's just that Fort Griffin was a terrible place for the enlisted men. They lived in small, miserable, filthy barracks, and under conditions so disgusting they were glad to be out on patrol. They'd fight anyone, including their own officers, and David"—she looked troubled—"well, David was so terribly unhappy. Because he'd been so badly wounded, he lost his place with Mackenzie. If he'd lived, I expect he'd have had to leave the cavalry."

As she talked, she'd been staring blindly at the scene in front of her, but when she actually began to see it, she was astounded at the mass confusion—milling cattle, shouting horsemen with ropes swinging, bawling calves pulled down for branding, the smell of burning cowhide. "Good heavens," Anne exclaimed, "is it like that every day?"

Justin smiled. "Not every day, but most. However, you can expect it to be less noisy and more beautiful when we get into Palo Pinto."

Anne was surprised that a man like Justin Harte was

sensitive to the beauty of the land. "Is that where you live?"

He nodded.

"What's it like?"

Justin, who had been staring dourly at a tussle between a cowboy and a calf that didn't seem to want its turn with the branding iron, took a long time to answer. "Mountains, streams, good grass in the valleys. It's fine winter range because the broken country protects the stock. There's some prairie, cedar brakes in the west. Cedar rail makes a good horse corral."

Anne laughed aloud. How like a man to speak of beauty and then equate it with winter range and cedar rails.

"Well, you seem to have perked up." He had finally turned to look at her.

"Certainly. Anything's better than washing other people's clothes in a cold creek," said Anne. "What are they doing over there? It looks like they're cutting off the calves' ears. Is that for some alternate version of son-of-a-gun stew?"

Justin's mouth twitched in the beginnings of a smile, and he explained that each outfit had its own way of marking the ears for further identification. Over the next half-hour Anne asked dozens of questions until at one point Justin said, "Mrs. McAuliffe, it's not necessary for you to pretend an interest in the cattle business."

Anne looked at him with amazement. The women he knew must be idiots, she decided. Or maybe he didn't know any women. That might explain his suspicious nature where her sex was concerned. "Mr. Harte," she replied, "I live on a ranch now. Of course, I'm interested in the cattle business."

After that, he answered her more readily and at greater length until finally Anne exclaimed impulsively, "You can be downright good company when you put your mind to it, Mr. Harte."

The relaxed expression disappeared from his face, and he suggested coolly that it was time she returned to her own camp.

Having meant her words as a compliment, Anne's lips compressed, and she whirled her horse, leaving without a word. What was the man's problem? she wondered. It almost seemed as if he wanted her to dislike him, which she had good cause to do. Unfortunately, she couldn't quite sustain the healthy animosity his behavior warranted. Embarrassing as it was to admit, she liked his looks, which was a stupid reason to put up with his rudeness.

Justin wondered how it was he always managed to end up saying something surly to Anne McAuliffe. He didn't think of himself as an unpleasant man, and he certainly didn't dislike her, which was probably where the trouble lay. He enjoyed her company more than he should and, consequently, always meant to stay right out of her path, but. . . .

"Say, Justin."

Justin looked up from his plate of steak and beans to find Homer shifting from foot to foot in front of him. He hadn't seen Homer in several days but had heard that the rancher, a shy man around women, was still eating at the Bar M camp, trying to work up the nerve to speak to the ladies.

"You seen any riders around you didn't recognize?" Homer asked.

"Hard to know them all. We got twelve outfits here."

"True, but, well, I moseyed around last night lookin' for a couple I seen yesterday, an' I never did find 'em."

"Probably riding night herd."

"Maybe, Justin, but I just got this uneasy feelin' about them two. You know what I mean?"

Justin set his plate aside, frowning now himself. He wasn't one to ignore uneasy feelings. He'd had enough during his years trail driving and had learned that there was usually cause, even if you couldn't put your finger on what the cause was. "Where did you see these—"

Both men lifted their heads sharply, listening to shouts in the distance that were coming closer.

"Stampede," Homer said.

"Damn." They were both astride and tearing out of camp in seconds with all the other men who had come in to eat.

Anne grumbled angrily to herself as she scraped leftover portions of stew from the plates. The men had inexplicably jumped up and left without finishing, without even washing their plates. Well, that's what she got for leaving her pots untended to go off riding with that sour-faced Justin Harte, although she hadn't thought the meal was *that* bad. The only benefit she'd got out of the morning's excursion was the discovery of some blackberry bushes on the way back, but now she'd have to do the picking herself. Sissie had managed to disappear while Anne was gone. The Lord knew where she'd got off to and why. Anne sometimes suspected that the girl could see into the future and, in this instance, had left to get out of berrypicking.

"Well, I seen some stampedes in my time," said Last Cauley. The men of the Bar M and a number of visitors were sprawled around the campfire, drinking their coffee, relishing the unexpected and well-received blackberry cobbler that Anne had provided, and swapping stories inspired by the stampede that day of a herd being driven in to the branding ground.

"One I remember best," the foreman reminisced, "well, it must have been in '68 or '69—I don't recollect —but I do know it was started by a boy named Dutch Henry Shannon. Had hair so blond, 'twas almost white, that boy did."

Anne cut into the last cobbler, glancing up from time to time to check on Sissie's whereabouts. Her sister hadn't returned till midafternoon, leaving Anne to pick all the berries. She passed along the first wedge of another cobbler to an eager cowboy and turned her attention back to Last's story.

"Now we was camped outside Abilene," said Last, who had once told Anne that he was named Last because his mother, at his birth, had announced to his father that he was the "last" baby she ever intended to have. "Done made the whole trail drive without much trouble 'cept for a few brushes with Indians, which didn't amount to much. An' young Dutch Henry, he pulled a long straw and got one of the first turns to go into town, see the elephant an' hear the owl, if you know what I mean."

The men all laughed knowingly, but Anne said, "I don't. What does that mean?"

Last chuckled. "Well, now, Miss Anne, it just means he went into Abilene to have himself a high old time, drinkin' an' dancin' an' such."

From the laughter that greeted this statement, Anne assumed that young Dutch Henry had done more than drink and dance in Abilene.

"Well, the boy come back afore dawn," continued the foreman, "an' happen he was a little the worse for the whiskey, so he laid right down an' went to sleep. Trouble was, he done missed the camp by a mile or more, so there he was, sleepin' out on the prairie in the high grass, an' our lead steer, an ole mossy horn we liked to call Mean Harold, he done come upon young Dutch Henry snorin' away in the high grass an' gave him a nudge with the horns. Well, sir, Dutch Henry, he woke up and seen that steer standin' over him, an' he jumped about six feet in the air with a yell we heard all the way back in camp. Course, you know what happened. Them cattle spooked an' stampeded all the way through Abilene with Mean Harold leadin' the way. Like to took us two hours to get 'em turned around even though the night man, he seen the whole thing an' had a start on 'em."

The men all chuckled appreciatively, but Anne, frowning and handing out another slice of cobbler, asked, "What happened to young Dutch Henry?"

"Well, Miss Annie, the whole herd done stampeded over Dutch Henry. Course, we went back to look once we got them cattle rounded up, but we never even found his hat."

"Oh, my God," Anne murmured, looking sick.

"Now don't you feel bad for Dutch Henry, Miss Anne. You can be sure, after a night in Abilene, that he died happy," said Homer, who, having finally managed to speak to her, blushed at his choice of topic.

"When it comes to trail-drive stories," Homer mumbled, "I reckon Justin knows more than any man here since, like as not, he's been on more trail drives."

Anne glanced up to see that Justin Harte was indeed standing at the edge of the circle, which surprised her. After their cool parting, she hadn't expected to see him anytime soon.

"That's right, Justin," Last said. "Whyn't you tell us the story about how you won all them buffalo hides off'n the Indians who wanted to rustle your herd?"

"How 'bout the story of Hobblin' Dan an' the buckskin britches?" Homer suggested eagerly.

"Let the ladies decide," one of the hands called out. "Miss Sissie?"

They looked around, but Sissie had disappeared. Now where had that girl gone? Anne wondered irritably. It was Sissie's second disappearance in one day, and she usually only hid out when there was work to be done, not when there were crowds of young men to flirt with.

"I've come to speak to the colonel," Justin said, looking less than convivial.

How like him, Anne thought and, just for spite,

urged, "Do tell us a story, Mr. Harte, and have a piece of blackberry cobbler for your trouble."

"There you go, Justin," Homer said. "No man in his right mind would pass up a piece of Miss Anne's cobbler." Homer was eyeing it wistfully, hoping, no doubt, to be offered the last piece.

Anne cut the remaining section in half and scooped out a portion, which she handed to Justin. "I think I'd like to hear about Hobbling Dan and the buckskin pants," she decided, earning herself a frown. "Will you have coffee?"

"Please," he said, his reply courteous, his tone impatient.

Justin took a bite of the cobbler, sipped the coffee, then began reluctantly. "Dan Trumper wasn't always called Hobbling Dan, as some of you know, not before '71 when we made that particular drive to Kansas, which was one of the worst I've ever been on. We had rain and mud the whole way, and Dan, he was wearing buckskin pants. Given the nature of buckskin, every time it rained, his pants would stretch out. He had to cut an inch or so off the bottom from one day to the next to keep the pants from tangling in his spurs."

The laughter started at this point, but Justin ignored it and continued as seriously as if he were discussing the price per hundred pounds of a steer on the hoof at rail head. "Finally, the day before we got to Abilene, the sun came out, and, of course, it dried up Dan's pants, and they shrunk right up to his knees, not to mention elsewhere, which may have been why they started to call him Hobbling Dan right about that time. Some folks say it was because he slipped in a cow pie in the railyard and broke his foot, but others say he was injured by his own pants." This observation caused howls of merriment.

"At any rate, he was fit to be tied over those buckskin britches. Just about everyone in Abilene laughed at him when he rode in barelegged from his boots to his knees, and all the way home he swore he was going to find the squaw he bought them off and shoot her, although I can't say as I know whether he did."

The men had been hooting with laughter, and Anne had to laugh herself, although she noticed that Justin was still perfectly straight-faced. Didn't he think the story was funny? she wondered. Evidently not.

"It's always been my contention," said the colonel, who had been listening to the tale-telling without any evident enthusiasm, "that it is the duty of an officer to see his men properly outfitted."

"Well, I wasn't an officer," drawled Justin. "I was the trail boss, and Hobbling Dan wasn't any enlisted man. But he *was* the best point rider I ever had."

"And a supporter of the Confederacy, no doubt," said the colonel disdainfully. "During the late war between the states, when I served under, among others, General Sherman, I was always appalled to see the lack of pride demonstrated by soldiers of the Confederacy, which showed so clearly in their ragged attire on the battlefields."

"I imagine," said Justin drily, "that it was less a matter of pride than the fact that most of them never saw a new uniform from one end of the war to the other."

As soon as the colonel had begun to talk, there was a sudden dispersal of men from the campfire, as if they had all been overcome with weariness at the same time.

"Nor did the soldiers of the Confederacy demonstrate a proper attention to the care of their weaponry or of their horseflesh. A good officer—"

"Look, Colonel, I didn't ride over here to refight the war. This afternoon we had a stampede."

"I'm aware of that," Morehead said. "As roundup captain, I should say that the responsibility for the stampede rests squarely upon your—"

"Upon your daughter, Sissie," interrupted Justin. "Everyone who was there when it started says that herd was ambling along peaceably until Sissie came tripping out of the woods, upsetting the cattle with a skirt full of pink ruffles down her backside. Then when they bolted, the man riding point couldn't turn them because he had to grab Miss Sissie and haul her back to safety."

"Down her *backside*?" roared the colonel. "Sir, I—"

"You either keep that girl in camp or send her home," said Justin, his voice filled with anger. "And that's an order. If you don't obey it, you'll leave yourself."

"Anne!" shouted the colonel.

Anne had been cleaning up and listening to their confrontation as it developed. She turned with her hands on her hips and glared at her stepfather, waiting for him to shift the blame to her, which he did.

"You are responsible for keeping Sissie here, Anne."

"I work from sunup to sundown and beyond in this camp," said Anne coldly. "And what for? To feed your pride because you think you're too good to let your men eat at someone else's chuck wagon the way they're supposed to. And then I wash your clothes, mine, and Sissie's, and she never lifts a hand. Maybe you'd like to tell me just when I have time to ride herd on her?"

"Anne," said the colonel threateningly.

"If you want her restrained, you do it. You're the one who spoiled her rotten as soon as David and I left New Orleans for a frontier posting. Sissie wasn't a useless featherhead when she was eleven, and there's not a reason in the world she should be now except that you couldn't be bothered to discipline her."

The colonel's face flushed, and he glared at Anne. "I took you in out of the goodness of my heart, madam, after your husband died, made the long trip out to Fort Griffin myself, and this is the thanks you show me? Well, I can tell you that if you wish to remain a part of this family—"

"Oh heavens, Colonel," Anne interrupted sarcastically, "I'd hate to have it said that I took advantage of the goodness of your heart. Why don't you just return the handling of the money I inherited from David to me, and I'll leave? Then you can get yourself another unpaid roundup cook and ranch housekeeper and seamstress for your daughter and—"

The colonel's fury abated rather suddenly, and she was cut off in mid-tirade and astounded to hear him say, "It's hardly proper, Anne, for us to air our family tiffs—" *Tiffs?* she marveled. "—in front of strangers." He shot Justin a venomous glance. "I shall see to it that my daughter causes no more trouble." Then he strode away.

Anne, still trembling, turned back to the pots. She had forgotten Justin's presence until he laid a firm hand on her shoulder. "You are an able debater, Mrs. McAuliffe," he said with quiet humor.

She glanced up at him and replied, her lips still thin with anger, "And you, Mr. Harte, are a prime source of trouble to me."

"And here I thought," he murmured, "that your sister was the source of the trouble."

Anne sighed and began to scour another pot with sand from the creek bed. "Sissie means well," she mumbled.

"You're remarkably tolerant. She strikes me as bone lazy and a careless, troublemaking flirt."

Her good humor returning, Anne shot him a mischievous glance. "Why, Mr. Harte, I do believe that you must have been victimized by some flirtatious female."

His face darkened, and Anne wished belatedly that she had kept her mouth shut. "Won't you have another piece of pie?" she asked in haste.

"Pie?"

"Well, cobbler." She picked up the last piece, which she had been saving for herself, and handed it to him. "In recompense for your trouble over the stampede." She gave him a friendly smile and poured him a second cup of coffee. His hand had felt pleasant on her shoulder, although she had been too upset at the time to savor it.

When Justin had eaten half the pastry, he put down his fork and asked, "Where's yours, Mrs. McAuliffe?"

"My what?"

"Your cobbler. I don't recall your having any."

Anne shrugged. "After spending the afternoon picking the berries," she said, "I've sort of lost interest in eating them."

"A very diplomatic answer. I can see why Homer is so taken with you."

"It's not me he's taken with," Anne replied, laughing. She wondered with a shiver of pleasure if Justin could be jealous of his friend, Homer Teasdale. He'd mentioned poor Homer's visits twice now. "It's my blackberry cobbler Mr. Teasdale likes. Why, the man hasn't said two words to me. Most likely he's sweet on Sissie."

"More the fool he, if that's so," Justin said.

"Why, thank you, Mr. Harte. It's nice to know you find me preferable to my sister whom we all know you can't abide." She grinned at him before he could take offense and hastily changed the subject. "Maybe sometime you'll tell me about trail driving since it seems that you're an expert."

"Not much to it," Justin said companionably and explained that he and his brothers had started by driving their own herd to Kansas from their mother's place in Palo Pinto and gone on to become cattle contractors, taking other people's herds up the trail between 1868 and 1874 when Justin had settled down to ranching and left the trail driving to his four younger brothers. He even told her that his one older brother had been killed at Vicksburg, while he, only sixteen when Texas seceded, had spent the war guarding the frontier against Indians with Captain Jack Cureton's rangers.

Eager to hear more, Anne said, "It must have been as dangerous on the frontier as on the battlefields."

Justin shrugged. "Hard to say. I lived through the Indian troubles; Ben died in the war." Then changing the subject abruptly, he asked, "Does the colonel always blame you for Sissie's escapades?"

Anne sighed. "I'm not his blood daughter, you know. Only Sissie is. The colonel married my mother when I was a little girl."

Justin looked surprised. "I didn't realize the colonel had a wife."

"Well, he doesn't. Mama died in '64 when he was off campaigning with Sherman, somewhere in Georgia I think. I may have been the only thirteen-year-old girl in the country trying to raise a sister by herself." She put the last pot back into the cupboard as she reconsidered her words. "Well, that's probably wrong," she decided. "Given the dislocations of those years, there may have been all kinds of children raising children."

"There were," said Justin, "but that didn't make it easy. I lost my father in an Indian raid not long after we took up land in Palo Pinto. My older brother and I, we had to work the ranch for my mother and do what we could for the younger boys, which isn't to say that she's not a strong woman. I expect she'd have kept things going even without Ben and me. You and my ma would probably get on real well."

"Why, thank you. I take that as a compliment."

Justin nodded. "It was meant as one," he said brusquely and picked up his hat.

Anne sighed and watched him go. A kind word from him always set him to flight.

CHAPTER

Three

"Mr. Teasdale," said the colonel angrily, "I think this whole conversation is insulting. You have availed yourself of my hospitality on a number of nights this week, and I find your conduct poor recompense for the welcome you have received. You may consider yourself *persona non grata* at my campfire in the future." With that, the colonel snapped shut a book of campaign memoirs he had been reading and strode off.

Justin and Homer watched him leave with ill-concealed irritation. They had come to the Bar M camp to question the two riders, Pullman and Cratcher, who had been seen talking to strangers several days in a row. From Last Cauley they had learned that the men had volunteered for night duty, a circumstance which made Justin doubly uneasy. However, the colonel took offense at the idea that his men were under suspicion and refused, over his foreman's objections, to call Pullman and Cratcher back.

"What's 'person aw grada' mean?" Homer asked.

"He meant don't come back and eat his food anymore."

"Well, son of a gun," exclaimed Homer. "I knew this conversation wasn't gonna come to no good. Now I'll never get acquainted with Miss Anne, an' things was goin' along so fine. I spoke to her two, three times the other night. You heard, Justin."

Justin suppressed a grin and said by way of consolation, "Maybe you don't really want to get acquainted with a woman who's sharp-tongued enough to hold her own against the colonel."

"There is that," Homer said, but he didn't sound convinced. "Guess I'll be gettin' back to my own campfire."

Justin nodded. "You got an extra man to put on night herd tonight?"

"I reckon."

"Good. I'll send two more of mine out and see if George Armistad can't spare a few. If someone's planning to rustle our cattle, tonight might be as good a night as any."

Homer pushed his hat back over thinning, faded red hair. "Now that we're into the Palo Pinto," he agreed, "there's a hundred places they could hide 'em come daybreak." Then he flushed as he stared over Justin's shoulder. "Evenin', Miss Anne."

"Mr. Teasdale, Mr. Harte." Anne, having seen the confrontation between her stepfather and the two ranchers, had given in to her curiosity. She hadn't caught so much as a glimpse of Justin since their last conversation and had concluded that he was avoiding her, although she had hoped, once the roundup moved into the Palo Pinto, that he might turn up to show her his home country. He hadn't, of course, and so she had gone out that morning to explore on her own and maybe flush him out of hiding as well, not that she'd had any luck.

"You know two riders named Pullman and Cratcher,

Miss Anne? They're part of your stepfather's roundup crew." Homer was holding his hat reverently over his heart.

"Of course, I know them," said Anne. "They're about as worthless as anyone we've had on the payroll since I've been here. Why do you ask?"

"Oh, we're just checking them out," said Justin.

"In that case, I suggest you ask Mr. Cauley, if he hasn't quit already. I saw him arguing with my stepfather." Well, at least Justin wasn't here to tattle on her. "Last thinks as little of that pair as I do." Evidently Justin didn't even know she had left camp that morning.

He nodded. "If you'll take some advice from me, Mrs. McAuliffe, it would be a sad day for the Bar M if you folks lost Cauley. He's a good man."

"I know that," said Anne, "but it's not much use to tell me. The colonel doesn't take my advice—or anyone's."

"You're to stay in this wagon, Sissie. Do you understand me?" Anne tossed several handsful of .44/.40 cartridges, a pair of socks, and a couple of leftover biscuits into a bag, which she hooked over her shoulder. "And if anyone should ask where I am, tell them you don't know."

"I *don't* know," said Sissie, shivering with fright.

"True, and I'm not going to tell you." Anne pulled a black shawl around her shoulders over her nightdress, grabbed the Winchester center fire repeating rifle David had given her for her last birthday, and hopped off the wagon.

Not five minutes earlier a man had ridden through camp, rousing the hands with the news that someone had shot one of George Armistad's men and was trying to drive off the herd. In seconds, the sleeping riders, whose idea of preparing for bed was to remove their hats and gunbelts, were up and astride their saddled horses.

Anne, who had explored the area thoroughly that morning, did not intend to be far behind. Although she had no horse to take her there, she knew a perfect vantage point overlooking a draw through which the rustlers might well drive the stolen herd.

"Remember," she called back to Sissie, "do what I told you, or you'll be one sorry girl." Sissie sniffled, and Anne rather imagined that her sister was burrowing, terrified, under the blankets at that very moment.

"Rollo, take six men and try to head 'em off at the Johnson Creek Ford in case they go that way."

Rollo Tandy chose his men and left at a gallop.

Justin headed down the hill with Homer and another group to pursue the rustlers from behind.

"Armistad's man hurt bad?" Homer called to him.

"Too early to tell," Justin replied. "Don't think so."

"Someone's laying down shots ahead of us, Justin. Who's up there?" called one of the riders.

"Don't know," Justin replied. "Let's hope it's one of ours. Sam Bannerman's taken some men toward the draw."

"That's rifle fire," Homer said.

From her vantage point in the tree, Anne watched the herd passing around the bend as she reloaded. Pleased, she nodded and took careful aim. She had chosen her spot well, and there was enough moonlight to reveal three of the rustlers. She sighted carefully at the near rider, led her shot enough to allow for his momentum, and gently squeezed the trigger. "Missed," she muttered in disgust, then repeated the whole procedure again. On her second try, she shot him out of the saddle, after which she emptied the rifle rapidly at the other two. Unfortunately, they were on the far side, too far for her abilities as a markswoman.

Shivering, Anne wished that she'd taken the time to put on boots. Her feet hurt, and they were getting cold. She reached into her bag for spare cartridges to reload the rifle, then pulled out the pair of socks, which she drew on. If her feet were bleeding, it was going to be painful to get those socks off later.

The next horseman to come within range was either Cratcher or someone who'd stolen his hat. She'd know his peculiar way of creasing his brim anywhere. With her father's ranch hand in her sights, she hesitated. Could he be trying to turn the cattle? Giving him the benefit of the doubt, she watched. No, she decided. You didn't turn a herd by urging them straight ahead. And Justin had been suspicious of Cratcher, with good reason it seemed.

For a second time she sighted carefully ahead of her target and squeezed the trigger. Not her best shot. She got the horse, not the man. Whether he'd survived the fall, she couldn't tell, and in the meantime the rough tree bark, against which she was supporting her arms, was exceedingly uncomfortable, even through the thick flannel of her nightdress. She shifted, looking for a better position, and then waited.

"Tie 'em up," said Justin. "We'll hang 'em tomorrow."

"That's illegal," objected a rancher from Tarrant County. "They have to be turned over to the authorities."

"The county seat's miles from here. We'll thrash it out in the morning at a meeting of the owners and foremen," Justin replied, his tone curt. "Rollo, you see that they're guarded. George, set out a night crew. See if you can't get the herd bedded down. Homer, you check the remudas. I'm goin' to see if we've lost any men."

Forty-five minutes later, Justin was reasonably sure that he'd accounted for everyone except Morehead's people. As little as he relished another run-in with the colonel, he intended to check there as well. He already knew that Cratcher had been injured; they had found the man unconscious in a thicket where he shouldn't have been, another matter to be investigated in the morning. In the meantime, Cratcher was under guard, and Justin intended to find out where his partner Pullman was. A visit to the Morehead camp, however, did not turn the man up.

As well as checking on Morehead's hands, he stopped by the chuck wagon and called quietly, "Mrs. McAuliffe." There was no answer. Justin squinted at the wagon suspiciously. It was unlike Anne McAuliffe to be sleeping through so much excitement. "Mrs. McAuliffe," he called again.

Sissie stuck her head out the back of the wagon and said accusingly, "You woke me up."

He believed that. "Is your sister all right?"

The girl looked uneasy and mumbled, "She's sleeping."

"Wake her up," Justin said.

Sissie stammered, "I don't want to. She'd—she'd be mad at me." When Justin insisted, the girl made what he took to be a pretense of searching the wagon for her sister. "She's not here," Sissie reported in a defensive voice.

"Then where is she?" he demanded.

"How would I know? I've been asleep." Sissie backed into her refuge and didn't re-emerge.

Justin stood a moment, thinking. There had been rifle fire early on that he couldn't account for, given his men's whereabouts. Swinging astride his horse, he headed toward the overlook from which the shots had come. If the rifle had been Anne's, why hadn't she returned to camp? With a feeling of unaccustomed panic, he guided his horse quickly through the trees, studying the terrain carefully in the moonlight. This should be about the right place, he decided, pulling up. He was nervous, sweating lightly in the cold spring air as he swept the area with keen eyes. "Mrs. McAuliffe?" he said quietly. There was no answer. "Mrs. McAuliffe!" He had spotted a flash of white in a tree to his left.

"How did you know where I was?" Her words floated down to him as if from a disembodied spirit.

He rode his horse under the branch and said, his voice rough with relief, "Get down from there."

"How can I? You're in my way."

"I'll drag you out of that tree if I have to, Mrs. McAuliffe." Confounded woman!

"You'd better not try it," she replied. "I'm armed."

"So I gathered. Were you shooting down into the draw?"

"I was, and I hit two of them."

"Somehow I'm not surprised. Now will you please get down?"

"No, I will not. I intend to stay here until I'm sure that the men in my father's camp are fast asleep."

"That's ridiculous," said Justin. "You'll freeze to death."

"No, I won't. I've brought my shawl, and I'm not going back into that camp in my nightdress, certainly not with my stepfather up and about. I'd never hear the end of it."

Justin sighed. He'd never understand how a woman's mind worked. "At least, come down out of the tree," he coaxed. "It can't be very comfortable, and if you fall out, you might injure yourself."

"Oh, very well," said Anne. "Give me your hand."

Justin rode closer to the trunk, reached up, and lifted her off her perch. "I could take you straight back," he muttered, "while I've got you across the saddle."

"I could shoot your horse," she replied. "How would you like that?"

Justin chuckled. "I believe you would. And as it happens, I put a high price on this horse."

"There's no need for you to wait, Mr. Harte, if you're in a hurry to get back to your bedroll. I can find my way to camp perfectly well. I got here on my own, after all."

"So you did." Justin dismounted, taking her with him. "And how badly scratched did you get on the way?" He ground tied the horse and sat down against the trunk of the tree, pulling her down beside him.

"Oh, I wasn't hurt much," said Anne, too stubborn to mention the damage to her feet. "You were right about my stepfather's men. Cratcher was helping to run that herd off. I got his horse, but I'm not sure what happened to him."

"Pity to shoot a good horse," said Justin.

"Well, I didn't plan to. I was aiming at Cratcher," said Anne indignantly. The warmth of Justin's body beside hers was radiating through her, making her feel a sort of bemused, simmering excitement.

"Well, you got him after a fashion. We found Cratcher unconscious out in the brush, and if we find his partner, we'll hang them both tomorrow. I suppose you're going to protest. Your stepfather undoubtedly will."

"Why should I?" asked Anne. "The messenger said they shot one of George Armistad's men when they took the herd." She leaned closer to him, letting her shoulder come to rest against the hard muscles of his upper arm.

"Are you cold?" he asked.

"A little," Anne replied.

Justin put an arm around her, and she snuggled against him, the softness of one breast against his side. She could feel him withdraw and knew she should move away, but somehow she couldn't, for suddenly she had the most unexpected and overwhelming desire to press against him.

"Anne?" His voice was tight and questioning, and he lifted her chin so that her face came into the moonlight that filtered through the branches above them. When she veiled her eyes, he said, "No, look at me."

Her eyes answered his unspoken question as she turned more fully into his arms, into the power and heat of him. She had hoped for a simple kiss but found herself overwhelmed by the force of his response. He locked her body against his full length in a quick movement that stretched her out beside him on the ground. Then he rolled her under the hard, heavy weight of his body, bringing his mouth down on hers in a kiss that made her tremble in the flash of her own ignited desire.

"Is this what you want?" he whispered when finally he had lifted his mouth from hers.

In answer, she pulled her arms free and wrapped them around his neck, drawing him back. Justin made a low, rough sound in his throat and took her mouth again. When he lifted his body away from hers, she could hardly stifle the whimper of protest in her throat. She wanted the pressure of him against her, or thought she did until he ran his hand with a firm touch from the taut curve of her waist to the underside of her breast. Her whole body quivered as she felt, even through the fabric of her gown, the rough pads of his fingers against her nipple, bringing fire there as well.

Then, as if he wanted to torture her, he moved his hand away again, and again the helpless protest whispered from her lips to his. Before she could save her pride by moving away, he sat up and reached for the hem of her nightdress, drawing it swiftly up to her waist and then pressing his hand against her belly. She went still with surprise, never having fantasized anything beyond his kiss.

He bent and gently kissed her. His tongue wooed her

lips while his hand stroked the sensitive skin at her waist. His mouth coaxed; his thumb brushed tantaliz-ingly across her navel and the soft flesh below. Trem-bling, she parted her lips for him, and as he took the invitation, his fingers slipped down to the silken curls between her thighs. Dazed, swept along by his swift, sweet aggression, Anne tightened her lips around his invading tongue, and drew it in. Her hips moved restlessly under his touch which advanced more inti-mately as he nudged his leg between hers.

Once her thighs were parted, he stroked her so perfectly, so tenderly in rhythm with his penetration of her mouth that she sighed once and arched up, convuls-ing against his hand, then fell back. He moved his lips to the tender curve of her shoulder, then his tongue to the intricate spiral of her ear, asking softly, "Do you want more?"

Anne, almost mindless with desire, pressed her hips against the hard thrust of his passion and nodded.

He inserted another knee between hers, and she curved to him with aching need, only to find his hand once again between her legs. "No," she whispered, "that's not—"

He cut her off with a deep kiss and slid a searching finger into her. Anne's body rose against it helplessly. He drew his hand back, and with care his fingers penetrated her again. And again. Until shudders racked her and her head tossed from side to side in the throes of a fulfillment that hadn't come the way she wanted it. When he withdrew and she was still at last, she whis-pered, "Justin, don't you—"

He silenced her with a soft, brushing kiss and drew the nightdress down to her ankles. "I'll take you back now," he murmured, and he did, leaving his horse outside the camp and carrying her silently to the wagon.

She couldn't speak to him without waking the others, so she was left confused. He'd given her great pleasure but taken none for himself. Why? She had certainly been willing, and he must have known that. She fell off to sleep with her questions unanswered but her heart now committed to a man who was an enigma to her.

Anne moved through her morning chores with an inattention born of fatigue and embarrassed happiness. On the one hand, she had had only two hours sleep and was dazed with exhaustion. On the other hand, she was astonished at her own wanton behavior the night before, but she was also feeling the first twinges of expectation and tentative optimism that she had known since David was wounded almost two years earlier. She cherished that small glow of hope as a primitive woman would the coal that could bring her campfire back to full flame. Anne's life had been in suspension, something to be endured, not relished, but that hour with Justin last night had brought her alive. She both yearned and feared to see him again.

If only she knew why he had held back. There were so many possibilities, some beautiful, some terrible. Perhaps he had remembered that she was recently widowed. Maybe he was afraid that she would be hurt by a more intimate relationship. But what if he simply didn't want the final intimacy? What if he had been shocked at her passionate response? Or most terrible to contemplate, what if his lovemaking had been an act of contempt? His attitude toward her had always been ambivalent and unfathomable.

"Miss Anne, you all right?"

Her brief happiness fast evaporating, she turned to find Last looking at her with concern. "Oh yes," she mumbled, "Fine, thank you. A little tired," she added, trying to smile at him, trying to banish the fears that had overtaken her. She would just have to wait, she told herself, to see how Justin treated her when next they met. But if he backed away again, she thought it would break her heart.

"Anne, Cauley and I are going over to the Crossed Heart camp," said the colonel. "There's a meeting to decide the fate of the men they caught last night."

"Then I'd better go with you," said Anne, firmly pushing away a cowardly desire to delay seeing Justin.

"Nonsense," her stepfather objected. "It's hardly a matter for women to mix in. When Pullman returns from night watch, tell him to take care of things until we get back."

The colonel left without waiting for any reply from her. Pullman? she thought sardonically. He was turning the outfit over to Pullman? She'd be surprised if Pullman ever showed up again, and no matter what the colonel said, she intended to be at the meeting.

She quickly finished the most pressing of her chores and set out to walk to Justin's camp. Once there, she sat down on the outskirts of the circle to listen to the discussion, which had already begun. It seemed to her that Justin had glanced her way when she first arrived, but he had given no sign of recognition. It wouldn't have hurt him to smile, she thought, or at least nod. Feeling overcome with misery, she wished she'd stayed away. Justin was proposing that the night guards be doubled. He reckoned that not nearly all the rustlers had been caught. "Any night they could try again," he warned.

"Nonsense," said the colonel. "The men are getting little enough sleep as it is, and there's no reason to think we'll be hit again, not after we successfully turned them back last night."

"That's easy for you to say, Morehead," snapped George Armistad. "Since the roundup started to the east, the bulk of your cattle are being held on your own range. You don't stand to lose as much if we're hit again, but those of us whose ranches are out here in Palo Pinto have most of our stock tied up in these herds. Besides that, you didn't have a man shot last night."

There were mutterings of agreement from the western ranchers.

"You're wrong, George," Justin said, "in thinking the Bar M didn't lose anyone. Cratcher was injured."

The colonel looked up nervously. "Cratcher?"

"That's right," said Justin. "Had his horse shot out from under him while he was trying to drive the herd off."

"I don't believe it," said the colonel. "Are you saying he was in with the rustlers?"

"I am," said Justin.

"It's a lie. Someone must have shot the wrong man."

"Not him, his horse," corrected Anne, speaking up for the first time. "I'm the one who shot at him."

"You! What were you doing away from the wagon?"

"Picking off rustlers as they came down the draw," said Anne. "And there's no mistake. I recognized Cratcher, and he was driving those cattle straight away from the camps."

"Then I say we hang 'im," George declared.

"You're going to condemn a man on the word of a foolish woman who should have been minding her pots instead of—"

"Mrs. McAuliffe did as much as anyone to stop that raid," said Justin, "although I agree that she shouldn't have been out there."

Anne looked at him as if he'd betrayed her, but he carefully looked away.

"Cratcher should at least be allowed to speak for himself," said the colonel. "It's hardly proper to condemn him without a hearing."

"I won't disagree with that," said Justin. "The man has a right to testify in his own defense. Rollo, you want to bring him here?"

"Did I hear it right, Morehead, that when Justin and Homer wanted to talk to your people who'd been seen huddlin' with strangers, you refused to call 'em in off night herd?" George asked.

"They're my riders, and I—"

"That sounds damn suspicious," said another of the cattlemen. "When the roundup boss tells you to call a rider in, you call the rider in."

The other owners muttered in agreement as Rollo shoved Cratcher into the circle.

"All right, Cratcher," said Justin, "now's the time to tell your side of the story if you want to talk."

"What side?" whined Cratcher. "I was just out night herdin' an' someone tried to drive the cattle off. They musta shot my horse to keep me from doin' anything to stop the raid."

"That's it?" asked Justin.

"What else?" said the rider more confidently. "I don't know why you got me tied up. I was just doin' my job."

Justin turned and looked at Anne for the first time. "Mrs. McAuliffe," he said formally.

She felt her heart sink; he was treating her as if she were a stranger. She swallowed hard and turned to the circle of ranchers who were awaiting her testimony. "When the word came that the herd was being driven off, I got my Winchester and went to a limestone bluff I'd seen that morning," she began.

"You aren't supposed to leave camp," snapped the colonel. "Harte ordered both you and Sissie to stay put."

Anne's lips tightened mutinously. She was tired of orders from men.

"Good thing the girl took a hand," George said. "I woulda been outa a lotta cattle if she hadn't. You go right on, little lady," he said to Anne.

"The bluff overlooked the draw," Anne continued, "and it seemed to me that if they were going to succeed, they'd have to come that way, which they did. I shot one of the first three. Then Cratcher came along, and I recognized him."

"Oh, now, Miss Anne," said Cratcher, his voice

wheedling, "how could you recognize me at night?"

"It wasn't hard," said Anne dryly. "The moon was up, you were riding that pinto you always use for night herding, the one you say has cat's eyes, and nobody could miss that hat of yours."

His hand rose automatically to the creased brim, and the other men stared at the hat, which indeed had a peculiar shape.

"Since I recognized you," Anne continued, "I waited. I didn't want to fire on you if you were trying to stop the raid, but you weren't. You were heading them straight down the draw, and you weren't shooting at any of the rustlers." She paused and gave him a hard look. "So I shot at you, missed, unfortunately, but I did hit the pinto, which seems to have kept you from getting away. Where's Pullman?"

Cratcher had begun to shift uneasily as she looked him in the eye and testified with such conviction. He shrugged nervously and answered, "How do I know? Maybe the rustlers shot him last night."

"Who says Pullman's missing?" demanded the colonel.

"He's missing," said Justin. "No one's seen him since he volunteered for night herding yesterday."

"He volunteered?" George exclaimed. "And Cratcher, did he volunteer, too?"

"He did," Last said.

"And you, Morehead, wouldn't let Justin call 'em back?"

"Look here, Armistad," blustered the colonel, "what are you intimating?"

"I ain't intimatin' nuthin'," George retorted. "I'm sayin' straight out, looks like you're mixed up in this."

"I'm for hangin' 'em," Homer said. The colonel turned pale, and Homer added hastily, "Oh, not you, Colonel. Cratcher an' the other one. I lost enough cows this year, an' I think it's about time we sent these damn rustlers a message they ain't gonna forget."

"The other one's about dead," said Rollo Tandy.

"And I'm innocent," Cratcher cried. "I ain't no rustler. You gonna believe a woman?"

"I do," George said.

"I don't know," said Major Sam Bannerman from Parker County. "I'd like to think on it, Justin. I ain't much for vigilante justice."

"Neither am I, Sam," Justin replied, "although I have no doubt about Cratcher and the other one."

"Even with a regular jury, it's gotta be unanimous," said Cratcher.

Justin ignored him. "Those of you in doubt, I'm willing to give you some time to think on it. We'll vote tomorrow, how's that?"

The various ranchers and foremen nodded and began to disperse. Cratcher, still protesting, was hauled away by Rollo, and Anne, who had hoped for a sign from Justin, decided that none was forthcoming and turned to leave.

Then suddenly, as she limped down the path toward the Bar M camp, Justin was beside her, his hand on her arm. "There may be more trouble tonight." She looked up at him. "I want you to promise me, Anne, that if they come at us again, you'll stay under cover."

"But—"

"Please." He held her eyes for a long minute. "I don't want to have to worry about you."

Anne stared back and nodded. "All right, Justin, I'll do what you ask."

He dropped his hand from her arm, evidently satisfied with her promise. "I've got to go now." He strode quickly back the way he had come as Anne looked at him. *He must care a little*, she thought, touched by his concern for her safety, but his hold on her arm hadn't been that of a lover. She shook her head and turned down the path again.

CHAPTER

Four

"Miss Anne."

She had been deep, deep in sleep and thought for a minute that it was morning and Justin had awakened her. Then, confused, she realized that it was still night, and she was sleeping in the chuck wagon, as she had for over a month.

"Miss Anne," the voice came again. Anne sat up groggily, pushing back her blankets. "It's me, Last Cauley."

She scooted by her sister and looked out. The foreman stood at the end of the wagon, holding a lantern, his horse behind him.

"I wouldn't a bothered you, ma'am, but Rollo Tandy, he's been bad shot. He's like to die, and don't no one know what to do. Then I recollected as how you'd said you did duty in the Army hospitals where your husband was stationed when they was shorthanded, an' how you'd helped the surgeons an' all, so I thought maybe—"

"Of course," she mumbled, finally awake and beginning to understand what he was saying.

"If you could hurry, ma'am. I know it takes ladies some time to dress, but—"

"I'm dressed," Anne muttered. "Since Mr. Harte seemed to expect more trouble, I never got undressed."

"God bless you, ma'am," Last said in heartfelt relief. "You are one mighty sensible woman."

Anne smiled to herself and said, "Let me have that lantern. I need to find my medical bag."

"You got a medical bag?" he asked, awed.

"Well, I've heard the men say often enough how dangerous roundup can be, so I thought I'd better bring what I could along." She looked over the racks of supplies in the wagon, glancing at her sister as she did so. Sissie hadn't even stirred, which wasn't any big surprise. Ah, there it was, just where she'd put it. Anne pulled out the kit and handed it to Last over the back of the wagon. Then she donned her shoes and shawl and scooted to the tailgate herself.

"If you wouldn't mind ridin' double with me, ma'am?"

"No, of course not," Anne agreed. She let him mount, handed him the medical bag and lantern, and took his hand to pull herself up behind him.

"How did Mr. Tandy get shot?" she asked as they rode away from the Bar M encampment.

"Well, Justin was right. The rustlers come back tonight, but not for the herd like we thought. They come for their partners. That stranger fella, he'd already died, but there was still Cratcher."

"If the colonel hadn't interfered," she muttered, "we might already have hung Cratcher."

"Oh, they didn't free him. Rollo may have took a bullet, but he put one in their fella, an' Mr. Harte shot Cratcher. Don't nobody need to hang that son of a—er—"

"And Mr. Tandy's wounds?" she asked.

"Bullet in the chest. I just hope he's still alive."

"Does Mr. Harte know you're bringing me?"

"No, ma'am, but he'll be glad for any help he can git. He thinks a lot of Rollo. Them two spent I don't know how many years on the trail together. Here we are."

Anne slid down from the horse and walked into the circle of men close to the campfire, her breath hissing in softly as she saw the amount of blood Rollo had lost.

"Anne, what are you doing here?" Justin demanded.

"I brought her," Last said. "I remembered as how she knew a lot about wounds from takin' care of soldiers an' all. You see, her husband—"

"I know about her husband," said Justin.

Anne knelt and cut away the blood-soaked shirt from Rollo's broad chest. "I'll need hot water," she said, looking up. Her eye had fallen on the cook; he just stared back at her. "Hot water!" she repeated.

"Rollo ain't havin' a baby, you know," the cook replied.

"Just keep your mouth shut, and get that water."

The circle of men sucked in their breaths. No one talked to the cook that way, not if they wanted to eat.

"Or maybe," said Anne, "you want to stand there watching him bleed to death while you make smart remarks." Addressing the circle at large, she then said, "I want something clean spread on the tailgate of the chuck wagon so we can lay him out there. You'll need to move him as carefully as possible so as not to increase the bleeding." The men began to follow her orders, even the cook. "Then I'll need every lantern you can light and hold up for me." She was already beginning to unpack her bag.

"Mr. Tandy, can you hear me?" There was no reply, and when Anne rolled back the foreman's eyelid, she was relieved to confirm that he was unconscious.

"Already had some water boiling," said the cook, bringing back a pot.

"Good," she said. "Was the pot clean?"

He gave her a look of pure dislike and said, "Are *your* pots clean?"

When Anne grinned at him, he looked abashed and carried the water over for her.

"Does anybody have any whiskey?" she asked.

"We're not allowed to have whiskey at roundup camp, ma'am," said one of the cowboys.

"Justin?" She turned to him.

"I'll get it."

The cowboys all grinned. Anne didn't as she examined the wound carefully, the men having turned Rollo so she could see his back. "It's a pity the bullet didn't come out the other side," she muttered as she grasped his wrist to take his pulse. Then she washed her hands, first in hot water and then in whiskey, selected from the bag the instruments she was going to use, and gave them the same treatment. "I want four men holding him, and you'll have to look sharp. This is going to be difficult enough without having him come around and move."

"Do you know what you're doing?" Justin asked.

Grim faced, she stared back at him. "I've seen it done," she replied. "If you've got any better ideas than to let me try, you're welcome to take over. I'd be surprised if he lives another hour unless we get that bullet out." Justin's lips compressed. "Well, make up your mind. Do you want me to go ahead?"

"Yes," he said.

Anne turned immediately back to her patient, drawing a deep breath, her head up, her eyes closed for a minute. She was terrified at what she was about to attempt. Then blocking everything, including the fear from her mind, she picked up a surgical tool, a legacy from an Army surgeon who had himself died of blood poisoning from an arrow wound received during Mackenzie's campaign in Mexico. Out of gratitude for Anne's help in his hospital and her hospitality on the lonely frontier, he'd left her his most valued possession, his medical bag. At the time, she'd never expected to use it.

She worked as quickly as she could, blotting up the welling blood when it obscured her path, and she did manage to remove the bullet. Although God knew what damage she'd done in the process, she thought unhappily. Once the bullet was out, she cleaned the wound as best she could and packed it to stop the bleeding.

Most of the men had watched with awe. One had fainted and dropped his lantern. Another had offered to find her cobwebs to pack the wound, and wincing, she had refused. Finally, she'd said, "That's all I can do," and stepped back, looking down at herself. Her hands and the front of her black gown were covered with Rollo Tandy's blood, and she began to tremble. Justin quickly pulled her over to a camp stool.

"More hot water, Hobbs," he called to the cook, who brought it immediately. Justin himself washed away as much of the blood as he could. "What do you think?" he asked. "Will Rollo make it?"

"I don't know," Anne replied unsteadily. "I'm no surgeon, and that was a bad wound. All we can do now is watch over him and pray."

"You want Last to take you back?"

Anne looked up in surprise. "Of course not," she replied. "I didn't go through all that to walk off and leave him."

"Hobbs," Justin called, "get Mrs. McAuliffe a cup of coffee and start some breakfast for her."

The cook was looking sullen but didn't refuse. However, when he had brought her the coffee and she had taken a sip, she sighed and said, smiling at him, "That's got to be the best coffee I've ever tasted in my life, Mr. Hobbs." The man looked mollified. "And I do thank you for your help," she continued.

"We're all grateful for Rollo's sake," he mumbled, and left to get her some food.

"Do you find Hobbs particularly appealing?" hissed Justin. "Or is it that anything coming down the pike in long pants will do?"

Although Mr. Hobbs was, surprisingly enough, a handsome man, Anne was first astounded, then infuriated that Justin would say such a demeaning thing to her.

He looked away as if he wanted to retract his words. "Do you want to move Rollo off the tailgate?"

"No," she said tightly. "I don't want to move him at all. I'll keep him as warm as possible, leave him right where he is, and hope for the best, and I'll need a man with me in case he wakes." Justin peered at her suspiciously. "To hold him down!" she snapped, rising to check her patient.

"Then *I'll* watch with you," said Justin.

Anne wondered bitterly why he was offering. Was it because he didn't trust her to care for his friend or because he didn't trust her with any of the men when he wasn't around? Well, she wasn't going to spend the night sulking. "This happened because they came for Cratcher?" she asked.

"They tried, much good it did them. One of the rescuers is dead. I killed Cratcher myself, and I think several more got away."

"Do the other ranchers think the colonel was involved?"

"Do you?" he asked sharply.

"I'm sure he wasn't. He's mule-headed, but he's not dishonest."

"That's the way I figured it." Justin frowned, then muttered, "Guess I'd better send someone back to tell them where you are, or did Last do that before you left?"

"They won't miss me," Anne replied. "They didn't the other night when I was with you." She brought up the subject deliberately because she wanted to find out what their time together had meant to him, why he kept blowing hot and cold with her.

His reply was a considering stare that silenced her. Sadly, she backed off, checked her patient again, then dozed off and on during the rest of the night. Had Justin put his arm around her in support, it would have been welcome, but he never did, and she wondered sadly what, if anything, he felt for her. She wished now that she'd never let him touch her.

Toward morning Rollo was still alive, but he was feverish and restless. Anne told Justin to get some sleep, and reluctantly he let another man take a shift by her patient while she went to the campfire to make up herbal infusions in the hope that she could lower Rollo's fever and give him a more peaceful sleep.

The cook watched her preparations with interest. Justin, from his blankets, watched as well, narrow-eyed, and she was uneasily aware of that suspicious scrutiny.

"I wouldn'a took you for a woman who knowed about herbs and such," said Hobbs.

Anne glanced at him. "I've spent five or six years out here on the western frontier at one fort or another," she replied, "and I've found there's a lot to be learned from the women who come out to settle this kind of country."

"My mother was such," said Hobbs. "She knew a million of them home remedies."

Anne nodded. When she had finished steeping the herbs, she had two different potions. "This is for fever," she said, pouring off one of the liquids into a cup. "And this is to bathe the wound in the hope that we can avoid infection. If you could make him a good beef broth, Mr. Hobbs, it would be strengthening. We might be able to get some into him later in the day if—"

"If he's still alive," Hobbs finished for her.

Anne nodded and said softly, "God willing."

The tea she'd made for fever had to be fed to Rollo drop by drop until it was gone. Then she uncovered and bathed the wound. The young cowboy who had been assigned to help her drew in a shocked breath, for he hadn't been present when Anne took the bullet out. Once she had finished, she covered Rollo again and sat down.

"You're lookin' mighty tired, ma'am," said the cowboy. "No reason why I can't set with him. I can do whatever you tell me to."

Anne nodded. She was exhausted, as much from the strain of dealing with Justin's changeableness as from her vigil. "Maybe someone could lend me a bedroll."

"Yes, ma'am," said the cowboy. "Hey, Hobbs!" he shouted.

"Sh—sh—sh," she hissed. "Mr. Tandy needs all the sleep he can get."

"Oh, yes, ma'am. Yes, ma'am. I didn't think." The boy blushed.

"What's going on?" Justin demanded, having unrolled from his blankets to come toward them.

"Gotta get Miss Anne a bedroll, so she can have a nap. Me, I'm gonna watch over Rollo."

Justin frowned at the boy. Then he studied his foreman. "How is he?" he asked Anne.

"Still alive," she said curtly.

"I can see that for myself."

"Then why ask?"

"Maybe a good, long nap would help your disposition, Mrs. McAuliffe."

"That and a few less questions," she snapped.

The young cowboy started to grin; obviously he had never heard anyone speak to Justin Harte that way.

By midafternoon Anne went reluctantly to Justin and said, "He desperately needs a doctor. Is there a town nearby?"

"Palo Pinto is the county seat, and it's not too far, but there's no doctor. He died just lately."

"Where then?" she asked, looking worried.

"Weatherford," said Justin, "but it will take a day, maybe two to get there."

"Two then," she replied. "We can't afford to jostle him."

"You think he's gonna make it?"

"I still don't know, but he needs care, expertise and medicine that I can't give him."

Justin nodded. "I'll provide the wagon and the men. Will you go with him?"

Anne's heart sank. Of course, she'd have to, but it meant leaving Justin without finding out what that night between them had signified to him. It meant not seeing his ranch, about which she had a wistful curiosity. Oh, well, she told herself, she really had no choice. "Yes, of course, I'll go," she agreed.

"And, Anne," he said softly, "I'm beholden to you. Except for my brothers, there's no one I'm closer to than Rollo."

Including me, she thought bitterly.

"We go a long way back. Live or die, I appreciate what you tried to do. Not many women would have the courage—"

"Oh, forget it, Justin." She didn't want his gratitude, and that seemed to be all she was going to get. "I'd have done the same for Cratcher."

Anne sent a rider to carry a message that Sissie was to pack and send Anne's things over. However, instead of her belongings, her stepfather arrived, protesting the loss of his camp cook.

"Morehead," said Justin, "I don't want to hear any arguments. You'll either agree to what has to be done, or you'll leave the roundup."

"Fine," said the colonel. "I'll leave the roundup and take my men with me."

"Just as you like," Justin retorted. "I'll work out the cost before you go."

"What do you mean?"

"Most of your herd's already been cut out. If you take your outfit away, that also means you'll leave owing us for the work your people won't be doing here and for any cattle of yours that we have to handle from now on."

The colonel looked shocked. "But that's not—you can't—that'll cut way into my profits."

"That's your problem, isn't it?" said Justin. "Now make up your mind. Are you going or staying?"

There was a long, angry silence. Then, with a resentful flush, the colonel muttered, "Staying."

"Fine, but Mrs. McAuliffe's going to Weatherford with Rollo. I'll send a man with them, and I'd advise you to send Sissie along as well. It's not a good idea for her to be here unchaperoned, the only female in camp."

The colonel agreed to that, too, but with ill grace, and Anne wasn't too happy with the idea of making the long, rough trip back to Weatherford with both her sister and a man who might well die before they arrived.

"I'm sending a rider named Abilene Harrison with you," Justin informed her. "He's a good hand and well able to protect both you and Sissie."

"Then I gather that I'm to drive the wagon."

"Of course not," said Justin. "He'll drive the wagon."

"In that case, I'll have to protect him," she said dryly. She could see that Justin was becoming exasperated and didn't much care.

"I just said that he'd protect you."

"Someone has to drive and someone has to ride shotgun," said Anne, starting to relish the conflict. "Or did you expect Sissie to do one or the other?"

"Sissie?" Justin snorted. "I can't say that I expect much of anything useful from your sister."

Anne nodded smartly. "Then it's drive or ride shotgun. I choose the latter."

Justin gritted his teeth. "I'll find another man to send along."

"Just as you like," she replied, and marched away, her eyes stinging. She hated to think that this was to be their last conversation, and she had to walk quickly into the woods before the tears showed.

"Anne," he said softly, putting both hands on her shoulders.

Damn the man! He moved like an Indian. She'd never heard him following her.

"Anne, I didn't mean to argue with you."

She whirled to look at him, her eyes bright with tears. "Am I going to see you again?" she asked.

His eyes blanked, and he replied cautiously, "I don't doubt we'll run into each other sooner or later."

She could hear the colonel calling to her from the camp. "Don't you want to see me again?" she asked.

A flash of pain crossed his face. "With all my heart," he said, but he looked as if he regretted it.

CHAPTER
Five

Anne entered the dining room, having just left the bunkhouse. Because the colonel refused to eat with the hands as most ranchers did, she had to serve every meal in two places, an addition to her workload which she resented. Last winter the colonel had even suggested that she prepare two entirely different meals, his more elaborate since he was accustomed to a more gracious standard of living. Wondering who had provided him elaborate meals during her eight-year marriage, and especially during his three years ranching in Parker County, she had flatly refused. Today the memory of his demands still rankled as she slapped serving dishes down in front of her stepfather and sister, then dropped wearily into her own chair.

"Anne, wait till you see the dress pattern I found in Emma Pickering's new *Godey's*," cried Sissie, and proceeded to discuss the frock she wanted Anne to make her with a length of blue-checked gingham Sissie had on hand.

Listening wryly, Anne passed a bowl of mustard greens boiled with salt pork to the colonel and helped herself to one of the catfish she had fried in cornmeal. At first the cowboys had been surprised to be served fish or, in fact, anything except beef and bacon, but they had got used to it and now occasionally volunteered to go fishing for her, although Anne herself liked to fish when she had the time. "I can't," she cut in, firmly quashing Sissie's plans.

"Of course you can," came the anguished response.

"I haven't even finished the riding dress I started for myself."

"Oh, goodness, you don't need a new riding costume. It's just going to be the same ugly black as the old one, so why bother? Unless you think Mr. Kimball's going to come by again to take you riding." Sissie giggled at the thought of Anne's suitor.

"Heaven forbid," Anne muttered under her breath. Ira Kimball was a Tarrant County farmer she'd met in Weatherford while nursing Rollo Tandy. A widower with three children, Ira was evidently looking hard for a new wife and had settled on Anne as a sensible choice.

"I certainly don't know what you see in him," Sissie observed. "The man's got all those children."

"So he does," Anne agreed. "And very nice they are too." She had liked the children better than Ira.

"I wouldn't want to marry a man with three children."

Anne was tempted to reply that a man with three children wouldn't want to marry Sissie. In fact, she herself had no desire to marry Ira Kimball, but the thought caused her mind to drift off, as it had repeatedly this last month, to Justin Harte. She'd heard nothing from him, not even a note of thanks for the time she'd spent nursing his foreman. Every day in Weatherford Anne had hoped to see Justin come riding in to check on Rollo, if for no other reason, but he hadn't. Since she'd been back at the Bar M, she'd expected him to call, now that roundup was over, but he hadn't. Picking disconsolately at her catfish, she tried to ignore her sister's nagging and finally suggested, suppressing a grin, that she might make time for Sissie's dress if Sissie took over the garden.

"The garden," Sissie wailed. "Why, I'd ruin my hands." She held up her soft white fingers of which she was so proud. "I don't know how you can grub around out there."

"Probably because it's the only way to get decent vegetables," Anne replied. "Now, would you be quiet for a minute so that I can talk to the colonel." Her stepfather looked up from his newspaper. "It's about the bunkhouse," Anne stated firmly. "I think you should get bunks. As it is, the men have to sleep in bedrolls on the floor."

"My dear Anne, cowhands are perfectly used to rough conditions," he replied patronizingly.

She tried to convince him, not for the first time, that they were losing their best hands because of the disgraceful living conditions and stood to lose their foreman, Last Cauley, as well because the colonel never took his advice.

The colonel shrugged and stated pedantically, "Women do not understand these matters, Anne. I, on the other hand, have been a leader of men all my adult life and am quite capable of running the ranch without your advice. Now, what have you prepared for dessert?"

"She made sour cherry pie," said Sissie, "and if you're through discussing the bunkhouse, I'd like to get back to the subject of my new gingham dress."

"Your sister won't have time. She's driving into Weatherford tomorrow to get supplies."

"Oh, goodie," Sissie cried. "I'll take my material along and hire a dressmaker."

"You'll stay home," said the colonel, "and do the cooking."

"Me?"

Anne had much the same reaction but ignored it to ask who was escorting her into town.

"You'll have to go by yourself," he replied.

She was amazed. Justin hadn't sent her off unprotected, but her own stepfather obviously didn't care what happened to her.

"You can leave at sunup tomorrow morning," he added. "Stay with Mrs. Pertle in Weatherford and be back before sundown Wednesday."

"You sent her off alone?" exclaimed Justin.

"Of course," the colonel replied. "She'll be making the trip in full daylight."

Justin's eyes narrowed. "When Sissie goes visiting, do you send her out by herself?"

"Sissie is younger and less self-sufficient," said the colonel stiffly. "Anne, on the other hand, is hardly a defenseless female."

"She's still a woman," said Justin. It was Anne's attractions as a woman that had drawn him against his will to stop at the Bar M when he should have been on his way to Fort Worth. "Now I'll have to go after her," he muttered.

"Before you finish your supper?" exclaimed Sissie.

"Yes," said Justin, much relieved. He couldn't recall a more unpalatable meal, even on a trail drive through the Indian Territories when they'd almost run out of supplies.

Anne was letting the team set its own pace, indulging in a daydream in which she attended a dance wearing a beautiful moss-green gown with a darker overskirt. She'd owned a dress like that once. She was dancing with someone; it didn't matter who, maybe Mr. Ira

Kimball. That thought made her giggle and endangered the daydream because Ira was portly and probably not much of a dancer. But then Justin suddenly appeared, looking so handsome in a fine suit of clothes, and he stared admiringly at her lovely gown . . . No, he couldn't do that because she was still in widow's weeds.

Anne sighed. She'd seen a handsome bolt of prune-colored china silk in Fort Worth on her way from Fort Griffin with her stepfather. The color was almost black. Would a dark, dark prune be considered acceptable for a young widow? If so, it would make a bold and unusual combination with her hair, and Justin, instead of shuttering his eyes, would look at her with open admiration and say . . .

It was just at that point in her fantasy that the horses, frightened by a snake on the road, reared and took off at a full gallop, dragging the wagon over a deep rut and pitching the inattentive Anne off into a ditch.

Justin saw the wagon careening toward him with no one on the driver's seat, and his heart lurched. Was it Anne's? He stopped the runaway team, tied his own horse to the back of the wagon and assumed the reins, sending the horses rapidly down the road while he scanned the edges. Half a mile away, he found her. She was sitting up, looking thoroughly dazed. Justin leapt from the wagon and knelt at her side.

"Do you think the prune will do?" she mumbled, then gave him a smile sweeter than any he had received from her.

"What prune?" he asked, confused.

"The prune silk. You don't think it's proper, do you? I knew I shouldn't have given in to temptation."

What in the world was she talking about? Because she looked so sad, he wanted to reassure her, but prunes and silk? "Are you hurt?" he asked.

"Oh, no," she replied. "I'm resigned to wearing black

because of David, you know."

David had been her husband, hadn't he? Justin scowled. "I was talking about you. Are you injured?"

"Injured?"

His breath hissed impatiently. She'd evidently bumped her head, if nothing else. Efficiently and as impersonally as he could, he ran his hands down her limbs, trying to ascertain if she'd broken any bones. When he glanced up, she was blushing. "Look, Mrs. McAuliffe—"

"Doesn't that seem a little formal under the circumstances?" she asked.

"I'm trying to determine if you've sustained injuries."

"Injuries?"

"I caught your team running away about a half-mile down the road; then I find you sitting in the dust making no sense at all, so it would hardly be surprising to discover that you'd been hurt."

"Oh," she said in a small voice.

Justin ran his fingers over her arms. "No bones broken there. Are your ribs all right?"

She gave him another soft-eyed smile and said, "Are you going to investigate?"

"Since you're undoubtedly wearing a corset," Justin replied stiffly, "I doubt that it would be much use."

"And I suppose you know all about ladies' corsets?" She giggled.

"Anne, would you please answer my question?"

"Of course," she said, and laid her head against his shoulder, her eyes closed. "Am I injured? I think I'm a little sleepy. Maybe I should have a nap."

"No," said Justin. "I'm going to put you on your feet, and we'll see if you can walk." He rose and lifted her gently.

"I don't want to walk."

"Walk," he commanded.

"Why should I? There's a wagon."

"Walk!"

"All the way to Weatherford?" she asked pitifully as she took a wobbly step.

"Now do you feel as if you've broken anything?"

"Possibly a wagon wheel."

"You, Anne. Have you broken anything—in your body?"

"No, I'm fine." She looked up at him with another sweet smile, her eyes still unfocused.

"So I see," Justin muttered. He walked her a few more steps and surmised that her bones were intact. Then he stared balefully at the colonel's wagon and decided that they could get into Weatherford and a doctor faster if he carried her on his own bay, so he gave the lead horse a smack on the haunches and sent the team clattering down the road toward the Bar M.

"Why did you do that?" asked Anne. She was leaning rather heavily against him. "It's bad enough that you expect me to walk. I certainly can't carry back all the supplies."

"We'll hire a wagon."

"Oh, I couldn't ask you—"

"At the colonel's expense," said Justin.

What a funny man Justin was! She'd never have guessed it—handsome, yes; funny, no. "The colonel's not going to like that," she warned, chuckling.

"Then he should have sent someone with you."

"That's what I thought," Anne agreed as she allowed Justin to lift her up into the saddle in front of him. Then she gave him a sleepy smile, wrapped both arms around his waist, and snuggled her head into the curve of his neck.

"Are you quite comfortable?" he asked dryly.

"Oh, yes, this is just lovely," she replied.

"Indeed, just lovely," Justin muttered in return. The soft pressure of her breast, the whisper of her sweet breath on his neck, the firm encircling of her arms about his waist all insured that the ride into Weatherford was going to seem painfully long.

"The colonel's going to be upset that I'm not staying at Mrs. Pertle's," said Anne, shaking out her napkin.

Justin shrugged. "You were groggy when we arrived, so I made the arrangements."

"In fact, when he gets the bills—"she laughed delightedly—"he's going to be very upset. Think of it. The hotel bill, the doctor's bill, this dinner . . ."

"I'll pay for the dinner," said Justin, and passed her a bowl of chicken and dumplings.

What nice hands he has, she thought, *long, square-tipped fingers*. Then she remembered how they'd felt, and her face flushed. She stared fixedly at the serving dish and said, "I think I'll start raising chickens."

"I thought it was pigs you were interested in."

"The colonel's being very difficult about pigs."

"Can't say as I blame him," Justin replied, grinning, "but I guess if you're planning a new project, you must be feeling better. Your head all right now?"

Anne shrugged. "The doctor said it was, though I don't see how he could tell. Whoever heard of a doctor who conducts consultations sitting out on the street in front of a drugstore?" She helped herself to biscuits. "Still, he took good care of Rollo. How's Rollo doing?" What she wanted to ask was why Justin hadn't come to see her earlier, but she wasn't sure she would like the answer.

"Pretty well, thanks to you. He can't sit a horse yet, so I've put him to studying tracts on breeding. Er—just cattleman's stuff," he added uncomfortably when she showed immediate interest, "nothing to discuss with a lady."

"Oh, for heaven's sake," exclaimed Anne, "you sound just like the colonel."

"Why, is he interested in breeding experiments?"

"The colonel isn't interested in anything that smacks of change," said Anne. "That's why he's doing so badly with the ranch. He runs it like a cavalry troop."

"So I've heard." Justin sipped his coffee and added thoughtfully, "Still, change is coming. We've got to bring in blooded stock if we want to keep a share of the Eastern markets. Our range-fed longhorns may be the best trail cattle in the world, but for beef they can't compete with other breeds."

"How could you afford to turn blooded stock loose on the open range?" she asked. "You'd probably find your investment long gone by the next spring to blizzards, or wolves, tick fever, rustlers."

Justin looked surprised. "It's obvious that you've learned something somewhere about cattle raising."

"After spending all that time at the roundup, I couldn't help picking up some information, could I?"

Justin chuckled. "I'd take bets your sister didn't pick up any."

"Oh, well, Sissie." Anne grinned back at him. "But you haven't answered my question."

"The answer is, of course, I can't afford to spend good money on a blooded bull and then turn him loose on open range. That's why I'll fence him in, and we'll bring the cows to him. Fact is, there's already ranchers out in the frontier counties that have thoroughbred bulls. More than you'd think. C.C. Slaughter in Young County's got thirty some bulls and heifers—shorthorns. Matthews and Reynolds in Shackleford have forty Hereford bulls.

"All fenced in? I thought you Westerners hated fences."

Justin shrugged. "The fences are coming. For a long time nobody did much fencing because they didn't own their land and because the wild cattle were there for the taking. Besides that, it costs too much if we'd had a mind to do it. Now with barbed wire, we can afford to fence, and with blooded stock in the herds, we'll have to."

"Well, I don't see how you can put a fence around land you don't own," said Anne.

"There'll be people who do that, too, but my brothers and I are buying land. Course, we own the water rights on our range, and the sections our houses stand on, but as we get the money, we're buying more."

"My stepfather isn't, not that I know of."

"Folks who think the open range is going to last forever are wrong, and they're going to find themselves in trouble ten years from now. It'll come to buying the land or losing it to settlers. At least, that's how I see it."

Anne nodded, fascinated with his view of the future. "It sounds reasonable to me."

Looking pleased, Justin ordered dessert and continued to talk. "Over the next ten years the cattle industry is going to change out of all recognition. You take the railroad. The Texas and Pacific's almost to Fort Worth, would have been there long since if it weren't for the panic in '73 when Jay Cook in Philadelphia failed."

"Philadelphia?" Anne looked dubious.

"The railroad lost their financing, and the line stopped dead in Eagle Ford." He accepted a cup of coffee from her. "It's taken us this long to get it built that last thirty miles, and the city had to set up a construction company and provide the men to work on the track, but it's coming, and that means we can ship cattle by rail if we want to."

He stopped briefly to sample the pie brought by their waiter, then continued earnestly, "I'm not saying the trail drives will die out right off; they won't. For one thing, you can only get about five longhorns in a railroad car. More than that and they'd injure each other. It'll still be cheaper for some years yet to send them up the trail, but sooner or later, we'll be breeding shorthorns and shipping them because they'll bring us enough more money per hundred weight to offset the freight charges."

Having signalled the waiter and paid the bill, Justin remarked with compunction, "You must be tired, Anne. I'd best see you to your room and let you get a night's sleep."

She nodded reluctantly and rose to accompany him from the dining room. "I envy you," she said wistfully, "having been on the trail drives during those years. It must have been an exciting life."

"I suppose it was. Most of the men who've driven herds up to Kansas or north and west to the feeder ranges, they'd agree it's as hard a life as you're likely to find, but on the other hand, there's a"—he stopped to choose his words—"I guess you'd say a companionship among men on the trail that you don't find elsewhere."

Anne nodded thoughtfully. "That's what my husband said about campaigning."

"He was right," Justin agreed, and he took her arm as they began to climb the stairs. "I've done that, too, but the thing about trail driving is, if you know what you're doing and have a little luck, it brings in a lot of money."

He sounded as pleased as a boy, and Anne, a step ahead of him on the stairs, looked back and laughed.

"Well, you can laugh," said Justin, "but I'm all set up now with a good ranch and plenty of stock, most of it paid for by trail driving. A lot of my money's still coming in that way."

They had reached the second floor and started down the hall to Anne's room. "And when the trail drives are over?" she asked.

"Well, by that time," said Justin, "my brothers and I'll own a big chunk of Texas range land and a lot of good beef cattle and horses." He opened her door, and she glanced up at him, her eyes bright.

"It's going to be an exciting time, isn't it?" she said. "The next ten years."

"It is that," Justin agreed. When he handed her the

key, their fingers touched, and she inhaled sharply. There had been a rapport, an excitement building between them all evening. Anne had forgotten her headache. All she could think of was the intensity of those dark blue eyes holding hers, the power that emanated from him. He seemed so much more alive than anyone she knew.

"Anne?" His hand closed tightly over hers, so tightly that the edges of the room key cut into her palm. Her lips parted, but she couldn't speak because she should have been saying good night, and that was the last thing in the world that she wanted to say to Justin Harte at that moment.

Justin had almost stopped thinking entirely. He released her hand only to slide his fingers to the slender curve of her waist. They were standing in the hall where someone could emerge from the stairwell or another room at any moment. Knowing that, he felt he had to be alone with her, if only for a minute. "Anne," he said again, his fingers sliding to her back where they rested against her spine above an elaborate cascade of black draperies that formed the back of her skirt.

When her fingers rose hesitantly to touch his face, he tightened his grip, swept her into the room, and closed the door. Anne had left one lamp lit before going down to dinner. At the door where they stood, their faces were in shadows. He turned to her, blocking out the light almost entirely and, with his hand at her waist, pulled her hard against the warmth of his body. With his left hand, he stroked her back, circling up until his fingers had reached the bare skin of her neck and she trembled against him.

Just another minute, he thought and ran his fingers up into the silken fire of her upswept hair, taking delight in the fragile bones of her skull, the vulnerable curves of her ears. Anne pressed against him, her body restless and seeking against the rising strength of his desire.

"This is madness," he muttered into her hair.

"Why?" she asked dreamily.

"We're not children, Anne. The way we're heading, I could—I could end up getting you in a family way."

There was silence for a moment, and then she said sadly, "That's not likely, Justin."

His body stiffened. "Have I mistaken your feelings?"

"No," she said.

"Then why did you say that?"

"Because I was married for eight years. Had you forgotten that? My husband and I loved one another. We wanted children so very much, but never . . . never . . ." The tears welled in her eyes, spilled over.

"Ah, Anne." He raised her face and kissed them away. "I'm so sorry. I know what it is to want children."

Of course he did, she thought miserably. He was a man building an empire, and he wanted children to pass it on to. But that meant she could never be his wife.

"Sweetheart, don't. Don't cry." He led her over to the bed, pulled her down into his lap. "Hush now. Someday—someday you might marry a man who already has children. Just because you can't have your own, doesn't mean you'll never have any to mother."

Anne thought bitterly of Ira Kimball and his three sweet little children. Unfortunately, she didn't want Ira Kimball; she wanted Justin. He was rocking her as if she were a child herself, and she resented his sympathy. It was his love she craved. Anne tightened her arms desperately around him, thinking of all the things she'd never have because she had given her heart to Justin so irretrievably.

"Anne," he said softly, his mouth against hers now. "Are you sure of this?"

She wanted to cry no, that what he was offering was not nearly everything she wanted of him. His fingers were already at the buttons that closed the tight bodice of her dress as she asked herself whether a little love, a brief love was better than none. When his lips touched the upper curves of her breasts as he slid the chemise over her shoulders, she knew that the answer was yes. Any love from Justin was better than none. He kissed one bared nipple, then the other as he freed her laces and pulled her clothing down around her waist.

She arched against him. "Hurry," she gasped urgently, feeling that every second her body remained separate from his was a second too long. If she couldn't have him forever, she wanted him now.

Justin was electrified by her urgent plea and began to strip her clothes away with careless haste. "Do you want the light out?" he asked as he ran wondering fingers into the red curls that had come loose across the counterpane. She was so beautiful, a lovely fire in his blood and under his hands.

"I don't care," she whispered, her fingers quivering on the buttons of his shirt and his trousers.

Justin rose to put out the lamp, and dropped his own clothes on the floor. Then he was back on the bed beside her, pulling the sheet up over their naked bodies. She rolled against him and trembled as her fingertips found the hard muscles and planes of his back.

"I'll make this wonderful for you," he promised. "Not just for me, for both of us." He had been taken aback by his desire to enter her at once, but he was also determined that he wouldn't. He had never been a selfish lover and he didn't want to start with Anne, who had become so important to him, who seemed like a part of him already, before he had even made her so. And it wasn't just passion; her mind was attuned to his in a way he'd never experienced before.

Anne didn't analyze her behavior. She simply reached for his mouth with hers while her fingers slid over his waist to the knotted muscles of his buttocks. Her first touch made his body, now fully aroused, buck against hers. She shifted to bring him into intimate contact.

"Anne, for God's sake," he said softly, but the protest was fruitless, for she could no more have taken her hands away from those hard muscles than she could have stopped her hips from moving in heated invitation.

"You're ready now?" he whispered against her ear, amazed.

"Oh, yes."

"You don't want more—"

"More than you can imagine," she murmured, laughter in her voice, "and soon."

Justin laughed in pleased response and turned her onto her back. "I think I should make you wait a bit." He supported himself on his elbows so that he could hold himself away from her and play with her breasts. Between her thighs he moved slowly, and he relished the shivers that ran over her as he stroked her so intimately, but with only the barest penetration.

Anne groaned, her voice husky as she said, "You're making me wild."

"You're making me happy," he replied. As he kissed her, he could feel the smile that told him he was pleasing her as well.

She let him continue his teasing strokes because he was driving her closer and closer to an explosion of feeling that she thought would be like nothing she'd ever experienced. However, as that climax loomed, her patience weakened, and she yearned to have him sheathed as deep inside her as he could go. "Now, Justin," she begged.

"Wait a bit," he murmured soothingly, but Anne was past waiting. She curved her fingers around his hard, flexing muscles and pulled him down to her as she thrust upward.

"Oh, God!" Justin moaned, his control shattered. His hands slid away from her breasts and under her to hold her firmly as he plunged again and again until she clenched around him and cried out wildly against his mouth in an outpouring of fulfillment. Then Justin too shuddered repeatedly until they were both still, sweat-sheened, sated. He felt as if he'd been given some miraculous gift. She was so passionately responsive, so loving, so much more giving in every way than he'd ever known a woman to be. But she wasn't for him, he reminded himself.

He gritted his teeth and rolled away. For a while they could be together, he thought—for a night—even if it was a terrible mistake. He buried his face in the curling silk that fanned around him, inhaled the sweet scent of flowers that lurked in the fine waves of her hair, while Anne, lulled by contentment, embraced him trustingly and slipped into smiling sleep against the hard wall of his chest.

CHAPTER

Six

Anne watched as the first gray light of early dawn filtered across his sleeping face. He wanted children, she thought unhappily, children that she couldn't give him. On the other hand, he seemed to feel as strongly for her as she did for him, although there was a reluctance in him, a withdrawal that she couldn't explain. She had noticed it long before the issue of children came up. Well, he had brothers who could marry; the family would continue. So maybe, maybe if he loved her enough, they could marry. She sighed and closed her eyes. If only he came to love her enough.

She dozed fitfully and reawakened to find him watching her with that intense blue stare. "You don't look happy, Anne," he observed. "Are you regretting last night?"

"No," she replied truthfully.

"You're a very passionate woman." She waited, wondering what he was getting at. "And you evidently loved your husband deeply."

"Yes, I did."

"Maybe when you woke up to find me instead of him—"

"Justin," she protested.

"In fact, maybe last night while I made love to you, you were thinking of him."

"David's dead, Justin. It was your arms I was in last night, your arms I wanted to be in."

"Yes," he said with a curious intensity, "my body, but you've been without the solace of a lover for months now."

"Years," she said coldly, angered at his implication. "I told you my husband was badly injured at Palo Duro. That side of our marriage, which was very good . . ." She stared at him challengingly, wanting to hurt him as he had her. "That side of our marriage was over two years before he died."

"And so you—"

"I what? Are you trying to say I'm a wanton?" she interrupted sharply. "A woman who turned to other men when her husband could no longer make love to her?"

"I didn't mean to imply that."

"I think you did, but you're wrong. I was faithful to David. Even after he died, I was faithful to him until I met you. And I don't know why you're saying these things. Is it that you think the worst of me for—"

"No," said Justin sharply, his arms tightening hard around her. "I just need to know I'm the only man in your mind as well as your arms when we make love." His mouth came down harshly upon hers.

Is he jealous, she wondered, *of a dead man*? He had already worked a rough thigh between hers, and she felt herself catch fire immediately.

"This time you won't hurry me," he whispered, his voice low and determined. "This time I'll make it last until I've burned away every image but mine."

What a strange man he was, she thought, so intense,

so overwhelmingly exciting. Perversely, she wanted to thwart his plans. She wanted to force him into an immediate joining. Wrapping her arms around his waist, she slid her hands up his back to dig her nails into his powerful shoulder muscles, but when she started to wrap her legs around him as well, he pinned her against the bed and, holding her helpless, began to explore her body with his mouth. He was relentless in his pursuit of her pleasure. Only when her breath was sobbing in her throat and her head tossing wildly on the pillow did he lower his body to hers.

"Say my name," he muttered.

She opened her eyes and stared into his. "Justin," she whispered, and he entered her with a deep, sure stroke. Her pleasure, for being delayed so long, was exquisitely intense, and she wanted to close her eyes and lose herself in the waves of excitement that pounded through her as he asserted his claim, but Anne had her own claims to make, and so she kept her eyes open, willing him to understand that she was joining her heart to his, not just her flesh.

When Justin closed his eyes, she objected. "You wanted to know that I belong to you. Watch it happen." His lashes lifted. "See," she whispered, her body rising to the rhythm of his penetration, her face tightening as the flush of ecstasy washed her cheeks.

And Justin did watch, fascinated, and he slowed his pace to draw out her pleasure and the pleasure he took as their mutual passion overwhelmed them. He watched as her throat arched in the final spasm of ecstasy, and as he found his own fulfillment in her, he was satisfied for the moment that he had banished the ghost of her first love.

Anne collapsed and let her eyes close at last, her sigh deep and satisfied as a smile softened her lips and she pulled his head down to the curve of her neck.

She was relaxed and warm beneath him. She was asleep, and he realized with compunction that she, trusting him, had found happiness and security in what he saw in himself as an exhibition of supreme selfishness. Justin knew that he had no right to make any claim on her.

"Anne," he said softly. "Annie." She didn't stir. He looked toward the window. The light was a little stronger, and when he estimated the time, he knew he had to dress and leave, had to do it immediately lest someone see him coming from her room and guess what had happened between them. She didn't need that kind of gossip, and neither did he.

Justin arranged a wagon and driver for her, studied the lists the colonel had given her, and expedited her purchases so that by noon the supplies were loaded, and the driver stood waiting for them to say their good-byes.

Was this it? she wondered. "When will I . . ." He looked at her questioningly, and she swallowed. "Do you think you'll be by the Bar M soon?"

"I don't know, Anne," he answered honestly.

She turned away, wondering if this was the final good-bye she had told herself he couldn't say. If only she'd had more time, surely, surely, he would never leave her like this.

"Take care, Anne," he said quietly.

She nodded and climbed up onto the wagon seat beside the hired man. "We'd best be getting along if we're to make the ranch by nightfall," she said to him. She didn't look back at Justin as they left. Pride had to count for something, she told herself, and he'd certainly never want her if she lost it. She wouldn't want herself.

Anne watched the days of June flow by in a surge of summer activity that should have made for a happier time than it did. Her garden flourished. The peach trees she had pruned in February bore rich, early fruit, and the yard was filled with racks of peach halves drying in the sun. Her flowers bloomed in profuse tumbles around the house. The riding habit she had designed and made turned out well. All the things over which she had control prospered, and she should have been content, she told herself, but disappointment underlay all her days.

She'd heard nothing from Justin—neither a message nor a visit. She could have wept but didn't. When she allowed herself to dream, she saw the two of them building that empire he had talked of, which made awakening all the more painful. It seemed unfair to her that they should be so perfect for one another and yet be kept apart by one insurmountable barrier. She almost wished that she had kept her sterility to herself.

Sometimes she let herself hope that he would decide he wanted her more than the children she could never bear him. In all ways but that one she would have been the perfect wife for him. They shared love and passion and ambition. No other woman could understand him better or work harder with him toward the realization of his dreams. There were times, however, when she questioned his love. Had he ever actually said he loved her? In the wild joy of their coupling, she couldn't even be sure of that.

And she had additional causes for uneasiness. The colonel had decided to send a large herd to Kansas and hired some stranger to lead the drive, a man neither Anne nor Last Cauley trusted, and that man had hired more strangers to accompany him. She had a terrible feeling about the whole matter, and Last was furious that his advice had been ignored. But again the colonel was adamant about having his own way, and the herd was gone.

Then there was her suitor, Ira Kimball, who, without any encouragement from Anne, had taken to calling more frequently. Sooner or later she knew that she would have to refuse a proposal from him. She didn't want to marry Ira Kimball, but every time the man showed up—once he had even come carrying flowers

—she heard Justin telling her that someday she could marry a man who already had children.

Would he want her to marry Ira? she wondered miserably. Should she? Maybe Ira Kimball represented her only chance at motherhood. She was twenty-five years old and considering a compromise with life. That thought made her terribly unhappy, and yet when Ira brought the children, she yearned for them. But did she want them enough to share the bed of a man for whom she had nothing but a mild fondness? Enough to give up her dreams of a love that surpassed even what she had felt for David during their best times? She couldn't, and she refused to believe that Justin would want her to.

When her thoughts became too heavy to be swept away by work, she put on her old riding dress and rode for hours, letting the wind and sun and speed clear the cobwebs of unhappiness from her mind. And she always returned at peace, although the colonel resented such frivolous, time-wasting, unwomanly behavior and grumbled for days.

Then at last Justin came. One day just before the noon meal he rode into the ranch yard, leading a second horse, and announced that he had brought a Goodnight saddle for Mrs. McAuliffe.

Anne's eyes rounded in joy. His visit was gift enough, but a saddle? Was it a courting present? The thought made her heart accelerate happily. Still, it was too expensive to accept, and that consideration evidently caused the colonel to snap rudely, "You've no call to bring my stepdaughter gifts, Harte. It looks damned suspicious."

"Colonel," cried Anne, aghast at his tone. The saddle might be over generous, but it was hardly scandalous, even if she was still in her first year of mourning.

"It's an expression of my thanks to Mrs. McAuliffe for saving Rollo Tandy's life," said Justin stiffly and so convincingly that Anne's pleasure ebbed a little. "Also, a Goodnight saddle is at least somewhat safer than an ordinary sidesaddle. Goodnight designed it for his own wife."

"My stepdaughter won't accept it," the colonel barked.

Anne glared at him, thanked Justin firmly—her own misgivings overcome by her anger at the colonel's interference—and invited Justin to share their midday meal. He was hesitant. What did that mean? Anne wondered. Surely, he'd planned to spend some time with her after coming all this way? She could hardly believe that the colonel's rudeness would put him off. It never had before.

When he nodded, she mulled over his reluctance as she preceded them into the house. Was he still ambivalent because she was barren? Or could he be worried that his pursuit of a new widow would look unseemly, tarnish her reputation? A tiny smile lifted her mouth as she thought of how much he had already compromised her. Not that anyone knew it but the two of them. Still, he was a serious and responsible man. Maybe he just needed a little encouragement. If that was the case, she couldn't think of a more pleasant task than giving it to him. Humming happily to herself, she began to put food on the table. As she took her own seat, Justin was saying that he had just bought four Hereford bulls.

"Waste of money," said the colonel. "We could have a hard winter in '77, and you'd lose them all."

"By next winter I'll have an ample store of feed." Justin explained that he'd found a nester on his land and let the man stay in return for a third of an agreed-upon acreage planted in feed for Justin's stock.

"Nonsense," was the colonel's opinion. "It's your land; you should have run him off. Looks like you're afraid of a fight. Sets a bad example."

Justin stared levelly at him and replied, "I've been in enough fights that only an outlander would think that."

Anne watched the colonel back off and had to hide a smile. "Where did you get the Herefords?" she asked.

"Two from Kentucky, two from Slaughter."

"Emma Pickering said the Slaughter girls buy all their clothes from the modiste in Fort Worth," Sissie broke in. The other three gave her blank looks, and she sulked.

"The animals bred from the new bulls—will you ship them by rail?" Anne asked.

"Anne!" her stepfather exclaimed. "That's hardly a proper area of interest for a female."

Sissie giggled, Anne snorted impatiently, and Justin, forking up the last bite of peach pie on his plate, said, "Would you allow me to familiarize you with the new saddle, Mrs. McAuliffe?"

"No," said the colonel. "She hasn't time."

"Of course, I do," Anne cut in, "and since Mr. Harte has been kind enough to provide me with a better saddle, I am anxious to try it out."

"Then Sissie must go along."

"Papa!" Sissie cried, "I'm to visit Emma. Have you forgotten? I'm sure Annie can figure out how to use her new saddle, or if she can't, she doesn't need Mr. Harte to tell her because Mr. Kimball would be ever so jealous if—"

"That's enough, Sissie," said the colonel.

Anne had already risen. "Have a good time at Emma's, Sissie. If you'll excuse me a minute, Mr. Harte, I'll change."

"Anne, come back here," commanded the colonel.

Anne ignored him. She had a new riding costume to don.

They pulled up in a grove of black jacks after an almost silent ride. Anne's hair, loose and blowing around her face and shoulders, made a glorious contrast to the black riding habit as she pulled off her wide-brimmed hat and smiled brilliantly at Justin. "I like it," she said, patting the horn of the new saddle. "I feel much more secure."

"Good." Justin dismounted and ground tied the horses. "The more I thought about it, the more I was sure that you wouldn't be a particularly conservative horsewoman." He smiled and lifted her down.

"You were right about that," Anne agreed, laughing. "Every time I feel melancholy, I saddle up and gallop it off."

"Are you often melancholy?" he asked, his hands warm at her waist.

"Often enough," Anne replied candidly. "It seems like forever since we said good-bye in Weatherford."

"Oh God, Anne!" He pulled her deeper into the grove of trees and into his arms. "I've thought about you, too." And before either of them could consider their actions, they were pressed against each other.

Anne, on tiptoe, wrapped her arms around his neck, and moved her hips urgently in answer to the blatant evidence that he was experiencing the same flare of passion.

"Anne, love," he groaned, "we can't, not here. Anyone could pass by and see us."

"I know," she agreed. But she wanted to touch him; she never had. Impulsively, she slipped her hand between their bodies to stroke the hard ridge of his passion.

"I can't believe we're doing this," he muttered as he quickly released his buttons.

"What *are* you doing?" She was momentarily confused, then quickly understood and closed her fingers around him, a sunlit smile flashing across her uplifted face.

"You make me act like an untried boy," he protested, but he was wasting his words. Her eyes were already glazed as her fingers pursued their curious exploration, and Justin's body stiffened, trembling. Completely out of control, he lifted her heavy riding skirts and astonished her by hurriedly relieving her of her feminine underpinnings.

"What—"

"Just cooperate," he muttered. "Considering the effect you're having on me, we don't have much time," he explained, lifting her.

"Oh, Justin," she gasped as she felt his unexpected entrance. Even as he penetrated her fully, he was sliding to the ground, his back against a tree.

"Now don't squirm," he warned, "or it'll be over before we've even begun."

Anne's knees were locked firmly at his waist, and she was experiencing the most delicious inner tremors.

"Stop that," he ordered.

"I don't have any control over it," she gasped. Her body wanted to move, although her mind still counseled cooperation.

"Oh, hell," Justin muttered, and he grasped her hips under the awkward mass of black skirting that flowed and bunched around them and guided her into a frantic motion that matched his own hungry upward thrusts. Anne was drowned almost immediately in a rush of heat that overwhelmed Justin at the same time.

"Lord," he mumbled as they collapsed against one another, breathless, "I haven't been in such a disgraceful hurry since I was sixteen." Anne raised her head from his shoulder, looked into his eyes, and burst out laughing. "This is hardly responsible conduct for two mature citizens," he observed wryly.

She giggled and moved suggestively against his thighs where she still straddled him. "Now, Anne," he warned.

"Now, Justin," she echoed teasingly, managing to give him another jolt of sensation before he lifted her away.

"This wasn't the riding lesson I was thinking of, you know," he mumbled as he helped her up.

"I'm not sure either of us was doing much thinking." She glanced around her. "I seem to have misplaced my under garments."

"They're probably lurking somewhere in the folds of those ridiculous skirts."

"Ridiculous skirts? I'd have called them suitably demure. You can't see so much as the tip of my boot when I'm in the saddle."

Justin nodded, grinning. "And they're voluminous enough to hide other activities when you aren't."

Anne had found the pieces of clothing so recently removed by Justin and was struggling into them. When she had settled her skirts, she pulled the pins from her hair, shook it out, and began to fasten it back in place.

Justin watched, fascinated. Finally he said, "I hear you have a suitor."

Anne glanced up and grinned. "Are you jealous?"

Stiffly, he said, "I have no right to be jealous."

"Haven't I given you the right?" she asked, hurt flashing quickly into her eyes.

"Oh, Anne!" He raised a hand to her cheek. "I shouldn't even be here, but I did miss you so."

Her face lit with happiness, and she moved toward him, but Justin, looking more somber than ever, held her away. "Are you going to marry him?" he asked tensely.

"Mr. Kimball?"

"Homer Teasdale," he corrected, scowling.

"Oh, I thought you meant Ira Kimball. He's the one who's been calling. I haven't seen Mr. Teasdale."

"Ira Kimball's courting you, too?"

"Well, I suppose that's why he keeps turning up."

"How often?"

"He's made three trips all the way from Tarrant County," she said, laughing. "Once bringing flowers, once bringing his children."

"And you're going to marry him?"

"How can you even say that after we—after we—"

"He'd be a good catch for you," Justin interrupted brusquely. "He has three little ones, doesn't he?"

"Well, yes, and they are lovely," she said wistfully.

"Then I can't imagine what's holding you back. He seems perfect for you."

"Indeed," said Anne resentfully. "Well, the children aren't his only advantage. He also has pigs."

"Pigs?" echoed Justin, startled out of his bad temper.

"Yes, he told me he had thirty fine pigs, a number of them pregnant sows."

"How very romantic," said Justin, a helpless grin taking over his mouth. "What woman could pass up three children and thirty pigs? It occurs to me, Anne, that you'll love Fort Worth. The streets are overrun with hogs."

She started to giggle. "Maybe I should refuse Mr. Kimball and just go into Fort Worth to catch my own. What do you advise?"

He stopped smiling and muttered, "You'll have to decide about Kimball for yourself."

Anne's eyes dropped unhappily. It was obvious that Justin did not yet believe he couldn't live without her. Well, she'd just have to help him change his mind, if he gave her the opportunity. "When are you coming to visit again?" she asked boldly.

"I doubt that Kimball would think much of—"

"Mr. Kimball doesn't come into it," she interrupted, no longer interested in teasing. "If he proposes to me, and he hasn't done so as yet, I do not plan to accept."

"Anne, I can't stand in the way of your happiness."

"You're not," she assured him impatiently. "Now about the next time I'm going to see you?"

Reluctantly he muttered, "I'll be back this way in mid-July when the Texas and Pacific tracks arrive in Fort Worth. There's to be a big celebration, and I—"

"Wonderful," Anne interrupted cheerfully. "You can stop to see me both coming and going. Just because the colonel's so grouchy is no reason for us not to see each other."

"If I do stop by," said Justin, frowning, "it had best

be elsewhere, Anne." He shifted uneasily and added, "There's a line shack up on Bushy Creek that's no longer used. Do you know the one?"

Anne nodded, but not happily. She could understand that he didn't relish the idea of coming to the ranch house, not when the colonel was always so inhospitable. "What about the Fourth of July barbecue in Weatherford?" she asked. "Sissie wants to go, so I imagine we will."

"Anne," he said, obviously startled, "we can't meet there."

"No, I don't suppose we can," she replied, disappointed but remembering her widowhood, "although Mr. Kimball doesn't seem bothered by—"

"Is he going to the barbecue?" Justin demanded angrily.

"Isn't everyone?" He *was* jealous, she thought smugly. Good. A little jealousy wouldn't hurt him a bit.

Anne slid out of her saddle into the dust of the yard. She was tired after the long ride from Sam Bannerman's Triangle ranch, where she had been invited to a quilting. Because of the distance, the sun was almost gone, just a red-streaked glow on the western horizon, and she imagined the colonel would be fuming after a day of Sissie's cookery. Anne smiled to herself and began to unbuckle the saddle Justin had given her.

She'd loved the quilting party where she had met most of the women in the area, one of whom she had liked especially. Sarah Bannerman, the young wife of Sam's son, Gus, was six months along with her first child and as pleasant a girl as Anne could remember meeting. Pulling her Winchester from the saddle boot and leaning it against a fence post, she thought about starting a quilt of her own if she ever found the time. Goodness knows, she had enough scraps. She'd made several dresses, hoping that she might see Justin somewhere when she wasn't on a horse. However, her scraps were black, and most people wouldn't appreciate a funeral quilt.

She heaved her loosened saddle from the horse to the corral fence. The horse wrangler was coming toward her and would take care of it and her mare. Now a man, she thought, might like a quilt with black in it, say black and red, or black, red, and gray. Maybe she'd make Justin a quilt for Christmas. She had particularly liked the blazing star pattern they'd completed that afternoon at the Bannermans'.

"Oh, Miss Anne, ma'am," said the wrangler, "I sure am glad to see you. Bowlegged Bennie's sick, an' we was hopin' you could take a look at him. Poor fella's feelin' lower than a dead snake in a dry creek bed."

Anne suppressed a smile. "I imagine that's pretty low," she murmured.

"Yes, ma'am, an' the boys got a heap of money bet on Bowlegged Bennie since he's the one's gonna win for us in the Fourth of July horse race. Last Cauley, as soon as he seen how sick poor old Bennie was, he said, "What we got to do is get Miss Anne to doctor him, her as saved Rollo Tandy's life when he had both boots in the grave.'"

"Well, in that case, maybe I'd better have a look at him." She found Bennie Schultz wrapped up in his bedroll, although it was a hot July day. "I hear you're sick," she murmured.

"Yes, ma'am," Bennie croaked pitifully. "Feel like I'm about to die, I do. An' if I don't improve none, I ain't gonna git to do me no dancin' with no pretty girls at the Fourth of July barbecue."

"Forgit the pretty girls," said one of the other riders. "It's the horse race you gotta worry about."

After listening to her patient's many symptoms, Anne announced that Bennie had a summer cold.

"That's all?" exclaimed Last, who had come up to hear the diagnosis. "He's just got a summer cold?"

"That's what it sounds like to me," said Anne.

"Summer cold's the worst kind," Bennie said defensively, as he sat up. "Still, if it's only a cold, I'll just eat me a few of them good onions you grow, Miss Annie. Nothin' like onions for a cold."

Another cowboy said garlic was better, and Bennie himself remembered that wrapping a dirty sock around the neck was thought to be a sure-fire cure.

"You're not going to get many girls to dance with you," said Anne, grinning, "not if you've been eating onions and garlic for two days and turn up wearing a dirty sock around your neck."

Bennie lay back on his bedroll, looking completely downcast. "I'm a goner," he said sadly. "Looks like I gotta choose between my health an' my love life."

"We'll choose for you," said Last. "Hobie's got a dirty sock here." The foreman snatched the offensive item from his wrangler's hand. "An' we'll bring you some onions an' garlic just to be on the safe side."

"I could make him up a tonic," Anne offered. "Of course, I wouldn't want to interfere with any of your time-honored remedies."

"Oh, ma'am," said Bowlegged Bennie, "if you got a tonic, I'd be mighty grateful. Raw onions don't set too well on my stomach anyways. I wouldn't want to be dancin' round with some pretty girl an' embarrass myself by breakin' wind or nothin', if you'll pardon my mentionin' such a thing."

"Certainly," said Anne. It was all she could do to keep from doubling over with laughter. "I'll send the tonic right down." She hastened out of the bunkhouse with her hand clamped over a wide grin.

Behind her, she could hear one of the riders hissing to Bennie, "See there. You done offended Miss Anne. No one talks about breakin' wind in front of ladies."

"Now she'll probably make you up somethin' really nasty tastin'," Last predicted.

"Oh, Lord, I hope not," Bennie moaned.

CHAPTER

Seven

On the bunting-draped platform erected in the courthouse square, after a stirring flourish by the Weatherford Cornet Band and a number of patriotic speeches, the mayor raised his hands for silence. "And now friends and neighbors," he said, his voice booming over the noise of the crowd, "it's my great pleasure to present the award for the winner of the Parker County Fourth of July Celebration Horse Race for the year of 1876, the centennial year of our great nation. The prize this year goes to the Bar M Ranch."

The Bar M hands, who seldom showed much enthusiasm for their outfit, cheered lustily. Beside the mayor stood Colonel Morehead, looking dignified, and Bow-legged Bennie Shultz, blushing and scuffing one boot toe against the other.

"To Colonel Bates Morehead, owner of the Bar M outfit, we present this fine centennial flag. Colonel Morehead." The mayor handed the flag to the colonel, who, bedecked in his cavalry uniform, saluted smartly.

"On behalf of myself and all those fine and loyal troopers of the Bar M . . ." At the word "troopers," all the Bar M employees scowled. ". . . I accept this flag on this proud year in the history of our nation, having myself been for so many years a humble defender of her flag, most specifically in the Army of the Republic . . ."

At the mention of the Union Army the rest of the audience, loyal Confederates all, commenced to scowl. However, the colonel was not put off by the cold reception and continued to speak proudly of his career in the defense of the country until the mayor, perceiving a dangerous restiveness, broke in with, "We thank you for those sentiments, Colonel Morehead, and now we'd like to honor Bennie Shultz, the man who won the race riding Pie Eye II. Bennie, would you care to say a few words?"

At the mention of Bowlegged Bennie and Pie Eye II, the crowd relaxed and cheered noisily while various cowboys bellowed questions at the successful jockey.

"How come you rode so good, Bennie?" shouted one.

Another cried, "What'd you do to the horse? Ain't never seen Pie Eye run that fast."

Bennie looked embarrassed but stepped forward bravely, and the mayor held up his hands for silence. "Well," said Bennie, "I reckon, folks, I owe it all to Miz Anne McAuliffe. 'Twarn't two days ago I was so sick I like to died, an' Miz Annie, she made me up a tonic which had me feelin' finer than a horse fly on a pile of—" Bennie stuttered to a halt amid shouts of laughter. Then he resumed, "That had me feelin' real fine. Now, I heard some of you boys askin' how come Pie Eye done run so good, an' I'd like to say that Pie Eye always runs good, cause he's a real fine horse, but I'll have to admit that ole Pie Eye run better'n usual today, an' agin it's all due to Miz Annie, cause I figgered if her tonic fixed me up when I was so sick, like as not it'd do wonders for ole Pie Eye, who warn't sick at all, so this mornin' I give him a couple of bottles of Miz Annie's tonic . . ."

Anne gaped at the cowboy. Her tonic had been concocted of bourbon whiskey, honey, strong tea, and her own special mixture of herbs. It was a recipe given her by a Tonkawa laundress, the wife of an Army scout at Fort Griffin, and was certainly never meant for dosing horses. She shuddered to think of what long-term effects it might have on Pie Eye.

"So, anyway," Bennie rambled on, "I fed that ole horse two bottles of Miz Annie's tonic, an' as you seen, he run like he was bein' chased by a mean and hungry panther."

"Thank you, Bennie Shultz," said the mayor hastily. "An' now folks, the barbecue's just about ready, an' the ladies have contributed many fine vittles, so I suggest that we all retire to the picnic ground for our festive centennial celebration."

The mayor had to talk louder and louder to make himself heard over a rising chorus of complaints from other outfits who were insisting that the outcome of the horse race be reconsidered. It was unfair that the Bar M horse had won after being dosed with some unknown and likely illegal tonic.

The awards ceremony broke up with another cornet flourish and a storm of controversy as the crowd surged toward the barbecue pits where whole steers had been cooking all day and where the tables were covered with delicacies made by the ladies of Weatherford and Parker County. Anne herself had brought three green plum pies, two cakes, and a crock of potato salad.

"Look what you've done," said the colonel angrily. "What should have been a triumph for the Bar M has turned into a scandal."

Anne snapped back, "I didn't tell him to give the horse that tonic, although I should have suspected when he asked for two more bottles. As for my causing bad feeling, your speech about the Union Army inspired a good deal more ill will than anything I did, especially considering that everyone in the audience is a dyed-in-the-wool Reb."

With that Anne jerked her elbow away from his bruising grip and set off toward the picnic tables to make herself useful serving beans, potato salad, and slices of cake and pie. Before the meal was over, five different men, three of them complete strangers, had sidled up to ask for the secret formula to her horse-racing tonic.

The Parker County Centennial Ball was in full swing, fiddlers fiddling, banjo players plucking, dancers whirling. Anne was feeling blue because, as Last had predicted, no one from the Crossed Heart outfit was in Weatherford that night. They were all attending a similar affair in Palo Pinto County, and her daydreams about whirling to Turkey in the Straw or Arkansas Traveler with Justin had died. Instead, she stood watching Sissie giggle in the arms of Steven Pickering while Lee Ann Bannerman glared. Mrs. Florence Bannerman and Mrs. Pickering, who had obviously hoped to unite the two families in marriage, were whispering together disapprovingly.

In Anne's group were the colonel, who was still peeved about her remarks on his acceptance speech; Ira Kimball, who had planted himself beside her more than an hour ago as if he had territorial rights; his three children, who were becoming sleepy and quarrelsome; and Sarah Bannerman, who had come over to chat and at the same time escape the pointed remarks of her mother-in-law, who thought it a scandal for a girl so far advanced in pregnancy to appear at a public function.

"And I don't care what she says," Sarah whispered. "If Gus ever manages to tear himself away from the whiskey barrel, I intend to dance too."

Anne smiled. She liked Sarah better every time she saw her and was much amused at a mental picture of

Sarah with her rounded belly and her young husband, somewhat the worse for the whiskey, bouncing around in a lively square dance and scandalizing all the judgmental old biddies, foremost of whom would be Sarah's mother-in-law.

"That's a pretty gown," said Sarah.

"Thanks." Anne smoothed out the tiny black-edged white ruffles at the neck. "It's likely to cause some comment I'm afraid." The dress was black, but it was covered with sprigs of tiny white flowers and had touches of white embroidered in black at the neck and wrists and on the flounces that draped from the bustle. Anne had put all of her extra time and thought into it in the weeks between her last meeting with Justin and the barbecue. "Your mother-in-law, for instance, probably disapproves of a widow in anything but solid black."

"Mother Bannerman disapproves of everything," grumbled Sarah.

"Lively music," said Ira Kimball, who could be counted upon to make some convivial remark every fifteen minutes or so.

"Pa," whined Merry Kimball, "can I have another cupcake?"

"Don't let her, Pa," said Anson, Merry's six-year-old brother. "One more an' she'll puke for sure, just like she done at the Baptist Church social."

"I will not," said Merry.

"Will too," said Anson.

Sarah wandered away, and Anne said, "Anson, why don't you ask your sister to dance?"

"Who me?" Anson looked horrified.

"Well, I think you're a big enough boy to join in the dancing," said Anne, as if she weren't quite sure but was giving him the benefit of the doubt.

Looking at it that way, Anson could hardly refuse, and the two children went off to join a square.

"You sure do have a way with young 'uns, Miz Anne," said Ira admiringly. "Only problem is, bein' newly come to Jesus in the Baptist congregation of Brother Hiram Foley, we don't believe in dancin'."

Anne sighed. That explained why Ira hadn't asked her.

"Miz McAuliffe, sure is nice to see you again."

"Why, Mr. Teasdale," Anne exclaimed, smiling at the heavily freckled rancher with his thinning, pale red hair. Poor Homer Teasdale was not a handsome man, she thought. "How have you been? I don't believe I've seen you since the roundup."

"No, ma'am," said Homer and ducked his head. "I wondered if you'd do me the honor of a dance."

"I'd be delighted." And off they went, leaving the colonel and Ira glowering after them.

For the next hour Anne, who loved to dance, almost managed to forget how downhearted she felt at Justin's absence. Ira and Homer kept her whirling through every set, Ira evidently inspired by competition to give up his Baptist principles for the evening. She even had a turn or two with several other men. Although she couldn't say that any of the group interested her, it was nice to feel young and sought after. She'd always had plenty of partners at the officers' balls she and David attended.

Her hour of gaiety, however, was shadowed when the colonel, who had left briefly, reappeared and announced that she was to stop dancing immediately, that her conduct was causing unfavorable comment among the married women of the community. Before Anne could protest, Homer interrupted by saying to her stepfather, "Say, Colonel, a coupla days ago my foreman seen two of your riders on my land. We wondered was there any particular reason for it."

The colonel gave Homer a black look and responded brusquely, "If my men were on your land, obviously they were line riders tracking some of our stock that had drifted."

"There wasn't no cattle of yours where Charlie seen

'em. That was over by the Muddy Fork where most of my herd's gathered, what's left of it."

The colonel scowled. "Just what are you getting at?"

"Well, I ain't makin' no accusations, but I've lost a lot of stock this year. We're keepin' a pretty careful eye out when we see strangers."

"If you recognized them as my riders, they weren't strangers."

"Charlie said they was your riders, but ain't nobody knows anything about them, an' you're always hirin' on new hands."

"Good men are almost impossible to find," muttered the colonel. "They're always coming and going."

"Don't have much trouble that way myself," said Homer. "At any rate, their bein' where they was looks suspicious. I'd like to know about them two. Charlie said they call theirselves Bud Smith and Bandy Hopper."

"Smith and Hopper are part of my crew, and they're camped on the line between my range and yours, which explains their presence on your land."

"No, it don't," Homer said stubbornly. "If they had business over there, when Charlie hailed 'em, they'd a stopped to talk steada gallopin' off guilty-like."

"I resent the implication, Teasdale," said the colonel. "Neither I nor my men are responsible for your losses."

"I wasn't accusin' you, Colonel. I was just askin' you what you know about them two riders."

"I have nothing to say on the matter," said the colonel and stamped away.

Homer sighed. "Reckon I made him mad again. I just don't seem to be able to get along no how with your stepfather, Miz McAuliffe."

"Not too many people do," muttered Anne. "You say when your foreman called to them, they rode off?"

"Yes, ma'am. Course it's possible that it didn't mean nothin', but most times when you see someone out on the range, they'll stop to pass the time a day, friendly-like, not ride on off in a big hurry."

Anne nodded. "We haven't had those two long. As I recall, they hired on after the roundup. I'll speak to Last Cauley about them, tell him what you said."

"That's mighty neighborly of you, Miz McAuliffe. Thank you," Homer answered. "Would you care to dance agin?"

As soon as Anne took an interest in the conversation between Homer and her stepfather, Ira had begun to shift uneasily from one foot to the other. When Anne spoke with Homer, Ira flushed and glared. When Homer asked her to dance, the farmer said peevishly, "It's my turn. You had the last dance."

Homer looked taken aback. "Well, I didn't mean to step on no one's toes, Kimball."

"Perhaps we could all sit down at one of the picnic tables instead and chat," Anne intervened diplomatically.

The two men eyed each other like fighting cocks but followed her obediently to a table. "Well," said Anne, wondering what she was going to talk about to two such halting conversationalists, "what shall we talk about?" They continued to glare sullenly at one another. "How are your pigs doing, Mr. Kimball?" she asked.

Ira brightened up, taking her polite question as a sign that she favored him. "Real fine, Miss Anne. Real fine. Reckon I got the best pigs in Tarrant County. Why one of our sows dropped a litter of eight fine fat little piglets. Fact is, Merry named her favorite after you."

"Did she?" murmured Anne, suppressing a desire to giggle. "That's very thoughtful of her."

"Yes, ma'am. Onliest problem is, Miss Anne turned out to be a male, so I'd sure appreciate it if you wouldn't mention that to her. Might make little Merry real sad. She's a tender little thing in her feelins', she is."

Anne nodded agreeably, but perceiving an opportunity to discourage any matrimonial intentions Ira Kimball might have toward her, she said, "Actually, it won't be a problem since I'm never likely to be at your farm to see my namesake."

"Oh, now, Miss Anne—" Ira protested.

"I didn't know you was interested in pigs, Miz McAuliffe," Homer interrupted.

"Oh, yes," said Anne. "I've always told the colonel that it was foolish to pay for bacon when we could be raising our own."

"Mighty sensible, ma'am," said Homer.

"Do you raise pigs, Mr. Teasdale?" she asked politely.

"No, ma'am, but I'd sure be interested in givin' it a try. I've heard all it takes is to buy a few an' turn 'em loose in the Cross Timbers. I got me some fine stands of oak, both black jack and post oak."

"Well, it's not quite that simple," said Anne.

"I'll say it ain't," chimed in Ira. "It's easy to see you don't know nothin' about pigs, Teasdale."

"Don't mean I cain't learn," Homer retorted.

"Of course, you can," Anne agreed. "The trick, as I understand it, is to train the pigs to come when you call, and you do that by feeding them corn now and then, which also firms up the meat at slaughter time."

"Well, Teasdale cain't do that," Ira said. "He don't grow no corn."

"But he could," said Anne encouragingly.

"Course I could."

"And, in fact, if you're interested, Mr. Teasdale, I have a very good pamphlet on swine raising. I'd be glad to lend it to you."

"Why, that's right kindly of you, ma'am," Homer said, giving her a melting look, as if she'd offered to give him a kiss rather than a treatise on animal husbandry.

Ira bristled as he saw his pig advantage disappearing and said, "Now look here, Teasdale, you know you ain't interested in pigs, an' there's no way you're ever gonna grow any corn. You're a rancher. Ranchers don't do nothin' like that."

"I can raise pigs if I want to," Homer said belligerently.

"You're just tryin' to shine up to Miss Annie here."

"Well, what if I am?"

"You ain't got the right. I'm the one who's been courtin' her."

Anne cleared her throat discreetly. "Ah . . . gentlemen . . ."

"Just because you're courtin' her don't mean I can't court her, too."

"But I've already spoken for her."

"You've done no such thing, Mr. Kimball," said Anne.

"See there, she ain't interested in you, Kimball."

"That ain't what she meant," Ira said. "She just meant I ain't actually asked her to marry me, but I—"

"Well, then! If you ain't asked, there ain't a thing in the world wrong with my courtin' her, too."

"Gentlemen!" Anne was glancing around nervously to see if their confrontation had been observed.

"Tain't right, courtin' a woman by makin' her think you're interested in pigs when you ain't."

"Who says I ain't?" Homer snapped. "I gotta mind to poke you in the nose, Kimball. I don't like your attitude."

"Now, look," Anne protested.

"Well, you just try it!" Ira shouted. "I'll poke you right back." Both men were teetering combatively on their toes with clenched fists and red faces.

"If I could get a word in," said Anne, teeth gritted.

"Daddy," cried little Merry, "why do you want to hit the man with the red face?"

"Quiet, Merry!"

"Yeah, quiet, Merry," said Anson. "Papa's gonna hit him right in the nose."

"Papa's going to do no such thing," said Anne firmly. "If either one of you hits the other, I'll never speak to you as long as I live." The two men stopped glaring at one another and turned to gape at her. "And furthermore, you're making a spectacle of yourselves and me."

"Oh, Miss Anne," said Homer, "sure, I didn't mean to embarrass you."

"No," Ira said pugnaciously, "you meant to embarrass me."

"Hit him in the nose, Papa," cried Anson.

"Yeth, Papa, hit him in the nose," echoed Anson's little brother, Woodul. "She's gonna be our new mommy. Papa promised."

"I'm sorry, Woodul, but I am not going to be your new mommy, and your father had no right to say so."

"What's that supposed to mean?" Ira demanded. "I done called on you three times. I even brung flowers."

"Prob'ly picked 'em in some creek bottom," said Homer.

"That's enough, Mr. Teasdale," said Anne. "I don't intend to marry you either."

Merry started to cry. "You promised, Papa. You said she'd be our new mama."

"Be quiet, Merry," said her angry father.

"Just go away, both of you!" Anne snapped.

"You done led me on," Ira accused her, "an' I resent it." He picked up his howling daughter.

"Me too," Homer said. "I thought you was gonna marry me."

"You have no reason to think any such thing," said Anne. "I've never said more than three words to you before this evening, unless you consider 'Good day, Mr. Teasdale' a promise of marriage."

Muttering angrily to himself, Ira stamped away with his two sons trailing him and his daughter in his arms. Homer stayed a moment longer, giving Anne a sad, hangdog look as if he hoped she might change her mind. She turned her back on him and sat down at the picnic table.

Behind her she could hear Mrs. Bannerman and Mrs. Pickering whispering about what scandalous creatures the colonel's two daughters were, Sissie for setting her cap at Steven Pickering, who was already spoken for, and Anne for leading on respectable land owners and for dancing in public, which was a thing no proper widow would do. But then, said Mrs. Bannerman, it was obvious that Anne McAuliffe was no proper widow. Look at the dress she was wearing. White flowers indeed! And white-trimmed ruffles! What was the world coming to? It was shocking indeed, said Mrs. Pickering.

"Don't pay any attention," advised Sarah, who had come back to sit beside Anne. "You can do a lot better than two silly men who can't talk about anything but pigs."

Anne sighed, feeling very sad indeed. She'd certainly like to do better, but the man she wanted to do better with was the one who seemed to feel that he had to stand off from her because she was a widow of less than a year's bereavement. She wondered what Justin would think of her dress. It had seemed reasonably innocuous when she had made it with him in mind.

"And I hope, Anne," Sarah said, "that when my baby's due, you'll come to the ranch for my confinement."

"I doubt your mother-in-law would approve," said Anne.

"I don't care," Sarah replied. "I want you with me."

"Then I shall be, Sarah," Anne promised her, but she had to quell the pang of envy she felt toward the young wife, so much in love and expecting her first child in the fall.

CHAPTER

Eight

Anne was riding the perimeters of the ranch, ostensibly to deliver pastries, but really to make sure the line riders were on duty and not out rustling Homer Teasdale's cattle. Last had wanted to come along, but she had argued that his presence would cause suspicion if any of their hands were, indeed, participating in the theft of other ranchers' stock. Mostly, however she had wanted to go by herself because she was to meet Justin, not that she told Last that. She just promised to look sharp and keep her Winchester handy in the saddle boot.

And, in fact, she would have done so without Last's admonitions because she disliked and distrusted both Bud Smith and Bandy Hopper, not only because of Homer's report but because they were the only men in the Bar M outfit who volunteered to stay out in the line shacks. Other riders had to be assigned to that lonely and onerous duty. However, her suspicions had not been confirmed. She met Hopper riding the line, and

Smith had been in his shack and had acted as if the delivery of a green plum tart was reason enough for some insolent remarks, which she had quelled by jerking her rifle from its sheath and giving him a look that would have frozen hot coffee.

Her last stop was at Bowlegged Bennie's camp, not that she suspected Bennie of anything more nefarious than dosing his horse with her cold tonic. Still, she could hardly overlook him when she was delivering food to others. When she reached Bennie's post, he had just ridden in to prepare himself a midday meal and was pathetically glad to see her. "Miss Annie," he cried, "it does my sad heart good to see your kindly face, ma'am."

Anne's eyebrows went up at this effusive if melancholy greeting, and she slipped from her sidesaddle and asked if he was suffering from another summer cold.

"Thank you, ma'am, no. I'm well in body if not in spirit." His round, boyish face reflected his misery.

Much as Anne wanted to ride on to her meeting with Justin, she found herself trying to explain away the colonel's having given Pie Eye II to Hopper, which Bennie took as a sign that he was about to be fired. "Ever'one knows that Pie Eye's part of my string," Bennie complained. "Don't an owner give a man's horse away, less'n he wants the rider to leave."

Anne was nonplused. She hadn't been aware that riders felt so possessive about the horses in their strings, which actually belonged to the ranchers for whom they worked. Nonetheless, she assured Bennie that the colonel, who ran his ranch on cavalry rules, rather than cow country rules, wasn't signalling any intention to fire him. At the same time, she did wonder why Hopper had been given Bennie's horse.

"Well, Pie Eye ain't my onliest trouble," said Bennie sadly, "though for sure I miss him somethin' terrible."

Anne suppressed a groan. She had been hoping to leave within the next two minutes.

"Yes, ma'am, the fact is that as well as losin' my horse, I've lost my heart."

For another twenty minutes she listened to Bennie's fears that Miss Rennie Sue Hicks, whom he had met and fallen in love with on the Fourth of July, might, in his absence from Weatherford, be transferring her affections to someone else, someone taller. Anne soothed his fears on this score by pointing out that short girls liked short men; that their names, Rennie and Bennie, rhymed, which was a very good omen; and that he could write a letter to Miss Hicks. Anne even agreed to write it for him since Bennie didn't know how.

"You sure are a nice woman, Miss Annie," he exclaimed. "If you wasn't so tall an' old, I reckon I'da fell in love with you instead of Miss Rennie Sue Hicks."

"I'm touched," said Anne. *Tall and old*? she thought to herself as she stepped up onto a rock and then into her saddle. *Tall and old*? "Good-bye, Bennie," she called, and headed away from the line shack at a brisk trot.

He wasn't there. As late as she was, Justin was nowhere around the dilapidated shack. Anne ground tied her horse, unsaddled, and spread the saddle blanket under a cottonwood tree beside the creek. What if he'd come and gone? What if he'd decided that because she hadn't arrived at noon, she wasn't coming at all? Anne could have cried with disappointment, but then she had another thought. She should be able to tell if he'd been there. He was traveling from Palo Pinto to Fort Worth to see the Texas and Pacific Railroad arrive, a grand event due to occur any day now. Therefore, his tracks would run from west to east. Hard as she looked, Anne could find no tracks of any sort, other than her own. She breathed a sigh of relief and went back to sit on her blanket.

Lord, it's hot, she thought and used her hat to fan

herself. There was nothing worse than wearing black on a hot day, which was another reason to dislike widow's weeds. She unbuttoned the jacket of her riding habit and then some of the buttons at the neck of her shirtwaist, after which she leaned her head back against the tree, thinking how wonderful it would be to see Justin again.

A half-hour later she was kneeling beside the creek to wet her handkerchief and pat her face and neck. Where could he be? she wondered. He was now an hour, maybe two hours late. She went back to the blanket and opened her saddlebags to take out some quilt pieces she'd cut, ignoring the food since she wanted to share it with Justin. She'd get his reaction to the color scheme, but without telling him the quilt was meant to be his Christmas present. Smiling, she took careful, tiny stitches as she put together the red, black, and gray scraps of material. It was going to be a work of art if she did say so herself.

An hour later she threw down the second square, stuck a pricked finger in her mouth, and glared toward the west. Where the devil was he? Then, leaning her head back against the tree, she sighed and reminded herself that he had a long way to ride. At least, there was a breeze now, although the temperature seemed higher. She closed her eyes.

When she opened them again, the sun was much lower on the horizon. *Good Lord*, she thought, *it must be four maybe five in the afternoon.* She looked around wildly. The clearing was still empty, which meant he wasn't coming. He had made this appointment himself, and he wasn't going to keep it, hadn't even sent word. He'd just left her to wait all afternoon in the heat.

Furious, Anne slapped the blanket onto the horse. Then she hoisted the saddle on as well and began to buckle it up. The horse danced protestingly at such rough treatment. "Oh, be still!" Anne snapped, and the animal turned its head to stare at her, perhaps sur-

prised at the sharp tone to which it was unaccustomed.
"Sorry, Horse," she muttered, for she had named it
Horse, much to the amusement of the cowboys. "It's
not your fault he didn't show up." She led the mare
over to a rock from which she could mount more easily.
Then her stomach protested noisily to remind her that
she had skipped the midday meal, so she delved into
her saddlebags for food, swung on, and ate as she rode,
grumbling to the horse about Justin's perfidy.

She was a quarter of the way home before her anger
gave way to sorrow and tears. "He means never to see
me again, Horse," she said miserably. "He could have
come to Weatherford to the celebration, and he didn't,
and now he's stood me up." Impatiently, she brushed
the tears away. "Well, I'm the one who asked him to
meet me. He's probably decided I'm a dreadful, forward woman, and he wants no more to do with me."
She blotted a second rush of tears with her sleeve.
"What was I thinking of to act the way I did with him?
Answer me that, Horse."

The horse had nothing to say on the matter, and
Anne took out her rumpled handkerchief. "He's probably found himself someone younger and shorter than
me," she said, recalling Bowlegged Bennie's remark.
"And someone who can give him babies." She tilted her
hat forward to shade her wet eyes from the westering
sun and nudged the horse into a gallop. She was going
to be very late getting home.

"Where have you been, Miss Anne?" Last demanded. "I was about to send out a search party."

"I was just taking my time," Anne replied. "Stopped
to have a chat with Bowlegged Bennie. You know how it
is."

"No, I don't know how it is, an' I don't want you
ridin' out to those line shacks anymore."

Anne, who was already in a bad mood, scowled.
"Neither you nor anyone else tells me what to do," she

announced, and tramped into the house without even unsaddling.

Last looked after her, astonished, and she knew she'd been unfair. He was just worried about her.

"Where have you been?" the colonel demanded as soon as she got in the house. "You're supposed to have been cooking supper."

"Sissie can to do it," said Anne angrily. "I'm tired, and I'm going to bed."

"Anne Martha McAuliffe, you do not talk to me that way," shouted the colonel.

"I just did!" she shouted back, and slammed the door of her room behind her. She was getting good and tired of the colonel and every other man she knew, for that matter. She threw herself down on her bed without even removing her dusty riding habit and gave way to stifled tears.

The railroad had arrived in Fort Worth on the nineteenth of July, accompanied by great fanfare. At the Bar M they'd got the news just yesterday from a passing rider. This morning, Anne had awakened thinking of Justin and decided she had to see if he would keep his second appointment to meet her at the abandoned line shack on his return from the railroad celebration. He had said three days after the first train arrived, and this was the third day. Maybe, she told herself, he was unavoidably delayed the first time. Since she planned to check the line riders again, there was no reason not to drop by Bushy Creek. She would give him a piece of her mind, for one thing.

The place was deserted as she slipped out of the saddle and wiped the perspiration from her face and neck. He wasn't coming this time either. Still, she was a bit early. It hadn't taken long to visit the line camps with only two riders around to receive their tarts. Bud Smith and Bandy Hopper were gone, and in fact, she thought they might have been gone for several days, which meant that even if they weren't rustling, they weren't doing their work either.

Anne ground tied the horse, unsaddled, and spread the blanket under the same cottonwood tree. It was hotter today than it had been before, and she was more tired, having slept badly all during the previous week. She ran her fingers up into her hair to lift the damp, escaping strands from her face. Well, she wasn't going to wait all afternoon this time. Goodness knows, she had enough things to do at home, more than enough, what with Sissie scatting all over the countryside visiting ranch families who had sons who interested her.

Anne sighed. She became more worried about Sissie with every week that passed. The girl was absolutely boy crazy. Because of her flirtation with Emma's brother Steven, Sissie wasn't invited to the Pickering ranch any longer. And when Anne herself had ridden over to visit Sarah Bannerman, she had received a cold welcome from Florence and Lee Ann. Anne hardly considered that the to-do caused by Homer and Ira on the Fourth of July had been her fault, but Florence and Lee Ann intimated that everybody in the county considered the incident the year's best scandal, next to Sissie's activities.

Anne sighed again and looked longingly at the cool waters of Bushy Creek. To relieve the heat, she took off the jacket of her riding dress and fanned herself vigorously with her hat. There wasn't a wisp of breeze, and the sun, as it rose to its highest point in the sky, was burning hot, even through the sheltering leaves of the cottonwood tree.

And there was no Justin riding into the clearing, not even whispering, hairless ghosts to break the shimmering silence of noonday. Chuckling over Last's warning that the ghosts of two scalped cowboys haunted the deserted shack, she rose from the blanket and went to kneel by the creek. First, she cupped water into her hands to drink. It was cool and felt wonderful against her face. Then she splashed her face and neck, and she felt even better, although the water wet her shirtwaist. Well, no matter. It was obvious that Justin wasn't coming. If he'd got an early start from Weatherford as he'd planned, he'd have been here by now. In fact, no one in his right mind would be out here at a deserted, haunted line shack on the hottest day of the year, no one but foolish Anne McAuliffe. She looked again at the cool waters of Bushy Creek. No one ever came here. That's what Last had said.

Impulsively, she stood up and began to undress. At least, she could cool off before she made the hot ride back to the ranch house, and as for Justin, she'd wipe him out of her mind—and heart. Blinking back tears, she dropped the last of her clothes onto the blanket and stepped carefully, barefooted, into the creek. And, oh, it felt wonderful, so cool and wet against her flushed skin. She immersed herself to the neck, holding up the straying curls and thinking it was a shame that men could go buck-naked into creeks and rivers if they wanted, whereas the whole world would raise a clamor if a woman did any such thing. A woman could only go for a swim in a creek haunted by scalped ghosts. Well, what the world didn't know wouldn't hurt it. She walked in further until she was waist deep with the water flowing around her. Cupping it, she dribbled it over her shoulders and breasts, reveling in the cool relief.

"Anne, what the devil do you think you're doing?"

Quickly she crossed protective arms around her breasts as she looked over her shoulder. Six or eight feet back from the creek stood Justin, glaring at her. "I can't believe what I'm seeing," he said.

"What are you doing here?" she snapped back angrily.

"I'm meeting you, of course. Why else would I have gone so far out of my way?"

"Obviously too far for you to have kept your last appointment," she retorted, edging into deeper water so that she could face him with her modesty preserved.

Justin flushed. "I shouldn't be here now," he muttered.

"You're quite right," she agreed. "You shouldn't, so go away."

"Very well," he said stiffly. "I'll leave as soon as you get out of that creek and put your clothes on."

"With you sitting there?"

"I didn't mean while I was looking," Justin amended hastily. "I'll turn my back, of course."

"Just turn your back and go," she ordered. "I'll get out of the creek when I'm good and ready. This is the second time I've spent a miserably hot day waiting for you, and I don't intend to ride home again in danger of heat prostration."

"Well, you've had your cooling-off period, so come out before you drown." She shook her head stubbornly. "Anne," he threatened, "you'll either do what I tell you, or I'll come in after you."

"No, you won't. Think of how foolish you'd look, riding the Weatherford Road soaking wet. Why my goodness, Justin, your spurs would rust." When he dismounted, she backed further into the water.

"Are you going to get out of there?" he demanded.

"No."

"Then I'm coming after you." He began to unbutton his shirt.

Anne stared at him, fascinated. His chest was deep and powerful, lightly covered with hair that trailed down to a thin line at his navel where it disappeared under his belt. His arms and shoulders rippled with well-defined muscles. His body looked no less threatening at the moment than his face, and her breath came fast and shallow as he sat down on a rock and yanked off his boots.

She couldn't believe that Justin was going to strip naked in front of her. Even though they had made love, she had never seen him naked, nor he her, for that matter. They had come together in the dark of night or the dimmest light of early dawn, even fully clothed, but never naked in full sunlight. How dark his skin was, as dark on his chest, arms and shoulders as on his face. He must work in the sun without his shirt, a sight, she thought wistfully, that she would like to see.

Then he stood and began to unbuckle his belt. "Are you coming out?" he asked again.

"I am not. And I doubt that you're going to take off your pants either," she retorted confidently.

"Well, you're wrong, so you'd better turn your back."

To her surprise he started undoing the buttons. About two seconds later he faced her naked, and he was magnificent. She simply stood in the creek, the water swirling around her, and stared. His thighs and calves were corded with muscle, beautifully formed, the result of years in the saddle she supposed.

"Damn it, Anne, I don't know a woman in the world who'd want to stare at a naked man." He sounded furious, and she raised her eyes to his, smiling a little.

"Why, Justin," she said, laughter overcoming her, "I believe you're flustered." He obviously was. For one thing he was fully erect, which no doubt embarrassed him. The sight was sending a flush of heat over her body, even in the cold water of the creek.

"I realize you've been married," he said, stalking angrily into the water, "but I doubt that most married women ever see their husbands unclothed."

Anne laughed. "I really can't speak for other women, but I guess I've seen about a hundred naked men."

"A hundred!" He looked astounded.

"At Fort Griffin in the summertime the river was always full of soldiers. I'd have had to walk around wearing a blindfold to miss them."

"Their officers let them do that? Your husband let you see them?"

"Those were the only baths they ever got. In the winter they didn't bother, and they smelled so bad, I suppose the officers didn't care who objected in summer."

Justin's hands closed around her shoulders under the water. "But you stared?" he said accusingly.

"I did no such thing," she retorted. "On the other hand, I couldn't hide in my house all the time, and there were occasions when I'd have walked into a tree if I'd kept my eyes closed when there were naked men in the river."

"You are the most provoking woman," he muttered.

"And yet you seem to like me." She reached a hand out under the water and touched him. "That's something a man, especially a naked one, can't disguise very well."

Justin flushed and pulled her closer. "Dear God," he muttered, "I promised myself I wouldn't do this again, that I wouldn't even come here to meet you."

"Did you?" said Anne. "Well, in that case, perhaps you should get out of the water, put your clothes on, and ride away."

"Anne, I can't leave you here. Someone might come by."

"Nobody ever does, Justin. The place is haunted."

"What sort of nonsense is that?"

"Last told me." She ran her finger through the droplets on his chest, touching one nipple as she did so.

"Don't do that," he growled.

Her finger moved on up along his neck into the line of his beard.

"Does Cauley know we're meeting here?"

"Of course not. He thinks I'm out checking the line riders, bringing them nice things to eat."

"You shouldn't be doing that either."

"Somebody has to do something to keep them happy,

or we won't have any hands left, not the way my stepfather treats them."

"But what if—"

"I go well-armed, and I can take care of myself, Justin." Her finger had slipped to his mouth, tracing it lightly, and he pulled her into his arms with rough force, lifting her feet off the creek bed, kissing her hungrily.

Finally he dragged his lips away and rested them in the soft curling hair above her ear. "If you can take care of yourself so well, what are you doing here with me?"

Anne had forgotten her anger as soon as she felt the delicious sensation of his mouth on hers again. Without answering, she turned her face to renew the kiss, and when his tongue probed her lips, she drew it in, stroked it, sucked on it as her body moved languidly against his in the cool water. Without releasing her lips, Justin lifted her and carried her out of the creek to the blanket she had spread under the tree. When he laid her down, the wool was rough under her skin, but she hardly noticed as Justin stretched out beside her, propped on one elbow.

"You're very beautiful," he murmured. He brushed his fingers over one nipple, then the other, watched them harden under his touch. "Very beautiful. And so responsive." He leaned over and licked her navel.

Anne felt deliciously vulnerable, lying naked in the dappled sunlight as he explored her. She moaned softly, moved restlessly under his caress.

Justin raised his head to study the red curls at the juncture of her thighs while his fingers trailed up between her legs. "Very beautiful. Wonderfully passionate." He touched her lightly, intimately, and her hips arched. "Do other men affect you the way I do?" he asked.

"What does that mean?" she asked, stiffening and trying to roll away.

He held her in place with a firm hand on one thigh. "I

heard there was an ugly quarrel in Weatherford on the Fourth of July, a quarrel about you between Teasdale and Kimball."

"Is that why you're here?" she asked, disappointed. "Because you're jealous of my suitors?"

"What difference does it make? I have no right to be jealous of your other men." He slipped his fingers between her legs and probed.

Anne's breath caught in her throat. "Leave me alone," she gasped.

"That's hard to do when your body tells me you don't want me to."

She turned her head away. What he said was true. She wanted his touch; she was already aching for him. He began to stroke her lightly, tantalizingly. He bent his mouth to her breast and suckled until trembling shivers ran over her body and her hips lifted to his touch.

When she was almost on the brink of explosion, he stopped and said, "You must have encouraged them. Otherwise, they wouldn't have argued over you."

Anne's eyes flew open. "I never encouraged anybody except you," she whispered, turning her head away because the tears had begun to gather. "And you make me regret that."

Justin groaned softly. "God, sometimes I think I must be crazy. I *am* jealous, and I want you so much." He knelt over her. "Do you know how much I want you?"

"As much as I want you," she said sadly.

"Then we'd better have what we want." He didn't sound very happy about it, but he lowered himself to her, parting her knees, and Anne gave a long trembling sigh as she felt him slide deep, deeper into her.

He made love to her slowly, taking his time, dallying and teasing, coming to her repeatedly all afternoon until the sun was low in the sky, when she stretched against him and said reluctantly, "If I don't start home soon, Last will send out a search party."

"He shouldn't have let you go in the first place," said Justin. "I don't know what the colonel's thinking of. The man should look after you better."

Anne tightened her arms around his waist and buried her face against the warm, bare skin of his shoulder, wishing with all her heart that the person to look after her could be Justin.

"We'd best get dressed, much as I hate to cover up that lovely body with anything but mine," he murmured. "God, sweetheart, I wish we could stay here forever."

Anne raised her head and smiled tenderly, and he smiled back and kissed her again, causing her heart to swell with happiness. She had known love with David, and she knew it now, not just hers for Justin, but Justin's for her. She had no doubt that he loved her.

"There never was a woman like you," he said wonderingly, and he dressed her himself, savoring the added opportunities to touch her, laughing softly as he puzzled over corset laces and tiny buttons. "You've got to promise me," he said quietly, "that you'll stop riding out to the line camps. I worry about you, Anne."

"Oh, Justin," she sighed, "it was necessary. Actually, I could use your advice about a problem we have."

"Oh?" He was buttoning his trousers. "What is it?"

"On the Fourth of July Homer told the colonel that two of our riders had been seen on his range, and when his foreman hailed them, they rode away fast. You may not know it, but Homer's been losing more stock this summer."

"I do know it," said Justin grimly.

"Well, the colonel, of course, didn't pay him any mind. He just got angry, but Last and I talked it over and decided that if I came out and checked the camps to see if the men were actually there, nobody'd be suspicious, not if I was bringing pastries."

"That's a dangerous scheme, Anne."

"Well, Last wasn't pleased about it either," Anne

admitted. "The first time I came out, the time you were supposed to meet me and didn't—"

"Sweetheart, I'm sorry. Did you wait long?"

"Long enough," she muttered.

"I told myself it was wrong to meet you," he said moodily. "I told myself the same thing this time, but somehow or other I just couldn't . . ." He sighed. "So anyway, what happened?"

"They were all at their posts the first time, but today both Bud Smith and Bandy Hopper were gone. They weren't in camp, nor riding the line, and although I'm no tracker, I don't think they'd been there for several days."

Justin scowled. "Teasdale just lost somewhere between two and three hundred head last night, most likely."

She gasped. "Do you think it was them?"

"Could have been. It's certainly something we'll have to look into." He finished dressing and helped her onto her horse. "I'll ride you halfway."

Anne nodded happily. She wasn't going to argue with any extra time they could have together.

"Teasdale doesn't have much left. Poor man's just about desperate," said Justin.

"I'm sorry," Anne sympathized. "I hope it's not our men who've been rustling his stock."

"Whoever it is," said Justin grimly, "we'll get 'em."

"We?"

"We're all losing stock, Anne. Hasn't the colonel had any problems?"

"Not that anybody's told me," she murmured. "Except for that trail herd he sent to market in Kansas. It seems to have simply disappeared along with the man he hired to boss the drive."

"But no losses here?" Justin asked, frowning. They came over a rise in the prairie, and he said, "This is as far as I go."

Anne pulled up her horse, and he reined his in close

and leaned over to kiss her. "This has to be our last time, Anne," he warned.

"What do you mean?"

"We won't meet again."

"But, Justin . . ."

"I have nothing to offer you, not a damned thing, and it's not right for me to take your love when I can't marry you." He looked grim and miserable. "I want you to promise that you won't come to the roundup in the fall."

She looked up, her eyes swimming with tears. "How can I promise that? The colonel will demand I go."

"Tell him no. Believe me, Anne, it's better if we don't see each other anymore." He put an arm around her, gave her one swift, hard kiss, then wheeled his horse and rode away, disappearing immediately into the splintering rainbows caused by the setting sun as it shone red through her tears.

CHAPTER

Nine

"What I don't understand, Miss Annie, is how you come to know about Homer Teasdale's herd bein' rustled?"

Anne stared bleakly at the hem of her riding dress, which was dusty and torn because she had ridden carelessly through the brush on her way home. She considered lying to Last because she was embarrassed that she had been meeting a man with no serious intentions toward her. Then impulsively, because it was obvious that Justin didn't want anyone to know, she blurted out, "I heard it from Justin Harte." Last frowned. "He was out at one of the line camps," Anne mumbled, regretting her answer already.

"Lookin' fer track, I s'pose," Last said. "Him an' Homer are long-time friends. He'd take it pretty hard, all the bad luck poor Homer's had."

Anne was relieved that Last had attributed such an innocuous motive to their encounter. She herself found it increasingly hard to understand what Justin's motives were. Lust, she decided resentfully. Much as it galled her to admit it, the colonel had been right in objecting to Justin's gift and attentions. "I hope Mr. Teasdale doesn't lose the Rocking T," she added.

"I hear tell he's been spendin' too much time in Fort Worth drinkin' an' not enough time protectin' his herds."

"Maybe he was celebrating the arrival of the railroad."

"Maybe," Last said. "Then again he coulda been feelin' bad 'cause of that fracas at the barbecue."

"Well, don't blame me for that. I never encouraged the man." Anne wasn't about to accept any responsibility for Homer Teasdale. "Any claim he thought he had on me was all in his head."

"You'll have to admit, Kimball'd been courtin' you."

"Not because I asked him to," Anne retorted. "I feel sorry for his children, but that doesn't mean I'm going to marry him. I've had one good husband, and I shan't take a second unless I find someone I like as well."

"Simmer down, Miss Anne. No one's sayin' you have to marry at all."

"Good, I'm glad to hear it," she snapped sarcastically. "Now maybe we could get back to the matter of Mr. Teasdale's missing herd and our missing riders."

"Well, them bein' gone sounds suspicious to me. Reckon I'd better go out there and have a look myself."

"And the colonel? Should we tell him?"

"Lemme think on it," Last said.

At noon the next day Last returned to the ranch and said to Anne, "You're right. Smith an' Hopper ain't there, and they probably been gone for some days. The onliest tracks I found was yours."

Anne frowned. "You mean I obscured their tracks?"

"No, twarn't that. Their tracks musta been washed out by rain, an' the only rain we had was before Homer lost his herd." He slapped his hat disgustedly against his thigh. "Well, far as I'm concerned, they're fired. I don't know where they are, but I'm gonna assign other men to their posts." Grumbling, he went off to do so.

Anne again considered telling the colonel but put it off. Having had so little sleep the night before, she didn't feel like another set-to with him.

"Hell, Colonel, we just took a quick ride into Fort Worth to see the big celebration when the railroad come in."

"Yeah, we wasn't gone more'n a day or two," said Bandy Hopper. "It gits borin' out there ridin' line."

"Line ridin's what you asked for," Last said.

"And you had no right to leave your posts without orders from your commanding officer," added the colonel.

"Yes, sir." Bud Smith all but saluted. "We was wrong fer doin' that, but it wasn't as if no harm was done."

"How do you know that?" Last demanded. "Homer Teasdale had two, three hundred head run off while you two was gone. We're still lookin' ours over to see what we mighta lost."

"Hell, we ain't lost no cattle," said Hopper.

"How do you know?"

"Well . . . well we seen the herds as we come in. The numbers looked just the same to me," said Smith.

"Me too," said Hopper. "The Bar M ain't been hit."

"Lucky for you," muttered the colonel.

"So you say you was in Fort Worth?" Last prodded.

"Yep, sure was one hell of a celebration, pardon me, ma'am." He nodded to Anne, who had been listening.

"Been a pack of people through here tellin' us about it," Last said. "An' not a one of 'em mentioned seein' either of you there."

"Well, actually we wasn't there the day the train come in," said Smith, shifting uneasily. "We heard about it, see, an' we wanted to go in an' take a quick peek, it bein' the first one an' all."

"How many days did you say you were gone?" asked Anne.

"Oh, not above two days, ma'am, just a day to ride in an' take a look an' a day to come back."

"Today's the twenty-fifth. That means that you must have left on the twenty-third. Is that right?"

"Don't rightly know, ma'am. Two days ago, that's all."

"And yet on the twenty-second I came by your line camp bringing tarts to the riders, and you weren't there, Smith."

"Well, likely I was out ridin' the line, ma'am."

"I didn't see you between Hopper's post and yours."

"Likely I was out west."

"I rode out west. You weren't there either, and it looked as if no one had been around for several days."

"Well, ladies, they don't know how to read sign."

"But I do," Last said, "an' I come to the same conclusion as Miss Anne."

"Well, there's likely some mix-up is all."

"I don't like mix-ups," Last said. "I think you two better throw your saddles on your horses and move on."

"Now see here," barked the colonel, "I do the hiring and firing."

"We didn't mean no harm, Colonel. An' honest Injun, we wasn't gone no more'n two whole days."

"They're lying," said Anne.

"Anne," said the colonel angrily, "I won't have you interfering in ranch matters."

"More the fool you are then," she said grimly. "If you'd listened to me before, you wouldn't have lost that trail herd."

The colonel flushed. "We'll hear from them."

"On a cold day in hell we will," said Anne.

"Watch your mouth." His fists clenched.

Beside her Last stiffened, and Anne held her breath, anticipating that the colonel was going to hit her. When she was a child he had beaten her, although never after she threatened him with his own sidearm when she was fifteen.

"These two stay on," said the colonel, controlling his fury. "But don't desert your posts again." He turned on his heel and stalked away.

Anne looked at Smith and Hopper, who were grinning insolently, and said, "He may be a fool, but I'm not."

Hopper stopped grinning and replied, "You're just mistaken, ma'am. We was there right when we said."

"Was I wrong too?" Last asked contemptuously.

"Look, Cauley, he said we could stay, so that's it."

"What's it," Last said, "is that I'm gonna have my eye on you. For starters, you're off line ridin'."

"Don't make no never mind to us," said Smith. The two turned and left.

"What do you think?" Anne asked.

"I think they was rustlin' Homer's cattle, an' Homer ain't the only one's lost stock around here. Only one as hasn't is the colonel."

"You don't think he's involved in the rustling, do you?"

"Nope. He's just bullheaded 'bout havin' his own way." Anne nodded her agreement. "Still an' all, you better quit takin' food to the line camps."

"It keeps the good men happy."

"But it puts you at risk with the bad ones, an' if them two should come to trial, we'd both be witnesses agin them. That bein' the case, I reckon we'd better watch our back trails. If you wanna go out ridin', I'll send someone with you."

Anne sighed. She no longer had a reason to insist on riding alone, other than her own desire to get away from the sound of human voices now and then.

Anne held her eyes open as wide as she could because when she let them close, a great wave of exhaustion swept her immediately into sleep. She knew cowboys could sleep in the saddle, but she was afraid she'd fall.

"Not too far now, ma'am," said Bowlegged Bennie, who, on the colonel's orders, had appeared at the Triangle ranch house that morning to take her home. When Florence Bannerman pulled her out of bed, Anne had had less than two hours sleep, having been awake the previous forty-eight delivering Sarah's baby.

"What was the emergency?" she asked Bennie, her mind fuzzed over with exhaustion.

"Roundup, ma'am," said Bennie.

Anne frowned. She'd already refused to go, and the prospect of another argument about it, when she was hardly conscious, was daunting, although not as daunting as the ordeal she'd just been through. She'd never delivered a baby who took so long. Not even her Tonkawa herb tea seemed to speed it up, and neither the doctor nor the midwife, sent for by Mrs. Bannerman, had arrived soon enough to help. In fact, by the time Sarah's son was born, everyone else except Anne had dropped into their beds with exhaustion. Even Sarah, badly weakened by three days of labor, was hardly conscious, and Anne, once she'd cleaned up mother and baby, had fallen asleep with her head on Sarah's bed and her hand on the baby's cradle.

Mrs. Bannerman, peeved that she hadn't been awakened for the event, and the doctor, badly in need of sleep himself, had roused Anne at daylight. Still, it had all come out right. In fact, Dr. Waller wanted the recipe for the tea, offering facetiously to take Anne into practice with him; young Gus had been ecstatic with his new son; and even Florence had softened toward Anne, tucked her into bed in one of Lee Ann's nightgowns, and later said a few unpleasant things about the colonel for insisting that Anne be dragged home before she could make up the sleep she'd missed.

"You're noddin' off again, Miss Anne," said Bennie. Obediently she widened her eyes and tightened her hands on the reins. That woke her up. Her hands ached abominably after two days of having Sarah clench them when the contractions hit. And her voice was almost gone because she had talked Sarah through each contraction, then defended her credentials and methods to a skeptical Florence Bannerman. Still, once Florence had seen her first grandchild, safe and sound in his cradle, and her daughter-in-law, alive and asleep, her whole attitude toward Anne had improved. And it needed improvement, thought Anne, remembering how critical Florence and Lee Ann had been on her previous visit.

"Here we are, Miss Anne," said Bennie encouragingly. "Now don't fall off your horse. Just let me—"

"What do you mean by staying away so long?"

Anne looked dully at her stepfather as he confronted her in the yard, red-faced and angry.

"You know very well you're supposed to cook on the roundup when it starts tomorrow."

"I told you I wasn't going," mumbled Anne, sliding down from her saddle with Bennie's help.

"Don't tell me what you'll do and what you won't. Get up on that chuck wagon. We're leaving right now."

Bowlegged Bennie tried to protest that Anne had had no sleep in several days, but the colonel eyed her narrowly and said, "Put her in the back of the wagon then. You can drive, Shultz." And that was the last Anne remembered except for jolting dreams.

She woke dazed and disoriented at the roundup camp, where the colonel insisted that she cook the evening meal immediately, which she did, half-asleep and uneasy that Justin would appear any minute to ask why she was pursuing him. However, by the time supper was over, she began to relax a little. Evidently Justin intended to ignore her presence, which would be a relief. Much as she longed to see him again, she couldn't face another hurtful confrontation. Anne was putting her pots away in the chuck wagon cupboard when he rode into camp with the Parker County sheriff. Both of them had guns drawn.

"Those two," Justin said, pointing to Bud Smith and Bandy Hopper.

The sheriff nodded and motioned to his deputies, who immediately began to tie the hands of the two Bar M men.

"Here now, what's goin' on?"

"Colonel, I'm arrestin' these two for rustlin'," the sheriff replied.

Smith and Hopper were thrown onto horses, and the party left, Justin having ignored Anne's presence.

"This is unconscionable," complained the colonel, "to come and drag off two of my men."

However, he received no support for his complaint. His outfit gave him resentful sidelong glances, for everyone knew that he had hired the two men and then insisted that they stay on when Last wanted to fire them. Anne supposed that the others felt their own reputations were tarnished by association. She sighed, thinking that the ranch would probably lose more men now that this had happened, and Justin . . . He hadn't even smiled at her. She climbed into the wagon and began her preparations for retiring, but then she heard Justin's voice saying, "We'll need to speak to Mrs. McAuliffe."

"Why?" the colonel demanded.

"The sheriff wants her testimony," was the answer.

Unwillingly, Anne climbed out of the wagon.

"Ma'am," said Justin, as if she were a stranger, "we'd appreciate your coming over to the Crossed Heart camp. You needn't worry, Colonel," he added. "I'll escort her there and see she's escorted back."

Sighing at the indignity of it, she allowed herself to be helped onto the horse saddled for her by their wrangler, although she was wearing only an ordinary dress and probably exposing her ankles to a whole camp full of men. She couldn't bear to check so she rode off with

Justin, her head held with stiff, pretended indifference.

As soon as they were out of the camp, he demanded to know what she was doing there. "I had no choice," she replied.

"Of course, you did. All you had to do was refuse."

"I did," said Anne angrily. "He dragged me home from the Bannermans' and had me tossed into the wagon when I'd been without sleep for two days." She sighed, all her exhaustion catching up with her. "I was delivering Sarah's baby."

"I didn't know you delivered babies," Justin mumbled.

"I have all sorts of talents, Justin, besides the ones you've made use of." She turned her head away from him.

"Look, I'm sorry . . ."

"We're both sorry, Justin. Just drop it."

In silence, they entered the Crossed Heart camp, and Anne hastily dismounted before he could help her. "Sheriff, you wanted to talk to me?"

"Yes, ma'am. I understand that you can testify that these two men, Bud Smith and Bandy Hopper, weren't doin' their work on the Bar M on the twenty-first of July the way they claimed."

"That's right," said Anne.

"She's lyin'," cried Smith. "She musta been out meetin' some man an' said she was lookin' for us to cover her own tracks with the colonel."

Anne felt a cold dread wash over her. If Smith's accusation got around, her reputation would be sorely tarnished. "I was taking pastries to our line riders," she said in a carefully controlled voice. "We have trouble keeping hands because of the way my stepfather treats them, so Last Cauley and I try to see that the men are well fed, if nothing else." Her eyes caught Justin's, and they both looked away quickly. "Besides that, we suspected these two because Mr. Teasdale said they'd been seen on his property."

Every time she glanced at Justin, her voice faltered, but the sheriff kept nodding encouragingly, so she inhaled deeply and continued, "I visited the camps several days before the nineteenth and they were on the job, but when I went back the twenty-second, they were gone. In fact, it didn't look to me as if they'd been there for a couple of days, although I'm certainly no expert on such things."

"You see," interrupted Hopper triumphantly. "She don't know what she's talkin' about. She admitted it her own self. The colonel, he heard all this, an' he didn't put no stock in it at all. He—"

"Then I rode west along the boundary line," Anne interrupted, her voice gaining conviction, "to be sure I hadn't missed either one of them. Mr. Cauley checked the next morning, the twenty-third, and the shacks were still deserted. He gathered from reading sign that no one had been there since the twentieth. Besides that"—she eyed the two contemptuously—"they lied to us about when and how long they'd been gone."

"Thank you, ma'am," said the sheriff. "You'll be an important witness when the trial comes up, if you're willin' to testify."

"I am," said Anne, exhaling unevenly. The two accused rustlers were glaring at her. "Is there anything else?" she asked the sheriff.

"No, ma'am."

"Then I'll be getting back."

Justin went to help her into her saddle, but she jerked away and mounted without aid. "Hold up, Mrs. McAuliffe. I said I'd escort you." He swung astride to follow her, and when they were out of earshot, said, "Anne, look, I'm sorry I snapped at you."

She turned her head away.

"I guess I'm upset about Homer," Justin mumbled. "The man's about done for as a rancher."

"And you blame me for his problems?" First the Bannermans, then Last. Anne was sick of being held responsible for Homer Teasdale. "Well, I'm sorry about Mr. Teasdale, but he's still got the Rocking T, and he must have a few cattle left."

"He's been drinking heavily since midsummer, and . . ."

She urged her horse to move faster, but Justin grabbed her reins and pulled her mount to a stop beside his. "Look, we're going to talk this out."

"Justin, you made it perfectly clear that you didn't want to see me anymore. Now can't you just let me get back to camp?"

"No, I can't." He dismounted, then lifted her from the saddle. Without putting up a physical struggle since there wasn't much she could do, she simply stood there, stiff and angry. "In a sense it is partially your doing that Homer fell to drinking. He loved you and—"

"Not because I encouraged it. You seem to have the idea, Justin, that I run around enticing half the men in the county, but that's not the case."

"I didn't say that, Anne."

"Well, what are you saying?"

"Oh Lord, I don't know. Just let me finish. Homer went into Fort Worth last week. The damn fool got in a poker game and lost the ranch to some gunfighter."

"Well, I'm sorry to hear it," said Anne, appalled at Homer's foolishness.

"Oh, sweetheart." Justin groaned and pulled her into his arms. "I've missed you so," he muttered.

"Who's fault is that?" she replied, her voice breaking.

"Anne, it's no one's fault. You know we can't be together."

"We already have been together."

"I know, I know, and I blame myself." He slipped his hands into her hair and tipped her face up to his, his mouth covering hers. His kiss was rough, desperate, and penetrating, and she felt herself almost immediately giving in to him all over again as he edged her off the trail. She was dimly aware that their horses had followed them, but Justin continued to kiss her hungrily, having pinned her body tightly against the rough trunk of a tree.

"I can't seem to get enough of you," he muttered as his hands released their bruising grip on her shoulders to drop over her breasts.

Anne shivered. "You've got to stop, Justin," she gasped when he released her mouth for a second.

"Now?" he said. "I can't." With urgent pressure, he ran his palms from her breasts over her waist to her thighs. Anne shuddered at the hard, fleeting touch between her legs, but he had moved on to lift and press her against the rigid swell of his passion. He caught her small moan with his mouth and began to press tantalizingly against her. "Lift your skirts," he urged.

"No."

"Do it."

"You're crazy," she whispered. "There are camps to either side of us. They'll—"

He stifled her protest with his mouth and dragged her clothing up himself, continuing to rub against her until she thought she'd faint for wanting him. In a wild flurry of motion, he was inside her, his hands beneath her buttocks to support her weight. As he held her against the tree and began to drive into her, a wild excitement overtook her, but she felt his jolting climax almost immediately. Justin had never done that to her before, and she tightened her legs around his waist, dimly aware at the same time of the sound of voices on the trail. He had started to release her, hissing in her ear, "People!" but she couldn't stop. She was locked around his waist, urging her hips against him. "Anne, for God's sake!" Her own climax exploded as the voices began to recede down the trail.

"Dear God, what are we doing?" he moaned.

Anne's head fell back against the tree as she pictured just how it would have looked to those men passing by—she with her skirts hiked up and her legs locked around Justin's body. Her reputation would have been ruined, which would have been unfair, because this time she had tried to stop him. Tears of relief welled from her eyes, and Justin, turning his head, tasted them and tightened his arms around her.

"Oh Lord, sweetheart," he said, his voice trembling, "I'm sorry." Where before he had tried to loosen her hold on him, now he moved his forearms under her to support her thighs and tightened his hands beneath her buttocks. "I didn't even make it good for you, but I will," he promised.

When she turned her face away from him, he followed and captured her mouth in a soft kiss. "This time I won't leave you behind," he said, beginning a tiny, seductive motion of his pelvis against hers.

"Don't," she protested.

"Sh-sh. Let me," he whispered back and continued moving his hips. He was still inside her, and she could feel the hardening, the filling. "Just relax," he crooned. "Let me do it all." He was kneading her gently, pressing and releasing, rolling against her.

"I don't want you to," she whispered.

"Of course you do. Imagine we're in a feather bed. A deep, soft feather bed."

She couldn't do that. She was against a jack oak, its rough, deep scored bark pressing against her back.

"Just relax and open up to me," Justin whispered. "You're sinking into a soft bed with my weight on you, inside you." He shifted position slightly, and she gasped. "That's perfect, isn't it?" He continued with small, rolling pushes. "I want to be deeper, and deeper," he whispered. "I want to feel you quivering all around me. Do you know you do that?"

She knew it. She could feel it happening. His fingers slid closer together, urging her to loosen, to open completely, trustingly, and she did. Helplessly, she felt herself flowing, melting around him, languid tremors widening around his penetration. She yearned for him to move faster and to take her completely, but he only continued the controlled, soft strokes that seemed to circle more widely inside her until she did find what she was looking for. She dissolved with him in one final liquid quiver that loosened all her muscles into boneless, drifting relaxation. It was a sensual dream, fading into a still, blind mist until he dispersed it with a sudden, hard thrust.

He couldn't, she thought dazedly, not when she had allowed herself to flower into defenseless vulnerability. Her eyes opened to the rustling dark around her, and her body woke from its dream as he continued to plunge. When she moaned sharply, he kissed her hard and thrust his tongue into her mouth as well. His grip had tightened and so did hers, and she clung in fear and wild excitement as he took her in two more thrusts to an unbelievable explosion of sensation. Her heart accelerated into runaway flight, and she tightened around him like a coiled spring, then was released in a passionate sensation that seemed to destroy them both. Their explosion was simultaneous, and when it was finished, he slid his forearms aside, loosened his grip, and allowed her to slip down until she was held only by the pressure of the tree behind her and Justin leaning weakly against her. They were both drained and silent.

Later, he stirred and helped her to rearrange her clothes. Then he straightened his own and lifted her into her saddle, after which they rode wordlessly back to the Bar M camp. To Anne, it seemed that they had been gone for hours, and she expected that all in camp would be asleep, but it was not so.

As she dismounted, the colonel stalked over and demanded to know where they had been. "It couldn't have taken that long for you to testify to what little you know," he said nastily. Then he turned to Justin and said, "I demand to know, Harte, what you've been up to with my stepdaughter."

"Since you never show her the slightest concern," said Justin scathingly, "I find your sudden interest in her welfare suspect."

Anne looked at the two of them as they scowled at one another, their hostility radiating for all to see, and it struck her that neither had any real concern for her. Wearily, she turned away and reached up for the horn of her saddle to pull herself onto the horse's back.

"What do you think you're doing?" The colonel grasped her arm roughly.

"Going home," she replied.

"You have duties here!" he shouted, his other hand raised as if to strike her.

Justin stiffened, appalled at the violence he sensed in the man, and started toward them, but Anne wrenched away from the colonel, mounted, and kicked the horse sharply into a brisk trot.

"Come back here!" her stepfather shouted.

She didn't even look his way.

"She won't change her mind," said Justin, "so you'd better send someone with her."

"The devil I will," said the colonel. "I don't brook that kind of disobedience."

Justin glanced around and spotted Bowlegged Bennie. "Shultz, saddle up and go after her. You'll have to escort her home."

"You don't command my riders, Harte," said the colonel.

"As long as I'm the roundup boss," said Justin, "I command anyone here."

"That's a fact, colonel," Bennie agreed as he tightened his saddle girth.

"If you leave, you're fired."

"And if he's fired, I go with him," Last warned. "There's certain rules to roundup, an' I won't be a party to breakin' 'em."

Justin gave the colonel a hard look. "From what I hear, you lost your profits from the spring roundup through your own bullheaded stupidity. Are you going to throw away your fall profits as well, because I can tell you, if you cause any more trouble, you're out, and no one is gonna bother with your stock."

The colonel's face turned a dull red. "You can't—"

"I can and will," said Justin. "Just try me. Shultz, be on your way." Bennie nodded and rode off. "Don't let me hear that you fired him."

Furious, the colonel whirled and stalked to his tent.

"Let me know if he makes any more threats," said Justin to Last. Then Justin mounted and rode toward his own camp. Anne's situation appalled him. Morehead had been about to hit her, and Justin felt responsible. Yet for all that, he still wanted her— desperately. He not only wanted her; he loved her. And he couldn't see her again, not ever, if he could help it.

CHAPTER

Ten

Anne trailed disconsolately through the lobby of the hotel in Weatherford. Even the new dress she'd made herself for Sam Bannerman Junior's wedding failed to cheer her, for she'd neither seen nor heard from Justin in two long months and had no assurance that he'd be attending today. Perhaps he'd miss the event just to avoid her, she thought gloomily. Perhaps he really didn't want to see her again.

She raised her eyes to glance at the clock over the mantel of the great stone fireplace and found herself looking into grim blue eyes. He had come! Her heart lifted with joy, a smile of pure delight irradiating her face, and she could see the immediate, if reluctant, softening of Justin's mouth, although he nodded curtly toward the stairs and strode off in the direction he had indicated. Anne suppressed her smile of pleasure. He evidently wanted to talk to her alone. Looking as demure as possible, she drifted after him toward the stairs. He was climbing them well in advance of her, but he paused long enough at his door for her to note his room. After he entered, she followed discreetly and slipped inside herself.

"Anne, what the devil . . ."

Ignoring whatever it was he had to say, she glided across the slightly threadbare carpet to him and slid her arms up around his neck, her heart melting with love. "Oh, Justin, you look so tired and so unhappy. Don't be." She tightened her grip and pulled his mouth down to hers, for Anne felt such a sweet caring, such a protective love for this complicated man to whom she had given her heart that she hardly knew how to assuage the misery and anger she saw in his face. He must have been as lonely for her as she had been for him. "Come," she murmured, drawing him toward the bed, pulling the tie loose from under his collar, sliding gentle fingers between the buttons of his shirt.

Justin sighed and murmured without much conviction, "Anne, we have to talk."

"Not now." She smiled at him with soft determination. "Later when I've chased away your troubles, whatever they are."

"For God's sake, Anne, you're one of my—"

"Troubles?" she finished for him and laughed. "Nonsense." She pulled him down onto the counterpane to overwhelm him with soft kisses. Never had she wanted to give so much, never so resolutely taken the lead in their lovemaking, touching and kissing him everywhere until she could see his outraged apprehensions fading away under her lips and hands. She teased him, gently, sensually, until they were both swept into the sweetest, closest of couplings and a depth of emotion that they had never achieved before in their tempestuous and enigmatic relationship.

When it was over, Justin, who had been exhausted, tense and anxious, relaxed into deep sleep, although it was early afternoon and she doubted that he was a man given to daytime napping. Anne cuddled contentedly against him, pleased to have erased the lines from his forehead, safe in her love and his. She had never felt closer to him, more loving of him, more secure in their union. Her heart told her that they were meant to be together.

She lay beside him for a half-hour or so, watching his beloved face in sleep, then rose reluctantly to dress and slip away. She still had to prepare for the wedding, to do her hair in a charming new style she had copied from a ladies' magazine. Much as she hated to leave him, propriety and practicality dictated that she go, and after all, she would be seeing him tonight at the reception after the wedding. Maybe the ceremony, combined with the beauty of their afternoon together, would be the impetus he needed to overcome his misgivings about committing himself to a woman who could not give him children.

It was the premier social event of the year. At dusk Hans Steinbrunner of Steinbrunner Mercantile had married his daughter, Gretchen, to Major Bannerman's younger son, Sam Junior, and all of Weatherford had been there along with all the farm and ranch families for several counties in every direction. Now the guests and wedding party had moved from the church to the Masonic Lodge for eating, drinking, and dancing.

Anne searched the faces swirling around her, hoping to spot Justin. Had he been at the church? Surely he wouldn't miss the wedding, although of course he might have overslept. A little shiver of sensuous remembrance ran up her spine. How would he act when they met? Would she see the memory of sweet passion in his eyes? Would he indeed, as she hoped, have changed his mind, decided that he wanted her more than he wanted children? Or was she indulging in foolish daydreams? Justin Harte, for all his passion, was a practical man. He was building an empire, and he wanted sons to run it. But, oh, how she wanted to spend her life with him. She ached with love for him.

Anne sighed dejectedly. Perhaps this was not going to be the happy evening she had anticipated. It was already turning sour because she was being systematically snubbed by the ranch families. She was afraid, being unable to think of any other reason for the ostracism, that Bud Smith's malicious allegations at the roundup camp had spread. The only friendly conversation she'd had was with Florence, who responded enthusiastically to Anne's query about Sarah's baby, but then Major Bannerman planted himself belligerently beside his wife and glared at Anne when she glanced up. *What now*? she wondered.

"How are you this evening, Major Bannerman? You've acquired yourself another pretty daughter-in-law today."

The major ignored Anne's attempt to make pleasant conversation and instead demanded angrily where she had been when it came time for her to testify at the trial of "those two dad-blasted rustlers."

Anne's heart sank. She'd forgotten that. Bud Smith and Bandy Hopper had been acquitted by a Weatherford jury because neither she nor Last had been there to testify. The colonel had sent Last off to Kansas to investigate the disappearance of the Bar M trail herd and the money its sale should have brought. Then the colonel had locked Anne in her room to keep her from attending the trial.

"It wasn't my idea to stay away," she mumbled, hoping Major Bannerman wouldn't ask further.

"What's that supposed to mean? The sheriff told me you'd promised to testify."

"I had every intention of doing so."

"Then why didn't you? I s'pose Cauley couldn't get back from Kansas, lookin' for that herd, although plenty of us are madder 'n hell that Morehead sent him, but there's no reason you couldn't have showed up. You were right here in Parker County," Sam Bannerman said.

"That's right," said Anne, resigned to admitting what had happened. "Locked in my room for two-and-a-half days."

"My land!" Florence exclaimed. "What'd you do that the colonel would lock you up, and you a grown woman?"

"Not much question there," muttered the major. "Everyone knows she was meeting some man."

"You believe Bud Smith, do you?" demanded Anne, her temper rising. "He's the one who started that rumor, the very man you wanted me to testify against." Her hands were planted belligerently on her hips. "Well, for your information, the colonel locked me up because I told him I was going into town to testify no matter what he said."

"Morehead didn't want you to?"

"He did not—not me and not Last Cauley."

Major Bannerman frowned. "Are you telling the truth, young woman?"

"Are you calling me a liar?"

"Why wouldn't the colonel want rustlers brought to justice? Unless maybe he was one of them."

Anne sighed. In truth, she didn't think that, angry as she was with her stepfather. "He had a falling out with Justin Harte at the roundup, several of them, as a matter of fact. I imagine he did it to spite Mr. Harte."

"I never heard about any trouble between Harte and Morehead, but I intend to get to the bottom of this. Come along, young woman." He engulfed her elbow in one huge hand and towed her through the crowd.

Anne was so angry that she would have pulled away had she been able, but escaping the clutches of a determined two-hundred-and-eighty-pound man was more than even a woman as angry as she could accomplish. Then she stopped thinking about prying herself loose because she saw where they were heading. Justin *was* there, looking very distinguished in a dark, finely tailored suit, his beard neatly trimmed. On his arm was a stunning blonde in an elaborate royal blue alpaca gown, which Anne was sure had come from the needle of some expensive, professional seamstress.

The sight made her self-conscious about her own black silk dress with its jet beading and fringed flounces, which Anne had made from a pattern she found in *Peterson's* and thought at the time a triumph of fashion. The blonde's dress had tapestry trim sewed on in vees across the front of the overskirt, velvet bows, and an accordion pleated hem. It was a beautiful gown, and she was a beautiful girl, thought Anne enviously, wondering if Justin was seeing her, if he thought himself infatuated or even . . . No, that couldn't be, not when just this afternoon. . . .

"Justin," rumbled Major Bannerman, "Miz McAuliffe here's got something to tell you, something mighty interesting."

Anne looked into Justin's eyes, and what she saw there chilled her. They were as cold and bleak as a winter sky, and his mouth tightened into lines of condemnation, which filled Anne with confusion and dread.

"Now, Major Sam," said the blonde, "mind your manners. I haven't been introduced to this lady."

Anne glanced at her as the major said, "Sorry about that, Penelope. This is Miz Anne McAuliffe. Miz McAuliffe, Penelope Harte."

Anne felt a great wave of relief wash over her. The girl was Justin's sister. How like a man to mention his brothers and ignore the fact that he had such a lovely sister. "I'm delighted to meet you, Miss Harte," said Anne, giving her a radiant smile.

"Mrs. Harte," corrected the blonde, laughing. "I'm Justin's bride, not . . ."

Anne missed the rest of it as the shock hit her. His

bride? She felt the room whirl, felt a veil of blackness closing in. His bride? She wouldn't faint, she told herself grimly. She wouldn't make a bigger fool of herself than he had already done. He had got himself married? Just since September? Through her mind flashed the pained memory that just this afternoon, in a blaze of love, she had all but thrown herself into his arms. She gave him one agonized look, then turned back to Penelope Harte. "My apologies for the mistake, Mrs. Harte," she stammered. "When was the wedding?"

"Why it was last Christmas," said Penelope. "We had the most gorgeous Christmas ceremony, didn't we, Justin?"

Last Christmas? Anne went cold. He had been married the whole time? He had been married before they even met in the spring?

"My wedding gown was made 'specially for me in New York City," said Penelope, "and I do believe it was the loveliest wedding gown Texas has ever seen, not, of course, that Gretchen's wasn't a pretty thing, but she got it in Weatherford, you know."

He had been married when he kissed her and touched her so intimately at the spring roundup?

"The local modistes are somewhat inferior to those of the great northeastern cities, don't you think?"

"I wouldn't know," Anne mumbled. He'd never once mentioned a wife, never once, not even this afternoon when Penelope Harte must have been somewhere close by while Anne and Justin were making love.

"Now this dress," said Penelope, "came from the Parisian dressmaker in Fort Worth, and I do think she did a creditable job, don't you?"

"I suppose so," Anne agreed. The first time he'd made love to her in the hotel in Weatherford, he must have come to her straight from his wife.

"Of course, I'd have ordered something more interesting had I had time," said Penelope, "but none of us got much notice, did we?" Then she lowered her voice and whispered, "This wedding was a bit rushed, don't you think? It makes one wonder."

"Wonder what?" Anne asked. She could hardly contain the fury that was forcing a rush of blood to her heart. How could he have done such a thing?

"Well, I don't think I have to put it into words," said Penelope in an offended whisper, glancing at Sam Bannerman. Obviously she had not expected to be asked for any explanation of a remark that had essentially been ill-meant and insulting. "When a girl gets married with practically no planning whatever, people just naturally wonder what the big hurry was." The major was talking to Justin, so Penelope Harte returned to a normal conversational volume. "My goodness, my wedding was seven months in the planning."

Anne dragged her eyes away from Justin and stared blankly at his wife, who had begun to describe the elaborate preparations for her own wedding, but interrupted herself to ask, "Is something the matter, Mrs. McAuliffe?"

Anne thought of how touched she had been by Gretchen Steinbrunner's wedding ceremony, how sadly she had been reminded of her own marriage when she too was very young and so happily infatuated with her bridegroom; of how she had daydreamed during the ceremony of what a marriage to Justin would be like because she had thought, in the sweet aftermath of their passion, that he truly loved her, meant to marry her after all. Well, there would be no marriage to Justin. Justin was already married, something he hadn't seen fit to mention, married to this shallow, vain, spiteful beauty.

"What could be the matter, Mrs. Harte?" Anne replied.

"Oh, do call me, Penelope," said Justin's wife. "That's a rather pretty gown you're wearing."

"I made it at home," said Anne.

"Did you? My goodness, aren't you clever? One can hardly tell."

"If you'll excuse me, ladies," interrupted Major Bannerman impatiently, "I've brought Miz McAuliffe over here to talk about rustling, not about ladies' wardrobes."

"I doubt, Sam," said Justin, "that Mrs. McAuliffe is as interested in cattleman's problems as anyone thought originally."

"Don't jump to conclusions, Justin," warned Major Bannerman. "Miz McAuliffe told me something mighty strange. She says she didn't turn up at that trial because the colonel wouldn't let her."

"Mrs. McAuliffe seems to have a lot of problems with her stepfather," said Justin dryly. "As I remember, she claimed to be at the roundup against her will."

"Well, I wouldn't know about that," said Bannerman, "but she says she didn't testify because More head didn't want her to, and when she said she was going to anyway, he locked her up in her room."

Frowning, Justin glanced at Anne.

"And kept her there till it was all over," the major added.

"Is that true?" Justin demanded.

Anne nodded curtly. How dare he question the truthfulness of anything she said? After what he'd done! She was so angry she couldn't speak.

"Kinda looks like, with him sending Cauley away an' lockin' her up, the colonel pretty much made sure those two rustlers were freed, much good it did them."

Although Bud Smith and Bandy Hopper had been acquitted, their bodies were found the next morning in a post oak grove not far from the Weatherford Road. They had been lynched by unknown parties.

"So what we gotta ask ourselves," continued Bannerman, "is why the colonel did that."

"That seems obvious!" snapped Justin.

Anne looked at him sharply. What ugly thing was he thinking now?

"Well, don't jump to conclusions. Miz McAuliffe says you and the colonel fell out a couple of times at the roundup, and she figgers he did it to spite you."

Justin flushed when Bannerman mentioned his arguments with her stepfather. Bitterly, Anne reminded herself that the colonel had had good reason to suspect Justin's motives for the attentions he had shown her; the colonel had known that Justin was married. No wonder he hadn't wanted her associating with or accepting gifts from Justin.

"You think that's likely, Justin?" asked Major Bannerman. "That he might of kept them from testifying to spite you?"

"It wouldn't be in the interests of any honest cattleman to prevent a rustler from being brought to justice. No matter what our differences—"

"But then my stepfather did have reason to be wary of you, didn't he, Mr. Harte?" Anne interrupted. As frequent as her own quarrels were with the colonel, she wasn't about to let Justin get away with implying dishonest motives to her stepfather, who had evidently been trying to protect his family.

Justin gave her a fulminating look and snapped, "Maybe you'd like to explain that remark, Mrs. McAuliffe."

"I seriously doubt that I need to, Mr. Harte." Trembling, Anne turned her back on him and walked away. The memory of how she and Justin had made love just hours earlier when his wife might well have walked in on them filled Anne with horror and fury, and the knowledge that she herself had initiated that lovemaking overwhelmed her with shame.

"Do come to visit us at the ranch, Mrs. McAuliffe," Penelope called after her. "Maybe you could make me a dress."

Anne shuddered. Visit them? When he had betrayed her? When she still loved him?

All she wanted now was to go back to the hotel, but she couldn't even do that without an escort. And how, she wondered, was she going to get through this evening? There weren't enough people in the hall to isolate her from the sight of Justin and his wife. Justin's wife! God, how could he have deceived her that way? He'd been married since the beginning. When he'd brought her that saddle, he'd been married. When he'd met her at the deserted line shack and carried her naked from the water and made love to her under the cottonwood tree, he'd been married. And when he'd taken her over her protests at the fall roundup, he'd been married then, too. And never once, never once in all the times they'd talked, had he mentioned a wife. This afternoon . . . Oh, God this afternoon, with his wife in the same town, no doubt sharing the very bed where they had lain.

She wanted to burst into tears, in the room full of laughing, dancing people. She'd probably have to watch him dance with Penelope, and what was she to do in the meantime? Because of him, she'd driven off her own suitors. What a hypocrite he was, objecting to their attentions, acting scornful because Homer and Ira had quarreled over her on the Fourth of July. So here she stood, marooned in the middle of this wedding reception where all the ranching families were avoiding her. Because she had been kept from testifying at that trial, there'd be no one to dance with, no one to talk to. She couldn't even look to her own family for company. The colonel was still furious with her, and Sissie. . . . Anne glanced around anxiously, wondering what had happened to Sissie. Well, there she was, flirting as usual, waving to Anne, tripping over to give her a hug.

"Isn't this fun?" Sissie cried. "Aren't you having a wonderful time?"

"Oh, wonderful," said Anne, if being on the verge of

tears was having a wonderful time.

"Did you notice that man over there in the corner?"

"Probably not," said Anne.

"Well, look," Sissie commanded impatiently. "Isn't he handsome? The blond one in the black clothes. Do you know who he is?"

"I've never seen him before," said Anne with an absolute lack of interest in the slender, somber fellow who was standing by himself like some sort of pariah. He didn't look like Sissie's sort of target. "What's wrong with him?" asked Anne. "He's the only person in the room with three feet of space around him."

"He's the gunfighter," said Sissie in an excited whisper.

"What gunfighter?"

"The one who won the Rocking T in a poker game. Surely you heard about it. They say Homer Teasdale went into Fort Worth and got as drunk as a hoot owl and lost the ranch to that man. Some people even say Homer tried to back out of turning over the deed, and the gunfighter threatened to shoot him. He looks dangerous, don't you think?"

"Actually, he just looks uncomfortable."

"Uncomfortable!" cried Sissie. "Why would he be uncomfortable?"

"Probably because no one is speaking to him."

"I'd love to speak to him," said Sissie. "Goodness me, I've never met a gunfighter."

"Well, don't stand on ceremony. Go introduce yourself."

"Papa won't let me," said Sissie, pouting. "When I asked Papa to introduce me, he said I wasn't even to look at him. Oh, there's Frank Steinbrunner. Yoo-hoo, Frank." Sissie went flitting off toward the bride's cousin, having lost interest in the gunfighter when someone new turned up.

Anne watched her go, thinking that her sister might well be the last person to speak to her that evening, unless the colonel came over to say something nasty. Her eyes swept the room and fastened on Justin, who was dancing with his pretty wife. His eyes caught Anne's for a moment, then moved on as if he hadn't seen her at all.

She swallowed hard and looked away. How could he love a woman, no matter how beautiful, who thought of nothing but clothes and gossip? Imagine intimating at the wedding reception that the bride had had to get married, saying it in front of the new father-in-law. Once again Anne's eyes drifted to the gunfighter. His blond hair needed cutting, she observed idly, and he certainly did look more uncomfortable than dangerous. She knew just how he felt—all alone in a room full of people who thought ill of him.

Behind her she caught a thread of conversation. "Poor Homer," the voice was saying. "Lost his heart to that wild redheaded girl and then the Rocking T to some hired gun . . . probably cheated poor Homer at the poker table . . . don't believe for a minute she was innocent in all that."

Anne's lips tightened. "Innocent of what?" she wanted to ask them. What was it they thought she'd done, and why did they assume that the gunfighter had cheated? If Homer was as drunk as people said, the young man would have had to be an idiot not to win.

Well, she thought defiantly, if no one else would treat him hospitably, she would. Maybe he'd like the company of another pariah. Anne caught up the black-fringed train of her gown and marched off toward the young man.

"Good evening," she said, with grim friendliness. "I'm Anne McAuliffe." She stuck out her hand.

He looked quite taken aback. "Ma'am," he stuttered, taking her hand as if it were a hot gun barrel on the point of explosion.

"And your name is . . ." she prompted.

"Ah . . . Pancho."

"Pancho?"

"Well, that's what folks call me. From when I was down in San Antone. I ain't a Mexican though," he added.

"You don't look like one," Anne agreed. "Do you have a last name?"

"Tighe," he mumbled.

"Fine. Would you like to dance, Mr. Tighe?"

"With you?" he asked uncertainly.

"Is there something wrong with me?" she retorted. He was a hard young man to befriend.

"No, ma'am. You're real pretty. It's just that . . ."

"Yes?" she prompted. "Maybe you've never danced before."

"Only in saloons," he replied, flushing.

"Ah. Well, I don't suppose it's any more difficult to dance with a respectable woman than with any other," she said and, taking his hand, led him resolutely toward the dance floor.

The poor fellow looked scared to death. Anne found it hard to believe that he was a famous desperado, and he certainly wasn't much of a talker. It was difficult to defy society, she reflected, by flirting with a gunfighter, when the gunfighter in question was too shy or too inarticulate to enter into the most rudimentary conversation.

"Are you enjoying the wedding reception?" asked Anne.

"Not much," he muttered.

"Why not?"

"'Cause you're the only person who's spoke to me since I got here. Do you know who I am?"

"Certainly," said Anne. "You're the young man who won the Rocking T in a poker game from Homer Teasdale."

"Oh. I figgered you didn't know who I was.

Otherwise, you wouldn'a come near me."

"Are you enjoying being a rancher?"

"Not much," he said again, looking morose.

"Why not?"

"I ain't never been a rancher before. Don't know how to go about it."

"Get yourself a good foreman," she advised.

"I don't know any."

"We've got one who'd probably like to leave," she muttered. "Well, since you don't enjoy dancing or ranching, what do you enjoy doing? Is gunfighting much fun?"

"At least, I'm good at it," he said defensively.

Anne nodded. "How did you get into the gunfighting business?"

"You sure ask a lot of questions."

"Well, I wouldn't have to if you'd carry your share of the conversation. So how did you become a gunfighter?"

"I don't know, just kinda fell into it, I guess."

The music ended and Anne, determined not to let him escape, slipped her hand through his arm and led him toward the refreshment table. "I'll have a cup of punch," she said, "and a piece of cake."

"You mean for me to get it?" He seemed doubtful, as if her request might be socially unacceptable.

"The gentleman is supposed to get the lady's refreshments," Anne assured him. He just stood there. "Do it," she ordered. Looking reluctant, he did. "Now get yourself some," she prompted. He did that too and allowed himself to be led over to several chairs near the dance floor. "So," said Anne, taking a sip from her cup, "you were telling me how you became a gunfighter."

"Well, I killed someone." She nodded encouragingly. "Then everyone said how good I was with a gun, so I just sorta took it from there."

"Ah." Anne sipped again.

"Do respectable ladies always wanna know about

things like that? If a man asked all those questions, he'd git himself shot."

"Respectable ladies," said Anne airily, "always have an insatiable curiosity about dangerous gentlemen."

Pancho Tighe looked pleased for the first time that evening. "Nobody ever called me a dangerous gentleman before. Well, not a gentleman anyhow," he marveled. "Sounds kinda classy. What'd you say your name was?"

"Anne McAuliffe. Mrs. Anne McAuliffe."

"Oh, oh. You got a husband who's gonna pull a pistol on me 'cause I'm talkin' to you?"

"I'm a widow. Did you make a good living as a gunfighter?"

"Pretty good. Made more money than I am ranchin', that's for sure."

"Well, you haven't been at it long. Perhaps you'll do better than Mr. Teasdale. Presumably rustlers would think twice about running off your cattle, seeing as you'd probably shoot them for doing so."

"That's if I had any cattle to run off."

"You could buy some."

"I ain't rich, you know."

"Maybe you could win some in another poker game."

"That's a thought." He had sipped some of his own punch and grimaced. "This sure is awful tastin' stuff."

"What did you expect?" asked Anne, laughing. "Whiskey?"

"Well, I wouldn'a minded," said Pancho.

"Eat the cake," Anne advised. "Eating wedding cake is supposed to be good luck, although you seem to have more than your share, having won the Rocking T and all."

"Well, I ain't sure if that's such good luck. Ah, would you like to dance again?"

"Very good, Mr. Tighe. I'd be delighted."

She stood up with alacrity, and they were soon whirling in a lively square dance. The other young ladies in their set looked quite astounded and not a little excited when it came their turn to give a hand or a waist to Pancho Tighe.

"Well, you've just fluttered a number of hearts," said Anne as they sank breathlessly into their chairs.

"Me?"

"Of course. All those girls are feeling quite daring for having danced with you."

Pancho looked immensely flattered. "This is the first time I've danced with any respectable ladies," he said. "It ain't so bad."

"Of course not. We'll make a social butterfly of you yet."

The young man laughed delightedly. "You sure are a funny lady," he said. "Your husband musta been one lucky man, since I don't reckon too many proper type ladies are all that much fun."

Anne sighed, remembering David and all the fun they'd had before he was wounded and all the unhappiness they'd had afterward. "It's hard to call a man lucky who's dead," she said quietly.

"Well, that's true, I guess," said Pancho. "I always figgered to die young, before I got old and ugly and stove up, you know."

"How old are you?" asked Anne.

"Twenty-two," he replied. "How old are you?"

Anne laughed. "You're not supposed to ask a lady her age, but because we're becoming such good friends, I'll tell you. I'm twenty-five."

"You're older'n me," said Pancho.

"Indeed I am. In more ways than one, I imagine. And that being the case, you can ask me to dance again before I'm too old to enjoy it." They had finished off their cake and put their cups aside.

"You sure do have pretty red hair," said Pancho, inspecting it as they danced.

"Why, thank you," said Anne. "If you don't look too closely, you won't even be able to see the gray."

"Ah, you're funnin' me. There ain't no gray."

"That's right," said Anne, and they laughed companionably together. It pleased her to notice that Justin was staring at them, his eyes angry. *What about?* she wondered. Was it because she was dancing with the man who had taken over Teasdale's ranch? *Well, good. Let him disapprove*, she thought defiantly. Anne hoped he dissolved in his own bile. She smiled gaily at young Pancho Tighe, and he smiled back, looking entirely smitten.

"How come you asked me to dance? Girls in saloons do that, but I wouldn't think respectable ladies, 'specially widow ladies ask men to dance."

"That's just it," said Anne. "I saw you in the corner looking lonely, and I was feeling just that way myself, so I decided to do us both a favor. Aren't you glad? You're obviously having more fun now than you were an hour ago."

"That's the truth. I'm havin' more fun than I've had since I won that damned ranch."

"Abomination!" shouted a powerful voice.

Pancho looked startled and stopped dancing. "I—I didn't mean to swear," he stuttered.

"And I didn't shout abomination," Anne replied, chuckling. "I believe that's Brother Foley of the Trinity River Baptist Fellowship. He doesn't approve of dancing and likes to show up at social events to let people know."

Over at the entrance to the hall there was a flurry of activity, several more bellows about the sins of the flesh, and Brother Foley disappeared from the gathering as abruptly as he had appeared.

"You think someone pulled a gun on him?" Pancho asked.

"More likely a contribution. I hear he gets lots of them from people who don't want their dancing interrupted."

"You figger he does it on purpose?"

"Did I say that? Now you were mentioning you hadn't had any fun since you won the ranch."

"I'll tell you," said Pancho, "bein' responsible for a whole ranch ain't that much fun."

"Why, I think I'd enjoy it," said Anne.

"Women ain't supposed to wanna own ranches."

"And men are supposed to, but you don't. If you don't when you're supposed to, why shouldn't I want to own one when I'm not supposed to?"

Pancho scratched his head as he led her back to a chair. "I'm 'fraid you're way ahead of me there. You ain't lookin' for me to give you my ranch, are you?"

"No," said Anne. "I have no designs on you or your property, Mr. Tighe." She had just seen Justin's wife kiss him affectionately on the cheek, and suddenly her little act of defiance with Pancho Tighe had lost its tang. "How would you like to escort me home, Mr. Tighe?" she asked. "I think we've both put in enough time at this social event."

"Well, I sure wouldn't mind gettin' outta here," Pancho agreed. "It's wearin', bein' among all these respectable folks. You sure you wanna be seen leavin' with me?"

Anne laughed and muttered, "In for a penny, in for a pound."

Pancho looked confused but willingly accompanied her to a room off the side of the hall where she retrieved her cloak and bundled into it for the walk back to the hotel. Not five minutes later she was bidding Pancho Tighe good night on the board sidewalk, having assured him that he need not escort her to her room.

She wondered, as she entered the reception area, if he had expected to spend the night with her. Anne laughed bitterly. If so, he was doubtless a somewhat disappointed young man, but she was sure that he would console himself with whiskey and poker at some nearby saloon, where the entertainment wouldn't be so "wearin'."

CHAPTER

Eleven

Halfway up the stairs to the hotel room she shared with Sissie, Anne noticed the sound of footsteps behind her and glanced over her shoulder. Her eyes widened in shock. It was Justin, his mouth set in a straight, grim line.

"I'm surprised you didn't invite him up," he hissed. "Or is he meeting you in your room later?"

"What are you talking about?"

"Tighe." He closed his fingers on her upper arm as they reached the landing, then pulled her down the hall to the left.

"My room's not this way," she gasped.

"Too bad. He'll just have to wait." Justin opened the door and yanked her inside.

"You're crazy! Let go of me." Why was he so angry? She was the one who had been betrayed.

"Do you know who he is, that man you were flirting with?"

"Of course, I know. His name is Pancho Tighe."

"He's a killer. He's the one who took Homer's ranch away from him."

"Maybe Homer shouldn't have put it on the poker table."

Justin scowled at her.

"What?" she demanded. "Am I being blamed for Homer Teasdale's foolishness again?"

"You're being blamed for making a spectacle of yourself over a hired gun. Can you imagine what people are saying?"

"My God, Justin, your hypocrisy astounds me! You're criticizing *my* behavior? As far as I know, Pancho Tighe isn't married. The same cannot be said of you, can it?"

"Everybody in north central Texas knows I'm married."

"Not everyone, Justin," she replied bitterly. "I didn't."

"You didn't know?" He looked stunned.

"That's right. *I* didn't know. For heaven's sake, I wouldn't—wouldn't get involved with another woman's husband. Did you really think—"

"I *thought* you knew, Anne." He ran a shaking hand into thick, dark hair. "The wedding . . . Everybody in this part of the country went to my wedding."

"I wasn't here. I lived in Fort Griffin with my husband when you were married, Justin."

"Well, I . . ." His hand fell to his side, his fist clenched. "You must have heard about it. People talked about it for months. Her father spent a fortune on that wedding."

"Maybe it wasn't as impressive as you thought," Anne said dryly, "because no one ever mentioned it to me, except, of course, your wife, who's obviously still impressed." She paused, trying to stem the outpouring of jealousy and disillusion; after all, her heartbreak wasn't his wife's fault. "She's very beautiful," Anne said grudgingly.

"Yes, she is." Justin looked bleak, drew in a slow, deep breath. "Anne, believe me, I assumed that you knew about Penelope."

"Then you have a lower opinion of me than I could have imagined," she said, her voice anguished. "If you assumed I knew about her, you also assumed that I'd see nothing wrong in—in making love with a married man."

"Anne, dear God!" He put his arms around her. "I'm sorry. I'm so sorry, but I did try to stay away from you. You know I tried."

"And I led you into sin. Is that what you're saying? What a slut you must have thought me."

"I never thought anything but that you were beautiful, and wonderful, a temptation I couldn't resist."

"Even though you had a beautiful wife at home?"

"She's . . . she's not—"

"Don't tell me what she's not," Anne cut him off. "You married her."

"I married her, but I want you," he groaned. His arms tightened around her almost unbearably. "I still want you," he muttered, his lips closing over hers.

When she tried to break away, he pulled her toward the bed, tumbling her down onto the feather mattress, his wife's feather bed, no doubt; the hotel certainly provided no such luxuries. Anne twisted desperately to avoid his weight.

"Don't," he muttered against her mouth.

She could feel his desperation as he continued to kiss her and ended her struggles by trapping her wrists and dragging them above her head, by pinioning her body with his while he used his free hand to undo the jet buttons on the bodice of her dress.

"Stop it, Justin," she gasped.

"Don't talk," he muttered. Having stripped the clothes away to her waist, he fastened his mouth hungrily on one straining nipple.

Anne gasped, for a lightning bolt of heat shot directly

from his mouth to her very core. She turned her head aside and whispered brokenly, "Don't do this, Justin."

He moved his mouth to the other breast and sucked deeply until trembling wracked her body. Then he shrugged out of his jacket. "Unbutton my shirt," he whispered.

Anne shook her head, tears wet on her cheeks. When she refused, he took her mouth again as he dealt with his own buttons. In minutes the rough hair on his chest was pressed against her sensitized breasts, and she felt the determination to resist him begin to slip away in a blaze of desire.

This would be the last time, she thought, the last time they'd ever have each other, and she wanted Justin as desperately as he seemed to want her. But desperately enough to ignore the fact that he had a wife? A wife whose existence he'd concealed from Anne all these months while she'd been falling hopelessly in love with him? Already Justin was pushing up her skirts, edging his knee between hers. He obviously thought her objections to deceit and to adultery so negligible that a few caresses would overcome them. Well, he was wrong. Spurred by her own hurt and anger, she bit his lip and when surprise loosened his hold on her, she pushed him away and rolled quickly to the side of the bed.

"Is this how you usually get your way?" she demanded. "If seduction doesn't work, try rape?"

His eyes confused, his fingers touching the blood on his mouth, Justin muttered defensively, "You wanted me," but he sounded unsure. "We want each other, Anne. At least let's have each other this one last time." There was a world of sadness in his voice.

"Wanting something doesn't make it right," Anne retorted bitterly. She was shivering with reaction as she sat on the edge of the bed to straighten her clothing. "Are you going to bring her back here to this room?" she asked.

"Don't talk about her," said Justin.

"How can I help it?" Anne yanked the corset strings hard, tied them carelessly. "I've just met her, just found out about her." She stood and shook out her rumpled skirts. "Do you expect me to ignore the fact that she exists?" Forcing her arms into the sleeves of her dress, she began to do up the buttons. "Am I supposed to forget that I've been committing adultery for months? That I did it again this afternoon? This afternoon, Justin! Where was your wife while we were—"

"She has her own room!" Justin snapped.

Anne turned her back, confused but still angry. Why did his wife have a separate room? Not that it mattered.

"Anne . . ." Justin had risen from the bed, his body magnificent in its partial nakedness. "Don't . . ."

She turned away, sweeping her fallen hair up, jabbing hairpins into it, her heart weeping. "Don't? Don't!" she echoed angrily. "When I said don't tonight, you paid no attention."

"Anne, you know you—"

"I know I've sinned. I know you led me into it."

"It would have been a sin," Justin muttered, "even if I hadn't been married."

"Not as great a sin," she said despairingly. "Not a sin against another person." She snatched her cloak up from a chair where he'd thrown it. "Not a sin spawned by a liar."

"I never told you—"

"It doesn't matter what you said or didn't say. It was all a lie. I suppose even what I thought you felt for me was a lie."

"No."

"I've been such a fool. And I feel sorry for her. Married to a man like you."

His face went blank and hard. "You don't know what you're talking about."

"David wasn't always kind to me," said Anne, "not

in the last years, at any rate, but he was always faithful."

"Even when he was out brawling in saloons?" asked Justin cruelly.

How he hated to hear about David, she thought. But why should he care? "Even then," she retorted with conviction. "And I know he loved me, which is more than I can say for you," she added, her hand on the door knob, her voice faltering into tears.

"Did you love me?" he whispered.

"What possible difference could that make now?" Anne mumbled as she slipped through the door and, weeping, made her way down the hall.

When she passed the stairwell, she thought she saw a trouser leg disappear around the corner. Just what she needed. Someone to witness her departure from Justin's bed, but then it was unlikely that anyone would know whose room it was she had just left. Or even who she was. She came to her own door, slipped inside and leaned against the wood, letting the tears flow unimpeded. How could she have loved a man who practiced that kind of deceit? How could she have deceived herself into believing he loved her?

"Repent," hissed the malevolent voice.

Anne whirled, terrified. Standing in the corridor between the horse stalls, she was looking for the livery stable owner so that she and Sissie could leave for the Bannermans' and the infare, as they called the traditional second-day dinner given by the groom's parents.

"For the sins of the flesh, the sinner burns on earth and in hell," the rasping voice whispered.

Anne peered into the gloom at the black-clad, scarecrow figure looming at her. "Get out of my way!" she ordered, trying to push past Brother Foley.

He grabbed her arm with his bony fingers. "I saw you. God saw you!"

"If you don't let go of me, I'll complain to the sheriff," she replied desperately.

"Adulteress," he hissed.

Anne shuddered away from him.

"If you don't have a care for your own soul, or his, think of his wife, the innocent victim of your lust."

Penelope Harte was not the only victim, Anne thought bitterly, but she didn't say that to Brother Foley. She had no intention of giving him any sort of confirmation for his suspicions.

"Repent. Seek God's forgiveness."

"How?" asked Anne cynically. "By making a contribution?" She knew how the man operated but had no money to bribe him, nor any inclination to do so.

"God looks with favor on those who support his works."

"Hypocrite!" hissed Anne and pushed him aside.

"The sinner shall not escape notice," he called after her, his voice malicious and threatening, "nay, neither in the eyes of men nor in the eyes of God."

Anne shivered as if someone had walked over her grave. How ironic it was, she thought miserably, that the accusation stemmed from the one time when she had turned Justin away, that she was being branded an adulteress when she had rejected love in the name of morality.

Wearily, she trudged across the ranch yard on a bleak day in mid-December. Before Gretchen and Sam Junior's wedding, she had almost decided to reclaim the money her husband had left her, which the colonel had been managing, and leave the Bar M. Instead she had stayed, determined to think better of her stepfather, who had tried to protect her from her own foolishness. However, the colonel was a hard man to think well of, and nothing was going right.

She pulled her cloak more closely around her and glanced up at the darkening sky, which threatened snow. Then she noticed a figure in black mounted on what looked to be a very ungainly horse or possibly a mule, then saw them disappear over the rise of land to the north. Who could that have been? she wondered. Usually, if there were visitors, she was called in to feed them, if for no other reason.

She felt a chill of apprehension as her eyes followed the mounted figure, but then she shook it off. Everything seemed to depress her these days. She climbed the two steps onto the porch and opened the door to find the colonel waiting for her in the big room, looking, as usual, like a thundercloud. *What now*? she wondered. Had he finally got word of Last or of the missing herd Last had been sent to find?

"I just had a visitor," said the colonel, his face clenched in simmering fury.

"Bad news?" asked Anne in as neutral a tone as she could muster.

"You could say that," he replied. He was wearing his high, black cavalry boots and slapping his quirt in a deadly rhythm against the leather.

Anne frowned and turned away to hang her cloak on a peg.

"Look at me," ordered the colonel. She turned, obeying his command. "My visitor claims that you were seen coming out of the room of a married man at the hotel in Weatherford."

Anne's lips compressed. The visitor must have been Brother Foley. "And who said that?" she demanded, determined to give nothing away.

"A man of the cloth," replied the colonel.

"What man of the cloth?"

"Foley," he snapped.

"Ah, yes," said Anne, "the preacher who blackmails people at dances."

"Don't try to change the subject. I want to know what you were doing in Justin Harte's room?"

"Why do you assume that I was in Justin Harte's room?" she snapped back.

"Why would a man of God say it if it weren't true?"

"There are men of God and *men* of God," Anne retorted, "and I don't intend to dignify any accusation of Hiram Foley's with an answer."

"Oh, you'll answer me," said the colonel, snapping the quirt across his boot again. "I won't have a woman in my house besmirching my good name."

It was on the tip of Anne's tongue to say that he seemed to care little enough about his own daughter's reputation, but she restrained herself, feeling that it would be mean-spirited to divert his attention from herself to Sissie. "I'm going to my room," she said, moving away from him, but the colonel closed iron fingers on her arm and jerked her around to face him.

"I want an answer."

"You won't get one from me," said Anne. She had never seen him angrier.

"Defiance won't work this time, madam." His voice hoarse with rage, he threw her against the heavy oak table and brought the quirt down on her back.

Anne was too stunned for a moment to react to the first curl of pain. It had been years since he'd beaten her, and then he'd never used a whip. At the second stroke, she struggled away from him, but he knocked her to the floor and brought the whip down a third time, burning an agonizing trail across her back.

"Papa!" cried Sissie.

Anne looked toward her sister and tried to rise.

"Get to your room!" the colonel shouted at the terrified girl.

As the quirt snaked down onto her shoulders, flicking her cheek, Anne saw Sissie flee. Quickly she turned her face away and pushed her hands under her. Better to keep her back to him as long as she could to protect her face, she decided frantically, even as she rose and the fire curled again across her shoulders.

She staggered against the table and grasped a heavy bowl into which she had dumped the last of the year's onions. Just after the next lash of the quirt, she whirled with the bowl in both hands and heaved it at him. Then she threw herself toward her room, gaining the door, slamming and bolting it while he was still recovering his balance. Her back was a solid sheet of pain, sticky with blood, and in the glass on her dressing table she saw that her cheek was bleeding as well.

With a strength born of desperation and terror, she drew a sobbing breath and forced her dressing table against the door. Then she leaned against the wall, her tears burning into the cut on her cheek. He'd never lay a hand on her again, she vowed, even if she had to kill him. But her Winchester was outside on the wall. Why hadn't she thought to get it? She closed her eyes and swallowed the rising panic. What was she to do?

She had to leave, but that meant deserting Sissie. Confused and trembling with pain, she tried to think through her options. Well, she'd have to leave Sissie behind. God knows, Sissie hadn't made a move to help her when she needed it.

First, the damage. How bad was it? She turned her back to the mirror and looked over her shoulder. There was blood aplenty staining through the tatters of her dress, but she had no time to take care of her wounds. It would be hard to do anyway since, to her, they were almost inaccessible.

She needed her heavy cloak, she thought desperately, but it was outside on the peg, and she dared not enter that room again. She'd have to escape through the window, take her horse, and get away. But what if he caught her, tried to stop her? The pistol! She had the .44/.40 that David had given her as a companion piece to her Winchester. It was in the drawer of the dresser, loaded, and although she had no extra cartridges, the rounds in its chambers should be enough to protect her. And she'd just have to do without the cloak, even though she knew the temperature was dropping steadily as night fell.

She jerked a blanket off her bed. Then with shaking

hands, she opened the dresser, took out the Colt single action, checked the cartridges, and moved at last toward the window. She felt weak already and wondered whether she would be able to ride at all. And where? Well, once she had the horse and was moving, she could decide that. As quietly as she could, she raised the sash and edged gingerly out the window at the rear of the house. Although she managed to spare her back the further agony of brushing against anything, her every movement was a source of pain, and she leaned one shoulder heavily against the wall for a moment, waiting for a wave of dizziness to pass. Then she carefully, silently closed the window, and made her way toward the stable, the Colt held ready in the folds of her skirt. The darkness, which came early in December, would conceal her as she slipped into the side door.

The interval during which she saddled the horse, mounted, and rode out, wrapped in a blanket, was a red blur of pain. Only when she was on her way did she remember that she had no money. She hadn't got any from the colonel lately, and he was always stingy with it, even though it was her own she was asking for. Well, once she got to Fort Worth, she'd retrieve her inheritance, but in the meantime, where was she to go? She guided the horse slowly out of the yard and headed for the Weatherford Road, trying to think beyond her pain to some course of action.

Since this was his fault, she ought to go to Justin, but she had no idea how to get to the Crossed Heart and knew she couldn't make it that far anyway. Besides, she'd never ask him for anything, not even shelter, nor would she cause his wife grief if she could help it. Inadvertently, she'd done the woman damage already.

She needed a refuge close at hand. The Bannermans'? Sarah would take her in, but Lord, how could she go there, her back cut to ribbons, and let them see what had happened? If that evil Brother Foley had told her stepfather, likely as not he'd spread the word everywhere, and no one would want her. Ultimately, of course, she'd go to Fort Worth, but she'd never make that tonight, nor even to Weatherford.

And then she remembered Pancho Tighe. Even if the young gunfighter had heard the gossip, he'd be unlikely to judge her, and in his way, Pancho needed help as much as she did. In fact, she thought fuzzily, maybe he needed a wife. And for the last few days it had begun to dawn on her that she might need a husband. She laughed softly, bitterly against Horse's warm neck. If people wanted to gossip about her, she'd go to Pancho Tighe. That would really give them something to talk about.

Then as the chill wind picked up, she huddled into her blanket and turned Horse toward the Rocking T and her future, whatever that might be.

CHAPTER

Twelve

The ranch house was dark, but from the bunkhouse she could hear occasional shouts and laughter. Could Pancho be there? As bad as she must look, she didn't want to expose herself to a pack of strange cowboys; on the other hand, she knew she'd never make it back into the saddle once she dismounted. Tears of self-pity were trickling onto her cheeks by the time she had managed to get their attention inside. The door swung open abruptly, and she fell against the barrel of a revolver, which was hastily withdrawn and replaced by strong arms into which she sagged. When she'd got her feet under her again, she looked up into Pancho Tighe's stunned face and mumbled, "I need help."

Pancho was staring at her with horror. "You're all bloody."

"I know. Do you have somewhere I could lie down?"

The ranch hands had fallen silent. She could see them dimly beyond Pancho's shoulder, sitting around a rough table lit by a coal oil lamp and covered with playing cards, mugs of coffee, and glasses of whiskey. "I don't feel well, Pancho," she mumbled. "If I could just . . ."

"I'll take you back to the house," he said quickly. "You need me to carry you?"

She shook her head emphatically, afraid he'd touch her back. Pancho looked confused at her refusal but took her arm and helped her across the yard toward the darkened ranch house.

"Do you have an extra bed?" she gasped as he fumbled in the dim, firelit room for the lamp.

"You can have mine, though I reckon this here's like to ruin both our reputations." The lamp caught, and he held it high to inspect her face, which was streaked with blood and dirt through which ran crooked channels made by her tears.

Anne tried to smile. "I'll leave as soon as I can," she promised. "After all, we wouldn't want people to think you're mixed up with a good woman, would we?"

"Glad to see you ain't lost your sense of humor," Pancho said with a weak chuckle. "The bed's over here." He led her into a second room, holding the lamp up as they moved. "'Fraid it's none too clean," he apologized, "but at least you can have it to yourself."

"Don't you have another?"

"No, but I got a bedroll. That'll do for me."

Anne wasn't about to argue. "I need medical attention," she mumbled as she lowered herself slowly and carefully onto the narrow, rumpled cot.

"Ain't no doctor here," said Pancho, astounded that she might think there was.

"You'll have to do it."

"Me? I ain't—"

"You can at least take off the blanket."

"Well, I reckon." He unwrapped her, then saw her back and gasped. "Who did this?" he asked in a tight voice.

"The colonel."

Staring in horror at the tattered rags of her shirtwaist and the dried blood, Pancho swore, then swallowed hard and mumbled, "I don't feel too good."

"You're a gunfighter," Anne retorted accusingly. "Surely, you've seen blood before."

"Not on a woman, I ain't."

"Well, there's no one but you to help me."

"I can shoot him for you," he offered hopefully.

"I appreciate the thought, Pancho," said Anne, "but I'd probably die of blood poisoning before you got back."

"Oh." He looked again at her injuries.

"Heat some water. You've got to cut and soak the shirtwaist away from the wounds."

"You mean take off your clothes?" he asked, shocked.

"For heaven's sake, Pancho, you must have seen a female back at some time or other."

"I ain't never seen a *respectable* female back."

Feeling the full irony of her situation, she wondered if he was really going to refuse to care for her because she was a so-called "respectable" woman. It was just her lack of respectability that had put her in need of his help. Maybe she should tell him why the colonel had beaten her. Dear Pancho, he hadn't even asked. Justin would have.

"Flesh is flesh," she said wearily. "Get the water heating. You do have a pot?"

"Sure, but—but if I get the shirtwaist off, your back's gonna start bleedin' again."

"Well, if that happens, you'll just have to stop it."

"How'my gonna do that? Well . . ." He thought about it. "Cigarette papers'll stop bleeding."

"Pancho," Anne groaned, "he must have hit me with that quirt six or seven times. Do you really think you have enough cigarette papers to plaster my whole back?"

"Well, what am I gonna do?" he asked desperately.

"It's got to be washed. We'll worry about the bleeding later, all right?"

"All right," he agreed reluctantly.

Justin stood in the door of his wife's room and studied the effect she had created. He was sure there was no other ranch house like it in Palo Pinto. What had they cost him, he wondered, all these silks and velvets, rugs, lamps, draperies, and fancy furniture? How many blooded bulls could he have bought with the money Penelope had spent to feather herself this luxurious nest?

The new ranch house, constructed from lumber shipped from East Texas and furnished from Marshall Fields in Chicago, had probably eaten up a year's profits. All that money just to build a place his wife thought fit to live in and to put clothes on her back she thought fit to wear, and for what? The new house was colder in winter and hotter in summer than the comfortable log house he'd had to move out of. And his wife, with her beautiful clothes, spent all her time in this expensive room escaping from the duties any other ranch wife would have taken for granted.

How could he have made such a terrible mistake, married a woman so little suited to him or his lifestyle? It had been her beauty, of course. He had thought her the most beautiful girl he'd ever seen when they first met, and when they were courting, she had been affectionate as well. But that hadn't lasted, not much beyond the ceremony. Penelope's affection for him, if she truly had any, was exhibited only in the most public of places. They no longer shared the same bed, or even the same bedroom. She claimed he kept her awake, that he snored, although Justin doubted it. No one else had ever complained, and he'd slept in the company of others most of his life.

Once he had believed that Penelope was cold to him

because she was inexperienced but that she would learn in his arms to enjoy intimacy. God knows, he'd taken enough trouble with her, but Penelope had hated the marriage bed and continued to hate it. Then Justin had found Anne and discovered that a good woman could be warm and passionate, could be everything he'd ever dreamed the woman he loved would be, and then he understood how much Penelope had cheated him. He knew that she'd married him, not for love, but because every other unmarried girl had wanted him and because she coveted his power and his money.

She wanted all that he possessed but gave nothing in return, whereas Anne had given him everything and had asked for nothing, only that he be free to love her. Well, he loved her, but he had little chance of ever being free. At the thought of their last meeting, at the thought of how much he'd hurt her, pain constricted his heart. Perhaps he had known all along that he was deceiving her. He wasn't sure. Had he wanted her so much that he'd kept his marriage a secret? Had he really believed that Anne knew he was married but came to him anyway? One truth was that he stayed away from home as much as he could and that he'd learned to blot Penelope completely from his mind when he was away so as not to be reminded of his disastrous marriage.

His eyes now followed her as she flitted nervously from dresser to wardrobe. Although she rarely picked up her own things—she had brought Calliope, her black maid, to do that—she was picking them up now, anything, he thought dryly, to avoid acknowledging his presence. She had been truly upset to see him appear in her door, to have him catch her in her nightdress.

"Gracious, Justin!" she exclaimed peevishly. "Must you stand there staring? You're making me nervous."

"I want a child," Justin said abruptly.

"Why—why, Justin, really I—" She was stammering, caught unprepared. "I—I don't know what you're—"

"We're going to resume sleeping together."

Penelope frowned. "You know I can't rest if you're in the same room."

"Then rest in the daytime. God knows, you don't do anything else worthwhile then."

"I resent that. I run this household."

"Calliope runs this household, and since you're not fulfilling that side of your wifely obligations, I think it's time you devoted yourself to motherhood."

She looked panic-stricken, but only for a moment. Then a veil closed over her eyes, and she stared at the floor for inspiration. When she raised her head, he knew from that bright look of innocence and regret that she was about to lie. "Justin, I have to tell you," she said softly, "that while I was in Weatherford, I saw Dr. Waller, and he told me it would be extremely dangerous for me to have children."

"Is that a fact?" asked Justin dryly. "In that case, I'll have to divorce you."

Although he was bluffing, she took the bait. The emotion that crossed Penelope's face when she heard the word "divorce" was more genuine than anything he'd ever seen reflected there. "You can't mean that," she cried.

"You knew when we married that I wanted children. We talked about it during the courtship, and you told me you wanted them as well."

"Well, yes, Justin, of course, but I didn't know then that it would be so dangerous. I didn't know—"

"You're lying," he cut in.

"I am not," she cried out, large tears welling in her eyes. "How can you say that? Dr. Waller—"

"We'll go straight to Weatherford tomorrow, and I'll talk to him myself." Penelope's face went white. "Just as I thought. You never saw Dr. Waller. Well, no matter. He can examine you, and if he says you can't have children, we'll get a divorce."

"You'd abandon me?" she asked pathetically. "How

would that look? Think of the scandal!"

"What scandal? People would simply think you ill-used and me hardhearted for ridding myself of you."

"I refuse to be divorced," cried Penelope.

"Then you'd best make up your mind to have children. You've only the two options."

"Oh, very well," she said sullenly, "but you know how I feel about that sort of thing. It's disgusting."

"Children?"

"No!" she snapped. "Not that I like that idea either. I mean what we have to . . . Well, you know. I'll need time to think about it. Maybe next year."

"Tonight," said Justin coldly.

"No!"

"Tonight. Or tomorrow we'll head for town and the lawyers."

"Oh, all *right*!"

"Good. Get in bed."

"I hate you."

"Perhaps you'll like the baby you're going to have," he said dryly.

Anne moved stiffly from the fireplace to the table. Cooking facilities at the Rocking T were primitive, but then Pancho didn't have many hands to feed. She put the basket of hot biscuits down on the table, pulled on the bell, summoning the men, and lowered herself gingerly into her chair. She had been here a week, and her back was healing, but it still gave her pain. As for Pancho, the two of them got along well enough, although he resented her lectures, for she had told him repeatedly that he should stop drinking and playing poker with the ranch hands and put them all to work.

Homer Teasdale's foreman had quit and disappeared when Pancho took over. Bobby Ambrose, one of the Rocking T cowboys, assumed some responsibility but made it clear that he didn't really want to be foreman, and Pancho certainly showed no leadership qualities.

He, thought Anne wryly, was perfectly happy to spend all his time winning back the wages he paid his men. In fact, she was not sure he could have made his payroll if he'd actually had to disburse the full amount. Well, it was a situation that couldn't go on, and so she had nagged him relentlessly until he and the other men were now going out by day to look after the cattle that were left. However, they still played poker and drank at night, a situation she knew most ranch owners would never put up with, much less participate in.

The men came straggling in, nodded to her, and sat down to eat. Pancho, the last to arrive, took his place at the other end of the table and, shoveling some beans into his mouth, said, "These don't taste as good as they used to."

"We're out of bacon," Anne replied.

"Good," said Pancho enthusiastically. "I'll ride into town to get some."

"Uh-huh," said Anne. "And get into a card game and lose the bacon money."

"I swear," he grumbled around a bite of steak, "you're worse than a wife, an' I still got to sleep by myself."

Anne grinned appreciatively. During her first few days, she had been made uneasy by the lewd looks and under-the-breath remarks of the hands. But Pancho put a quick stop to that, not by becoming angry with them but by his wry comments about how ill-used he was in offering his hospitality to a respectable widow, who not only wouldn't have anything to do with him, but who had co-opted his bed so that he had to sleep by the fire on a bedroll. Once he'd said it often enough, the men took the situation to heart and stopped snickering and grinning.

"What you'd better do," said Anne, "is bring back some pigs."

"What for?" Pancho's fork stopped in midair.

"You've got a fine oak grove out there. You can turn

the pigs loose, they'll eat the acorns, and you'll have all the bacon you need."

"I don't wanna raise pigs," said Pancho. "Cattle's bad enough."

"Pigs start stampedes," said Bobby Ambrose. "You probably didn't know that, ma'am."

"We wouldn't be running the pigs with the cattle. The pigs would be in the woods."

"Cain't trust 'em," said Hap, another of the cowboys. "They'd prob'ly get loose in the herd just for spite."

"What herd?" muttered Pancho, but nobody paid him any attention.

"Fresh hog meat's mighty good," said Jocko, a black cowboy, who had been herding at the Rocking T for years.

"No sensible pig's going to leave a good oak grove full of nuts just to associate with a lot of foolish cattle," said Anne sternly. "Now, Pancho, if you're going into town . . . What town are you going into?"

"Fort Worth," said Pancho happily. "I'm goin' into Fort Worth."

"Good," said Anne. "Fort Worth is a wonderful place for pigs. You won't even have to buy one. You can spend your poker winnings on whatever you want. Just catch me a pig off the street."

Pancho gave her an insulted look. "How 'my gonna do that? Can you see me ridin' home with a live pig across my saddle? I'd prob'ly get laughed outta Texas."

"Don't be so sensitive," said Anne. "Tell you what. If you bring me a pig, I'll make pies every day next week."

"Do it, Pancho," urged Hap. "Why, for a week of Miss Anne's pies, I'll even build a fence around the oak grove so the pigs cain't get out."

"There you go," Anne exclaimed. "All your problems are solved, Pancho. Hap will build a fence; just be sure you come home with the pig." Pancho scowled at her. "And while you're there, you ought to buy yourself a blooded bull."

"Them things are expensive," Pancho objected.

"Well, you're the one who's a first-class poker player."

"Ain't that the truth," said Jocko. "I ain't been paid yet. Lost all my money in advance at the card table."

"If you buy yourself a good bull and breed it to your best cows . . ." All the riders blushed at such talk from a woman. "You'll make a lot more money on your cattle next fall."

"How do you know so much about it?" asked Pancho.

"From listening to other ranchers."

"Does the colonel do that?"

"Of course not," said Anne. "Everyone knows what a terrible rancher he is."

"Yep," agreed Bobby, "if the colonel don't do it, like as not, that's just what you should do, Pancho. All them big ranchers like Slaughter an' Harte, they buy blood stock." Anne's lips compressed at the mention of Justin. "Yep, you sure oughta get yourself a good bull."

Pancho groaned. "Everybody's always tellin' me how to spend my money, an' I ain't got that much. Pass the beans." Since Anne was glaring at him, he mumbled, "All right! I'll think on it."

"Heard somethin' mighty interestin' in town, Justin," said Rollo Tandy. "Took particular note 'cause she saved my life."

Justin, who had been going over the year's accounts, looked up sharply. "Who are we talking about?" he asked.

"Miz McAuliffe," said Rollo.

Justin grunted, concealing the painful lurch of his heart when he heard her name.

"She's left the Bar M. Heard it from two of the hands who'd quit. They said she just up an' disappeared."

"Where did she go?" Justin asked, not sure that he wanted to be told. She attracted men like flies. Heaven

knew how many proposals she'd had since he last saw
her. Had she accepted one? The thought of her married
to someone else twisted his gut.

"No one knows," Rollo replied. "Like I said, one
mornin' she wasn't around, an' no one was answerin'
any questions. The hands said Miss Sissie looked
mighty upset but wouldn't say nothin', an' the colonel
like to bit off anyone's head who even mentioned Miz
McAuliffe. No one's heard a word from her since."

"Probably doesn't mean anything," said Justin, but
through his mind flashed that scene when he, Anne,
and the colonel had quarreled at the fall roundup. He
had had an overwhelming conviction that the colonel
was about to hit her. Still, if the man had attacked her,
someone would have known. And if she'd gone somewhere, she must have gone of her own accord. The
colonel wouldn't have driven her away; he got too much
free work out of her.

"Likely she's gone visiting," he murmured.

"Onliest woman she was that friendly with, from
what I hear, was Miz Sarah Bannerman, an' Miz Sarah,
she went over to the Bar M to visit, an' lil Sissie burst
into tears an' run into her room when Miz Sarah asked
after Miz McAuliffe. Then the colonel, he glared an'
told Miz Sarah to go on home an' mind her own
business, which didn't set too well. Miz Sarah
Bannerman, she's real upset."

"Ma'am," Bobby said, "I wonder if you could come
out to the bunkhouse. We got a man down sick."

"Oh?" Anne had been building a fire in preparation
for making lye soap since there seemed to be no soap at
all at the ranch. Pancho had plenty of good oak ashes
which Anne had cleaned out of the fireplace, and there
was more than enough grease. For some reason, the
men had poured it off into jars and kept it for heaven
knew how many months.

"What's the problem, Bobby?" she asked, walking

along beside him to the bunkhouse through the cold morning air.

"It's Jocko. He's got him a earache, like to drive him crazy, an' Hap, he said best cure for a earache was to clip some hair an' stick it in the bad ear. Well, Jocko got mad an' hit Hap, so now we got one cowboy with a earache an' one with a bloody nose, an' Pancho's been gone off into Fort Worth these two days to catch a pig and win some bull money, an' I don't know what to do. Hell, I ain't no foreman."

Anne had to laugh, although she knew having two hands incapacitated was no joke. "Well, let's see," said Anne, entering the bunkhouse. "First, the nose."

"Don't worry about it, ma'am," said Hap. "I took care of it."

"What did you do?" she asked, eyeing his nostrils with amazement.

"I 'membered Pancho sayin' cigarette papers was good fer bleedin', so I stuck a couple up my nose."

"Oh, yes," said Anne. "Is it working?"

"Seems to be," said Hap.

"Good, I guess that takes care of that." She looked over at the black man who was rocking back and forth on the bench, holding his ear and groaning. "Hurts pretty bad does it, Jocko?" she asked sympathetically.

"Yes, ma'am, an' Ah ain't cuttin' off mah hair an' stickin' it in mah ear neither."

Anne nodded. "Probably wouldn't work anyway," she guessed. "I've never heard of any such thing, and my husband was an officer in a company of black buffalo soldiers for a year or two."

"An' Ah ain't puttin' no 'baccy juice in mah ear."

She looked astonished. "Why would you want to do that?"

"'Baccy juice, that was Hap's second damn fool idee."

"Well, my granma always said it worked," said Hap.

"Ah'm a punch yer nose agin," said Jocko. "An' after

that Ah'll go find yer granma an' punch her nose too."

"No, you ain't."

"Your granma's dead, Hap," said Bobby.

"I know just what to do for an earache," Anne interrupted hastily. "We'll put a bag of hot salt on it. You'll feel better in no time at all, Jocko."

"Well, that don't sound so bad."

An hour later Jocko was fast asleep with his bag of hot salt. Hap, the cigarette papers still protruding from his nose, and Bobby had made a hasty exit, driven off by the smell of Anne's lye soap. Anne, bundled up in Pancho's heavy jacket, was stirring the grease into the pot of water and ashes with a large paddle. Left alone in the yard, she was able to concentrate on her stirring and her tests, both for the color of the mixture when it was allowed to cool and for its consistency.

She had just achieved what she considered the perfect condition for a pot of lye soap and was raking the coals from under the pot to let it cool when a voice said, "I couldn't believe it when I heard you were here. Now it seems you've stooped to living with a killer."

Anne's shoulders stiffened, but she continued her task.

"Have you any idea how much time I've wasted trying to find you?"

She raked the last of the coals out and straightened slowly. "Good morning, Justin," she said. "Did you have any particular reason for coming here?"

"Of course I did," he practically shouted at her. "Rollo told me you'd disappeared. I didn't know what the hell had happened to you."

"As you see," she said coolly, gesturing to the ranch yard, the cooling pot of liquid soap.

"If I'd known you'd run off to live with a worthless, gun-slinging gambler—" he began bitterly.

"There's a difference, Justin," she interrupted, "between living *in* the house of and living *with*."

"Who's going to make that distinction?"

"Not you, obviously."

"If one word of this escapade gets around . . . Good Lord, Anne, are you sleeping with him?"

She blinked twice to clear the stinging tears. "It's none of your business, Justin."

"Are you married to him?"

"Was I married to you?" she retorted bitterly. "Go home to your wife."

"Anne, for God's sake," he exclaimed, swinging down from the horse, "you have to think about your reputation."

"Justin, for God's sake," she mimicked angrily. "I don't recall that you ever thought of it."

He flushed, and his fingers clasped her shoulders. "I ought to shake you," he grated.

Anne gasped as the pain from the healing scars hit her.

"Get your hands offa her before I shoot you in the back."

Justin released her and whirled.

"Hands over your head," Pancho said, his voice soft with menace. Then he recognized the man he was threatening and looked confused. "Mr. Harte?" His gun stayed steady on Justin's chest, but his eyes wavered to Anne. "You all right, Annie?" he asked.

She could barely nod, so dizzy was she from the pain. Tottering toward Justin's horse, she grasped the stirrup to keep herself upright. He, fortunately, didn't notice because his whole attention was focused on Pancho Tighe.

"You got business with Miz McAuliffe?" asked Pancho, dismounting carefully, the gun steady.

Just as carefully Justin replied, "Word got around that she was missing."

"Oh, yeah. Well, her stepdaddy—"

Anne shook her head at him. She didn't want Justin knowing anything about her problems.

"She had a fallin' out with her stepdaddy," Pancho

finished lamely. "So she's—ah—stayin' here a few weeks until she can—ah—until she . . ."

Anne could see him floundering because he didn't know how much he was allowed to tell Justin. "Until I can make arrangements to go elsewhere," Anne finished. "Not that it's any of Mr. Harte's business."

"Ah-huh." Pancho looked from one to the other.

"Did you buy a bull?" she asked, wanting to get the conversation away from herself as rapidly as possible.

"No," said Pancho, "but I got this here horse. He's a beauty, ain't he?"

Anne eyed the horse. "Pancho, you were supposed to buy a good bull. You don't need a horse."

"Cain't have too many good horses," said Pancho defensively.

"Nonsense."

"That's all the thanks I get?" he exclaimed with exaggerated disappointment. "Here I brung you that pig you been dyin' to have."

"A pig?" Anne let go of the stirrup as Pancho lifted a squirming burlap bag off the horn of his saddle.

"Yep. Caught him in Forth Worth. There's a man with a bullet in his shoulder 'cause of you an' yer pig."

"You shot someone to get the pig?"

"I shot someone who thought it was pretty funny 'cause I was tryin' to catch one."

Anne took the squirming sack and peeked inside. "Oh," she cried ecstatically, "isn't he a beauty?" She noticed, to her surprise, that Justin was looking forlorn.

Pancho, on the other hand, looked pleased and asked, "What are you gonna do with him?"

"I'm going to take him into the house," Anne replied. "It's too cold for him out here."

"Into *my* house? I don't want no pig in my house."

"Just till the cold snap ends," Anne promised. "Then we'll turn him out into the woods."

"When was it you said you was headin' for Fort Worth?" Pancho grumbled.

"As soon as I get the pig settled," said Anne, then turning back to Justin, added, "Good day, Mr. Harte." She kept her voice cold and marched away, leaving the two men standing in the ranch yard. Anne wanted to turn her head and take a last look at Justin, but she restrained herself. How dare he come here making accusations? Her whole predicament was his fault. She clutched her pig, which squirmed protestingly inside its burlap bag.

Justin rode disconsolately into Fort Worth, thinking of Anne's teasing, loving relationship with Pancho Tighe, and it broke his heart. He was losing even the chance to dream that someday she might belong to him. And ridiculous as it seemed, he was jealous that the gunfighter had been the one to provide her with her heart's desire—a pig. Penelope, damn her, wasn't satisfied with having got her greedy hands on a whole year of his profits, while Anne turned misty-eyed at the gift of a pig, not even a bought pig. Tighe had probably chased down that pig on the streets of Fort Worth.

CHAPTER

Thirteen

Anne watched curiously as Pancho worked on his gun. "Why doesn't it have a trigger?"

"'Cause I thumb the hammer," said Pancho. "It's faster. If I used a trigger, I'd be dead by now."

"I don't see how you can hit anyone if you have to whip the gun out and shoot instantly. There's no time to aim."

"That's a fact," he agreed, "but pistols ain't that accurate anyway. If I'm gonna shoot someone, I'm gonna do it when I'm six, seven yards away. Beyond twenty yards a pistol's no good at all hardly. At two hunnerd yards you'd have to aim eight feet above a man's head to hit him."

"You're not serious."

"Course I am. If there's one thing I know, it's guns, an' up close there ain't nobody better'n me."

"Even Marshall Courtright?" She'd heard tales about Long-Haired Jim Courtright, the marshall in Fort Worth.

"Well, he's good," Pancho admitted, "an' I don't aim to pick no fights with him." His eyes narrowed. "Get back in the other room. Someone just rode up."

"I didn't hear anything."

"You don't never hear anythin'. Now get back, an' I'll find out who it is."

"My goodness, Pancho, just because we have a visitor . . ."

He waved her to silence and approached the door cautiously, gun in hand. "Who's there?" he shouted, standing to the side. Anne heard boots mounting the steps.

"Last Cauley," came the reply.

"Oh, my goodness!" Anne turned back from the bedroom, raced toward the door, and flung it open.

As she greeted her stepfather's foreman, Pancho was grumbling, "What if it'd been somebody else? You'd a got shot. I'd a got shot. You're a crazy woman, you know that?"

Anne ignored Pancho and gave Last a hug. "Come in and sit down, Last. I thought you'd disappeared forever."

"An' I been thinkin' that about you," replied Last.

"How long have you been back?"

"Long enough to search the whole damn county for you. Once I found you was gone—"

"Oh. Well, I'm afraid I had to leave."

"Yeah, I know why you had to. That's why your stepfather just lost his foreman."

"Oh, Last, I am sorry. I wouldn't want to think you'd quit because of me."

"Wasn't much of a job anyway. 'Specially after he decided to blame me when I told him them boys he hired to trail his stock north done sold the herd in Kansas an' took off for Oklahoma with his money."

"I'm not surprised," said Anne.

"Me neither, but I was surprised when it turns out he expected me to go after 'em." Last slapped his hat disgustedly against his thigh. "Now, Miss Anne, what I wanna know is why you're livin' here with this boy?" He glared at Pancho, and Pancho glared back.

"Don't criticize Pancho," said Anne. "He took me in and cared for me when I had nowhere to go."

"That's real nice. What's he want in return?"

"Not a thing!" snapped Anne. "He's been sleeping by the fireplace ever since I got here."

Last grunted skeptically.

"You got a big mouth, Cauley," said Pancho. He hadn't lowered the gun an inch.

"Just calm down, Pancho," Anne begged. "You too, Last. No one here's going to shoot anyone else. Why, the two of you are just about my best friends in the whole world, and I don't intend to lose either one of you."

Both men looked embarrassed and stopped eyeing one another like bulls pawing the ground with lowered horns.

"You need a place to stay, Last?" asked Anne.

Pancho bristled.

"Well, Miss Anne," said Last, "that's mighty hospitable of you, but the fact is, this ain't your ranch."

"Oh, well." Anne looked embarrassed and glanced sideways at Pancho. When he continued to glare, she gave him a narrow-eyed, prim-mouthed look.

"Got room in the bunkhouse," Pancho muttered reluctantly.

"There, you see. Now sit down, and I'll fix you something to eat, Last, and then you can take your bedroll out. I guess, Pancho, you could use a cup of coffee and a slice of pie."

"Another slice a pie?" Pancho looked astounded. "That's sure as hell the onliest time you ever let me have two in one day."

Last grinned, then started to laugh. "I can see she's got you as buffaloed as ever' other man she comes across."

Pancho looked embarrassed. Anne's own smile faltered. Goodness knows, she'd never had Justin buffaloed. But she shook off that unhappy thought and busied herself warming a plate of food for Last, pouring coffee and slicing pie for Pancho.

"You'll never believe what he told me about guns," she said conversationally as they ate.

"Reckon you're gonna tell me," grunted Last around a mouthful of stew.

"Pancho claims that at two hundred yards with a pistol, you'd have to shoot eight feet above a man's head to hit him."

"Did he mention the left drift the riflin' causes?"

"I didn't think she needed to know ever'thing," snapped Pancho.

"Fact is, she probably does," said Last. "She shot two, three rustlers when they hit the herd at spring roundup."

"Did she?" Pancho looked at Anne with new respect.

"Well, actually I shot the horse instead of the rider one of those times."

"What were you shootin'?"

"A Winchester .44/.40 my husband gave me for my birthday."

"Sounds like a good man," said Pancho.

Anne smiled at him. Justin had never reacted to any mention of David so nicely.

"So you shot the horse, huh? Well, a rifle at long yardage, it's gonna shoot low, too."

Anne sighed, beginning to feel that she was back in school, not that the schoolmistresses had taught marksmanship between the piano lessons and embroidery class.

"Pancho," she said later in the evening when Last had gone off to the bunkhouse and Anne had put on her heavy winter nightgown and come back into the main room.

"You shouldn't do that," he said.

"Do what?"

"Come in here in your night rail."

"Oh, sorry."

"It don't look right."

"Fine," she snapped impatiently. "You'll never see my nightgown again. Maybe you'd like me to wear a bag over my head too since my face still shows."

Pancho grinned.

"What I wanted to mention," she persisted, "was that you need a foreman, Pancho, and Last needs a job."

"Uh-huh." Pancho looked dubious. "He prob'ly wouldn't wanna work for me."

She glared at him.

"Well, I'll think on it."

"Like you thought about buying a blooded bull? Think about it seriously while he's still here. If you let it go, he'll leave, and you'll have lost your chance."

"What'd I have to pay him?"

"It's not only the pay," said Anne. "You'd have to actually come up with the money. There's no way you're going to get Last Cauley to lose his wages to you at the poker table before he ever gets his hands on them."

Pancho groaned.

"So what are you going to do?" she demanded.

"Well, I ain't gonna make no decisions till tomorrow. He won't be ridin' off before breakfast, will he?"

"I suppose not," said Anne, "but don't dally."

"I don't see why I couldn't go in to buy my own bull," said Pancho.

"Don't worry. Last won't waste your money. I'll take two cards, Hap."

It was Christmas Eve, and they were playing poker in the bunkhouse. Anne, who had just learned how and had no money, was allowed to play for beans. The arrangement was that if she lost twenty dollars worth of beans in a week, she provided an extra round of pies. So far she hadn't been forced to, not that she was such a good player, just a cautious one.

"You want more coffee, Miss Anne?" asked Bobby Ambrose, who had been looking brighter since Last hired on as foreman.

"No, I want to try the whiskey," said Anne. The cowboys exchanged glances and hastened to tell her about the evils of whiskey. "Then why are you drinking it?" she asked as she poured three or four drops into her coffee cup. She really was curious about the taste, but mostly she loved to shock them, and she had.

"Well, we're men," they declared defensively. "We're used to it . . . We're not ladies . . . Will we have to stop drinkin' if we don't let you?" came the various answers.

Anne grinned, took a sip, and grimaced. "Nasty tasting stuff, isn't it?" she murmured. Smug looks passed among the hands. "Still, it's Christmas Eve." She flashed a radiant smile around the table and met renewed uneasiness.

An hour later Anne and Jocko were harmonizing on a spiritual.

"Ain't that pretty?" said Hap sentimentally as he wiped a bright red neckerchief across his eyes. "Why, Miss Annie, you sing jus' like black folks."

"*Ah* sing jus' like black folks," said Jocko, sounding highly incensed. "She sings good, but not that good."

"How true," said Anne. "It's an honor to sing with you, Jacko. You have a bea–u–ti–ful voice."

"Jocko."

"S'what I said." She took another gulp of her whiskey, which didn't taste so bad once she got used to it. "I win," she exclaimed triumphantly, and laid down her hand.

"Miss Anne, you ain't got anything there," said Bobby.

"Oh, shut up, Bobby," Pancho ordered. "She thinks

she's got a straight. Anyone can see that, so if Annie thinks she's got a straight, tha's good enough for me."

"All right, boss, whatever you say, but I ain't payin' up in real money. Give her some beans. She collects enough of them beans, she won't never make us no more pies."

"'Snot true," said Anne, hiccupping graciously behind her hand. "I bake ev–er–y week. Beans or no beans. 'Sa schlander. Oughta make bean pie nex' time."

"Bean pie prob'ly be good," was Jocko's opinion, "'specially with a little hog meat in it. How's that pig a yours doin', Miss Annie?"

"Jus' fine," said Anne. "He's a bea–u–ti–ful pig, an' I thank you ver–y mush for him, Pancho," and she leaned over and kissed him on the cheek.

Pancho looked astounded, and Hap cried, "An' you said there wasn't nothin' goin' on with you an'—you an'—"

"Gettin' kissed on the cheek ain't nuthin'," Pancho mumbled.

"Tha's right," said Anne. "He's jus' like my—my ba–a–by brother."

"I knew you was gonna ruin my reputation one way or another. Deal the cards, would ya, Hap?"

"How come I alus has ta deal?"

"'Cause you ain't quite as drunk as the rest of us."

Anne opened one eye, then closed it hurriedly. She tried the other eye, but it didn't feel a bit better. In fact, both eyes felt as if they'd been peppered with sand, and her head—oh Lord, her head—there was a blacksmith in there pounding on an anvil. She groaned and flung herself over on her side. That snapped both eyes open at once because she rolled right into another body. Pancho's. She jostled him roughly and got only a sullen mumble. A second jostling brought him awake, but he looked as dazed as she felt.

"What are you doing here?" she demanded.

After a long, shocked silence, Pancho said in a weak voice, "I don't know."

"Did you take advantage of me?" Anne demanded.

"I don't know."

"What do you mean you don't know?"

"Do you?"

"No," she admitted. The last thing she remembered, and that was pretty fuzzy, was a chorus of Merry Christmases and the beginning of a journey, a very long journey with she and Pancho helping each other toward the ranch house. It had been cold; now it wasn't. But then Pancho radiated a lot of warmth. Anne sniffed and decided she'd rather be cold. "You don't think we . . ." she began hesitantly.

"I sure hope not," said Pancho, looking completely stricken.

She sat up and patted him consolingly on the shoulder. Through her mind passed the unbidden thought that this situation could be to her advantage, but she put that idea away as quickly as it came to her. The blacksmith in her head was becoming more energetic, and she clenched both hands to her temples and groaned.

"Me too," said Pancho.

Then Anne noticed that he was stripped down to his trousers, no shirt, no boots, no socks—if he wore socks. He hadn't asked her to darn any while she was here. She was wearing her nightie, which was all encompassing, although she'd certainly like to know how she'd gotten into it. That was not part of her dim memories. Maybe they had done what they both hoped they hadn't.

"What do you do when you feel like this?" she asked.

"Since I ain't never woke up in bed with a respectable woman," said Pancho, "I don't know."

"I meant from the liquor. What do you do for the headache and the nausea?"

"Well, sometimes I throw up," said Pancho. "I groan a lot."

"Oh, you're a big help." She climbed out of bed and yelped. It was cold! Someone had forgotten to feed the fire. "'Scuse my nightgown," she mumbled, wrapping up in a blanket. Pancho had just dived completely under the remaining covers. "Aren't you going to get up, Pancho? Are you going to let me start the fire all by myself?"

"I ain't got no clothes on."

"You have too, you shirker."

"I do?" He peered under the covers. "I do. Well, turn your back."

Anne laughed; Pancho was modest. As she left the room to warm up last night's coffee and to try to alleviate the terrible pain in her head, he was mumbling. "I can't believe I done this. What would my ma think?"

What indeed? Anne thought sadly. Her life seemed to go from bad to worse, and she had no reason to expect any improvement. Still, things might not be as ominous as they seemed. That unbelievable and terrifying suspicion that hovered at the back of her mind might be nothing at all, just female vapors.

Anne woke up feeling sick, not for the first time that week. For several days she had told herself it was the result of her night of whiskey drinking and poker, but that was four days ago, and it became harder each day to maintain any belief in that fiction. However, she dragged herself out of bed and fixed breakfast for the hands as usual, although the very smell of food turned her stomach. As for eating, well, she couldn't and didn't, which Pancho commented upon. Anne shrugged lightly and muttered, "Not hungry." He frowned. She wished fervently that they'd all finish breakfast and leave.

Eventually all did except Pancho, who lingered over his coffee until she finally gave up her attempt to conquer her nausea and made a dash for the bedroom and the chamber pot. Pancho followed along behind her and said, "I thought you was sick. It's that whiskey, ain't it? I told you not to drink whiskey. Look where it got you. First we wake up sleepin' in the same bed, embarrassed to death, not knowin'—"

"Oh, shut up," said Anne.

Pancho looked surprised. "An' then you're sick, an' stay sick. It's been four days, an' you ain't looked good a single one of 'em."

"Thanks a lot."

"Well, I don't mean you're not pretty. You're always pretty, but you're pale as a bedsheet dryin' in the sun. Ain't no doubt in my mind that you shouldn't never touch whiskey."

"I'm not sick from the whiskey," she snapped.

"You're not? Oh Lord," he cried, beginning to look even more worried. "You got some real bad disease, ain't you? If you've been feelin' poorly for this many days, something's wrong. Reckon I'd better go get the doctor."

"Now there's an unusual excuse for going into town to look for a poker game," said Anne. She was sitting on the floor, and she leaned her head sideways against the bed. She really hated throwing up. It was one activity that made her feel terrible before, during, and after.

"That's a mean thing to say. You really think I'd go into town to get you a doctor and stay to play poker?"

"Oh, stop worrying, Pancho. I'm not sick."

"Course you're sick. I just seen you throw up."

Anne sighed. "I'm probably with child," she muttered.

"What? What's that?" Pancho turned as white as the bed sheets he'd been mentioning.

"I'm—probably—with—child!" she shouted.

He looked horrified, but no more than she felt. In truth, it was the first time she'd really admitted it to herself. Although she must now be close to two months

along, she still felt a stunning sense of disbelief. She'd
wanted a child for eight years and never had one, and
now, when a child was the very last thing she needed,
she was going to have one. Anne groaned and leaned
her head back. Maybe she was wrong. As terrible as
these two months had been, she might well have missed
her monthly flow because of the strain she'd been
under. That was probably it, she tried to tell herself,
although she wasn't really sure she believed it. In the
meantime, Pancho looked as if he might faint.

"You can't be," he was mumbling to himself. "We
only done it once. I didn't think we had at all, really. I
can't even remember it. Don't seem like you could
be—be—you know! Not if I can't remember it."

Anne glared at him. The fool obviously thought that
it was his baby. Good! Maybe he'd offer to marry her.

"I can't marry you," he cried desperately.

"Why not?" she snapped.

"Well, because—because I ain't never thought of
gettin' married. I never figgered on marryin' nobody.
Sure not you!"

"What's wrong with me?" she demanded angrily.

"Nothin'. I like you a lot. It's jus' . . . well, hell,
Anne. It'd be like marryin' my sister."

The anger drained out of her face. Poor Pancho. In
his way he did love her, just as she did him, but he was
quite right. Marrying Pancho would be like marrying a
brother.

"It's not yours, you dolt," she mumbled. Tempting as
it was to let him think he'd fathered the child, she
couldn't do it to him.

"It's not?"

"That's something you can't tell after only four days.
Don't you know anything about it?"

"How would I know?" asked Pancho. "It's not my
baby? Then whose is it?"

"None of your business."

"Well, he'll have to marry you."

"He can't." Oh Lord, what was she to do? She was carrying Justin's child, and he was already married. A wave of sheer terror hit her. "He can't," she said in a small, hopeless voice.

"Why not? Is he dead?"

"No, he's not dead."

"You mean he won't marry you?"

"That's right."

"I'll kill him."

"Wonderful idea, Pancho. Then he really would be dead, wouldn't he?"

"Well, yeah. You're right about that. But if he's alive, I don't see why—"

"Just let it go, Pancho," she said wearily.

"But if he don't marry you, ever'one's gonna think it's my baby 'cause you been livin' here. Ever'body's gonna think I took advantage of a good woman."

"Maybe you did," said Anne, her mouth quirking.

"It ain't funny," said Pancho. "I'll get shot in the back, most likely, where I cain't do nothin' about it."

"Oh, stop worrying. I'll move into Fort Worth. It's about time anyway." The idea terrified her. "Since I'm not going to announce to anyone that I'm with child, people will forget all about my having been here." She'd be all by herself—no family, no friends. "Hardly, anyone knows me in Fort Worth, so you won't have anything to worry about, will you? No one will think you got me in a family way and then deserted me."

"But what'll you do? All by yourself in a strange town. That's not gonna be any good. You won't have no money. You won't have a husband."

"I'll have the money my husband left me. I just have to see the lawyer in Fort Worth to get it back from the colonel."

"Yeah, the colonel." Pancho frowned. "He's got ever' thing else you own, don't he?"

Anne sighed. "That he does. My sewing machine, my clothes, my rifle, everything."

"I'll get 'em back."

"I appreciate it, but—"

"No buts about it. I'll get ever'thing back. He'll either give it to me, or I'll shoot him. How's that?"

"It would be a great help, Pancho. Thank you," said Anne, for she understood that his offer was as much to salve his own conscience as it was to help her. Poor Pancho. He was probably going to feel guilty about this forever. "That's really good of you," she said, pulling herself wearily to her feet and kissing him affectionately on the cheek.

"Don't do that," he said. "It don't look right."

Anne laughed, thinking that it was a little late for anyone to be worrying about what looked right as far as she was concerned. "I'll tell you what, Pancho. Tomorrow I'll go into Weatherford to see a doctor, just to be sure I really am . . . you know." She didn't even want to say it again. Maybe if she didn't say it, she wouldn't be. "And while I'm seeing the doctor, you can stop by the Bar M to get my things, and then I'll go on into Fort Worth. That's the best thing."

Pancho was frowning mightily. "Even if you're not— ah—expectin', what are you going to do in Fort Worth? That's a rough town, you know. All them trail drivers an' buffalo hunters an' freighters an' railroad workers —ever' kind of riffraff you can imagine."

Anne laughed, but without much humor. "Sounds just like Fort Griffin. I ought to feel right at home."

"But you won't have a husband to protect you in Fort Worth."

"No," said Anne sadly. "I won't have David." And to herself she thought, *Or Justin.* Oh Lord, it was going to be hard, hard to see any kind of life ahead for her and for the child growing inside her body. Maybe after she got the money, she'd leave Texas entirely. Never see

Justin again or Sissie or Pancho. She felt like crying. Instead she gave Pancho the best smile she could muster and said prosaically, "Well, I'd best get supper on, hadn't I?"

"Did you have any trouble?"

"Nope," said Pancho, "not so you'd notice. Oh, he wasn't too friendly at first, but when I jammed a gun in his ribs, he decided to gimme your stuff. Miss Sissie packed it all up. An' here's your sewin' machine. I asked her three times if she was sure she'd got ever'thing that belonged to you."

"Those things of my mother's, did you get those?"

"Yep. Ever'thing on your list, although the colonel tried to tell me you didn't have no right to that teapot and them little cups, but Miss Sissie she packed those up, too." He was studying her anxiously. "Sure you don't want me to go into Fort Worth with you?"

"No, Pancho. I know a woman who takes in boarders there. I stayed at her house with the colonel when I first came from Fort Griffin."

Pancho nodded. "Now if you need help," he said, "you get word to me, hear?"

"I hear, and thank you, Pancho. You've been a good friend."

"No, I ain't," he said, scuffing one boot toe in the dust. "If I was really a good friend, I'd marry you."

"No, you wouldn't, and you shouldn't." He'd asked and she'd told him what the doctor said, that she was indeed with child.

The stage driver had finished loading her few possessions into the boot and on top of the stage. Anne thought she'd never felt more desolate in her life, even after her husband's death, but then the colonel had come for her, and she'd been comforted by the thought that she had family to go to. Now she had no one. There was only her and the illegitimate child she carried and the prospect of never being able to share that child with his father. What a future to look forward to! Soon they'd be outcasts, she and her baby. She swallowed hard and said, "Bye, Pancho. Take care of yourself."

"You too," said Pancho as she climbed aboard. "You too Annie."

CHAPTER
Fourteen

"I hope you're satisfied," said Penelope. "At least now you'll leave me alone."

"As soon as I have a doctor's confirmation," Justin agreed. "It's not as if you're a joy to take to bed."

Penelope flushed but retorted confidently, "There are hundreds of men who'd be delighted to have me for a wife."

"Only until they'd actually had the experience."

"Get out of my room!" she shrieked.

"Not, my dear wife, until a doctor tells me that you actually are with child. Then I'll gladly move out until, of course, it's time to beget our second child."

Penelope turned white. "I won't have another one."

"Yes, you will," said Justin.

"Land sake," cried Elsie Gilchrist in answer to Anne's knock, "it's young Miz McAuliffe. Is the colonel in town with you? No? Well, I hope you're not looking to stay here. I'm full up to the rafters. Can you believe this is the same place you saw last winter? More folks than you can shake a stick at since the railroad came."

"I'd take anything," said Anne, remembering the thronged streets and the mushrooming tent city she had seen at the edge of Fort Worth as the stage rattled in. "Maybe I could share a room if you have any female boarders."

"Jesus be praised, girl, I haven't an extra bed anywhere. I wouldn't even know where to tell you to try." The woman looked more pleased than dismayed. "If I was you, Missy, I'd get right back on the stage. Give me a couple of months' notice, and I'll promise you a bed, but not today."

At that advice, Anne, exhausted after a rough, five-hour trip from Weatherford, slumped to the floor. When she regained consciousness, the badly flustered landlady was waving a bottle of smelling salts under her nose and saying, "Lord have mercy, what a to-do!"

Anne blinked.

"Well, you've come around at last." Elsie squinted at her. "You're not ill, are you?"

"Just very tired," Anne whispered.

"I don't want you bringing sickness into my house. Still, if you're not sick maybe I could fix you a pallet in the kitchen. 'Twouldn't be much for a young lady like yourself, but . . ."

"I'd be so grateful, Mrs. Gilchrist."

"I suppose I could do that. Perhaps it's my Christian duty." She didn't look particularly happy about it.

In the offices of C. Bain and Co., Anne was on the verge of tears. Her belongings, which she had left with the stage driver, had disappeared; the money given her by Pancho had been sadly depleted by the outrageous rent Mrs. Gilchrist was charging for a pallet by her wood stove; and now this young houligan, who was to have carried Anne's luggage to the boarding house, wanted to be paid for no work. "Why don't you just trail me down to the marshall's office," said Anne, "and see how he feels about young men who attempt to extort money from widows?"

"I want to be paid here and now!"

"Oh, go away," she cried as, in search of a handkerchief, she fished her Colt out of her reticule.

The boy, gaping in surprise, whirled and sprinted from the office. Anne herself scowled at the stage-line agent, who was backing up with his hands over his head.

"Be you a lady bandit?" he gasped.

"I am not. I'm a lady victim."

She stuck the pistol back into her bag and stamped out the door toward the jail on Second and Commerce Street, which she had now passed twice. The marshall, Long-Haired Jim Courtright, who looked rather splendid in his light Stetson, his coat and string tie, and his vest with its star and watch chain, promised to investigate, but Anne was afraid she'd never see her possessions again. At least, what little money she had had been on her person. She doubted that Mrs. Gilchrist would have let her stay otherwise, no matter how miserable the accommodations. Still, with thousands of people living in tents, Anne dared not complain. At least, she had a roof over her head. But what about clothes? She had only what was on her back, what little her carpetbag held, and no money to buy any new clothes.

"Well, Miz McAuliffe," said the colonel's lawyer, "the problem is that the courthouse burned down. Surely, you heard about it."

"No, I didn't," said Anne, "although I noticed that a new one was going up."

"Yes, ma'am. Well, it burned down. Let's see. Last March, and all the clerk's records went with it."

"But I don't see what that has to do—"

"I can't very well transfer that much money when I

don't have written permission from the colonel."

"Why do you need his permission? It's my money."

"But he's got it, and then," continued the lawyer, "the papers are all gone."

"You mean you don't have copies in your own office?"

"Not of the county clerk's records, no, ma'am."

She looked at him suspiciously. "Obviously it's not possible for you to represent me."

"Of course I can, Miz McAuliffe. Why, I won't even charge you till things get straightened out."

Anne found that news a great relief and changed her mind about going to another lawyer. Given the state of her finances, she couldn't afford to.

"First thing, I'd best send word to the colonel. The second thing is to write to the courthouse in Jacksboro. That's the county seat of Shackleford County, where, as you know, Fort Griffin is located. Like as not, they have a copy of your husband's will which I'll admit I don't recollect at all. There's been a press of business between the last time I saw you, Miz McAuliffe, and now."

"I suppose so," she said dubiously, "but my husband left the money and property to me, not to the colonel."

"I don't doubt you, ma'am."

"I just turned it over to him to manage because I—"

"Perfectly natural," said the lawyer sympathetically. "A new widow doesn't want to be bothered with business."

"But I do need money now."

"If I might make a suggestion, maybe you should return to your stepfather until this matter is resolved. Then—"

"No!"

Mr. Dawson raised his eyebrows. "I'm sure he—"

"That's out of the question."

"Hmm. Well, you're safe enough with Miz Gilchrist, and I'll send word by the next stage to the colonel and to Jacksboro. Bain and Co.'s a real reliable line."

"Is it indeed?" Anne responded coldly. She had yet to see the return of her property.

"Why, we'll have this cleared up in no time at all."

"I hope so," Anne murmured with heartfelt fervor.

"Marshall, my Winchester's not here," said Anne, who had just had her belongings returned by Long-Haired Jim Courtright himself. The marshall was highly indignant that thieves felt free to steal from widows in his town.

"You didn't mention a rifle, ma'am."

"I didn't? But I must have." She shook her head, distraught. "It's a Winchester .44/.40. I had it wrapped in a feather star quilt, light blue and white." The loss of her rifle was the last straw. Lawyer Dawson was putting her off, urging her to return to the Bar M. Mrs. Gilchrist expected her second week's money, which—if Anne gave it to her—was the last of the money Pancho had paid her for cooking while she was at the Rocking T.

"We found it," said the marshall gently. "Should have known it was yours. After all, how many men wrap a rifle in a quilt?" He smiled cheerfully at her. "No need to weep, Miz McAuliffe." Anne had burst into tears.

"My land," cried Mrs. Gilchrist, bustling down the stairs. "You're not in trouble with the law, are you?" She looked as if she wouldn't be a bit surprised.

"No, it's just that they found my things." Anne dabbed her eyes with a handkerchief handed her by the marshall.

"Gracious me, don't sound like anything to cry about," said Elsie Gilchrist severely. "More like something to thank the good Lord for. You could do with a little more church-going and a little less gadding about."

Anne cut disconsolately across the square, threading her way among the wagons and horses with her black skirts raised above the mud. It was mid-January, and she had just made another visit to Lawyer Dawson, whose opinion it was that his letters to the colonel and to Jacksboro must have been lost in a stagecoach robbery. Otherwise, he couldn't imagine why he had had no word.

Anne was feeling quite desperate. She had given Elsie, after the woman's innumerable hints, the last of her money and had no idea what she would do when that week's advance payment ran out. She had been seeking employment for several days, soliciting jobs from people as diverse as the owner of Peers House, which hired female waiters but not her, and the editor of the newspaper, who never hired women at all. No one had a job for her—not as a clerk, not as a waitress, not as a schoolteacher.

Well, maybe someone wanted a good cook. Tomorrow she'd look for work as a cook. Tomorrow she wouldn't be so fussy about the location of the business. If she had to, she'd try down toward Hell's Half Acre, but the thought of the painted women and the gamblers and the ruffians racing their horses in the streets and shooting off pistols and rifles made her shiver.

"I do not need ze chef, madam," said the owner of LeBeau's Paris Cafe.

Anne nodded. She hadn't really thought he would, but tomorrow her paid-up lodging ran out. The little Frenchman went back inside his establishment, and Anne leaned against the wall, inexpressibly weary.

"You're a cook?"

She looked up in surprise. A middle-aged woman was eyeing her narrowly, a woman wearing clothes that were a little bright in color for a person her age, but very well made and exceedingly fashionable, especially the hat. It was downright—what word could adequately describe that hat?—ornamental, Anne thought with the first flash of humor she'd felt in days. Perhaps this was some newly wealthy person looking for a household cook. Anne's spirits lifted. In a private home, she'd have a room of her own. She could leave the pallet in Elsie's kitchen and the tension caused by Elsie's hostility, for the landlady, a widow, had somehow got the idea that Anne was pursuing Mr. Ephraim Barker, a butcher with whom Elsie had been keeping company for years.

"Yes, ma'am," said Anne, "I am."

"What sort of cooking do you do?" asked the woman.

"Plain or fancy. I can follow any kind of recipe."

"Can you now? My name is Hannah McDivot."

"Anne McAuliffe," Anne responded promptly.

"Ah, a fellow Scotswoman."

"Well, my husband's people were Scots, at any rate."

"You're married?" The woman began to turn away.

"A widow," said Anne hurriedly. She wanted to grasp the woman's hand, not let her leave in case she had a job to offer. "My husband was a cavalry officer."

"You wouldn't be interested in my job."

"Yes, I would," said Anne eagerly.

"The name Hannah McDivot means nothing to you?"

Anne shook her head.

"I run a sporting house," the woman said bluntly.

"A sporting house?"

"Aren't you the innocent?" She laughed with a wry twist of her mouth. "Now, I'm sure you wouldn't be interested. Girls live at my house, Mrs. McAuliffe, and men come to visit them. Since it's a rather high-class establishment, of its kind, I serve food, wines and whiskey before the gentlemen go upstairs with the ladies of their choice. Now do you know what a sporting house is?"

Anne flushed, her mind whirling. Now she understood. The question was, could she work there? Or perhaps the question was, did she have a choice? "What does it pay?"

The woman named a figure, and Anne felt a sinking disappointment. It wasn't enough to live on even if she could bring herself to accept. "That includes a room and food," said Hannah McDivot.

"A room?" asked Anne warily.

"Your room would be on the first floor, Mrs. McAuliffe, not upstairs where business is conducted."

"Oh." Anne flushed again.

"As I said, you wouldn't be interested."

"Oh, but I would," she cried desperately.

"Why?"

"Because I haven't a penny to my name, and I'm about to be ejected from my boarding house because I can't pay."

"Well, you are in a pickle, aren't you?"

"I am indeed." More than Hannah McDivot knew, but then Anne had no intention of telling the woman that she was with child as well as penniless.

"Very well, you can have a week's trial. Nothing will be expected of you but cooking. However, if you should wander out of your kitchen and my customers mistake you for one of the girls, you'll have to fend them off yourself. I've no time for the defense of virtuous women."

Anne shivered, wondering whether that was going to be a problem. "What am I supposed to do if one of your customers accosts me, shoot him?"

Hannah looked at her in surprise, then burst into laughter. Anne herself smiled hesitantly. "If you've a gun and the nerve for it, blast away," said Hannah. "Just give warning, and try not to kill the rich ones."

"I'll keep that in mind," Anne agreed. She would have shared the laughter had she not been so scared. "May I come tomorrow morning?"

"Better make it noon. We're not early risers."

"Noon then," said Anne. "Good day, Mrs. Mc-Divot."

Hannah nodded sharply and turned down the street, her silken flounces whispering richly.

God help me, thought Anne. *What have I gotten myself into? Well, what choice do I have?* she amended, and set off to announce her departure to Elsie.

A streak of mischievousness made her do it at the dinner table in front of the amorous Mr. Ephriam Barker. He was obviously disappointed, Elsie less so. "Where are you going then?" she asked.

"I've got a job as a cook," said Anne.

"Where?"

"What does it matter? It's the only one I could get, so I took it." Her brief spurt of defiance died as she thought of her new job at the sporting house. She hadn't even seen the place, but she had a fair idea of where it might be—in Hell's Half Acre, likely, where life would be as dangerous outside as it was in.

"I had a visit from Brother Hiram Foley this afternoon," said Elsie. "Do you know that godly man?"

Anne's face paled.

"Ah, I see you do. I think it's just as well you're going, Mrs. McAuliffe," said the woman smugly.

Anne thought so too.

Anne wore a voluminous apron at all times, an apron with deep pockets, in one of which she carried her Colt revolver. If she could have carried her rifle, she'd have done it. She hated this place, not the cooking, but the goings on upstairs. Even as desperate as she'd been, she didn't think she could have done what those girls were doing. It seemed to her a desecration of the act of love.

How did Hannah's girls feel about it? she wondered. And who had driven them into such a life? Lying men and mean-spirited women, Anne decided bitterly. People like Justin and the colonel, Brother Foley, and Elsie

Gilchrist. Well, she would survive despite them all. Anne patted the gun in her pocket and went back to her sauces.

No beef, beans, and biscuits here. Hannah wanted the meats in rich wine sauces. She served game and fish, the freshest vegetables available and fancy desserts. The first week had been difficult for Anne, who hadn't done any cooking of this sort since she'd lived in New Orleans. The work, however, got easier. But the sounds that floated into her kitchen never did—the raucous laughter and music from the front rooms where the men were entertained before they went upstairs, the sounds from above. She hated it all.

Except for Hannah. She rather liked the owner, who was as down to earth and blunt-spoken as a woman could be, but intelligent and knowledgeable for all that. Anne hadn't been there a week before Hannah called her into the office, eyed her sharply, and said, "You're with child, aren't you?"

Although Anne was now two-and-a-half months gone, she hadn't thought it was noticeable, and she was feeling better. What could Hannah have seen? Still, there was no use denying her condition. She'd show sooner or later. "How did you know?" she asked.

"I've a sharp eye for such things," said Hannah, "as you might expect. Do you want to get rid of it?"

"What?"

"Do you want to get rid of it?" Hannah repeated. "You said your husband died last January, so obviously it's not his. For a woman like you, an illegitimate child is going to be a burden."

"But I . . . How?" Anne felt both surprised and frightened.

"Oh, I have a connection. Don't look so horrified, girl. It's done all the time, especially in places like this. There's some danger, of course, but most women carrying babies they don't want are willing to risk it."

Get rid of her child? Anne had never thought of such

a thing. "I don't know," she mumbled.

"Better consider it. Your life would be easier."

"I suppose it would." She went back to her kitchen.

What an irony! she mused as she basted a chicken with wine and butter. At one time she'd thought Justin wouldn't marry her because she was barren. Now she carried his child, the child he'd seemed to want so much, and she had been offered the opportunity to get rid of it. Could she do that? Lord, what a sinful thing, and yet how in the world would she ever support herself and a baby? Mr. Dawson was still putting her off. He'd had no word from the colonel, he said, and Anne didn't know whether the colonel had simply failed to receive the message or was punishing her by withholding the money. Nor had the lawyer received papers from the courthouse in Jacksboro, although he assured her he'd sent for them.

Anne sighed. What kind of life would this child have with no father? And a mother who cooked for a living in a house of ill repute? Tears welled up, and she wiped them away. She cried so easily these days, although she'd never been much for crying before she'd met Justin. Hannah had advised her to decide soon, within the next two weeks preferably. The longer she waited, the more dangerous the procedure became. Oh Lord, what was she to do?

Well, if Dawson could secure her inheritance within two weeks, she'd move away. She'd say she was an Army widow, which was the truth. She didn't have to say when David had died. Then she could raise the child in some semblance of respectability. But if the money didn't come through, and she was caught here in Fort Worth, in this house . . . She shook her head, glad that she could put the decision off.

Anne stepped out of the railroad depot, carrying the hoard of precious spices she'd just picked up from the train. Coming toward her down Main Street over newly laid tracks was the small, mule-drawn streetcar that traveled round and round between the courthouse and the Texas and Pacific train station. Ordinarily Anne would have walked the distance back to Hannah's, if only to enjoy the fresh air, the exercise, and the time away from that place, but she was finding it almost impossible to adjust to the hours there. She still woke early, although she had to stay up late providing refreshments for Hannah's customers.

Giving in to exhaustion, she climbed aboard the small car, paid her nickel, and sat down on one of the two seats that ran lengthwise down either side. There were two other passengers, one of them a brawny fellow lured aboard by the driver and not required to pay. Soon enough she found out why, for they had gone less than a block when the little car jumped the tracks and plowed into a mud puddle. Anne and the others had to dismount. The two males were called upon to help lift the car back onto the tracks with much swearing by the driver and grumbling by the customer who had paid. The free rider took their accident with less annoyance.

After a second derailment, the driver called to his passengers, "Back in a minute," and headed into a saloon directly opposite where they'd stopped. No sooner had he disappeared through the swinging doors than the small mule, whom Anne wouldn't have credited with the ability to move that fast, bolted toward the river, dragging the car behind him.

"Oh, hell," murmured the brawny passenger. "He's runnin' away agin," and the man saluted Anne and leapt off.

"Best bail out, ma'am," said the second passenger, and he too leapt out.

"Jump, lady!" pedestrians and riders were calling to her from the street and sidewalks. Anne began to panic. Both men had fallen hard, and the mule was picking up speed in his dash for the Trinity River. If she jumped, she might lose the baby, Justin's baby, and all because of a feckless streetcar driver. Well, she'd paid her nickel, and by God, she wasn't jumping off the car.

Getting angrier by the minute because she couldn't stop the mule by ordinary means, she formed a new and rather desperate plan. She had no idea what its outcome would be, but still she had to try before she ended up in the river. Taking a shaky breath, she drew her pistol from her black silk, drawstring bag and sighted at the mule's head. Pancho had said a pistol was fairly accurate within seven feet or was it yards?

"She's gonna shoot the mule," people were crying on the street.

There'd be a slight drop to the bullet's path but not much. She wasn't two hundred yards away.

"Let him have it, lady!"

And a drift to the left because of the rifling, whatever that was. Last had said so.

"Don't be afraid, sweetheart. Just squeeze that trigger!"

She did. She even saw the bullet ricochet off the mule's skull, and the mule staggered, slowed, veered left, and stumbled to a stop.

Anne dropped her pistol into her reticule and dismounted into the mud, her skirts lifted demurely. The crowd cheered as, scowling, she slogged toward the saloon, where she found the driver having a beer, chatting with the bartender, and obviously very surprised to see a redheaded woman in widow's weeds drawing a Colt Frontier revolver from her silk handbag and pointing it at him.

"I ought to shoot you right between the eyes," she said. The driver's mouth fell open. "Just as I did your miserable mule."

"You shot my mule? Why'd you do that?"

"Don't you recognize me?" she demanded. "I am the lady you abandoned in the streetcar."

"I was comin' right back. Jus' stopped for—"

"Your mule ran away with me."

"Oh, well, he does that sometimes."

"I could have been killed because of your irresponsible behavior." She cocked the gun, and the driver blanched.

"Ma'am, you wouldn't shoot me just 'cause—"

"You deserted your post, you rotten shirker."

"But I'm a family man. Sure, you wouldn't shoot a man with a wife and two babes."

"I'd be doing them a favor," Anne declared.

A throat was cleared behind her, and gloved fingers came to rest upon her arm.

"Unhand me," she snapped, "or I'll shoot you too, whoever you are." She kept her eyes pinned on the driver.

"Now, Miz McAuliffe, you wouldn't want to shoot the marshall of Fort Worth, would you?" asked Jim Courtright.

"I wouldn't," she agreed, "unless, of course, you try to come between me and this worthless, lazy—"

"Now, Miz McAuliffe, I realize you're mighty upset, but still I can't very well let you shoot Tad Boynton here."

"See!" cried Tad. "The marshall ain't gonna let you."

"How is he going to stop me?" asked Anne, raising the pistol and pointing it at his head.

"If I was you, Tad," said the marshall, "I'd keep my mouth shut. This lady just bounced a bullet off the skull of your mule. Now that's shootin'!"

"I ain't no mule!" cried Boynton. "She'd hang."

"Maybe I'd consider it worthwhile!" snapped Anne.

"Now Miz McAuliffe, I think we ought to come to some sort of compromise here," said the marshall. "I'm sure you don't want to kill no one."

"Well, I *might* consider a compromise," said Anne, who was beginning to calm down.

"Oh, thank you, ma'am," cried the driver. "Anything, anything at all."

Anne nodded. "First, I want my nickel back."

"Yes, ma'am." The driver thrust his hand into his pocket, hurriedly shuffled through the coins there, and came up with a nickel.

"Put it on the bar," she ordered. "And since I had to do your job, under extremely dangerous conditions, I want your day's pay."

"My day's pay!" he cried. "How'm I gonna—" She raised the pistol again. "Yes, ma'am. My day's pay." He put more money down on the bar.

"Does that look like the right amount to you, Marshall?" she asked, glancing sideways at Long-Haired Jim Courtright, who seemed about to burst into laughter.

"Yes, ma'am, sure does."

"Good," said Anne. "If you would pick it up and put it in my reticule."

The marshall swept up the money and dropped it into her bag. The driver looked very unhappy. "Do you have any quarrel with this, Mr. Boynton?" she asked him challengingly.

"I ain't about to quarrel with a lady holding a pistol on me," he replied sullenly.

"Good. Now turn back to the bar and put both hands on it. You're not to move until I'm out on the street. Do you understand?"

"Yes, ma'am."

"Don't worry, Miz McAuliffe," said Marshall Courtright, now laughing irrepressibly. "I'll cover your back."

"Thank you, Marshall," said Anne, and she turned smartly and marched out.

Behind her the marshall said, "Let that be a lesson to you, Boynton. It don't pay to take off from work the way you do, not when you've got redheaded ladies aboard."

It was late morning by the time Anne got back, and she stopped by Hannah's office to tell her that there would be no abortion. Her panic at the possibility of miscarrying Justin's child had convinced her that she couldn't bear to give it up, not for any reason.

"You're making a mistake," said Hannah.

Anne sighed. "Perhaps so, but I can't do anything else, although I do thank you for your concern, Hannah."

The woman nodded. "How about a game of chess?" They played occasionally in the early afternoon.

"Wonderful," said Anne, and her face lit with the special radiance that showed there in moments of happiness, even fleeting happiness.

"Oh my," said Hannah, "you and I could make a lot of money if you were interested in becoming a sporting woman."

Anne laughed. "I'm afraid I haven't the disposition for it, Hannah. I'd more likely shoot your customers than accommodate them. In fact, today I did shoot the streetcar mule and came pretty close to shooting his driver."

"Good Lord," said Hannah, "I never thought I'd have to worry that my cook might give the place a bad name."

CHAPTER

Fifteen

"They're ready for the first course now," Hannah called in at the door to the kitchen. Then she disappeared in a rustle of striped taffeta and velvet bows.

Anne loaded a large tray with bowls of sherried turtle soup. So important did Hannah consider this dinner meeting of wealthy men that no other food would be served to the house's customers that night. Anne was walking carefully down the hall, balancing the tray, when hands grasped her waist from behind. Her impulse was to whirl and heave the hot soup on whomever it was, but she restrained herself. Making a scene and losing the first course, along with its china, wasn't going to get that raise Hannah had hinted at, and Anne would need the extra money once she had to stop working.

She lowered the tray to a hall table as the man behind her, who reeked of whiskey, whispered amorously into her ear, "Pretty, pretty red hair."

Anne gritted her teeth and slipped her hand into the pocket of her apron.

"Let's go upstairs," said her admirer.

"I don't go upstairs," she replied quietly as she began to edge the gun out. Maybe she could scare him away. If not, she'd have to shoot him, preferably in some spot that would allow him to run away. With all the racket going on out on the street, who, except the recipient, would ever notice one more gunshot? "I'm not one of the sporting girls. You'd best get back to the parlor."

"But I like you," said the voice behind her. "And Hannah always lets me have the ones I like."

Anne whirled and jammed the gun into his stomach. Then she gaped. "Sam Junior, what are you doing here?"

Young Sam Bannerman blinked at her and smiled foolishly. "Why, it's Annie McAuliffe," he mumbled. "Pretty, pret–ty Annie McAuliffe. I saw you at my wedding."

"Indeed you did."

"I liked you then, too."

"Thanks a lot. Now get your hands off me."

"An' I'm so glad to see you here at Hannah's. I never thought I'd get to go to bed with you."

"And you were right; you never will."

"Aw, Annie." He squeezed her.

"Sam Junior, I have a gun in your stomach. Do you realize that?"

"Aw, Annie," he crooned again, seemingly quite unintimidated by the idea that she might put a bullet in his gut. "You wouldn't shoot Sammie. All the girls love Sammie. Let's go upstairs."

"I don't *go* upstairs, Sam Junior."

"Everybody in Hannah's house goes upstairs, everybody that's worth going upstairs with." He wrapped burly arms around her and hugged her, squashing the gun between them.

Good Lord, she thought, if she pulled the trigger now, she'd shoot herself as well as him. "Sam Junior, let go of me. I'm the cook here."

"Tha's all right," Sam said. "You can put your clothes on after we get through an' cook me supper."

"Don't be disgusting."

"Aw right. I'm not hungry anyway." He'd been trying to kiss her but having no luck.

"Think what a jackass you're going to look when it gets around town that you were trying to drag the brothel cook off to bed."

"I don' mind," said Sam, finally managing to trap her head for the kiss. She bit his lip. "That wasn't nice," he mumbled.

"Shame on you, Sam!" Anne snapped reprovingly. "What are you doing here when you have a lovely young wife at home?" She had to put off struggling for fear the gun would discharge. "Let go!"

"No–o, no–o," said Sam, trying for another kiss, then planting one hand on her bottom and lifting her almost off the floor.

Anne was really beginning to be afraid. "If you don't stop, I'll go out to the Triangle and tell Gretchen," she warned, "and that's after I tell your father."

"Papa knows where I am. He's here too," said Sam, giving her a pinch.

Anne tried to knee him but wasn't successful because she didn't have her feet on the floor, whereas he had managed to get his hand over one of her breasts. "I warn you, Sam, I'll tell your wife."

"That's enough, Anne," said Hannah coldly. "One thing we do not do here in my establishment is report to wives on our customers' activities."

"Then make him let me go."

"This is the one I want, Miss Hannah. I'm gonna carry her right on upstairs."

"I think you'd best let her go, Sam," advised Hannah.

"I think so too," said Anne, giving up caution and struggling violently. "I've still got the gun, and if you keep squeezing me, it's liable to go off and kill us both."

"Nobody's gonna shoot Sam Junior," said the young man, squeezing her again.

"What the devil's going on here?"

Anne recognized the voice and groaned.

"Nothing to worry about, Mr. Harte," soothed Hannah. "Just go on back to the Blue Room. I'll be right along."

"Anne, what are you doing here?" Justin demanded.

"I'm working," she snapped, "if this lout will ever let go of me."

"Working here?" he roared.

"She's my cook," Hannah explained.

"You're a cook in a house of prostitution?" he demanded indignantly. "Let go of her, Sam."

"I won't," said Sam. "She's mine, an' I'm takin' her upstairs."

Since young Bannerman towered over Anne, Justin simply planted a powerful fist on his jaw, knocking him back four feet. Anne went two of those feet with him before Sam lost consciousness and released her. She fell against the table, which sent the soup tray flying, and the pistol discharged when her fingers tightened involuntarily on the trigger. The bullet shattered a wall sconce.

"By God, this is too much!" exclaimed Hannah. "I've a good mind to fire you, Anne."

"You don't need to bother," said Justin. "She's quitting." He helped her off the floor and said, "Put the gun away before you shoot someone."

"I'd like to shoot Sam Junior," muttered Anne.

"Don't talk nonsense. You have to leave before anyone else finds out that you've been working here."

"Leave!" cried Anne, incensed that Justin Harte would try to interfere in her life again. With both herself and his child to support, she couldn't afford to lose this job.

"That's right. With me, and right now."

"Hannah!" wailed Anne.

"I just don't want any trouble," said Hannah. "What am I supposed to do with him?" She pointed to Sam, who looked like a giant blond bear, lying unconscious in her hall and completely blocking access to the kitchen and the door that led to the backyard outhouse.

"Is this what you were bringing? This soup?" Justin asked, pointing to the puddles and shattered china on the carpet. "You were going to serve it to the men in there?"

"I was, and look at it. That oaf ruined it, and it was a triumph."

"Hannah, get someone else to take over for her in the kitchen. She's leaving."

"What about my butterflied lamb roast?"

"Cattlemen hate lamb. I'll be back to the meeting as soon as I find some safe place to put her, Hannah."

"I'm not going anywhere with you, Justin Harte," said Anne. "And if you try to make me, I'll call the marshall."

"Not to my house you won't," snapped Hannah.

Justin was scowling impatiently. "Have you got a place I can go to talk to her?"

"Upstairs, second door on your right, and keep it quiet," said the madam.

Before Anne could protest, he'd removed her gun, clamped one big hand over her mouth, the other around her waist, and dragged her upstairs. No amount of struggling on Anne's part could get her loose before he'd kicked the door shut behind them.

"Do you know what goes on in this room?" he asked when he had taken his hand away from her mouth.

"Of course I do, and how dare you bring me up here?"

"It was bad enough that I found you living with that gunfighter, but now working in a bawdy house!"

"Well, what are *you* doing here?" she asked nastily.

"I'm here for a meeting and nothing else!" he snapped back. "We're not talking about my behavior anyway, but yours is outrageous. Letting that killer—"

"Don't you say anything bad about Pancho. He was there when I needed him."

"What does that mean? Why would you need Pancho Tighe? I'll admit the colonel's no bargain, but at least you were safe and respectable at his house. Why in God's name did you ever leave?"

Anne was so angry she was literally looking at him through a red haze. "You want to know why I left the colonel's house? All right, Justin, I'll tell you." She began to unbutton the front of her dress.

"What are you doing?" Justin asked nervously.

"I'm going to show you why I left the colonel's house." She stripped the top of her dress away and turned her back to him. She could hear Justin's indrawn breath. "You see the scars, do you? Well, if you think they look bad now, think how they looked in December when he took his quirt to me."

"What happened?" he asked, his voice subdued. "Did he find out about you and Tighe?"

"There wasn't anything to find out about Pancho and me. Brother Foley found out about *us*, Justin. Do you remember dragging me into your hotel room in Weatherford?"

"Yes."

"Well, Hiram Foley saw me coming out; then he cornered me in the livery stable the next day and tried to blackmail me. And when that didn't work, he went to the colonel, and that, Justin, is why the colonel beat me. I left the Bar M that night." She dragged the top of her dress up over her arms and began to button it. "Maybe you think I should have stayed. Maybe you think I got what I deserved."

"Dear God," said Justin.

"Oh, yes, dear God."

"But to go to Tighe."

"Who else could I go to? You? Would you have wanted to take me in? Would your wife have been glad to see me? Brother Foley's no doubt been blackening my name all over Parker County. You're worried about my reputation because I'm living in a whorehouse?" She laughed bitterly. "I don't have any reputation left. I went to the one person I thought might take me in, might not judge me."

She turned to face him and stared hard at his pale face, at the lines of anguish that deepened there as she talked. "I was a bloody mess and only about half-conscious when I got to the Rocking T, and he took me in, took care of me, and let me stay there till I was well enough to leave on my own. And he didn't ask anything of me. Do you understand me? Pancho Tighe didn't want anything from me. That's more than can be said for you, Justin, isn't it?"

She had to pause momentarily to control the quiver in her voice. "You've given me nothing but grief, Justin Harte; he gave me nothing but kindness. He even gave me twenty dollars when I left so that I'd have some money when I got to Fort Worth. Well, you can imagine how long twenty dollars lasted here. I was about to be thrown out on the street when I found this job."

"For God's sake, Anne, I'd have helped you."

"Would you indeed? What would you have done for me, Justin? Given me lectures on my shocking conduct? Or maybe money? And if I'd taken money from you, what would that have made me? Just what you've accused me of being. That's what I'd be if I took your money!"

"Anne," he groaned, "I never meant for any of this to happen."

"No, I'm sure you didn't," she admitted wearily.

"You can't stay here. If Foley's spreading slander about you, you'll be treated badly."

"Oh, I hardly think Hannah would care about anything he had to say."

"I'm not talking about Hannah. You certainly can't stay in this house. No matter what you're here for, you'll have more trouble of the sort you had with Sam Junior. I meant you can't stay in Fort Worth." He paused, frowning anxiously. "You'll have to come back to the Crossed Heart; I can't think of any other way."

"You're going to take me home to your *wife*? Well, that's got to be the ultimate hypocrisy. I suppose you think she'll welcome me."

"She's already invited you," he said dryly. "Don't you remember?"

"I do," said Anne. "The night I found out you were married."

Justin flinched. "We've got to talk about that, but as far as Penelope's concerned, you can be sure she'll find all sorts of uses to make of you, and it would never occur to her that I might be in love with another woman."

Anne's eyes flicked up to his. Love? Her heart stumbled over itself.

"She's too damned self-centered," Justin continued.

"It doesn't matter," said Anne wearily. "I can't go to the Crossed Heart."

"You have no choice. Come for a while, at least until I can—damn! How in God's name am I going to straighten this out?"

"There's no straightening it out," said Anne, thinking of the one last thing he didn't know.

"Oh, I'll find a way," said Justin. "I can put a gag on that damn preacher. I'll drive him out of Texas if I have to. As for the colonel, he's running close enough to the edge where it shouldn't be hard to tip him right off."

"Leave the colonel alone."

"You're being mighty forgiving."

"I'm not forgiving at all, but Sissie needs him. He may not be much of a father, but he does seem to love her, and I certainly have nothing to offer her."

"You never cease to surprise me, Anne. I guess you're about the strongest woman I know, except maybe my mother." He was staring at her with the strangest expression. "But that doesn't mean I'm going to leave you to fend for yourself. I got you into this mess, and I'll take care of you until I can get you out of it. Now let's pack your stuff. You can stay in my room at the hotel tonight."

"Where are you going to stay?" she asked suspiciously.

Justin sighed. "I guess Hannah will give me a bed. Tomorrow we'll head for Palo Pinto."

Anne didn't argue with him, but she thought to herself that if she left his hotel early enough in the morning, she could hide out until he was gone. Then maybe Hannah would take her back.

They were about three hours out of Fort Worth, passing through Parker County, the ride having been made in virtual silence. Anne had spent the time asking herself how she could have slept that long when her plan had been to be up and gone before he returned to the hotel. She supposed it was the fact that for the first time in weeks she had been able to sleep without fear of some drunken lecher bursting into her room. On the other hand, a nagging voice at the back of her mind accused her of oversleeping because she couldn't bear to part with Justin. *How pathetic*, she thought with self-contempt.

Well, it was useless to worry about the reasons now. She was on her way to impose on the hospitality of Justin's wife, whom she didn't even like. She could remember a time at the spring roundup when she had looked forward to seeing the Crossed Heart. Then she'd been prepared to like anything that belonged to Justin. Maybe even then she'd harbored hopes of living in Palo Pinto with him, but hardly as his wife's guest. *Stop it!* she told herself sternly and asked, her voice sharp, "Where are we going to stay tonight?"

Justin glanced sideways at her. "Well," he said hesitantly, "we can make camp. There's a place we'll hit right about sundown. Or we can drive on after dark to Weatherford, but—"

"But if we appear there together, people will talk," Anne finished for him, "and although there's not a whole lot of damage that can befall my reputation at this point, there's still yours to consider," she finished bitterly.

"We'll do whatever you want, Anne."

"Make camp, I guess," she decided. "I'm still tired."

"Was the work that hard at Hannah's?"

"It wasn't so much the work as the strange hours. And the place made me nervous. I hated it."

"I can see why after witnessing that situation with Sam Junior. Had that happened before?"

"Once or twice," she admitted. "Not that bad. But Sam Junior? How could a young bridegroom act that way?" Justin looked embarrassed, probably remembering, she decided, that he too was a bridegroom.

"Gretchen's a sweet girl," Justin muttered. "I reckon she'd be mighty unhappy to hear about his goings on."

"Well, ease your mind, Justin. I'm not planning to tell her. In fact, I doubt that I'd be welcome at the Bannermans', so I wouldn't get the chance if I had a mind to." Anne sighed. "But I do miss seeing Sarah," she added.

Justin glanced at her unhappily. "Anne, I am sorry about all this. I can't tell you how many times I've asked myself why it was I never mentioned my wife to you."

"I can understand," she admitted reluctantly, "that you might have thought I knew you were married, but if you did, you also must have thought it didn't matter to me, in which case you'd have no reason to keep her a secret."

Justin stared bleakly at the horizon and shifted on the wagon seat. "I wasn't exactly keeping her a secret. I just—I just don't like to talk about her. In fact, I try not to think about her if I don't have to." He sighed and admitted, "My marriage hasn't worked out, Anne, which I'm afraid is something you'll see for yourself when we get to the Crossed Heart."

"I didn't notice anything in Weatherford. She seemed—she seemed to love you."

"Oh, she puts on a front in company sometimes, but the truth is I don't think she ever even liked me."

"That can't be, Justin. Why in the world would she have accepted your proposal?"

"Money, land, and cattle," he replied succinctly. "She liked the idea of being a great lady."

Anne glanced at him, frowning. How could Penelope not love Justin?

"She couldn't be nice enough to me while we were courting. Then once we were married and she found out what ranch life was like, she hated it, and everything else about being married. And me . . . Well, let's just say we were both disappointed." He stared somberly ahead. "I certainly don't love her. Sometimes I wonder now if I ever did. I guess I was misled by her beauty, thought the rest of her must be as beautiful as her face, which was a stupid assumption for a man my age to make.

"At any rate, I don't even like her anymore, much less love her, but she is my wife, so I owe her some loyalty, I reckon. Enough not to talk about our problems if I can help it. And so I don't." He hunched his shoulders, pulled his hat down against the wind.

"Besides that, I guess I thought it wouldn't be tactful or kind to mention my wife to you, not when I cared for you so much. When we were together, I was always torn between what I wanted, which was take hold of you and never let go, and the right thing, which was to stay away from you for all our sakes. I did try," he added lamely.

"I know you did," Anne admitted, "and if I'd known why, you'd have had some help from me, but I thought"—she swallowed hard—"I thought you were backing off because I was barren." She could hardly get the words out, given her present situation.

"Oh Lord, Anne, if I'd been free, I'd have married you in a minute, children or no children."

She turned her head away, tears stinging under her lids.

"And I'm afraid that's something else I've got to tell you," he continued reluctantly.

"What?" She turned to stare at him with wide-eyed alarm. Had he guessed about their baby?

"Penelope's with child."

Anne closed her eyes. That had to be the most painful news of all. Penelope, whom he didn't love and who didn't love him, would bear him the heir he wanted, while Anne's baby went fatherless. Well, by God, she'd love it and cherish it enough for both of them.

"Anne, I'm so sorry," he was saying. "I was afraid this would hurt you."

"No, no." She gritted her teeth and said what she had to say. "Congratulations, Justin. I know how much you wanted children. You—you and Penelope must be very happy."

"Happy?" Justin laughed bitterly. "She isn't. Penelope didn't want a child. I insisted."

"Oh?" Anne clasped her hands tightly together in her lap and bit her lip as hard as she could. She wanted to weep. She couldn't bear to think of them together, making that baby. "Well, maybe after she's had it she'll feel differently."

"Maybe," said Justin, but he didn't sound very hopeful.

"No," she said, her teeth chattering.

"It's all right." He'd slid under the blankets beside her. "I'm just going to hold you. You're freezing, sweetheart. If you don't warm up, you'll be sick."

He was right, of course. The temperature had plummeted at sundown, and she was so cold in her blankets, she was shaking. She could already feel the warmth of him behind her, beginning to alleviate the cold, and she had the baby to think of.

"Relax," he murmured, wrapping her in his arms and pulling her back against him. "You're so tired. If you're warm, you'll sleep."

She did. She willed herself to because she'd need every ounce of energy and courage she could muster to walk into Penelope Harte's house tomorrow.

CHAPTER

Sixteen

"It's about time you got back. I don't know how you could go off and leave me when I'm so sick."

"You weren't sick when I left," said Justin, knocking snow off his hat.

"Well, I am now, and it's all your—"

"Penelope," he interrupted, "we have a guest."

For the first time Penelope seemed to notice Anne standing behind Justin, her cloak and hood white with snow.

"I met Mrs. McAuliffe in Fort Worth and thought you might like some company, so I talked her into coming back for a visit."

"Mrs. McAuliffe?" It was obvious that Penelope couldn't place her.

Anne slid her hood off and began to divest herself of the cloak.

"Oh, now I remember. In fact, who could forget that hair? What a—a *bright* color! We met at the wedding in Weatherford, didn't we?"

"Yes," said Anne. "You were kind enough to invite me for a visit."

"Did I?" murmured Penelope. "I don't remember, although you'd think I would. Gretchen's wedding was the last social event I've attended because, you see, nothing *ever* happens out here but snow. It's freezing in this house. You'd best put your wrap back on, Mrs. McAuliffe."

Justin muttered something under his breath, and Penelope whirled toward him and said sharply, "I don't want to hear another word about your ridiculous log house and how much nicer it was. A woman who's forced to live in the middle of nowhere ought to have a decent-looking house."

"And a cold one," muttered Justin.

"I'm afraid, Mrs. McAuliffe, you'll find your visit most uncomfortable. Not only is the house cold . . . My father's house in Fort Worth was never cold, and it was a frame structure, so don't tell me, Justin . . . Oh, well, what do you care if I freeze to death?" She shivered and rubbed her arms petulantly. "Not only is the house cold, but we haven't had a decent meal in days. Calliope's sick!"

"What's wrong with Calliope?" Justin looked concerned for the first time.

"Isn't that just like a man? He worries more about the maid than his wife," Penelope remarked to Anne, then turned irritably back to Justin. "How do I know what's wrong with her? She claims to be too sick to take care of the house or cook, so all the cooking has to be done by some old cowboy, and the food is inedible. You'll have to hire a cook, Justin. You can't expect me to—to endure all sorts of discomforts and not have a decent thing to put in my mouth. I'm sure Mrs. McAuliffe will agree. Really it's—"

"I can cook, Mrs. Harte," Anne interrupted quietly. She could see how this visit was going to go. Still, cooking for cowboys and even for Penelope Harte was bound to be easier and less nerve-wracking than cooking for a bunch of sporting women and their customers.

"Can you?" exclaimed Penelope, her tirade stemmed. "Why, that's wonderful news. It's so nice of you to offer."

Anne nodded, removing her gloves. "Perhaps I should take a look at Calliope. I've some medical skill."

"Oh, Calliope will get well. You know how these people are. They fall ill when they get tired of working."

"Calliope's a good woman and not given to malingering," said Justin. "I'd appreciate it if you would see her, Anne."

"Well, Justin, if you're worried about someone's health, you might worry about mine."

"Is anything particular the matter?" Anne asked.

"Of course, something's the matter. I'm sick every morning. I don't suppose Justin told you, but—"

"Yes, he did. You must be very happy."

Penelope gave Anne an astonished look.

"However, I'm afraid your nausea is quite common in women with child. It will pass."

"Well, that's an insensitive thing to say," Penelope snapped, "but then you wouldn't know how I feel. You've never had a child."

"Penelope," warned Justin.

How ironic, Anne thought, that Justin should try to protect her from that particular hurt when he'd seen to it that she no longer had to feel sensitive about being barren. "Sometimes sipping tea and nibbling on dry bread or toast before you rise in the morning helps," Anne suggested.

"And who's to bring me the tea?" demanded Penelope. "My maid claims to be sick; my husband deserts me. Am I to have some cowboy"—she said the word with great disdain—"coming into my own boudoir?"

Anne realized that she was expected to offer morning tea service but couldn't face the possibility of confronting Justin in bed with his wife. "I'd best have a look at your servant," she suggested instead.

"Don't you want to sit down and rest?" asked Justin. "Have a cup of coffee, something to eat?"

"And who's supposed to make the coffee?" demanded Penelope. "That cowboy cook disappears as soon as he can and leaves me here all by myself. I hope you don't expect me to make it."

"I can do without the coffee," said Anne hastily, "but perhaps I could freshen up."

"Of course. In what room do you want Anne to stay, Penelope?" he asked his wife.

"Oh, any room," she replied, waving her hand indifferently. "Goodness knows what kind of condition they'll be in with no one to clean these four days."

"Calliope's been sick for four days?"

"She has. I've quite lost my patience with her." Behind them the door opened, and Rollo Tandy stepped in. "How many times do I have to tell you to knock, Mr. Tandy?" Penelope demanded.

"You can stop telling him," snapped Justin. "He's lived with me longer than you have."

"Why, Miz McAuliffe," exclaimed Rollo, "never a face was more welcome, I swear."

"Rollo, it's good to see you," Anne replied, her spirits lifting. "You're looking healthy."

"That I am, thanks to you, and I'll tell you, we could use your healing touch. We've got a maid here with a real high fever. It worries me, I can tell you."

"I don't see that it's any of your business, Mr. Tandy," snapped Penelope. "Calliope's my servant."

"I seen people die of fevers that high," Rollo continued, ignoring the mistress of the ranch. "Might lay my whole crew low."

"My goodness!" cried Penelope. "You think it's catching? I visited her myself just yesterday."

"Yesterday?" echoed Justin. Everyone turned to stare. "You haven't even looked in on her since?"

"Well, I wouldn't know what to do for her!" snapped Penelope.

"I'd best see her now," said Anne.

Justin led her toward the back of the house, saying, "This is a poor welcome, I'm afraid."

Anne shrugged; she'd had plenty of those recently.

As Anne settled in, she found herself caught in the crossfire between Penelope's selfishness and Justin's intransigence. The only sign of generosity or hospitality exhibited by Penelope was an offer of any black fabric Anne might find among the supply of material on hand at the ranch, but then Penelope didn't like the color on herself and expected Anne to return the favor by making an elaborate dress for a party she was planning.

No matter what the motive, Anne was delighted to accept the offer. She investigated the storeroom as soon as she had time and found enough fabric, thread, and trimming to stock a dry-goods emporium, which convinced her to start immediately on several wrappers, a loose sort of dress that was both popular and figure concealing. She reasoned that if she began to wear the style before her regular clothes appeared tight, espousing wrappers ostensibly for comfort now that she was the housekeeper and cook at the Crossed Heart, no one would guess later that she had to wear them for concealment. In fact, she was surprised at how little change there was in her body and wondered if she could be mistaken about her condition. Would she be happy about that, happy to miss her only chance of having a child of her own? How terrible to feel so torn and so frightened about something that she had wished for wholeheartedly during all the years of her marriage.

Shrugging her troubling thoughts aside, she selected three bolts of black fabric and took them to her room. One was a fine cashmere, which she would never have taken had she not realized that Penelope would never use it. Justin's wife thought black "most unattractive," a remark she had made while eyeing Anne's black dress.

Well, it was a lovely, soft material and would certainly do very well for special occasions during the cold months and even into spring. If she was ultimately forced to attend Penelope's ball, she'd need it. The other two fabrics were lighter and would be appropriate for common use and next summer as her confinement drew near in August. Where would she be then? she wondered as she began to cut the first dress from one of the patterns she had brought with her. No need to make a muslin trial run for these dresses since they wouldn't be fitted.

By the time to begin preparing the evening meal arrived, she had two dresses cut out and was feeling pleased with herself. Not so Penelope. "Where have you been?" Justin's wife demanded petulantly. "I couldn't find you."

"I was in my room taking advantage of your kind offer of fabrics from your supply."

"Well," said Penelope indignantly, "I thought you'd want to start a dress for me before you did your own."

"Oh?" Anne smiled through a desire to give the girl a well-deserved slap for such blatant selfishness. "Goodness, I thought you'd want something fashionable, which, of course, would require a good deal more thought in the choice of the style, the fabric, and the trimmings. Whereas I just need something everyday for cooking and cleaning."

"Oh." Penelope looked appeased. "Well, of course, I would want something fashionable. What are you making for yourself?"

"Wrappers."

"Wrappers!" exclaimed Penelope. "You can't be serious. They're so unflattering."

"They're comfortable," Anne replied. "Did you want to come into the kitchen with me while I start dinner?"

"Oh, no," said Penelope hurriedly. "In my condition, you know, I need lots of rest."

"Of course," Anne muttered, thinking that in her own condition, she did too, but she kept her mouth shut and went off toward the kitchen.

She was rolling out dough for pies when Justin came in through the outside door. "You make a picture to gladden a man's heart," he said quietly.

Anne drew a shaky breath and kept working.

"I'm ashamed at how little hospitality you've received, Anne. You've been doing the work of three women ever since you arrived."

"At least I'm earning my keep," she muttered, flipping the round of rolled out dough onto the top of the first pie.

"You don't need to earn your keep in my house." He touched a finger to a spot of flour on her cheek.

Anne drew back sharply. "Are you saying that I've already earned it?" she inquired sharply.

Justin flushed and dropped his hand. "You know I didn't mean that. I was trying to tell you how grateful I am for your kindness and help."

Anne sighed. "And I received your thanks ungraciously enough, I'm afraid."

"You've good reason to be sharp with me, with all of us. How's Calliope?"

"Weak, but she'll live."

"And my wife. Is she giving you trouble?"

"I believe she's gone back to bed to conserve her strength and decide what kind of fashionable dress she wants me to make her."

"Damn," Justin muttered. "You don't have to sew for her. You're already doing all the work around here, and you're not my wife, after all." He stopped abruptly. "My God, Anne. I'm sorry."

"Well, it's the truth, isn't it? I'm not your wife." She bit her lip and turned away. "We don't seem to be able to stop hurting each other, do we?"

"And you're the last person in the world I want to hurt," he replied. "This must be terrible for you."

"It's better than Hannah's," said Anne wryly.

"I suppose it is at that, but we must both consider what I can do to set your life right."

Turning earnestly to him, she said, "For one thing, you've got to stop Penelope from giving that ball. Can you imagine, after all the gossip about us, what people would say finding me here. Say to her, to me, to each other?"

"They'll say nothing," said Justin grimly.

"You're fooling yourself. Even if I leave before—"

"It's too soon," he broke in.

She looked at him in surprise. "Too soon? I should never have come in the first place."

"Do you really want to go?" His eyes were anguished.

Anne turned away, her fists clenched on the table. Then she breathed deeply, lifted another crust and flipped it over onto a second dried apple pie. "I have to leave, go to a place where there's no gossip about me." She began to crimp the edges of the crust.

"I know you're right," he admitted. "I just don't want to face it." He leaned back against the table, his booted feet crossed. "Have you a preference? At least, I can arrange it for you."

He didn't want her to go! Her heart exulted, and it was hard to think of anything else. If only she didn't have to leave him. Well, she did have to. And she knew it had to be somewhere far away, where she'd never see him again, the thought of which made her want to weep, both for herself and her child.

"My party will be the second weekend in March," Penelope announced. The three of them were in the sitting room, Penelope and Anne on either side of the hearth, Justin at a table making entries in the ranch journal. "You must send riders out to all the country families, Justin, and, of course, I hope some of my friends from Fort Worth can come."

Anne shivered and shot Justin a pleading look.

"How are we going to put up all those people?" he asked. "The weather's bound to be bad. Usually if you have a big party, some folks expect to camp out, but that could be unpleasant to impossible this time of year."

"The ranch families can stay in the old house," said Penelope indifferently. "I'm sure they won't mind."

"Especially since it's warmer than this one," he muttered.

"I'm tired of hearing about that!" his wife snapped. "Now, the people from Fort Worth will expect better accommodations. They'll have to stay here with us. Why, it will be an adventure! Sharing rooms and all—we used to do that when I was a girl." Her laugh trilled out excitedly.

"Better postpone it till after roundup," said Justin.

"No!" She gave Justin a look of such hatred that Anne drew in a shocked breath and bent over her needle. Then Penelope turned to Anne. "And what are you doing, Anne? You're always such a busy bee."

"Quilting," Anne replied.

"Here, let me see." Penelope held her hand out imperiously for the work. "Well, my goodness, it's got black in it. Whoever heard of a quilt with black? How gloomy." She examined it closely. "We used to call this toenail stitching when I was a girl, not that I ever cared for quilting myself. I always think it's so country!" She handed the piece back to Anne, who examined it herself.

"I suppose it is toenail quilting," she murmured indifferently as she noticed how large her own stitches had become. Well, she was tired after a full day's work, exceedingly tired.

Justin had risen from the table to look. "I like it," he

said. "Especially the colors."

"How like a man!" exclaimed Penelope. "Men have such odd taste."

"What's toenail quilting?" he asked, ignoring his wife's rude comments.

"It means the stitches are so large and sloppy," said Anne, "that you catch your toenails in them if you try to sleep under it."

"Well, it looks good to me. It's a handsome piece."

"Thank you." She smiled, thinking, here was yet another irony; the quilt had been meant for him. Perhaps in her heart she had wanted to give it to him as a wedding gift, for their own wedding night. She stared down hard at the pattern and blinked. "Perhaps I'll give it to you when I leave," she murmured, "in thanks for your hospitality."

"I'd treasure it," said Justin.

"Well, I don't know why anybody'd want a quilt with black in it," said Penelope angrily. "I don't know why you'd put black in it."

"Probably because, being a widow, I have a lot of black scraps," said Anne, and picked up her needle again.

"As far as I'm concerned," Penelope confided, "the only good thing about being with child is that I don't have to have him in my bed anymore."

Anne froze, quite sure that she didn't want to be a party to this conversation.

"I think it's disgusting, don't you?"

Maintaining a determined silence, Anne bent her head industriously over the wrapper she was hemming.

"Well, don't you?" Penelope demanded querulously. "You were married. You know what I'm talking about."

"My husband and I had a very happy marriage," Anne muttered.

"Well, I certainly don't see what—what *bedroom* things have to do with a happy marriage, unless you mean he left you alone at night," said Penelope. "You aren't trying to tell me, are you, that you enjoyed having him . . . well, you know. Goodness, it's so uncomfortable and embarrassing and—and de*grad*ing."

"It's an expression of love," said Anne shortly.

"Love!" cried Penelope. "It's an expression of lust, and I'm sure no decent woman does more than endure her husband's demands. Of course, maybe you didn't mind so much because you didn't have to worry about having children," said Penelope maliciously.

Anne gave her a straight, cold look and said, "Read your Bible, Penelope. It has a few things to say about a wife's duties to her husband and his to her."

Penelope flushed. "Well," she said defensively, "I can tell you, the whole thing came as a great shock to me. I had no idea when I got married what was . . . well, you know."

Anne did know. With no mother to advise her, she had gone to her marriage equally untutored, but her husband had been a patient and considerate lover, and Justin, who was a superb lover—well, she couldn't imagine that he had been anything but gentle with his new wife.

"I'd be curious to know just what it was you liked about it," said Penelope nastily.

"And I think this is an exceedingly tasteless conversation," said Anne as she folded up her sewing and rose to leave. *Poor Justin*, she thought. She understood more each day why he had been unfaithful.

Anne wore her new cashmere wrapper for the first time on Sunday, and Penelope laughed aloud when she saw it. "Goodness, Anne, why in the world would you want to make an ugly thing like that when we have such truly lovely styles these days? Your figure isn't unattractive. Why hide it under a sack?"

Could Penelope be suspicious? Anne wondered. If so, she'd have to be sidetracked, but how? Then Anne had an idea. "These fitted lines that are so popular now are hard to make, Penelope, especially if you don't have a friend to do the fitting. Of course, I'd love to have one if you'd be willing to help," Anne added, barely able to breathe at the thought that Penelope might agree.

"Me?" Penelope looked astounded. "I don't know anything about dressmaking."

Anne let her breath out slowly. "Well, in that case I guess I'll just have to be satisfied with my new wrapper."

"I certainly wouldn't be," said Penelope. "Perhaps we can get a seamstress out to the ranch. Here's Justin. We'll let him decide. Now tell the truth, Justin, don't you think that's an ugly thing Anne has made for herself?"

Justin eyed the new gown. "It's a Mother Hubbard, isn't it?" he asked. "I read a newspaper article about those." He grinned at Anne. "The editor didn't seem to care much for them."

"I should think not," said Penelope.

"As I remember, he said that such a voluminous dress not only used up huge amounts of fabric and disappointed male admirers but frightened horses and caused serious accidents."

"There, what did I say?" cried Penelope. "At least, you agree with me on something, Justin." She gave him a complicitous smile.

"Obviously neither you two nor the editor has tried to cook for a horde of ranch hands or clean house in a fitted gown and a tightly-laced corset," said Anne dryly.

"That's certainly true as far as I'm concerned," said Penelope, "and I do believe, Justin, that you'll have to get a dressmaker out for me. If this is an example of Anne's talents with a needle, I'll simply have to have a professional dressmaker before the party. I wouldn't be caught dead in such a garment on a social occasion."

"I believe I'll retire," said Anne sharply.

"It's only eight o'clock," Penelope objected.

"I've had a long day." Anne rose with determination and left.

Behind her she heard Penelope saying, "My goodness, it's not as if she's doing anything she's not used to."

CHAPTER

Seventeen

"And who's this lovely redheaded lady cooking in the Crossed Heart kitchen?" cried an exuberant voice. When two arms circled her waist loosely, Anne stamped down hard on the booted toe behind her and was gratified to hear the yelp that followed and feel the immediate removal of the arms. "I believe," said the voice, as she turned, wooden spoon ready to strike, "that my attentions are unappreciated."

Anne looked up into a bearded, laughing face that had Justin's blue eyes. *One of his brothers*, she thought.

"I've lost my heart," said the stranger, clapping his hand dramatically over his chest and staggering into a chair at the large kitchen table. "Who might you be, love of my life?"

Anne couldn't help smiling. "Anne McAuliffe," she replied.

"And I'm David Harte, at your service, at your feet." He jumped up and swept her a dashing bow.

"I'm deeply touched," she murmured. "Is it that

you're hungry and want to eat before the dinner hour, or have you been so long on the trail that any woman would look good?"

"Dear lady, how can you think it's not your own fair self who has stolen my heart. Not your cooking, which smells ambrosial, and not my hard and lonely life, which I'll admit warrants every feminine sympathy you'd care to—"

"David!" interrupted Justin from the back door. "They told me you'd come in." Justin strode across the kitchen to embrace his brother. "Why are you so late returning?"

"Well, brother, I delivered the herd to Kansas. Then I picked up another and took it up toward the Indian Territories. Didn't you get my letter? All's well."

"It always is when I send you. Anne, have you met my brother David?"

"I have," said Anne, smiling.

"The lady's broken both my heart and my toe," David added, laughing, "and just because I gave her a small hug."

Justin scowled. "Watch yourself with Mrs. McAuliffe," he snapped.

"Mrs.? You're married, sweet Anne? Someone has won you ahead of me?"

"I'm a widow," said Anne quietly and turned back to her stew, for Penelope had appeared in the doorway to greet her brother-in-law and ask where her new gown was.

David looked taken aback. "What gown, Penelope?"

"The one from Kansas City. I gave you the measurements, and . . . Oh, you're teasing me, David."

"I never got to Kansas City, love," David replied. "We only went as far as Wichita. And then I took another herd up near Indian Territory. No time for gowns, Penelope. What luck that you have plenty."

"Plenty!" she cried. "I don't know what you mean by plenty, and I'll never forgive you, David Harte, never!"

Her voice rose hysterically, and she ran out of the room in tears.

"Well, hell," said David, "I don't know how she expected me to buy her a dress in Kansas City when I never even got there."

"Don't worry about it," Justin muttered.

Anne had to fend off David's cajoling as she put platters of chicken and dumplings down on the long table.

"Having won my love, can't you at least give me a smile, sweet Annie?" he teased.

"I presume you mean you're in love with dumplings."

"That too," said David, his merry laughter echoing around the room.

"And where did you get the chickens?" Penelope demanded.

"A farm woman brought them yesterday."

"Don't you think you should consult me about such purchases?"

Anne glanced at her. "You were asleep, and Justin said to buy them. If that's a problem, you two must settle it between yourselves." Out of the corner of her eye she could see that David was enjoying the byplay. Well, Anne wasn't and wished Penelope would stop sniping at her.

"I am the mistress of this house!" snapped Penelope.

"Fine," said Anne. "You do the cooking tomorrow."

"Why don't you tell us about the trail drive, David," said Justin.

"Really, Justin, I haven't finished with what I had to say. I am, after all, the mistress of this house, and—"

"And since I have fallen head over heels for Miss Anne and her chicken and dumplings," David interrupted cheerfully, "I shall make her mistress of her own house where we two shall live happily on love and chicken and dumplings and relieve you, dear Penelope, of any cause for concern."

Both Justin and Penelope scowled.

"Why, David," said Penelope peevishly, "you've always said you were in love with me."

"Ah, but you can't cook."

"Well, I hardly think cooking of much importance," said Penelope, "not among people of means, at any rate."

"How wrong you are. When a man's hungry, there's nothing he appreciates more than a good cook, especially a pretty one." He beamed at Anne.

"That's enough, David!" snapped Justin.

Anne gritted her teeth. She found David's foolishness charming, but obviously Penelope didn't, and there was an ugly tension building up to which David seemed insensitive and to which Justin was contributing.

"Mr. Holquist tells me he shot a deer today," said Anne, in an attempt to defuse the situation. "Maybe I'll make some venison sausage."

"Do we have to discuss things like that at dinner?" Penelope asked disdainfully.

Justin slammed his fist down on the table, and everyone jumped. "Just what was it you wanted to discuss, Penelope? We all know that you're the mistress of the house because you've told us so, and I'm afraid you're the only one at the table who's interested in your wardrobe, which seems to be another favorite topic of yours."

Anne watched the cowboys shifting uneasily in their seats and decided that she'd wasted her time plucking all those chickens. The hands had probably stopped tasting their food ten minutes ago.

"So now we're going to hear about David's trip," Justin continued, and it was an order, not a request.

"Oh, by all means," cried Penelope. "Let's do hear about running a bunch of dusty cows all over the countryside. What could be more interesting?"

Justin's lids lowered, and he stared her into silence. Then he turned to his brother. "What about the second herd you picked up?"

"Well, I took the train back to Fort Worth," David obliged. "Sure is nice to have the railroad coming in there now. Say, Justin, how much do you think that's going to cut into our trail-driving business?"

"Not much for a while, although it will eventually," Justin replied. "It's still a lot more expensive to ship by rail than it is to drive them to market. We might have five to ten more years of making good money at it."

David nodded. "Well, anyway when I got to Fort Worth, I heard of this rancher up near the Indian Territories who wanted a herd delivered, so I thought, well, hell, why not?"

"It's taking a chance this time of year."

"His risk," said David. "I did it on commission." Justin nodded. "The best of it is he wanted to pay with a draft on his bank, but it turned out they couldn't find any paper in the house, so he made his woman rip a piece off her petticoat, and he wrote the bank draft on that, so there I was two days later carrying in a lace-edged bank draft."

The cowboys, who were usually silent during the meal, all guffawed, and Justin grinned at his brother. "Just as long as the bank honored it," he said.

Anne had risen during the story to clear away the empty chicken platters and put out the cakes she had baked.

"My Lord, look at that," said David. "Cake! Why, I ain't seen a homemade cake in three, four months, I reckon."

"You've certainly gone out of your way, Anne," said Penelope. "Could it be you've set your cap for David?"

"No, it couldn't," Anne replied.

"Well, that's bad news for me," said David. "Here I'd

hoped I was making an impression on you, Miss Anne."

"If our mother could hear the way your grammar has deteriorated, David," said Justin, "I doubt she'd let you have a piece of cake."

"It's associatin' with all those ignorant cowpokes," said David, grinning. "And speaking of book learning, I'm reminded that I've brought presents back."

Penelope immediately perked up. The hands finished their cake in record time and drifted out while David went for his saddlebags.

"Aha, now let's see. This is for Miss Penelope." Penelope reached eagerly for her bundle. "And these are for you, Justin, a book on cattle breeding an'—"

"Oh, look," cried Penelope, pulling out a beautiful shawl made of a heavy material with a raised design. "It's gorgeous, David."

"It's called a broche," said David.

"I know that, silly." Penelope whirled around with the shawl on her shoulders. "Now, I hope we don't have to talk about cattle breeding tonight," she admonished gaily.

The two men gave her impatient looks. "Then I found a couple of history books I think you'll like, Justin, knowing you inherited Pa's love of history."

"You couldn't have pleased me more, David," said Justin as he paged through the books.

"And, Miss Anne, this is for you."

"For me?" Anne looked astonished.

"Open it up."

Penelope stopped admiring her shawl and frowned as Anne examined the gift. "Why, David," said Anne, "it's so beautiful." He had given her a small filigreed locket. "I have a picture of my late husband I can put in it." She smiled up at him. "His name was David too."

"But it must have been meant for me," Penelope broke in. They all turned to her, startled. "Well, wasn't it? How could you have brought a gift for Anne when you didn't even know she'd be here?"

"Penelope," warned Justin.

"Oh, of course," said Anne, flushing and putting the little locket back into its box.

"Well, didn't you mean it for me, David?" Penelope demanded.

"Go to your room," said Justin.

The look of astonishment on Penelope's face was almost comical.

"No, Justin, really—"

"Be quiet, Anne. Penelope, you're to go to your room immediately."

When Penelope started to speak, he rose from his place, towering and furious, and Penelope rose as well, backing away. "I hate you!" she screamed in a high, childish voice, her fists clenched. "I hate everything about you!" She whirled and ran from the kitchen.

"David," said Anne softly, "this was very thoughtful of you, but I really can't accept it."

"You might as well take it," said David, "because, by God, if you don't, I'll throw it away, and that would be a shame, wouldn't it, for it is a pretty little thing."

"Put it on, Anne," said Justin in a voice that brooked no argument.

He circled the table, took the locket from her, and fastened it around her neck. Anne closed her eyes, trying to steel herself against the touch of his fingers. "If it was meant for Penelope—" she stammered.

"It wasn't meant for Penelope," said David. "I brought a number of things back with me, some just in case I found some pretty lady I wanted to give a gift to. No offense meant, Justin, but if I'd given it to Penelope, she'd never have worn it. She wouldn't have figured it cost enough to be worth her notice."

"No offense taken. And he's right, Anne," said Justin. "That was a childish display on Penelope's part."

"Well, I'm for bed," said David. "Good night, Miss

Annie, and thanks for a fine dinner."

Anne nodded. "Thank you for the locket, David."

As he left, Justin was scowling. "Was she right?" he asked. "Are you setting your cap for my brother?"

Anne rose from her place and gave him a cool look. "I'm not setting my cap for anyone, Justin. I'm leaving. After tonight I hardly think I can stay any longer."

"If you're worried about Penelope, she'll have forgotten all about this by morning, which isn't to say you'll find her any more pleasant."

"It doesn't matter—pleasant or unpleasant. She's set on that dance, and I can't be here when it occurs."

Justin's teeth clenched. "Where would you go?"

Anne had been thinking about that. She had to make another try at getting back her inheritance, and perhaps the way to do it was to go to Fort Griffin and get a copy of the will. "Fort Griffin," she replied.

"Good Lord, Anne, why would you want to go there? That's the roughest town on the frontier."

What Justin said was true, but since she didn't want to get him involved in her problems with the will, she couldn't tell him her real reasons for going there, nor that she didn't plan to stay. "I hardly think Fort Griffin's any worse than Fort Worth," she pointed out. "At least, I have friends in the area."

He had closed both hands on her shoulders and asked in a tight voice, "Officer friends? Are you—"

"Oh, stop it," she cut in sharply. "If you won't help me—"

"I didn't say that, Anne. I just want you to go where you'll be safe."

"Well, Fort Griffin's far enough away so that I should be safe from gossip, if nothing else."

"You overestimate the danger. I haven't heard anything."

"Who would dare accuse you to your face?"

"What a mess this is," Justin muttered. "Well, let me think about it." He brushed his thumb longingly over her lips. "I can't bear to let you go. That's the real problem."

Anne turned her head away to hide her anguish. When he touched her, she wanted to be in his arms. She wanted it even when he wasn't touching her.

"This is the one I want," said Penelope, pointing to a ball gown featured in the latest *Godey's*. The traveling seamstress, who had arrived in time to prevent Penelope from driving everyone to distraction with her wardrobe worries, stared at the elaborate gown with dismay. "I have a lovely lilac satin that would be perfect for it," Penelope added, "and I want the yoke and undersleeves in a deeper violet."

"It will take days to make a dress that difficult," said the seamstress.

"No matter. The ball is more than a week away. Surely that will give you time enough."

"I suppose so," said the woman, "but doesn't Mrs. McAuliffe want a gown as well?"

"It's quite unnecessary," said Anne, who was actually relieved. She was finally beginning to notice bodily changes and did not want to risk fittings with a sharp-eyed dressmaker. "I think you should devote the time to Mrs. Harte's ball gown," said Anne, "and now if you'll excuse me, I need to check on Calliope."

"Nonsense, Anne," said Penelope. "My maid is fine, and Mrs. Kilhane may need your help in the fitting."

"Do you have a pattern?" asked the seamstress.

"No," said Penelope. "There was no pattern included."

The seamstress sighed. "We'll have to do it in muslin first," she said to Anne.

Anne nodded, knowing the problems well enough.

"Well, Mrs. Harte, if you'd be so good as to take off your dress, we'd best make a beginning." The dressmaker took another worried look at the picture, and

Anne wondered whether the poor woman was up to the construction of such an elaborate dress.

Penelope, in the meantime, was eagerly disrobing. "Oh my, I'm going to look so-o beautiful in this," she said. "The lilac satin will be perfect for my hair and coloring, don't you think so, Anne? Lilac makes my eyes look just like pansies."

Anne suppressed an inelegant snort as she turned with a length of muslin in her hands to find the dressmaker staring in dismay at Penelope. "You're with child," said Mrs. Kilhane.

Penelope flushed. "Well, what of it?"

"Mrs. Harte, this gown is snugly fitted from shoulder to hip. It won't look right on you."

"It will," said Penelope, her voice rising.

"But, ma'am, your waist's already thickened."

Anne was surprised to see the truth of the dressmaker's observation. Although she knew that Penelope was not as advanced as she was, Justin's wife had seemingly put on more weight.

"Mrs. Harte, believe me," said the poor seamstress, "you'll not like the way this dress will look on you."

"I will," said Penelope. "I'll just lace tighter."

"You shouldn't do that."

"I'll do whatever I please! This is the dress I want, and I intend to have it!"

At this point she was shrieking, and Justin threw open the door, demanding to know what the problem was.

"This idiot woman," cried Penelope, "said I can't have my ball gown. She said I'm too fat, and it's your fault, Justin!" Penelope was screaming at him, tears flooding her cheeks. "Well, I'll have it! I don't care! Calliope and Anne can pull my laces until it fits!"

"You'll do no such thing," said Justin. "Would you excuse us please, Mrs. Kilhane, Anne?"

Anne was so relieved to get away that she practically

ran from the room with the seamstress hot on her heels. Behind them Justin's fury and Penelope's hysteria warred for dominance as Anne closed the door.

"Would you care for some coffee, Mrs. Kilhane?" Anne whispered in a shaking voice.

Several minutes later Justin stalked through the room, grabbing his Stetson off a hook by the door. "Throw her corsets away," he instructed Anne in a hard voice.

"Do it yourself!" Anne snapped back. "She's not my responsibility."

Justin glared at her. "And you, Mrs. Kilhane. I don't care what kind of gown you make her, but be sure it's something that won't injure my child." With that, he clapped on his hat and walked out, slamming the door.

"Oh Lord," exclaimed Mrs. Kilhane. "What am I to do, caught between the two of them?"

"Look at that," said David. "A beef pie, and a thing of beauty. You made it just for me, didn't you, Annie?"

"That's right, David," said Anne, "just for you and all the other ignorant cowpokes." Grins and chuckles ran around the table as the men scooped out portions of the large beef and vegetable pies that marched down the table.

"Ah, well, even if it's not for me alone, I shall enjoy it, nonetheless," he announced, "and your gravy, Mrs. McAuliffe, has a touch of the gods' nectar."

"And your tongue, Mr. Harte," Anne retorted, "has a touch of the Blarney stone."

"Anne's quite right," said Penelope repressively. "I hardly think a simple meat pie is reason for such fulsome compliments, David."

"Is that a fact, Miss Penelope? Well, I notice you've helped yourself to a healthy share, for all it's just a simple meat pie. In fact, now that I look at you, it's easy to see that you're benefiting as much as anyone from Anne's fine cooking."

"What's that supposed to mean?" Penelope demanded.

"Why, you're becoming as round-faced and pretty as a chubby little girl." David grinned happily at his teasing compliment, but an ominous flush mounted in Penelope's cheeks, and Anne gritted her teeth against the outburst she knew was coming.

"Chubby! Are you saying I'm fat, David?"

"Of course not, but you have put on a bit of weight, sweet Penelope," said David, entirely missing the signs of the impending storm, "and very becoming it is."

"Yes, she's truly radiant," said Anne quickly. "I don't know when I've seen you looking more beautiful, Penelope."

"You stay out of this!" snapped Penelope.

"Is that how you respond to a compliment?" asked Justin, his voice tight with irritation.

David was looking confused and turned to his brother. "Did I say something wrong?"

"Penelope's with child," said Justin shortly.

"Are you? Are you, really, Penelope? Little Penny! That's wonderful!" David jumped up to kiss her cheek.

"Wonderful?" cried Penelope. "Wonderful to have your brother-in-law say you're fat? Wonderful to have your dressmaker tell you can't wear the ball gown you've chosen?"

"That's enough!" Justin snapped.

"I didn't say you're fat," said David. "Anne's right. You're radiant. Congratulations, love!"

"Congratulate your disgusting brother!" she screamed at him. "He's the one who's happy about this." Penelope's eyes were filling with tears, and her hands were trembling. "He's the one who did this."

"Well, I should hope so," said David humorously, "since he's your husband. Now calm down, little Penny."

"Don't call me Penny."

"All right. Calm down, pretty little mother."

Penelope's face turned from pink to bright red, and she flung her empty cup at David, leaving him gaping after her.

"Well, I've heard that mothers-to-be were a bit temperamental, but I meant no harm."

"Oh, hell," Justin muttered. "Don't worry about it."

Anne stared at her plate. She'd also thought that the beef pie was tasty, but now she had no appetite for it.

Anne leaned wearily against the table and brushed the damp wisps of hair away from her face. Although the weather outside was cold, the kitchen was hot because the stoves and hearth had been lighted day and night, and she had been cooking almost continuously, preparing for Penelope's grand ball. It was to be a gala affair, but Anne thought that by the time the party actually occurred, she'd be too tired to care—even if all the guests denounced her. Weary past words, she sank into a chair for a moment's rest. Sometimes at night before she fell into a dead sleep, she thought she felt her baby stir and wondered whether this kind of effort could harm it. It galled her that Penelope lounged about in her room, eating and complaining and giving out orders, completely indifferent to her own child, while Anne worked like a slave.

"My goodness, don't tell me the estimable Mrs. McAuliffe is sitting idle when nobody's looking?"

Anne looked up to find Penelope in the doorway, giving her a particularly inimical look. What now? Had another session with the dressmaker set Penelope off? Sent her looking for someone to take her wrath out on?

"What would all your admirers think?" asked Penelope. "All those men who think you work so hard, that you're so wonderful. Of course, I know why you're doing it. You just want to ingratiate yourself with them. You don't even care who. You want them all to love you, don't you? The cowboys, that stupid Rollo Tandy that Justin thinks so much of, Justin himself. You want to make me look bad with my husband, don't you? And David. You want David to hate me."

Anne just stared at her.

"You want them to think I'm not a good wife. And you'd like to get your claws into David. Well, he won't marry you. Why would he? A woman of your sort?"

Anne caught her breath in alarm, then lifted her chin challengingly and said, "A woman of my sort?"

Penelope sneered. "Oh, you know what I mean. It makes me wonder what else you're doing. Just cooking wouldn't make them nose after you, and you told me yourself you enjoyed—you liked your husband to—"

"I told you I *loved* my husband," said Anne coldly.

"David and Justin are going to see through you. You just wait. They won't want you around very long."

Anne stood up and rubbed the small of her back absently. It had been aching for several days now, probably because she'd been on her feet so much. It couldn't be the weight of the child shifting, not yet. "Well, I don't know about Justin and David," she said quietly, "but it's obvious that you don't want me around, Penelope, so perhaps the best thing is for me to pack and leave." She went over to the stove and lifted a large pot of antelope stew off the fire. "I'll be ready to go by tomorrow morning."

"Go?" Penelope sounded shocked.

"Of course. I'll tell Justin tonight."

"You can't."

"Of course, I can. I'm a guest here, not a servant."

"But the ball—"

"Hire somebody."

"There isn't anybody." Penelope looked panic-stricken. "You're the guest of honor."

"The guest of honor?" asked Anne dryly. "Since when am I the guest of honor? I'm the cook."

"The invitations said you were the guest of honor."

"Well, the guest of honor's leaving. Make David the guest of honor if you have to have one."

"David can't cook," Penelope wailed. "You mustn't leave. You can't. It'll ruin my party. You'll miss the party yourself. You don't want to miss the party."

"I don't care a thing about the party. I never did, and you know it. Now I'm going to my room and take a nap."

"Yes, yes, take a nap. That's a wonderful idea. You're tired. You'll feel differently when you wake up."

"I most certainly will not. When I wake up, I'll start packing." Anne walked determinedly out of the room, leaving Penelope in tears.

When Anne awoke, it was dark outside, and her room was lighted only by a candle. Justin sat in a chair beside the bed, watching her thoughtfully. "What did she do to you?" he asked.

Anne sat up and swung her legs to the floor. "It doesn't matter, Justin. I'm going to pack now."

"I'd like to know what she said."

"What did she tell you?" Anne countered.

"She said she didn't know what she could have done to offend you, but that you insisted on leaving. She's been crying now," Justin added dryly, "for about six hours."

"She's worried about who's going to do the rest of the work for the party."

"I'm aware of that. I wish I could cancel the whole damned thing, but the invitations have gone out."

"She said people had been told I'm the guest of honor."

"So she mentioned. I hadn't been aware of that."

"Has it occurred to you, Justin, that no one may show up? With me as the guest of honor, she may have offended everyone from here to Fort Worth."

"I doubt that's so," said Justin, "but if no one comes, it'll be interesting to see how she takes it." A smile quirked his lips.

Anne looked at him in surprise, then smiled herself.

"That's not a very charitable thought," she murmured.

"I'm not feeling particularly charitable, and I'd still like to know what it was she said to you."

Anne sighed. "She seems to think I'm trying to usurp her place by ingratiating myself with every male in sight and in the most despicable ways."

"Does she?" murmured Justin. "Well, you couldn't possibly merit the opinion the men have of her. It's far too low, and you're far too well thought of. She's just about worked you into the ground, hasn't she?"

"Yes, she has," said Anne, "and I am very tired, and I want very much to leave here."

"I know that I have to let you go," he sighed, "but I can't do that until I've made the arrangements, and I don't see how I can before the ball. Anne, you've made no plans, have you? How can you go now?"

She stared down at the toes of her shoes peeping from beneath her black skirts. What he said was certainly true. She had no money, no place to go, and no assurance that she'd have any more luck retrieving her inheritance this time. Feeling trapped and miserable, she blinked hard, but the tears still began to spill down her cheeks.

"Oh, Annie," said Justin, "my sweet love." He rose from his chair and took her in his arms.

"Justin, don't make this any harder."

"At least let me hold you a minute," he said. "I promise I'll make it right, but you must stay long enough to let me. As for the ball, I don't care if the guests go hungry. Why don't you get back in bed and stay there? Let her worry about how she'll handle the work."

"She'd just try to force Calliope to do it all, and the poor woman's not up to it. As for Penelope, all this crying isn't good for your child."

Justin frowned. "She's using her condition to manipulate anyone who'll let her."

"The hysteria is still bad for the child."

"But not your responsibility. You look thinner every-day, Anne. It worries me."

She leaned her head against his shoulder. "I'll feel better tomorrow after a good night's sleep. The preparations will just have to be a bit less elaborate. But, Justin, I have the worst feeling about this ball."

"No one's going to hurt you, Anne. I won't let them."

"There's no way you can protect me from gossip."

"Believe me, Anne, since you've been here, I've talked to all kinds of people, and I've heard nothing."

"And I've told you, no one would say anything to you."

"You don't know men. If there were rumors about my—my affairs of the heart, the men I know would be joking with me about them."

"They would?" asked Anne in surprise.

"Oh, yes. There are men who find such things amusing, who'd even think the better of me for being unfaithful to my wife, and without knowing what my marriage to Penelope is like."

Anne bit her lip. "The better of you and the worst of me."

Justin nodded. "That's true, I'm afraid, but still I've heard nothing."

"Justin, Brother Foley spoke to my stepfather, went all the way out to the Bar M to do it. And then when I was living at Elsie Gilchrist's, he spoke to her, too. I don't know exactly what was said, but—"

"Perhaps those are the only two. Maybe he wanted to make trouble for you because you wouldn't pay him, but he was afraid to make trouble for me."

"I suppose it's possible. Maybe."

"Try not to worry." He let her go, leaned forward, and kissed her lightly on the forehead. "Anyone who'd think evil of you has to be a scoundrel or a fool, Anne. Now sleep in tomorrow. I'll swear you're thinner than you were when you came, and you were too thin then."

How ironic, she thought as he left. She wasn't thinner.

Maybe her face, but not her body. She put her hand against her middle, thought of her baby, and smiled. No matter what happened, she'd have Justin's child. Then she remembered that she wasn't the only woman in the house carrying his seed, and she felt a familiar rush of resentment.

CHAPTER

Eighteen

Anne watched fondly as Sissie, humming in front of the mirror, inserted a few last hairpins. Her sister had arrived two days before the ball, having discovered Anne's whereabouts from the rider who delivered the invitation. And the intervening months had made changes in Sissie. The girl was guilt-stricken that she had not defended Anne against the colonel and had evidently been frantic since December because she could not discover where Anne had gone.

"I'm ready," Sissie announced. "Shall I see to things in the kitchen while you finish dressing?"

Anne nodded. That was another change. For a week, Penelope had been driving everyone crazy with her worries about whether the preparations for the ball would be finished in time. She hadn't offered to do any of the work, but she'd given in repeatedly to attacks of panic. Sissie, on the other hand, had pitched in and helped.

"Do you think David will like my dress?" Sissie

asked wistfully. That was the last change. David Harte had turned his teasing, flirtatious ways from Anne to Sissie, and poor Sissie, having met her match at last, was totally smitten, so much so that she had actually turned shy.

"I'm sure he will," Anne murmured absently, "as pretty as you look." Sissie gave her a grateful smile and tripped away, while Anne sighed and rose from the bed to dress.

The weather was poor. Yesterday and the day before had brought intermittent cold rain; today, cutting winds had arrived with the guests. As a result, Penelope was disappointed in the attendance. Anne, however, was somewhat relieved since there would never have been enough beds or even floor space for all of them in the two houses and the bunkhouse. Penelope's last tantrum had occurred when Anne refused to take a female guest into her room so that Penelope could have a bed to herself.

However, Anne was adamant. She didn't want to undress in front of some sharp-eyed woman. Sissie, who was already sharing her bed, was no cause for concern since the girl wasn't particularly observant and wouldn't have given Anne's condition away had she realized it. But the last confrontation with Penelope sapped the last of Anne's energy, and as she got herself into her black cashmere wrapper with its velvet trim, she wished desperately that she could fall back into bed instead of attending the party.

The only thing she could say for the event was that it had brought Sissie to her and that so far no one had looked at Anne amiss, much less spoken an unkind word to her. In fact, Sarah Bannerman had been ecstatic to see her, and Florence had been downright friendly, giving Anne hope that her presence would not set off the storm of malicious whispers she had expected. Perhaps Justin was right. Perhaps the preacher had only denounced her to the two people with whom

he'd found her living. Sissie hadn't believed Brother
Foley's accusations, had, in fact, been quite indignant
on the subject and assured Anne that she had heard no
ugly rumors elsewhere.

Anne looked into the glass and smoothed her hair
into a tight bun. No pretty ringlets for her. The last
thing she wanted to do was attract attention. With luck
she could manage to spend the whole evening in the
kitchen. She went straight there, thinking wryly that the
guests would have to leave the rooms that had been
cleared for dancing if they wanted to greet the guest of
honor. However, her tactic worked only until
midevening when David arrived to drag her off for a
dance, and after that she never got back to her pots
because she was passed from one partner to the next.

As she caught her breath between dances, she took
time to wonder who was tending the kitchen. Calliope,
she supposed, and various older women who had
congregated there to chat. Anne would rather have been
among them. Much as she loved dancing, she was
simply too tired to enjoy it, and she was receiving
unpleasant glances from Penelope as each new partner
turned up to claim her hand.

Well, at least here she could keep an eye on Sissie.
David was monopolizing her sister's evening just as he
had teasingly promised earlier. Not only that, but it
looked to Anne as if Sissie might be falling in love
instead of succumbing to her usual fleeting infatuation.
Love, if it was that, might well be a painful experience
for the girl since David, although delightful, hardly
seemed serious in his pursuit.

Finally, when one of her partners turned to insert a
remark into a heated conversation on the evils of
barbed wire fencing, Anne managed to slip away,
heading for the kitchen. In the hall, however, Justin
grasped her arm and whisked her into his office.

"You're making a spectacle of yourself," he hissed.

Anne felt overcome with confusion. He was angry

again, and she was too tired to counterattack.

"You're a widow," he said accusingly, "and yet you've danced with every man in the room."

The injustice of his condemnation seemed more than she could bear after such an exhausting day, and Anne burst into tears.

"Anne?" questioned Justin, looking surprised and worried at her reaction to his words. "What's the matter?"

"What do you think's the matter?" she hiccuped. "I'm so tired all I want to do is go to bed and sleep for a year. Do you imagine it was my idea to be out there dancing? Your brother, on a goodhearted impulse, dragged me out of the kitchen, where you evidently think I belong. And I—and I—"

"Oh, Annie," said Justin. "Lord, I've done it again, haven't I?" He put his arms around her and cradled her head into his shoulder with one large hand. "Poor girl. Penelope's worked you like a slave, and then when my brother's thoughtful enough to see that you have a little fun, I attack you for it."

"Justin, it's all right," she mumbled. "Just let me go."

"No, I won't," he replied, his arms tightening around her, and he lifted her tear-stained face and covered her mouth with his own.

Anne trembled in his arms, first at the gentleness of his kiss, then at the dizzying forays of his tongue. She drew back and gasped anxiously, "What if someone walks in?"

"They can't," said Justin, laughing low in his throat, "not when we're leaning on the door," and he pressed hard against her and claimed her mouth again.

She could feel his arousal and instinctively moved her hips to accommodate it. When his tongue plunged entirely into her mouth, a wonderful, hot weakness washed over her until panicked caution reminded her that, as closely as they were embraced, he might be able to feel the changes in her body. She couldn't let him find out that she was with child. Frantically, she pushed against his chest, but he responded by tightening his arms.

"I want to make love to you," he said in a low, rough voice. "I ache for you. Every night I dream of you."

"Let me go, Justin! This is madness."

"Yes," he agreed, drawing her toward the door that led from his office to the yard, sweeping his own heavy jacket off a peg and draping it around her as he tugged her outside. "But it's a madness you feel too." He pulled her behind him across the empty, wind-whipped yard and into the deserted stables. "I'm going crazy living in the same house with you and never touching you, Anne. I have to be alone with you," he pleaded softly, "if only for a little while."

"Justin," she protested, but he had already wrapped her again in his arms, and the hard warmth of his body was so compelling. She wanted to stay safe against him for just a moment, to enjoy the security and power of his embrace, to feel again the heat of his desire for her and her own for him.

Justin swept aside a pile of riding tack, lifted her onto a rough table, and stood before her, his hands at her elbows. "Anne, love," he said softly, "I watch David flirting with you and I can't stand it."

"Oh, Justin, he means nothing. You know that."

"I do know it," he agreed, "but I wish it could be me. I want to laugh with you the way he does. I want to spend long hours talking with you. Anne, you're the only woman I've ever known I could talk to that way, and God, how I want to love you." He dropped his hands to her knees, parting them, and reached down for her skirts.

"Justin!"

He laughed softly. "Annie, do you realize this table's the perfect height?" He'd already lifted the front of the loose gown to her thighs. "It's perfect, and you're perfect, and I'm dying of desire for you."

"Oh, Justin," she protested, her voice trembling as she edged away from him, "I can't be your lover."

"You already are, Annie," he retorted. "You love me. And you want me. You tremble when I touch you."

Mutely, she shook her head, pushed his tormenting hands away. "I won't take what belongs to another woman," Anne declared stubbornly, even as her body ached for him to continue, to pull her forward and impale her on the thrust of his desire. Instead she curled her legs protectively under her on the table, pulled her skirts tightly around them so that he could no longer tempt her.

"What belongs to another woman?" Justin echoed bitterly. "I wonder if you know how ironic that is. You'd hardly be taking anything that Penelope wants. She'd rather die than have me lay a hand on her."

Anne knew that to be true, having heard it from Penelope herself. How unfair it was that she should want Justin so much, love him so much, and have to refuse him because of the claims of a woman like Penelope. "We'd best get back," she said sadly.

"You don't want that," he protested as his hand slid lovingly around her neck. "Do you know what my idea of heaven is?" he murmured, brushing his mouth lightly, undemandingly against hers. "An empty house and a bed with you and me in it, making love for about four years, and after four years we'd—"

"Justin," she whispered regretfully, "we haven't got four years. Or even four minutes."

"How about four hours then?" he bargained hopefully. "At least stay here and talk to me, rescue me from all that boring conversation in there."

"You know we have to get back," she protested halfheartedly, thinking all the while how good it would be to spend time with him here alone where no one would interrupt them. Talking wasn't a sin. Talking took nothing from Penelope, who wanted his company no more than she wanted his loving. If there was evil in this, it seemed more theoretical than real. Still, she'd do well to remember that Brother Foley had separated her from her home and family for the appearance of sin, not the sin, about which no one had known at that time but she and Justin. Now because of the baby, everyone would know.

"People will miss us," she said, her voice dull and discouraged.

"Let them," he muttered, drawing her into the loose circle of his arms.

She leaned her head against his shoulder and shivered.

"Are you cold?" he asked.

"Afraid."

"Oh, Annie, I forget how hard this has been on you, but don't be afraid. I'll straighten things out, and as for tonight, you said you're tired. Just go to bed. If anyone asks where you are, I'll say Penelope worked you into exhaustion, and you retired. As for me, I went out to have a cigarette."

"Lies," she murmured.

"Not wholly. You'll really be in bed, and I can have a cigarette if it will make you feel better." Anne was shivering again, and he sighed. "You are cold, aren't you? I guess we'd better return."

Reluctantly, he backed away from her, and she slid off the table. When they had slipped across the yard and into the office, Justin looked out into the corridor, gave her a quick, hard, anguished kiss and let her go.

Minutes later Anne was in her nightgown, curled in her bed, a sort of peace washing over her as her eyes closed. He had been kind and loving, even in the face of her refusal. She laid the palm of one hand against her stomach and whispered to her child, "He was so close to you tonight. He didn't know it, but we did." Then she drifted into sleep, tears of regret still on her cheeks.

* * *

"Where have you been?" asked Penelope.

"Outside."

"Outside? What were you doing outside?"

"What the hell do you care?" he snapped.

"I want to know where you were."

Her voice was beginning to rise. To forestall another scene, he replied, "I was having a cigarette and getting away from the inane chatter of your friends from Fort Worth."

"And where's Anne?" Penelope demanded suspiciously.

"I sent her to bed."

"She's the guest of honor!"

"Well, the guest of honor's been working sixteen hours a day for days, in case you haven't noticed it. Then she spent most of the evening in the kitchen, which didn't seem to bother you. The woman was asleep on her feet."

"She was dancing," said Penelope.

"Yes," said Justin. "I know David meant well, but that finished her off."

"She had no right to go off to bed. What are people going to think?"

"They'll think twice about coming to visit you if they know you use your guests as unpaid servants."

"They'll think I gave a boring party," she countered.

"Everybody else seems to be having a good time."

Penelope looked around, mollified. "Well, I guess they are. Yes, of course they are. Anne's just a boring person."

Justin laughed and turned away from his wife. Boring was the last thing Anne was. Penelope, certainly. But Anne? Never.

"Why are you laughing?" Penelope called after him.

Sissie was gone and the rest of the guests with her. Calliope had taken on the cleanup duties because Anne had yet to overcome the exhaustion that hit her at the party. She'd slept most of the day after, all of the following night, and was late rising the second morning. Dressing, once she'd dragged herself out of bed, seemed the greatest effort she'd ever expended. Anne stared wearily at the corset in her hand. Why put it on? She wasn't going to lace it tightly anyway. She was about to toss it onto the bed when the door to her room burst open and Penelope entered.

"I know what you're doing," she said in a high, angry voice.

Anne felt a moment of panic at being caught wearing only a chemise and one petticoat, but she reached quickly for the second and held it in front of her while she tried to look calmly and questioningly toward the angry woman in her doorway.

"Acting like you're so tired. Leaving the party early and going to bed! You want it to look as if I worked you so hard you got sick. You're trying to make everybody hate me."

Anne closed her eyes. She didn't feel up to another of Penelope's tantrums.

"Well, if you don't like it here, if you think I'm so awful to you, why don't you just leave. Go away."

With weary effort and a wry smile Anne opened her eyes again to look at the furious girl. "What you mean is that Calliope's better and I've taken care of your party so you don't need me any longer."

"That's right. I don't need you anymore, and I want you out of here."

"Fine," said Anne. "Now would you leave so I can get dressed?"

Penelope's eyes narrowed, and she stepped forward suddenly and yanked the concealing petticoat out of Anne's hands. For a minute the two of them stood frozen. "You're with child," gasped Penelope, and she began to laugh. "Little Miss Butter-Wouldn't-Melt-in-Her-Mouth, and you're in a family way. Being a widow isn't good enough, you know. Your husband's long dead. If it were his, you'd be a mother by now, which means I was right about you, wasn't I? You're a slut!" Penelope's voice was strident with malicious pleasure. "Pack your things. I want you out of here before noon. I want you—"

"What's going on?" Justin demanded, appearing in Anne's doorway.

Anne felt a terrible pain in her chest. She'd been so careful not to let him find out, and now stupid Penelope was going to give it all away.

"She's with child. Look at her! She's carrying someone's bastard. I won't have her in my house!"

"That's enough, Penelope."

"Don't tell me that's enough. She's probably bedded every man in—"

Justin whipped her around and pushed her into the hall, slamming the door behind her. They could hear Penelope's triumphant laughter as her footsteps receded. Justin, leaning against the door, his face as white as parchment, stared at Anne. "Is it true?" he asked, studying her waistline. "My God, it is." He looked dazed. "I'm surprised I didn't realize it last night," he muttered.

Anne bent for the petticoat Penelope had snatched away and then dropped. She turned from him, pulled it over her head, then reached for her dress.

"The gunfighter," came Justin's voice, low and pained. "You went to bed with the gunfighter."

For a moment she was confused. Then she realized that because she had put on so little weight, Justin must think she was in the very early months of pregnancy. Penelope had thickened more than Anne, so, of course, he assumed the child was Pancho's. Dazed at how fast everything had happened, she decided impulsively to let him continue in his mistake. It seemed for the best.

"Tighe." Justin's voice grated viciously. "He must have taken advantage of you when—"

"Don't blame Pancho," Anne cut in.

"Then why?" His face was tight with anguish when she turned to look at him. "How could you . . ." He paused to gain control. "Anne, I know you love me. Why would you sleep with him?"

Anne turned her face away as the tears started.

"Gratitude, I suppose," Justin muttered.

Well, he'd found his own explanation, which spared her from telling any more lies. She brushed futilely at the slide of tears.

"God, sweetheart, don't cry. I'm not condemning you." His voice was suddenly gentle as his hands came down on her shoulders. "How could I? It's my fault you had to go to him. I put you in his debt." Justin wrapped his arms around her shoulders. "Sh–sh–sh. Don't cry now. Does he know you're carrying his child?"

Anne shook her head silently, letting Justin take her denial any way he would.

"Do you want him to marry you?"

She shook her head again. Surely Justin, who had always been so jealous, wouldn't want her to marry Pancho. She pulled away and dropped into the rocking chair. Was self-interest taking over? Did he want to salve his own guilt by providing her with a husband? "It's not really your responsibility, Justin," she assured him, knowing that she couldn't let him go to Pancho.

He stared at her, frowning and silent. Finally he said, "I'm not going to desert you, Anne. Did you think I would?"

What could she say to that? She looked away.

"You should have trusted me enough to tell me as soon as you knew."

Trust Justin? It was hard to believe even now that he was taking her supposed intimacy with Pancho so well. And there was something she couldn't quite identify underlying his kindness and concern. Resentment? Reproach? Disbelief? Whatever he was feeling, she *had* to distrust him. Anne stared bleakly at the window, hunting for the right thing to say. "I wouldn't need to be taken care of," she explained slowly, feeling her way toward a new approach, one that would keep him away from Pancho, "not if I could get back the money David left me."

"David?" He looked momentarily confused.

"My husband."

"Oh, I see."

Pride wouldn't carry her through the next months, so she'd let Justin do something to get the money back. He was a powerful man; he had forced his will on the colonel before. "David was fairly well-to-do," she explained, "and I'm his heir, but the colonel won't turn over control of the estate."

Justin's concern turned to anger. "You'd best tell me about it," he ordered.

Good, she thought, he'd taken the bait. She told him everything she knew, including the story of a mysterious visit by Lawyer Dawson to the Bar M after she'd left Fort Worth, something she'd learned about from Sissie and found highly suspicious. If Dawson had really been acting in her interest, he'd have made that trip while she was still in town and pressuring him about the money. Instead he must have been reporting her disappearance to the colonel, and Sissie had said the two men quarreled.

"Anne, it sounds like they're in collusion," said Justin, his voice grim.

"I've wondered about that myself, but I don't know what I can do."

Justin was sitting on her bed, his head bowed, deep in thought. Then he said decisively, "We'll leave for Fort Worth as soon as you can get ready."

"We? You can't go with me, Justin. What about Penelope?"

"I'll take care of Penelope." He was frowning. "I know just how to keep her quiet."

Anne shivered at his grim expression, the forceful tone of his voice. Penelope, who'd thought herself the winner, had evidently stepped wrong again.

"We'll leave tomorrow morning, and believe me, Anne, she'll never say a word to anyone about your— ah—condition."

"What about Brother Foley if I reappear in Fort Worth?"

"Brother Foley's more vulnerable than you might think. I've been doing a little investigation of Brother Foley, and I intend to have a talk with him as soon as we get to town."

"But—"

"If he ever so much as mentions your name again, I can have him denounced to his congregation for seducing a fourteen-year-old girl."

"Is that true?" whispered Anne, startled.

"It's true," he replied, his voice harsh with distaste, "and she's evidently not the only one, but she's the case I can prove. No, Anne, Brother Foley's going to learn discretion—at least where you're concerned."

Anne shivered, glad that she wasn't Justin's enemy. He rose and knelt by her chair, took both her hands into his. "It'll be all right, Annie. I can take care of the colonel and Foley, but it breaks my heart to think of how afraid you must have been." He tipped her bowed head up to look into her eyes. "You're not by yourself anymore," he promised.

She sighed, her concealed fears ebbing for the first time in months. "Thank you, Justin. You're being a good friend."

"Friend?" His mouth twisted bitterly. "Anne, you're the only woman I've ever loved, the only one I ever will love."

"Which means there's little prospect of happiness for either of us," said Anne.

He rose abruptly. "Dry your tears. Calliope's about to serve the midday meal."

"Oh, Justin, I can't!"

"Be courageous one more time, sweetheart. You need

to see how I handle Penelope. It's the only way you're going to feel safe."

Puzzled, she looked to him for an explanation. He was so confident she had to feel reassured herself, and so she rose and went with him to the table.

Penelope flushed when she saw Anne in the doorway. "Why is she still here?"

"Did you plan to send her away hungry, Penelope? If so, your hospitality is less than impressive," said Justin. "However, rest easy. Mrs. McAuliffe will be on her way this afternoon as soon as Calliope's ready to go."

"Calliope?" His wife looked confused.

"Of course. After all Anne's kindnesses to you, I know you wouldn't want to send her unescorted into Forth Worth. What would people think, as you're so often saying." He poured syrup on a biscuit and continued blandly, "And don't suggest that I escort Mrs. McAuliffe myself. I haven't the time, Penelope. You and I have a busy two weeks ahead, getting ready for our move."

"Our move?" A satisfied smile settled across Penelope's lips. "Well, Justin, I'm glad you finally see things my way." She glanced triumphantly at Anne. "But I'm not sure I can be ready to move to Fort Worth in so short a time, not if my maid's away. I'm afraid Mrs. McAuliffe will have to do without Calliope. One of the men can take her. She'll like that."

"Calliope's going to Fort Worth with Anne," Justin repeated mildly. "Calliope can see a doctor while she's there, then join us later in Mitchell County."

"Mitchell County?" Penelope's face turned pale.

"That's right. I've had enough of life in Palo Pinto, too much luxury and socializing. It's a bad influence on you."

"No," said Penelope, her voice small and frightened.

"In two weeks. David can run this place if he wants to, he or one of the other boys. You and I will be living in a dugout by the end of March. It'll be a new experience for you, Penelope, and I may even have the pleasure of delivering my own child."

"You're doing this to punish me," she whispered. "You're trying to protect—"

"Watch what you say," he warned, his face absolutely expressionless. "Do you understand?"

"Yes," she whispered.

He nodded and cut into his steak.

CHAPTER

Nineteen

"We'll go to Peers House for dinner," said Justin.

"Oh, I really don't think we should."

"Anne, will you stop worrying about being seen with me. As far as anyone knows, I'm just a gentleman trying to do a good turn for a widow lady, and there will be no gossip about you, now or later."

She looked at him in surprise. They were entering the restaurant, so he ended the conversation, and only after they had given their orders, did he continue. "Penelope will never say anything about you because she'd rather die than move into a dugout on the frontier." Justin grinned sardonically.

"Would you have liked that?" asked Anne.

"Of course."

She nodded wistfully. "It would be fun to start a ranch out in new, unsettled country."

Justin, who had been about to take a sip from his cup of coffee, put it down and stared at her. "You really mean that, don't you? God, how I wish—" He stopped himself.

Anne turned her head away and fastened her eyes on the young waitresses as they came and went in the dining room. Finally Justin grunted and continued, "So Penelope's neutralized. And as for Brother Foley, I saw him last night. He now understands that if he ever mentions your name again, he's likely to end up run out of Texas in a coat of tar and feathers."

They were served a hearty soup and began to eat as they discussed the meeting they'd had that afternoon with a very nervous Lawyer Dawson. "I wasn't sure that he was in collusion with your stepfather," said Justin, "until he tried to deny having gone to the Bar M. Now I'm beginning to wonder if the two of them aren't out to steal you blind."

"It's hard to believe that my own stepfather . . ." Anne stared at her soup bowl, her appetite waning. "Perhaps this is some sort of retaliation for what the colonel considers a blotch on his honor."

"Whatever his motives," said Justin, "you'll get back every penny you inherited."

"Not if he's already spent it," Anne replied gloomily.

"If he's already spent it, there's his ranch. We're going to my lawyer tomorrow, Anne. He'll handle the rest. If we have to go to court, so be it."

"How am I supposed to pay your lawyer? The reason I stayed with Dawson is that he offered to defer payment."

"Which is suspicious in itself. I know very few altruistic lawyers," said Justin dryly. "As for Barnett's fee, don't worry about it. I'll—"

"I don't want you paying my bills," she interrupted.

"You need help, Anne."

"I know, but I can't take money from you."

"Let me make this suggestion." He paused as the waitress put platters of beefsteak and potatoes in front of them. "First tell me, how long do you think you can go on hiding the fact that you're with child?" He had lowered his voice to a murmur.

Anne shrugged. "With the type of clothing I'm wearing, I'd say for quite some time. Possibly three or four months." She didn't really believe that, but she couldn't let Justin know how far along she was.

"How do you feel? Are you still tired? Do you experience the illness Penelope's always complaining of?"

"No."

"Then I have an alternative suggestion to make. I own a house here in Fort Worth, a rather large one."

"Really?" Anne looked astounded. "But Penelope—"

"Penelope doesn't know about it. She's not interested in my business ventures, only the money they bring in," he added bitterly. "And this place wouldn't appeal to her. Penelope wants something grand up on the bluff."

"But surely she'd settle for—"

"A boarding house? Hardly. I acquired it in repayment for debt. If you want to manage it, you can."

A boarding house. That sounded feasible to Anne.

"The town is running over with people. They're living in tents and wagons because there's no other place for them. Then there are others passing through, and the hotels can't accommodate them. I think a well-run boarding house with a good table would make a lot of money here." He stopped talking and raised his eyebrows questioningly.

"Of course," said Anne with growing enthusiasm. "It sounds perfect."

"Until you get going, I'll pay you a salary. As soon as you're making money, you'll get a percentage of the profits as well."

She nodded eagerly. That way, if she made a go of the business, she'd be able to pay her own legal fees, and if she got her inheritance back before the child was born, she could go somewhere else, where she wasn't known. "Thank you, Justin."

"Don't thank me. I don't want to put you to work. If you weren't so damned independent . . ." A smile flashed radiantly across her face, and his breath caught in his throat.

"Of course I am, and I'm going to make you lots of money. What shall we call it?"

"Since you're going to be the proprietress," he said, smiling at her enthusiasm, "I'll leave it up to you."

"Panther House," she said promptly, attacking her beefsteak and potatoes with relish. Fort Worth was called Panther City because a Dallas newspaper had once claimed the town was so quiet that a panther had wandered in and fallen asleep in its streets. Since the coming of the railroad, however, Fort Worth was anything but quiet, and the residents had adopted the name with a sardonic enthusiasm, even to adopting live panthers as mascots.

Justin laughed at her name choice for the boarding house. "You really liked that story about the pet panther at the fire station, didn't you?"

Anne agreed merrily. "Indeed I did. I'd love to have seen it when he got loose and had the firemen climbing hot stove pipes and diving through windows. It must have been a sight."

Justin grinned. "Probably wasn't so funny if you were one of the firemen."

"I suppose not," Anne agreed.

The waitress brought their pie, and Justin took a bite. "This doesn't compare with yours."

"Just keep that thought in mind," said Anne, smiling, "and mention it to your friends. Maybe I can serve meals to others beside my boarders."

He sighed. "I suppose I'd be wasting my breath if I tried to slow you down." He paid their bill, and they went back into the street to return to their hotel. "Tomorrow we'll see my lawyer."

"What's that man doing, Justin?" They both stopped to watch a rider on a black pony as he stood up in his stirrups with a long stick in his hand.

"By God," said Justin, "they've got gas lamps now." They watched the man open the three vents and light the street lamp. "Streetcars, gaslights—it's really getting to be a big city."

Anne grinned. "And wagons bogged down in the mud, and pigs rooting under the buildings."

"Well," said Justin laughing, "it takes time." Then as he heard shouts and gunfire, and as riders came whooping down the street, he swept her into the doorway of a hardware store and shielded her body with his. "I want you to promise me," he muttered in her ear, "that you won't go out at night by yourself."

"What's going on?" she asked.

"Just cowboys shooting up the town. They don't mean any harm, but sometimes people get hit by stray bullets, and I don't want you to be one of them, so stay in at night, and stay out of the third ward entirely. There are more murders and beatings there than all the rest of the town put together."

"I don't even know where the third ward is."

"Hell's Half Acre," he explained brusquely. "And you do know where it is. You lived there."

When the shouting riders passed on down the street, he took his arm from around her, and they resumed their walk to the hotel.

"Three months is plenty enough time to have straightened this out," said Henry Barnett, "particularly if there's no mention of your stepfather in the will."

"None at all," Anne assured him, "but the courthouse fire occurred after I transferred control to the colonel."

"Doesn't make any difference," said Barnett. "Now you're sure he was going to handle the money, not Dawson?"

"That's the way I understood it." She studied the lawyer. He was a neat, distinguished-looking man, short of stature, with a salt-and-pepper beard and fine but very conservative clothes. No flowing cravats or colorful waistcoats for Henry Barnett.

"I ask because we need to know who we're going after, who it is that's unwilling to turn the money over. I'm not sure exactly how Dawson figures into this, but it doesn't look good, not when he's insisted he never went to see your stepfather. If the case goes to court, would your sister be willing to testify that Dawson visited the ranch?"

"I don't know," said Anne. "The colonel is her father. Although she might want to, she could be afraid to appear in court, or he might stop her."

"Stop her? I hardly think if we subpoenaed her—"

"When I was supposed to testify at a rustler trial in Weatherford, he locked me in my room."

"Indeed." Henry Barnett frowned. "Why did he do that?"

"I always thought it was to spite Justin."

"Probably was," Justin agreed. "He and I had words a number of times at the roundups last year."

"I'd heard he's a choleric man," mused Justin's lawyer, "but these incidents certainly shed new light on his character. Well." Henry Barnett placed both hands flat on his desk as if shaking off some disturbing insight. "Well, Mrs. McAuliffe, I don't want you to worry about this. We'll get your money back, and if by chance your stepfather has used it for his own purposes, we'll take whatever assets of his will make up the difference."

"According to Sissie, things aren't going very well at the ranch," said Anne, wondering what she'd do if the colonel didn't have any assets.

"We'll see," said the lawyer. "Time and events must dictate our course of action, and in the meantime, may I suggest, insist in fact, that you not deal personally with Colonel Morehead. Leave that to me."

Anne was more than happy to agree to Barnett's suggestion.

"Now there's one other thing, Henry," said Justin briskly. "While Mrs. McAuliffe's waiting for this matter to be settled, she's going to take in boarders at that old Tate place I own, so if she has any legal problems with that, I'd like you to handle them, and I, of course, will foot those fees, as well as your fees on the inheritance matter."

"Justin," Anne interposed.

"Until she's able to repay me," Justin added grudgingly.

"Of course," said Henry, glancing thoughtfully from one to the other. "Incidentally, Justin, I hope you'll tell your wife I was sorry to miss her ball, especially since everybody who went has told me how fine the food was."

"Anne was responsible for the food," said Justin.

"I'm glad the guests were pleased," said Anne, flushing with pleasure. Penelope had never said anything complimentary.

"They should have been," muttered Justin. "Penelope just about worked you to death."

Henry's eyes narrowed on his client. "And how is Mrs. Harte?"

"As difficult and expensive as ever!" snapped Justin.

"Ah." Henry frowned and tapped his fingertips together contemplatively. "Well. Mrs. McAuliffe, I'll keep you up to date on the matter of your inheritance."

"He's a good lawyer," said Justin as they left the office. "Honest and thorough."

Anne nodded. "Too bad I didn't know his name and have the money to hire him three months ago," she said. She was wondering uneasily what Henry Barnett suspected about her relationship with Justin.

Panther House had a full quota of boarders the day it opened. Half of them Justin had brought in; the other half Anne acquired by running newspaper advertisements, and since her item announced that she also served meals to drop-in guests on a first-come, first-served basis, her dining room held more people every night. She hired a pale, timid young girl named Lilyanne Whitten to help with the cleaning and had almost decided to find another employee to work in the kitchen. She also opened accounts with R.L. Turner to buy her groceries and with Dodd and Company on Houston Street to provide her with various household furnishings.

Just two weeks later, she was on her way to purchase new tables, accompanying chairs, and tableware for her restaurant venture, which was now flourishing with the help of one Maggie Riley, a stout, goodhearted woman of forty with a deft hand in the kitchen. As Anne made her way toward the purchase of the much-needed furniture, she was enticed first by the sight of Henry Cobb's newsstand on First and Houston, which had a marvelous array of reading material. She'd buy—let's see—a copy of *Godey's* for sure and perhaps *Harper's*. She thumbed through and saw a pattern she could use. Yes, *Harper's* definitely. She purchased the two and, tucking them under her arm, continued her walk toward Dodd's.

It was market day on the courthouse square, and the southwest corner was thronged with wagons, some covered, some open, and men in all manner of dress who had come for the event. And pigs. The pigs wallowed in the mud, ran in and out under the buildings and entangled themselves among the crowd. Somehow or other, they weren't as attractive as the nice pig Pancho had brought her. For one thing, Pancho's had been smaller, and obviously he had cleaned it up before he carried it home. Anne smiled and wondered how the gunfighter was doing. She'd heard nothing of him since he left her in Weatherford, but she hoped that all was well with him and that her pig was thriving in the

Rocking T oak grove. As for these pigs, well, they certainly made a terrible stench, but on the other hand, she supposed that if she could catch one and have it butchered, it would taste better than it looked.

She smiled and ducked into Dodd's to choose her furniture, hoping that they'd be able to deliver it immediately to accommodate the customers who could now be found lined up out into the street at Panther House as they waited for a meal. They seemed to like the name as well as her food.

"Mrs. McAuliffe," said Henry Barnett, eyeing the throng of hearty eaters at her tables, "you must be comforted to realize that if you never get your inheritance back, you're quite capable of making a good living at what you're doing now—which is not to say that you won't get your inheritance," he added hastily.

Anne had been unable to conceal the alarm she felt. Although she was making money here, she couldn't stay. How many people would come to her boarding house if they knew she was carrying an illegitimate child?

"My dear young woman," Henry admonished, "I was just passing the time of day. I surely did not mean you won't retrieve your inheritance. I have talked to Dawson, and it is obvious to me that whatever's going on, Mr. Dawson is part of it. He hemmed and hawed and backed up as fast as a man could, which will do him no good whatever. I now have a copy of your husband's will."

"If you could get it, why couldn't he?"

"Presumably because he didn't try. They hadn't received any requests but mine, which is something I intend to point out to Dawson when next I see him. Also I sent word to Colonel Morehead that unless he wants to be sued in open court for trying to cheat a widow, he's to be here for a meeting of all the parties concerned on April twentieth. Is that agreeable to you?"

"Yes, certainly," said Anne, trying to hide her dread of facing the colonel again, even with Mr. Barnett's help. "Would you care to sit down to dinner?" she asked.

"I fear you have not one empty chair, Mrs. McAuliffe."

"We can eat in my parlor."

"In that case, I'd be delighted. It's been a long time since I've had a home-cooked meal."

"I'm not sure you could call this home cooking," said Anne, "not on the scale we're doing it now. Aren't you married, Mr. Barnett?" she asked, then wished she hadn't lest he think she was expressing an interest in him.

"I am a widower. My wife died two years ago."

"Oh, I'm sorry. I know how hard that is."

Henry held her chair at a small table in the parlor. "I loved her mightily," he added, surprising Anne with such a blunt statement of emotion from so reserved a man. "I doubt I'll ever marry again."

She nodded and went out to fetch their food, smiling slightly to herself. Was he warning her off? Well, he needn't worry. She wasn't likely to marry again herself, not when she couldn't have the man she wanted. She returned and placed a heaping plate in front of Mr. Barnett, a smaller one at her own place.

"So as I was saying, the meeting will be April twentieth. If your stepfather and Dawson do not attend, we will immediately file a complaint, but, of course, the matter would be expedited if we didn't have to do that."

"How long if we do?" she asked, thinking she didn't have very long.

"If we can get the case on the spring calendar, maybe another few months."

April, May, June, she counted to herself. In June she

would be just two months from giving birth. She might have to appear in court unable to disguise her condition. Anne bit her lip.

"Now, don't you worry, Mrs. McAuliffe," Henry said, looking worried himself as he searched her pale face. "We're going to get the money for you."

"I have every faith in you, Mr. Barnett. It's just that so many things have gone wrong in the last year or so."

"So it must seem," Henry agreed. He went on explaining what he intended to do on her behalf, but Anne was thinking, what if the colonel had spent her money, and all that was left was the Bar M? She remembered wryly that she had once told Pancho she wouldn't mind running a ranch. But could she? Could she run a ranch and raise her illegitimate child? In Parker County where everyone knew her? Oh, well, she thought, as she saw Mr. Barnett to the door, she'd worry about it if and when she had to.

Anne climbed the steps to Panther House, having attended St. Andrew's Episcopal Church for the second time. No one had looked at her askance, so she presumed that Justin had indeed managed to stem the gossip. She had enjoyed the sermon by a pastor so different from Brother Foley and his ilk, but even more she had enjoyed the greetings of the church members, who had welcomed her warmly. She felt almost lighthearted as she opened her front door.

"Oh, Miz McAuliffe," cried the little maid, Lilyanne, "there's a gentleman to see you."

Anne's first thought was Justin, and her heart began to race.

"He's ever so handsome, the young gentleman. Thin and blond-haired."

"Blond?" Anne echoed, disappointed. It wasn't Justin.

"I took him to your parlor. I hope that's all right. He said his name was Mr. Tighe."

"Pancho?" Anne laughed delightedly and headed down the hall to her quarters. "Pancho," she cried as she closed the door behind her. "What are you doing here?"

"Well, I reckon I could say I came in to visit you, but the truth is I didn't know where you was until I heard last night about some redheaded lady who's the best cook in all of Fort Worth."

Anne chuckled. "So what did you come in for? No, don't tell me. To find a poker game?"

"Reckon that was part of it," he admitted, "but I particularly come in to see Madam Rentz's female minstrels. You ain't heard about 'em? They do this French dance called the cancan, an' it's an eye opener."

"Oh, Pancho." She laughed and patted him on the shoulder. "How are you?"

"Why, I'm fine. More to the point, how are you? You're lookin' good." He eyed her curiously. "Are you still—ah—"

"Yes, I still am."

"You sure don't look it, for a lady who's been—ah—that way for a while . . . you know."

"Hard work will keep you thin under almost any circumstances I suppose," she replied dryly.

"You own this place?"

Anne shook her head. "Justin Harte owns it. I'm running it for him, and I get part of the profits."

"Never did like him much," muttered Pancho. "What about that money from your husband?"

"I have a lawyer trying to get it back."

"He ain't done it yet? Look, I'm still willin' to go shoot the colonel."

"Thanks, but then I'd have to go to court for sure, wouldn't I?"

"I guess. I try to stay clear of courts myself. So, you got a place for a tired, hungry gunslinger to stay?"

"I guess I could find a bed for you, but I run a respectable house," she warned him teasingly. "No gambling, and I don't want you coming in late at night, drunk and noisy after an evening spent watching the ladies doing the—what was it?"

"The cancan. Why, you oughta come along with me, Annie. You never saw nothin' like it in your life. All them legs an' petticoats an' ever'thing."

"I'll skip it," said Anne hastily. "I don't imagine there are too many female spectators."

"Suit yourself," he answered agreeably. "So, what's for supper? I ain't had a decent meal since you left."

Anne frowned. "Are things going badly at the ranch?"

"Nope. That Last Cauley, I reckon he's a real good foreman 'cause he tells me we're gonna turn a profit this year."

"Good for you, Pancho. You may become a staid, respectable citizen yet."

"I sure hope not. Ain't nothin' like that in my plans. You ever gonna tell me what I'm gittin' to eat tonight?"

Anne grinned. "Antelope stew and dried apple pie."

"Sounds good to me. When do we set down?"

"Miz McAuliffe, I hated callin' you down here to the jail," said Jim Courtright, "but this young fella insisted that you'd wanna get him out."

"My goodness, Marshall Courtright," said Anne, eyeing the law officer, "you do look the frontiersman today." The marshall was wearing fringed buckskins, rather than the suit she'd been accustomed to.

"Oh, well, when you seen me before, I'd been havin' my picture taken regular. My wife, she always wants me to git gussied up when I'm gonna have my picture taken, an' for a while there all these tenderfoot, Yankee photographers kept comin' 'round lookin' out for gen-u-ine western he-roes. Last one come 'round, I offered to put a gen-u-ine western bullet in him, so I ain't had no more trouble."

"You didn't!" exclaimed Anne, grinning. "Why,

they'll think we're downright uncivilized, Marshall."

"We are, ma'am," declared the marshall. "If you don't believe me, ask your friend Tighe what he was doin' last night."

"I'll be sure to do that," said Anne, intrigued. "What's the procedure for getting him out?"

"Just pay his fine, an' he's free to go. You sure you wanna do this? He's a gunfighter, you know."

"Yes, I know, Marshall, but he's also a friend."

The marshall shook his head as if he couldn't believe it, but he had Pancho brought from one of the two cells.

"Well, you certainly are a sight," declared Anne. Pancho had trailed in looking wrinkled, muddy, and red-eyed. "I hope you feel better than you look."

"It ain't the best jail I been in, but it ain't the worst. Thanks for gettin' her over here, Marshall."

Anne paid the fine, and the two of them left as she asked, "What were you arrested for?"

"Oh, 'twasn't nuthin'. I was just down at Henry Burns."

"And that is?"

"It's on Main near Second," said Pancho evasively.

"Uh-huh. What is it, a sporting house?"

"No!" said Pancho, looking shocked. "It's a saloon." Anne waited.

"An' they got these pits out back," Pancho continued reluctantly. "For prize fights, dog fights, cock fights, an' such. That's illegal, only I ain't never heard that the police ever done nothin' about it before," he added resentfully, eyeing her sideways to see if he'd satisfied her curiosity.

"Go on," said Anne.

Pancho sighed. "So when someone yelled 'police!' I didn't hurry gittin' out. I jus' figgered it was 'cause the challenger was winnin' over the house fighter. When that happens, Burns he has 'em yell 'police' so ever'one will run off an' he won't have to pay the hunnerd dollars he offered to anyone as could beat his man. Problem was, this time it turned out to be the police," said Pancho indignantly. "I guess the marshall, he just gits sick of all the ruckus an' decides to take out after some illegal activity or other once in a while. Anyway, I got arrested. You heard enough, or you wanna know ever' bad thing I done since you last saw me?"

"Are you telling me they have men fighting one another at this place?"

"Sure. They always have some big fella works for Henry Burns challengin' anyone who thinks he can win in a fist fight, an' folks make bets an'—"

"Oh, so that's the attraction," said Anne, "the gambling."

"Matter a fact, I didn't make any bets. I just watched. The odds are bad if you bet on the house fighter, an' you can be sure the other fella's not gonna win, so what's the sport there? I been in jail half the night." He sounded and looked doubly resentful. "They wouldn't even let me git my fine paid till mornin'."

"That's good. I'd just as soon not be awakened in the middle of the night."

"Why, I wouldn't send for you in the middle of the night, Annie, not when you're ah—ah—"

"All right, Pancho, maybe we shouldn't talk about that since no one else knows."

"Oh, sure. Sorry. What's for breakfast?"

CHAPTER
Twenty

"**I** want Harte removed," said the colonel savagely. "He may be her paramour, but he has no legal status here."

Henry Barnett and even Lawyer Dawson looked shocked and embarrassed. Anne almost groaned aloud. This was just what she had feared when she entered Henry Barnett's office to find that Justin had come in from Palo Pinto for the meeting.

"What did you call me?" Justin demanded. His hostility, which ten minutes earlier seemed to be directed at her, causing her great confusion, was now turned, understandably, against the colonel.

"I called you her paramour," the colonel sneered, not in the least intimidated. "It's well known that you two have been consorting adulterously."

Anne shivered. What would he say next? Did he know she'd stayed with Pancho or about her sojourn at the sporting house? Before he got through with her, even her own lawyer might turn against her.

"Well known to whom?" Justin's voice was tight and deadly.

"I heard it through a man of the cloth." The colonel looked smug, evidently thinking that no one would question the word of a preacher.

"Brother Foley? The blackmailer?" asked Justin sarcastically.

Colonel Morehead flushed. "What does it matter who? I hardly think my stepdaughter will be prepared to go to court on the matter of the inheritance when such revelations would come out."

"In other words, *you've* taken to blackmail, too," said Justin, his eyes like ice. "Well, Colonel, if you make any allegations of that sort against Mrs. McAuliffe, the result will be an immediate charge of assault."

"Assault?" The colonel looked amused. "Calling a trollop a trollop is hardly—"

"Physical assault!" snapped Justin. "On the unsupported word of a man whose reputation is exceedingly unsavory, you physically assaulted Mrs. McAuliffe, causing her grave bodily harm, as Henry here would say. For that alone, you ought to be put in jail. Given the present circumstances, your threats against Mrs. McAuliffe's reputation and your misappropriation of her property—"

"She signed—"

Henry Barnett, who had been listening, astounded, through the whole vicious exchange, roused himself and interrupted. "Any papers Mrs. McAuliffe signed in the past are irrelevant, Colonel," said Henry. "She has asked to have her property returned, and she has a perfect right to get it back. Furthermore, slandering her will not change the fact that if you do not return her inheritance, you will be guilty of theft and charged with it."

The colonel flushed and began to bluster, but Henry cut him off. "If you have assaulted the person of my client as well as defrauded her, I think we should call in the marshall immediately. You, Dawson, being a party to all this, will come in for charges yourself."

"I haven't done anything," quavered Dawson.

"You led Mrs. McAuliffe to believe that you were performing legal services for her, when, in fact, you were representing the illegal interests of her stepfather."

"She didn't pay me anything." Dawson was sweating, his collar beginning to wilt under the rusty black of his suit.

"Irrelevant. You're a party to fraud and theft. I shall move to have you disbarred as well as charged. And you, Colonel, should come in for criminal charges."

Anne started to protest, but Henry frowned and cleared his throat warningly. "Mrs. McAuliffe, if you're worried about your sister, let me remind you that you are of age to take over her guardianship. With your inheritance returned, you'll be able to provide for her, so I see no problem in bringing the whole matter to court."

"Now—now, just a minute here," stammered the colonel.

"Are you ready to turn Mrs. McAuliffe's property over to her?" Henry demanded.

A sly smile came over Morehead's face. "What there is of it," he said, shrugging.

"There was quite a bit, sir, when it came into your hands. Every penny will have to be accounted for and repaid from your own funds if need be."

"See here now, you can't—I mean if I had reverses in handling her—"

"Every penny!" Henry reiterated.

"Texas law doesn't allow you to attack a man's livelihood," Dawson pointed out.

"But Texas law does allow me to send him to jail for theft," Henry said. "Is that what you want?"

The colonel looked so shaken at this juncture that

Anne wondered with a sinking feeling what he had done with her inheritance.

"She was living in my house, eating my food," said the colonel. "Accepting my familial protection. That has to be taken into consideration."

Justin snorted.

"As I understand it," Henry said, "Mrs. McAuliffe, during her stay at the Bar M, served as your housekeeper and cook. Did you pay her a salary?"

"Of course not. She's my stepdaughter. She owed me!"

"On the contrary. Since you wish to charge her room and board, you then become liable for her wages at a fair rate. That will have to be figured into the accounting."

What came out during the next few hours was that the colonel had maintained his accustomed lifestyle and tried to recoup years of ranching errors by spending Anne's money. He had made ill-advised investments in town that failed and bought cattle to replace those he had lost in the trail herd that disappeared.

"I'd have repaid her," said the colonel defensively. "I still intend to. In fact, I'll allow her to come back to the ranch while—"

"Absolutely not," Justin interjected. "She'll never live in your house again, and given your disastrous record as a rancher, I don't see any prospect for the return of her inheritance." He turned to Henry. "I think we should take him to court, Henry, make him sell up and pay her right away."

"You can't do that," said the colonel, turning pale. "You'd be taking Sissie's share," he appealed to Anne.

She bit her lip and turned away. She knew she had to consider Sissie.

"I must agree with Mr. Harte," said Henry. "You, Colonel Morehead, are not to be trusted, nor are you a competent rancher. I too see no prospect that Mrs.

McAuliffe will get her money back. However, if we put you into bankruptcy—"

"What sort of debts do you have on the ranch?" asked Justin briskly, as if it had all been settled but the details. "Have you borrowed against it?"

"No," said the colonel sullenly.

"How much do you owe the merchants from whom you get supplies? It will all come out if we go to court, so don't bother lying."

The colonel flushed and turned to his lawyer for assistance, but Dawson just squirmed in his seat and looked helpless, so glaring, the colonel detailed his debts.

"What would you say his ranch is worth?" Henry asked Justin. Justin made a guess, and Henry continued thoughtfully, "Well, if he sells out, Mrs. McAuliffe should get at least part of her money back."

"Could I suggest a compromise?" murmured Anne, who had been thinking hard if silently. "I'd be willing to have him pay me over a period of two or three years."

"Anne, there's simply no prospect of his doing that," Justin pointed out. "Nor do I think you could trust him."

"I don't trust him," said Anne, glancing at the man she both hated and feared. He was beginning to look smug, evidently thinking that he was about to get a reprieve. "What I propose is that I be given title to half the Bar M with a fair division of the land, the water rights, and the cattle." She frowned and added, "Perhaps some third party and the lawyers can agree on the value of the ranch and what a fair split would be. Then the rest he could pay off over a period of time."

"I still don't think you'd get the rest of the money," said Justin.

"I would if someone else were running the Bar M."

"What?" exclaimed the colonel.

"If we had a competent foreman with the final say

over both halves," said Anne, ignoring him, "and I took half of the colonel's profits each year, I'd soon be paid off. It's good land and should have made money."

"It might work," said Justin thoughtfully, "if we could find a good foreman. For that matter, Henry, Anne's got a lot more sense about ranching than the colonel has."

"The devil she does!" shouted the colonel. "I won't put up with this! We'll go to court!"

Mr. Dawson cleared his throat hesitantly. "I wonder if I might have a word with my client?"

"By all means," Henry said, "step out in the hall, if you like."

The colonel looked absolutely apoplectic, but Dawson managed to drag him out of the room. They were gone ten minutes, and when they returned, Dawson said, "If we can agree on someone to take over management of the ranch, Colonel Morehead will sign the papers."

"Can all this be legalized, Henry, so that he can't back out or cheat her again?" Justin asked. When Henry nodded, Justin said, "Good. Set it up so that no money comes into his hands until Anne gets her share."

Anne peeked sideways at her stepfather and shivered at the sheer malevolence she saw in his eyes. Well, she wasn't going to back off. He'd stolen from her, and he would pay her back, but then she remembered with a sinking heart something she had forgotten during the pressure of the negotiations. She was going to bear a child come late summer, and this solution might well hold her in the area. She stared hard at her hands, which she had folded tensely in her lap.

"Are you sure you want to do this, Mrs. McAuliffe?" Henry Barnett asked, a worried frown marking his usually impassive face.

She tried to think of some other resolution but couldn't. "Yes," she said reluctantly. "It's the only way to protect both Sissie and me." But she did wonder what Henry Barnett's reservations were. He didn't know about the baby.

"I hope that girl appreciates how far you're willing to go for her," Justin muttered.

The colonel was directed to stay in town until the agreement could be implemented, and he stalked out immediately thereafter.

Justin then said, "If we're through for now, Henry, I'll escort Mrs. McAuliffe home." He looked almost as grim as the colonel.

Anne wondered uneasily whether she wanted to go with Justin. That unexplained hostility she had seen in his eyes earlier had reappeared. However, she shook off her apprehensions, picked up her parasol, and preceded him from the lawyer's office.

"It's very kind of you to come in for this meeting, Justin," she said once they were out on the street. "It's a long ride from Palo Pinto."

"Especially since you don't seem to have needed me. You're a very canny negotiator yourself, although I'm surprised that you've tied yourself to this area. Are you going to stay here and bear Tighe's child?" His voice was grim with tension.

"I don't know," said Anne nervously. "I wasn't thinking of that when I suggested the compromise. Still, I guess if the foreman we get is reliable . . . I wish it could be Last Cauley, but I wouldn't want to take him away from Pancho."

"Yes, it's obvious that you have deep feelings for Tighe." He glanced coldly at her, and his hand on her elbow was hurtful as he assisted her across the street. "The gunfighter has, after all, been staying at your place."

Ah, thought Anne, that explained the strange looks and the suppressed anger.

"In fact, I hear that you paid a fine to get him out of jail."

"He repaid me," she replied defensively.

"How?" asked Justin.

"In money!" Anne snapped. "What are you accusing me of?"

"I guess I didn't think you'd take up with him again as soon as I was out of sight."

"I haven't taken up with him. He was a guest at my—at your boarding house."

"He's no guest of mine."

"True, he's gone home, so why are we arguing?"

"How could you go back with him?" Justin's voice grated with anger and resentment. "I'm doing my best to see that things work out for you. What has *he* done for you since he got you with child, beside ask you to rescue him from jail, that is?"

"Oh, for heaven's sake, Justin, stop it, will you? Do you want to take the boarding house back? Is that it? Do you want to find someone else to manage it?" She tipped her parasol aside and glared at him. "I suppose I can ask for my half of the Bar M to be along Bushy Creek and move out to that line shack where we used to meet before I knew you were married." When he paled, she knew her shot had gone home. "You don't like to be reminded of your culpability in all this, do you?" she snapped.

"Anne, I . . ."

She turned sharply away from the square and strode down the street toward Panther House, leaving him behind. She wasn't sure whether she wanted him to follow her or not, but he didn't.

Once out of sight, she trudged along disconsolately, wondering when he'd got to town. He hadn't even called on her, hadn't stayed in his own house. Was he being discreet or judgmental? she wondered as she climbed the steps and opened her door. She glanced into the dining room as she put her parasol into the hall rack, noting that the midday meal had yet to be cleared away. Well, the work would take her mind off the fact that the man she loved had turned on her and that her stepfather had wanted to rob her and that Dawson, whom she'd trusted, had betrayed her. Whom could she trust? she wondered. No one but herself, obviously. She was on her own.

Anne heard no more from Justin. She assumed that he had gone home to Palo Pinto. Was their tie to one another finally broken and all because she had gotten Pancho out of jail? She felt increasingly alone and lonely, even though the boarding house continued to prosper and kept her surrounded with people and conversation. Her customers ate her food with relish as they discussed the local election in which the reform ticket under Beall lost to the incumbent, Mayor Day. As a result, crime continued to escalate in Fort Worth and particularly in Hell's Half Acre.

One night a drunken cattle broker came lurching into Panther House, having mistaken it for one of the many houses of ill repute that were scattered all over town. He grabbed young Lilyanne with the loudly stated intention of taking her upstairs for a two-dollar "quickie." The poor child was terrified, and Anne had to drive the man into a corner with her Winchester prodding his chest while a boarder, who thought the whole incident hilarious, went for the marshall.

Jim Courtright arrived and said, looking rather amused himself, "Here now, fella, you can't invade respectable houses makin' lewd suggestions," whereupon the drunk replied, "All right, Marshall, if I can't have the young one, I'll take the redheaded one, but you got to make her put away the rifle. I ain't fond of that weird stuff with women."

Anne sighed in disgust, and Jim Courtright asked if she wanted to bring charges.

"I certainly do, Marshall. Good grief, people aren't safe in their homes anymore."

"Yes, ma'am," said the marshall, looking glum. "And you can thank your local government and your local merchants for that. Everytime I try to crack down, they complain it hurts business."

"So I've heard, and please don't call them *my* local government. No one ever gave me the vote."

The marshall grinned. "I reckon, Miz McAuliffe, if we had you for mayor, things'd be different."

"Indeed they would," said Anne.

"All right, fella, off you go. If you're lookin' for a sportin' house, I can recommend one," said the marshall as he hauled Anne's would-be customer away. It had taken her forty minutes to console the terrified little maid.

As well as local government, the boarders often discussed national government, for Fort Worth, an enclave of the Democratic Party, had been incensed to hear in March that the House of Representatives in Washington had elected Hayes president when all knew that Tilden had really won the election. His Fraudulency they called the new president and raised toasts at table to his ill health.

As April warmed into May and Anne added more fullness to her clothes to conceal her six-month pregnancy, thousands of longhorns were driven through town and north across the Trinity River, and the railroad yards were piled high with buffalo hides from Jacksboro and goods that had been brought in by rail to be freighted west on wagons. The tent city grew, and the streets swirled with newcomers and residents. The city's recently formed baseball team, the Panthers, in their white knee pants and red stockings, beat Texarkana and Dallas, and the boarders discussed baseball and the dad-blasted hogs that roamed the streets and the Headlight Bar where a man could ride his horse right in and have his drink served to him in his saddle. Amidst all the activity surrounding her, Anne worried because the compromise had not yet been finalized with her stepfather.

Then finally she received word from Henry Barnett

that she was to come to the courthouse where Colonel Morehead would sign over half of his rights to the Bar M. What did Sissie think of all this? Anne wondered. Did she feel that she was being deprived of her inheritance? And what was Anne herself to do? She had no idea as she walked toward the courthouse. As yet there was no agreement about who would manage the Bar M, and she was receiving no income from it; nor could she expect any for at least a month. The little she had saved from her earnings at Panther House would never support a move away from Fort Worth, and her pregnancy could not be concealed forever. Every day now she expected someone to notice—a boarder, Maggie, someone.

Her eyes bleak, she mounted the steps to the courthouse, sick with anxiety about her own future. She should have let them make the colonel sell; she should have taken what she could get. Why hadn't she? She had told herself it was because of Sissie, but her heart said Justin was the reason. She couldn't bear to sever their tenuous connection, although maybe their last quarrel had accomplished that, and what was she to do now?

These thoughts were wiped away when she heard a terrible commotion and furious shouts coming from the building. Alarmed, she stepped out of the way as the doors burst open releasing three large, disgruntled pigs and a crowd of men behind them, shouting and driving them out of the halls of justice. Anne started to laugh and couldn't stop. Here she had been feeling the tragic queen, only to be swept aside by a pig stampede.

"Well, ma'am," said a stranger in a brown Stetson as he remounted the steps and eyed her disapprovingly, "I reckon it looks funny to see fourteen grown men drivin' three pigs, but if you was tryin' to carry on a trial, an' suddenly you found them hogs runnin' up an' down the aisles disruptin' the proceedings, you wouldn't think it was so funny."

"I'm sure I wouldn't," gasped Anne, trying to stifle

her laughter. "I'm sure I wouldn't, sir, and I think you have done an admirable job as a pig herd."

She clapped a gloved hand over the last giggle and walked into the courthouse, feeling immensely cheered. Her life might be grim, but delightfully ridiculous things were always happening around her.

A short time later she became part owner of the Bar M. Much good that would do her if a competent foreman could not be found to run it.

CHAPTER

Twenty-One

"Get your cloak, Miss Annie."

Startled, Anne looked up from the sewing machine where she had been working on a baby dress. "Last?" She couldn't believe her eyes. She hadn't seen the man since December. "Last, how wonderful of you to visit me."

"There's no time for visitin', Miss Annie. You gotta come along with me."

"What is it?" she asked, alarmed at the grim look on his face.

"Pancho's been shot."

"Oh Lord," cried Anne. "How bad?"

"Bad enough. You comin'?"

She nodded and swept her light cloak off the peg. "How did it happen?" she asked as they hurried down the hall and out the door.

"What you might expect, given the boy's habits. A gambler shot him over a hand of poker." Last helped her into a buggy and whipped up the horses.

"Where is he?"

"Over in the third ward," said Last in disgust. "I wouldn't take you there for nuthin', but he cain't be moved."

Anne bit her lip, thinking that his wound must be serious indeed. "At the poker table?" She couldn't believe it. "He always said he was the best gun alive up close."

"Yeah, well, if you live the kinda life Pancho did, sooner or later someone's gonna take you by surprise, an' then it don't matter how good you are."

"I suppose so," Anne replied, "but you're not to worry, Last. I'll take care of him. I didn't let Rollo die, and I'm certainly not going to let Pancho, although I do wish I'd nagged him more about the gambling."

"You cain't hold yourself responsible for anything that happens to a fella like Pancho Tighe, Miss Annie. He was bound to get hisself shot sooner or later."

Anne sighed and muttered, "He's a lovable fool all the same."

"You love him?" Last glanced at her, surprised.

"Of course," said Anne. "No one was ever kinder to me when I needed a friend."

Last grunted skeptically and drew the buggy up in front of a noisy saloon. "Here we are. Now, just ignore anythin' you see or hear in this place." He rushed her through the large, raucous crowd where the men drew back and the noise stilled like a spreading pall around them. "This way," said Last, ushering her quickly from the barroom into a hall.

"What's back here?" she asked.

"The bed he's lyin' in," muttered Last.

"A bed in a saloon?"

Last looked embarrassed. "Other things go on in places like this 'sides drinkin' an' gamblin'."

"Oh, I see."

Last swung open a door and allowed her to enter ahead of him. In the small room, Pancho lay on a narrow, rumpled bed, his blond hair sweat-soaked, his face paler than she'd ever seen it, but still he gave her a weak smile as she knelt beside him.

"Glad you could come, Annie," he whispered.

"Well, of course I came, Pancho. Now what have you done to yourself?"

"'Twasn't me. 'Twas that gambler with the belly gun." He closed his eyes for a moment, then resumed, "An' don't ask me a bunch of questions 'bout belly guns. I ain't up to no shootin' lessons tonight." He motioned to Last, who stepped out into the hall again.

"Why weren't you staying at Panther House?" she asked.

"Had me a little visit from Justin Harte awhile back."

"Oh dear, I am sorry," she groaned. "What did he say?"

"Didn't much like my stayin' at your place less'n I planned to do right by you an' my baby." He grinned at her.

"I knew he thought that," Anne mumbled contritely, "and I should have told him you weren't the father."

"That's all right, Annie. I aim to set ever'thing right. Now in just a minute here, we're gonna play out this little scene, and I want you to go along with whatever I say. You understand me? I might not make it through this one, Annie, an' I got it all figgered out what I wanna do, so you follow my lead." He closed his eyes again, a grimace of pain crossing his face.

Anne, with growing anxiety, said, "All right, Pancho, whatever you want, but you're not going to die if that's what you're thinking. I'll make you well."

At that minute Brother Foley stepped in the door. Behind him a respectably dressed man whom Anne had seen at the courthouse entered as well.

Pancho opened his eyes and called out in a stronger voice, "Bless you for comin', Brother."

Anne was stunned. Could he be welcoming that sleazy hypocrite?

"You can do the Lord's work tonight, Brother Foley," said Pancho, "by savin' this sinner."

All her anxiety evaporated, and she glared at Pancho. Was she the sinner he was talking about? Of all the nerve.

"An' retrievin' the good name of this fine woman I done wrong to." Pancho shot a warning look in her direction. "I aim to confess my sins, Brother, while I got the chance."

"Hallelujah," mumbled Brother Foley, glancing nervously from side to side. Whether because of the punishing grip Last seemed to have on his arm or the sight of her at Pancho's bedside, the preacher looked scared, perhaps suspicious, certainly not spiritually exhilarated. She herself was nonplused. She'd heard about deathbed repentance, but she wouldn't have thought Pancho a likely candidate, and anyway, his color was better.

"I killed a few men in my time," said Pancho solemnly, "but none of 'em was worth much. God prob'ly didn't care one way or another."

Anne rolled her eyes. If this was Pancho's idea of making his peace with God, he needed some help. She opened her mouth, only to have him increase the pressure on her hand so much that she gasped and shut up. In glancing at the abused hand, she noticed that blood was staining the blanket and wished he'd finish with Brother Foley so she could have a look at his wound.

"This good woman was the victim of my lust," said Pancho loudly, giving her hand another warning squeeze. Anne's eyes flew open. He had some grip for a man who was making a deathbed confession, she thought wryly, and she could have sworn she saw his lips quiver in a smile.

"It was—ah—demon rum. When she'd been hurt by evil and unkind men"—he gave the preacher a mean look, and Brother Foley paled with alarm—"I took advantage of her by—ah—plyin' her with demon rum."

More like demon whiskey, thought Anne, remembering their Christmas Eve poker game. What was Pancho up to, anyway?

"Disguised in—ah—lemonade."

Lemonade? She hadn't seen a lemon since 1870.

"And then I had my evil way with her."

Pancho looked downright smug. Anne supposed he was pleased with his own performance and wondered if he'd seen this whole melodrama on the stage of some saloon between poker games.

"I offered her hospitality in her time of need, an' then I took advantage of her."

Anne frowned at him. Just what did he think he was doing? Confessing to something neither one of them was even sure had happened. It was bad enough to have her name tarnished through association with Justin, but this was something else entirely.

"An' then Brother Foley, I compounded my sins by turning her away when she was with child."

Brother Foley gaped; Anne glared. That was really the last straw. He could at least have kept that aspect of her situation out of it.

"Will God forgive me?" asked Pancho in a voice that didn't sound a bit contrite.

Last gave Brother Foley's arm a shake, and the preacher mumbled, "Do you repent your sins?"

"I'll do better'n that," said Pancho. "I aim to make right the wrong I done."

Anne's head swiveled back toward Pancho. What did that mean?

"I want you to marry us here and now, Brother Foley," said Pancho. Now Anne gaped.

"I could do that," stammered the preacher.

"Course you could," Pancho agreed. "That's why you're here."

"What are you going to do if you live through this, you idiot?" Anne hissed into his ear.

"Divorce you, what else?" he whispered back. "Think I wanna be married to a drunken woman?"

Anne clamped her hand over her mouth to keep from laughing, but then her eyes fell on the blanket. "You'd better let me have a look at that wound," she murmured.

"Right now, Brother Foley," said Pancho. "I want to give the child my name."

"Oh, Pancho," she whispered. That was it? He'd changed his mind? Maybe he was delirious with pain.

"Shoulda done it months ago."

"Let us pray," said Brother Foley.

"Let's not," said Pancho. "Let's get on with the weddin'."

Last shoved the preacher toward the bed and snapped, "Make it short."

Brother Foley gave him an alarmed glance and immediately began the ceremony. Anne wondered wildly what to do, but when she was asked if she took Pancho Tighe to be her wedded husband, Last gave her such a poke that she stammered yes. Just seconds later she was hearing the minister pronounce them man and wife and tell Pancho he could kiss his bride.

"We ain't got time for kisses," Pancho whispered. She looked at him in alarm, for his face was now gray. "Lawyer, you got those marriage lines?" The other man produced a document which Pancho signed with difficulty, then Anne, then the preacher, then the two witnesses. "Now the other," said Pancho. Four signatures were affixed to the second document, Anne being excluded from this signing. "That's it," Pancho sighed. "Now, Pinson, if you and Last could explain all this to Brother Foley out in the hall, I'd like a word with Annie."

The two men hustled the preacher out. Anne began to cry. "Oh, Pancho," she said, "you didn't have to do this."

"Seemed like a good idea to me," said Pancho. "I ain't done that many kindly things in my life. Maybe God'll forgive me all the other stuff 'cause I done somethin' good before I died."

"I'm not going to let you die."

"You know, Annie, I ain't forgot how nice you was to me at that weddin' when ever'one else acted like I had the cholera or somethin'. You're as good a friend as I ever had."

Anne leaned over and kissed him on the forehead.

"I wouldn't mind a better kiss than that, seein' as we're married now. I never did get the one I expected the night I walked you home."

Obligingly she kissed him on the lips.

"That qualifies as better. Now stop cryin'," he ordered. "I ain't partial to saltwater kisses. Just makes me thirstier, an' no one wants to give me nuthin' to drink, this bein' a stomach wound, though I don't see what difference—" He coughed, and a pink froth stained his lips. "Well, that ain't what I wanted to tell you. Now, you take a good look at them weddin' lines, Annie, an' memorize the date."

Anne picked up the wedding certificate, which was dated December 14, 1876. She looked at him, puzzled. "That way it looks more like it's my child," Pancho explained. "The will, it leaves the Rockin' T an' ever'thing else I own to you."

"Pancho, you're not going to . . . Look if you'd just let me see the wound." She was thoroughly frightened now.

"Annie, you don't wanna look, believe me." He shifted slightly, grimacing. "It's all gonna work out. I 'member you said once you wouldn't mind runnin' a ranch, so now you got a ranch to run, an' a name for your baby an' ever'thing. Purty smart, ain't I?"

"What is your name?" she whispered, trying to blink back her tears. "You signed the marriage certificate Pancho."

"Oh, shucks, I didn't think. My real name is Edward, but it's still legal under Pancho."

"I wanted to know what to name the baby."

"You gonna name it after me?" He looked unaccountably pleased. "Ain't that nice? I never figgered I'd have no baby who was almost mine. Let's hope it ain't a girl. Edward won't sound too good on a girl."

"Edwina then," said Anne, sniffing.

"That sounds downright dumb."

Anne smiled at him. "It's better than Panchette."

At that Pancho grinned widely and chuckled; then his eyes closed, and he lay still.

"Pancho?" She touched a trembling hand to the pulse in his neck. There was none. "I'd rather you lived," she whispered, "I truly would," but he could no longer answer her.

Twice widowed, Anne thought drearily. She sat in her parlor at Panther House, rocking and going sadly over the arrangements she had made: a fine rosewood coffin for Pancho from Fakes and Co.; Henry Barnett summoned to handle the new inheritance; Panther House turned over to Maggie, who would do a competent job running it for Justin.

"Miss Annie?" Last eyed her with a worried frown from the doorway. "You decided where you wanna lay Pancho to rest?"

"We'll take him home to the Rocking T, Last, but"— how she hated to get into this—"but before we go maybe you could—could explain a few things to me. I'm not sure I understood everything Pancho told me after you left with Brother Foley."

"Well, it's simple enough," said the foreman, looking as embarrassed as Anne felt. "Soon as the doctor told Pancho he wasn't gonna make it, the boy sent me for that lawyer, an' they made out the will leavin' the Rockin' T to you. Then they fixed up the marriage lines an' backdated 'em." Last's cheeks were a dull brick red, and he stared at his scuffed boots. "So—so there wouldn't be no question about the—ah—the baby."

His embarrassment brought home to her what a shock the knowledge of her pregnancy must have been to him. She only hoped he wouldn't ask who the father was; perhaps he believed it was Pancho.

"So if anybody asks, just say you an' Pancho married last December, but then you had a fallin' out, an' he hadn't even knowed about the baby till he come here awhile back."

"What about Brother Foley?" Anne asked, dreading the answer. How she hated to be in that man's power again. "He didn't know the document was falsified when he signed it. Does he know now?"

"Brother Foley's not gonna say any different from what we say. He cain't afford to, 'cause a somethin' Justin Harte told Pancho about him."

"Good Lord, is this Justin's plan?"

"I don't know, Miss Anne. I'm just tellin' you what Pancho told me right afore I went off to get you the night he died. Anything else you want to know, you'd have to ask Justin now Pancho's gone."

Anne wondered if she'd ever see Justin again to ask. If he'd arranged the marriage, that surely meant he'd washed his hands of her.

"At any rate, you just stick to that story, an' ever'thing will be fine. I s'pose you're comin' back to town after we bury Pancho?"

"No," said Anne. "I'll live at the ranch."

"All right, if that's what you want." But Last looked doubtful of that arrangement.

"Pancho left it to me," said Anne defensively. "I don't take that lightly. Will you mind working for a woman? Is that your objection?"

"Some women I would," Last admitted. "But I

reckon you'd be all right. I was just thinkin' about the—the baby."

"Lots of babies are born and brought up on ranches," she pointed out.

"But there won't be no other woman there."

"That's not unusual either. The Bannerman women will come over when it's my time. Now about your working for me, Last. I'm probably going to be asking more of you than you imagined." She told him about the colonel's handling of her estate, at which Last cursed angrily, and then the settlement she had proposed, at which he chuckled.

"You are a smart one, Miss Annie," he said, looking a lot more relaxed. "So what is it you want from me?"

"I want you to run both ranches. My half's been signed over to me, but I'll never get the rest of my money unless there's a knowledgeable man running things, and you're as knowledgeable as any I know. Would you be willing to take both outfits on?"

"You think the colonel's gonna agree to that?"

"He's been trying to delay the final settlement by not agreeing to anyone who's been proposed, but what objection could he raise to you? He hired you himself at one time, and the Bar M has gone steadily downhill since you quit."

"So I hear, but it wasn't doin' too good when I worked there."

"That's because he never listened to you. I will." She glanced down at her bare fingers. She had taken off David's ring, but had none to commemorate her so brief marriage to Pancho. "I don't mean to mislead you, Last. I intend to learn everything I can about ranching and to take an active part," she continued, dragging her thoughts once again from the past.

"It bein' you, Miss Annie, I wouldn't expect nuthin' else, but just you remember, some of that active part of yours, it's gotta be the bookkeepin', 'cause I ain't a man for writin' nor for figurin' neither. I sure hope you are, or else we're in trouble afore we even git started."

"Miz McAuliffe," said the little maid, popping her head in the door, "Mr. Barnett's here to see you."

"Show him in, Lilyanne," said Anne. "Maybe we can get everything settled now and be on our way. I know just where I want to bury Pancho. There's a big oak—"

"Sure you ain't gonna bury him up there with the pigs? I don't think he'd like that."

"We have more than one now?"

"Damned pigs're all over the place. The one he brought home was a sow an' dropped a litter."

Anne smiled broadly. "Trust Pancho to find me the perfect pig. But you needn't fret, Last. I don't mean to bury him in the oak grove. I meant by that lone tree up on the hill. There ought to be a carpet of wild flowers up there by now. Don't you think he'd like it?"

"Well, I never heard Pancho say nuthin' about flowers, but maybe he would, seein' as you cain't bury him under a poker table."

"Oh, Last." Anne giggled. "I can't believe you made me laugh about his funeral, but then Pancho and I were both laughing when he died." She blinked back tears.

CHAPTER

Twenty-Two

"He were a good man to work for," said Bobby Ambrose solemnly. "Leastwise when he didn't want me to be foreman."

"An' as good a poker player as I ever seen," said Jocko, by way of eulogy.

Anne, weeping for Pancho beneath her black veils, scattered wild flowers on his grave.

"And fast with a gun. He was real fast with a gun," said Hap.

"Amen," agreed Last, and they all turned away to walk down the hill toward the ranch house.

"What happened to the gambler?" Anne asked.

"Why, Pancho killed him," said Last. "Even after he took a bullet in the belly, he shot that gambler dead through the heart."

"Good," said Anne vindictively and then wrested her thoughts away from Pancho. "I guess we'd better make some plans now."

"Yes, ma'am. First thing, Bobby said he seen some

Bar M riders nosin' around down by the herd. Made him kinda nervous, seein' as what happened to Homer Teasdale."

Anne frowned. "I can't believe it. The colonel's hired more rustlers?"

"No way a tellin', but we know he ain't the best judge of men."

"Maybe we should camp out with the herd to be on the safe side."

"What's this we? You ain't campin' out by no herd."

"I don't see why not."

"You're with child, Miss Anne. Cain't have a woman with child sleepin' rough by a noisy herd of cattle, an' if'n we was to pitch you a tent, them rustlers might notice," said Last dryly. "No, ma'am, you better stay home. I'll leave Bobby at the ranch house with you, just in case someone unfriendly comes by."

"Rustlers aren't going to bother with the ranch house," said Anne.

"They might figger, you bein' a woman owner, they could scare you off easy. You 'fraid to stay at the house?"

"Certainly not," said Anne indignantly, "and I don't need Bobby to look after me either." Then she caught Last grinning. "Aren't you the clever one?" she muttered. "Just for that, you get to slaughter one of the hogs."

"Not me!" exclaimed Last. "Me an' the boys, we don't know nuthin' 'bout hogs. You wanna do anything with them hogs, you'll have to figger it out yourself. Read one a them pamphlets you're always tellin' me about."

Behind them Hap was saying, "I just plainly hate hogs."

"Not me," said Jocko. "I like to eat 'em."

"Well, maybe we oughta put you to hog herdin'."

"If you two start squabbling again," warned Anne, "I

won't bake a pie from now to Christmas." The quarrel immediately subsided. "And I want a garden," she continued. "It's late but not too late, so who'll help with that?"

The cowboys behind them started to edge away. "Bobby, you kin dig Miss Annie's garden," decided the foreman.

"Ah, come on, Last. Why me?"

"'Cause while we're out lookin' for rustlers, you're gonna be back here protectin' Miss Annie, that's why."

"How come I'm the one gotta stay?"

"'Cause you're a pretty fair shot. Jocko cain't hit the broad side of a barn, an' Hap ain't much better."

"It seems to me you ought to have your best shot out by the herd," said Anne.

"We are gonna have our best shot out by the herd— me," said Last. "Now, I thought I was supposed to be your foreman. You gonna argue with me over ever' little thin'?"

"Of course not, Last." She smiled sweetly at him and, grabbing Bobby's arm, said, "Let's all get to work. You, Bobby, I'll show you where I want the garden." The two of them went off, Anne bubbling with plans, Bobby grumbling that he'd as soon dig a well as dig a garden.

"Do we need a well?" Anne asked.

In early June Anne woke to the sound of gunfire. She rolled her now cumbersome body from the bed, grasped her Winchester, and ran toward the door. Another shot rang out, followed by the high squeal of a pig, and her mouth tightened in lines of anger. Someone was shooting at her pigs. She slipped quickly out onto the porch and crept along in the shadows toward the sound of gunfire. *Be cautious*, she warned herself. *Wait till he's closer.*

It was a moonlit night, and a rider, coming fast, was silhouetted clearly, whereas she was hidden in the shadows of the overhang. She lifted the rifle carefully to her shoulder and followed his progress through the sights. He passed the bunkhouse first and fired into it. Well, the man wasn't one of hers. Bobby returned fire but missed. Anne led the rider, aimed for his head, hoping to hit him in the body, and squeezed off her shot. He yelled and fell out of the saddle. When he tried to rise, she shot him a second time. This one wasn't going to trial only to be let loose. Then she waited to see if he had companions.

"By gosh, ma'am," said Bobby, when they had both ventured out into the yard, "I don't know why you need me here. You're a better shot than I am."

"I just had a better angle on him," said Anne diplomatically. "Is he dead?"

"He is that."

"Good, drag him into the stable. You want a cup of coffee and a piece of pie when you finish?"

"Now, that sure sounds good." After disposing of the body, they trudged into the house, where Anne donned a robe over her voluminous nightgown and warmed up the coffee.

"You know what I've been thinking about?" she asked as they sat down to eat. "I'd like to try beekeeping."

"Beekeeping?" cried Bobby, obviously appalled. "You ever been stung by a bee?"

"Think how nice the honey would taste on flapjacks in the morning. I wake up every morning now thinking of honey."

"Yeah, well, you'll likely git over that after—ah— after your—ah—baby's born, an' me, I sure don' wanna be around no bees."

"Oh, I'd do the beekeeping," said Anne, wishing the men wouldn't all stammer and blush when her pregnancy came up. How did they think they got into the world? "There's nothing to beekeeping. You chop down a bee tree, lure the bees into your own hive and—"

"An' git yourself stung half to death."

"No, you don't. You wear veils."

"Veils?" She could see that Bobby was trying to picture himself in a veil.

"Like those widow's veils I wore for Pancho's funeral. Why, I can get years and years of use out of those even when I'm out of mourning."

"You gonna chop the tree down? 'Cause don't none of us have no veils."

"Well, that's a minor problem," said Anne. "We can work it out."

"Ain't nobody gonna like it, Miss Anne, a bunch a bees around here. Like to start stampedes an' stuff."

"Oh, Bobby, that's what you all said about the pigs, and look how successful they've been, which reminds me, I think that raider shot one of my pigs. You better go get it before some wild creature does. We'll butcher it tomorrow while the meat's still fresh."

"Ah, Miss Annie," groaned the cowboy, "you want me stumbling around in the dark lookin' for a dead pig?"

"Of course, and as for the bees, I think they're a wonderful idea. I have this pamphlet on beekeeping. It would be a real waste not to put it to use."

"I swear," grumbled Bobby, "I kin sure see why some folks think women shouldn't never be 'lowed to learn readin'."

Anne grinned. "Now you know that's nonsense, Bobby. I learned about pigs from a pamphlet."

"Yeah, an' I bet you read about blooded bulls in some book, too, an' I ain't enjoyin' bringin' in lady friends for that mean ole bull out in the pasture. He don't never act like I'm doin' him any favor. An' I didn't like puttin' up the smokehouse too much or diggin' the garden."

"Well, there are drawbacks to everything," said Anne philosophically. "Now if you could just go find my poor murdered pig, we'll be having fresh pork roast by the end of the week."

In late June Anne sat under the shade of the porch roof, rocking and shelling peas. Her garden was doing well for all Bobby's grumbling, not that he had anything to grumble about. She had done most of the work once he finished the digging, and she was suffering the consequences—a distressing sprinkle of freckles across her nose, even though she had been very careful about wearing a sunbonnet when she went outside.

Well, today was the day she had set aside for her freckles. Once the last man had ridden out, she went into the house to mix buttermilk and cornmeal, which she then plastered carefully onto her face. After that, she covered the whole thing with a stocking into which she had cut eye and mouth holes. The remedy couldn't fail to deal with her June crop of freckles; Gretchen Bannerman had stopped by to visit and given her the recipe, which the girl had had from her own mother, a fair-skinned German woman who suffered horribly from freckles.

Anne had been uneasy when Gretchen rode up, having feared that at any minute the girl would denounce her for that horrible incident with Sam Junior at the sporting house. Instead Gretchen wanted to hear about Anne's romantic, secret marriage to Pancho Tighe, which, much to Anne's surprise, had fluttered every female heart in Parker County once the news was spread by the hands at the Rocking T. Gretchen also brought messages from Sarah and Florence, who both offered to come for the birth of Anne's baby.

Again, Anne was uneasy. On the one hand, it was nice to know that she'd have help if the doctor didn't arrive in time, which he rarely did. On the other, suspicious Florence Bannerman might well realize that the dates didn't quite add up as they should. Anne doubted that her child would be late arriving, as would have been more convenient. She was now making up for her early slenderness by becoming huge, or so it seemed to her. Florence would likely think the child had been conceived when Pancho took her home from Sam Junior and Gretchen's wedding, which would protect Justin from gossip but not Anne. Well, there was no use worrying about it. Pancho had done his best for her.

In the meantime, she planned to have a lovely, lazy day, shelling peas and hand-stitching clothes for her baby. By the time the men returned at sundown, the stocking would be gone, the buttermilk and cornmeal washed away, and her freckles magically dispersed, if Mrs. Steinbrunner's time-honored recipe for freckle removal did its work. With that thought in mind, she smiled, and continuing to rock and shell her peas, stared contentedly at the dust motes drifting in the sunlight that now beat down from almost directly overhead into her ranch yard. It was a good life, she thought, and things were going well.

The night the unknown rider had come through and shot one of her pigs, the herd had also been hit but not driven off, and her men, who had been waiting in ambush, had killed two more outlaws. The rustlers had evidently thought her an easy mark. Well, they had learned differently. She and Last could protect the Rocking T.

The sheriff, coming out to investigate the raid, had addressed her as Mrs. Tighe. How strange it had seemed, since she'd never really been married to Pancho. She thought of him often, wondered if he'd approve of the things she was doing with the ranch. He'd probably have laughed at the garden, the pigs, and the bees. She had her own hive now. Bees weren't any problem to work with, not if you were a widow. You just put on your Sunday best and got to it.

And what would he think of little Edward—or Edwina? She laid her hand against the curve of her belly, which seemed so enormous, and felt the child as it stirred. Pancho had found a way to protect her and the baby. Maybe Justin had had a hand in it, too. Since she'd had no word from him, she'd never been able to ask how instrumental he'd been in Pancho's dying actions.

Her eyes drifted lazily over the horizon as the peas continued to fall into her pan. A rider. She squinted against the sun. None of the men were supposed to return before nightfall. Carefully, she laid her pan aside and reached for her Winchester. Would they attack her in broad daylight? she wondered. Did they know she was by herself?

The rider came steadily toward the ranch house until finally she rose and moved further back into the shade of the roof, bringing the rifle to her shoulder. Then her breath caught in her throat. It was Justin. She recognized his blood bay. She recognized that powerful, familiar body in the saddle, although his face was obscured by his hat. Then last and saddest, she recognized his grim expression when he took his hat off to her. Whatever he was coming for, she thought unhappily, it was not a friendly mission. But still, she wouldn't greet him by pointing a rifle at him. She lowered it to the rough, wooden floor of the porch and waited.

"Why did you put your gun down?" he asked disapprovingly as he drew level with her.

"Because I knew who it was," she replied. Her legs were trembling as she went back to her rocking chair and resumed her pea shelling. "What can I do for you, Justin?" she asked.

He dismounted, threw his reins around the hitching post, and climbed the steps, looking grimmer than ever. But when he had come under the shade of the porch roof, he stared at her in amazement and then began to laugh. "Anne, what the devil?"

Confusion swept over her. Why was he laughing?

"What's that on your face?" he demanded.

Then she remembered, and her hands flew to the stocking that covered her buttermilk and cornmeal mixture. What a fool she must look, she thought miserably, and fled into the house, where she ripped the stocking off and splashed water onto her face until she had washed away her freckle-removing preparation. When she returned, she found Justin sitting in the second rocking chair.

"What was that?" he asked, grinning. "Have you decided to become a lady bandit?"

"It was a preparation to make freckles disappear," she muttered resentfully.

Justin's grin widened. "I'm afraid it didn't work."

Anne touched her nose and burst into tears.

"Annie," said Justin in surprise, "it's nothing to cry about. Here now, sweetheart." He was out of the chair in an instant and wrapping her, swollen belly and all, in his arms. "Don't cry. Are you feeling ill?"

"Why are you being so nice? You rode up looking like a thundercloud."

"I suppose I did," said Justin, "but there never was a woman like you for overcoming my bad humor and in the damnedest ways. I come riding along, drowning in my own spleen, and there you sit with a stocking over your head. How can a man stay angry with a woman like that? Now, sit down." He put her gently into her rocking chair. "Can I get you some water or something?"

"No, of course not. What are you doing here, Justin? After the way you treated me when we last met, I thought I'd never see you again. Oh!" Suddenly she thought she knew. "It must be about the boarding house. Isn't Maggie running it to your satisfaction? I did the best I could to train her."

"Everything's fine at Panther House, Anne. She's not the manager you were, but it's still making money, in which, incidentally, I think you should have a share."

"I don't want a share," said Anne sullenly. "I'm

getting along very well, thank you."

"So I heard. I'm glad Tighe did the right thing."

"You don't look particularly glad. What was your part in that?" she snapped. "He said before he died that you'd come to visit him."

"I did," said Justin. "If he was going to keep seeing you, I thought he should take responsibility for you and the child."

"Well, he did," said Anne. "He did the best he could."

"I know, Anne. I'm sorry he was killed. Obviously, he cared for you in his way, although he wasn't man enough to do the right thing while—"

"Shut up!" said Anne furiously. "Pancho did care for me, which is more than you—"

"Go on," said Justin when she stopped herself. "More than I what?"

"Nothing." Anne drew a shaky breath. She'd almost told him, and she didn't want him to know. "So why are you here?"

He was still staring at her.

"Has Penelope decided she wants me to keep house for her again?" Anne asked sarcastically. As her pregnancy advanced and her discomfort increased, she found herself more and more often thinking bitterly of Penelope, pampered to death out there in her beautiful house because she was carrying Justin's acknowledged child, a child she didn't even want.

"Penelope doesn't change," said Justin wearily, "except to get more difficult as her time draws nearer."

Anne could believe that. She could just imagine how selfish, vain Penelope would react to the last months of pregnancy. In fact, she shuddered to think what would happen when the woman actually went into labor. "Is her health good?" Anne asked politely, wanting to snarl at Justin instead of showing courteous interest in his wife. He must have got Penelope pregnant not a month after Anne herself conceived his child.

"Seems to be. And your health? How are you, Annie?"

She shrugged. "I'm fine. We're prospering here." She almost wished he'd go away.

"So I've heard. What I came to talk to you about was the night rider you had."

"Are you investigating the rustling again?" she asked.

"I am."

Well, she might have known he wasn't here out of any personal concern for her, not after he thought she'd been consorting with Pancho.

"In fact, we've formed a cattlemen's association to try to deal with it."

"And you've come to ask me to join, or don't they accept women owners?"

"I don't know," said Justin, looking surprised. "But there's no reason why they shouldn't. You weren't an owner when we first organized, but I'll give you a copy of the rules if you want to join."

"Of course," said Anne. "I'd join any organization set up to protect us from these thieves."

"Unfortunately, your stepfather doesn't feel the same," Justin muttered.

"I suppose that comes as no great surprise."

"Have you had more trouble with him?"

"No, Last is running both ranches now. The colonel pretty much ignores him since he's under court order not to interfere."

"I'm glad to hear it. Now tell me about the attack."

"Well, a man came riding through here and shot one of my pigs," said Anne.

"Ah, one of your pigs and died for his trouble, I hear."

"That's right. I shot him," said Anne, giving Justin a challenging glance. Justin seemed surprised at her hostility. He obviously didn't think *she* had any reason to be angry with *him*. She sighed. Well, why should he? He didn't know he'd fathered two children. "Besides the one I shot, I had men staked out near the herd. They got two of the four trying to run my cattle off."

"The sheriff told me you made sketches of the dead men."

"That's right."

"I'd like to see them."

Anne rose with slow care and walked into the house. Justin, watching her, thought how much more courageous she was than his own wife, who was no longer even willing to get out of her bed unless she had the opportunity to buy something, and did nothing but complain from morning till night, so much so that no one ever willingly went down the hall that led to her room.

If he'd waited just a year, just a half year, he could have had Anne. Instead he'd let himself be enticed by a beautiful face with no character behind it, and now he had to spend the rest of his life with Penelope. Well, at least he'd have their child. One. He doubted that he'd ever get another from her. He and Calliope had to watch her all the time to keep her from doing things to endanger the one she carried. Damn woman!

Anne returned and handed him the sketches.

"Do these look like the men?" he asked.

"I think so," she replied.

"A handy talent," Justin remarked as he studied the faces.

"Just one of the many boring, fashionable arts a young lady is expected to master," said Anne dryly. "I was surprised to find a practical use for it. Embroidery and piano playing certainly haven't helped me much in defending the Rocking T."

"Speaking of defense," he said, glancing around, "you're not here by yourself, are you?"

"Yes, I am," she bristled. "We've had no trouble

since that one incident. I keep my gun handy, and I'm as good a shot as any of them, better than most."

Justin smiled. "Another of your fashionable talents?" Then his smile faded, and he said, "You still shouldn't be here alone. What about your neighbors?"

"I've only seen Gretchen Bannerman."

"Good Lord, she didn't find out about the baby?"

"No, she came because she thought my marriage to Pancho was so romantic." Justin frowned. "I didn't tell her that losing two husbands, shot over cards, isn't very romantic. She also said Sarah and Florence would come for my confinement. So except for Gretchen and the sheriff and the rustler, I haven't seen anyone but my own people since I brought Pancho's body home."

"It seems to me that Sam Bannerman might offer you some help beyond that of his women," Justin muttered. "Still, at least you'll have someone with you when your time comes. I don't know a neighbor who'd willingly help Penelope. I'd probably have to deliver my own child, even in Palo Pinto, if it weren't for Calliope."

How embittered he looked, thought Anne sadly. But she was too. "Tell me about the cattlemen's association," she urged, longing to keep him with her, realizing how foolish she was to let resentment color what little time they had together. What did it matter why he'd come? He was here. She kept him talking for an hour or more about the rules the association had made to control roundups and cattle drives so as to thwart the rustlers who plagued the whole area.

"Would you care to stay for the midday meal?" she asked when he seemed to have run out of things to say.

Justin hesitated, then grinned at her boyishly. "Did you know you have the best creek for fishing in the county? Homer and I often fished it on a hot day, as much for the pleasure of sitting under the trees as anything."

"I didn't know," said Anne. "I've been so busy, I

hadn't even thought of fishing."

"Come along then," Justin coaxed. "I'll hitch up your buckboard."

"All right," she agreed eagerly. "I'll pack a lunch." She ran inside, thinking that for a few hours she could pretend they were a courting couple instead of two ex-lovers caught in a hopeless tangle of their own making.

"How beautiful you look," he said later as he helped her onto the high seat, his smile warm and approving.

"Oh, Justin, how can you say that? I'm as fat as one of my own pigs." Her courtship fantasy went flying as she realized how foolish it had been. She'd be delivering a baby in not much more than a month, and she felt as if it might be the day after tomorrow.

He laughed. "I take it your pigs are thriving. What other innovations have you brought to the Rocking T?"

"Well, you may laugh, but my hands appreciate my innovations once they get through complaining about any part they have to take. They don't like pigs, of course, but they do like bacon and ham. They all complained about my beekeeping."

"You're raising bees!"

"Yes, and everyone enjoys the honey," she snapped defensively. "Who better than a widow? All the veils protect me."

"You're always in mourning for someone," he muttered. "I've never seen you wearing anything but black."

"And I've put beds into the bunkhouse at the Bar M, which means we have better riders and they're not always leaving us, and I sent the cook Pancho hired over there so Sissie isn't cooking for them."

"I'm sure they appreciate that. Do you ever see her, or is she too busy with her social life to visit her sister?"

"The colonel won't let her come, and I'm not welcome in their house," said Anne miserably.

"Sweetheart, I'm sorry."

Her chin rose, and she added, "And of course, I have a garden. It's doing well. Then I followed your example and leased a portion of my land over on Bushy Creek."

"You rented our place?" He looked as if she'd betrayed him.

"Yes, Justin, I did," she snapped.

"Well, of course. Why not?"

But he didn't look happy about it. Well, why should he care? You'd think he'd want to forget all that.

"Who did you rent it to?"

"To a farmer in return for a corn crop."

"For your pigs, I presume."

"For my pigs, and for my chickens when I get them, and to make hominy. I've plenty of use for corn." Justin pulled up the horses and helped her down from the wagon. "And I've had the men dig me a cellar to keep lard and sausages and such, and honey, preserves, pickles and canned fruit, and, of course, later I can store potatoes and turnips in the cellar. Next month I'm going to start drying peaches."

"I wish you were my wife," he muttered.

"Why?" she asked dryly. "Because I'm thrifty?"

"No, because I love you. Because you're the kind of woman I should have married."

"Oh, Justin." Her heart melted toward him. "Let it go," she murmured unhappily. "It's no use speaking of what can never be." Still, it gave her joy to hear him say he still loved her. She'd doubted it again and again. "At least, soon you'll have a child of your own to love," she said consolingly.

"Yes, and so will you."

"And so will I," Anne agreed, staring into the waters of the creek as they bubbled past the tree under which he'd seated her. *Your child*, she thought. She raised her eyes to his. "Are we going to fish?"

"Let's eat first," he replied, lifting down the picnic basket.

"Well, that's a sluggard's plan," said Anne. "Eat first

and work later? How do I know once you've eaten my picnic lunch, you won't want to take a nap, and I'll have to do the fishing?"

He set the basket aside and dropped down beside her, threading his fingers into her hair. "Anne, love, I can think of other things I'd rather do than eat or fish." His mouth closed gently over hers before she could even draw breath. She was amazed at how quickly he could stir her passion. Even as close to term as she was, she still wanted him. He was pulling her down into the grass with him before she could protest.

"Don't you want to hear about my garden?" she asked rather desperately.

"Not really," he mumbled.

"I've planted Irish potatoes and English peas." His lips were exploring her neck. "I've set out sweet potato slips," she informed him, closing her eyes against the delicious seduction of his mouth.

"Anne," he groaned, "will you be quiet and kiss me back?"

"Oh, Justin, don't torture me. You know how I feel about this, and anyway, I'm hardly an object for romantic attention, not in my present condition."

"To me you are, love." He leaned over and laid his lips against the curve under which their child lay. "Do you know, sometimes I wish I were Pancho Tighe?"

"He's dead, Justin."

"Yes, but he gave you a child. That would be a thing worth dying for."

"Justin, don't. Don't talk that way." Anne didn't think she could stand to hear another word. She was so tempted to tell him that the child she carried was his, but she realized sadly that he might not believe her and that she would only add to his burdens, which she didn't want to do. Telling Justin the truth could only cause more grief.

"I didn't mean to make you sad, Anne," he whispered, rolling away from her reluctantly.

They ate their picnic lunch, fished with willow poles, catching perch and sunfish, but Justin wouldn't stay to eat them.

"I'd best move on," he murmured after they'd driven back. "I don't want to cause talk when your life is finally straightened out."

He unhitched her buckboard and stabled her horse, bade her good-bye in the ranch yard with a sweet, light kiss, and rode away before her men had even returned from their work.

Anne's eyes followed his disappearing silhouette with such a sad yearning. It was so unfair. Justin would not be with her when their child was born. He'd be with Penelope who didn't want a child. He'd never know the joy that Anne took in their baby. Nor, although he seemed bent on ignoring her scruples, would they ever make love again, not while he was married to Penelope.

Well, well. She turned and mounted the steps, sat down in her rocking chair, and once again began to shell peas for dinner.

CHAPTER

Twenty-Three

Anne straightened slowly with her hand at the small of her back. All day she had been halving and pitting peaches, then spreading them out on the drying racks in the hot sun. When finally she had finished, she wiped the sweat from her forehead, then moved her hands to the full curve of her stomach. The baby was kicking again. In fact, she sometimes thought she had a herd of babies in there. Heaven knows, she'd grown big enough to stable a herd. No concealing her condition now. Pancho had made a respectable woman of her in the nick of time, although his method of doing it had been sadly drastic.

Curiously she turned toward the oak grove and an ominous, panic-stricken chorus of squeals. The last thing she needed was pigs among her peaches, but good grief, there they were, with Hap riding behind, shouting as if he had in mind to cause a pig stampede right through her yard.

"Stop that!" she yelled at him. Her warning was

futile. Obviously he couldn't hear her over the sound of his own shouts and the squeals and grunts of the pigs that were heading this way. She fired her rifle into the air to get his attention, but by then it was too late. Although most of the animals veered off toward the trough where she fed them corn from time to time, one big sow, obviously not too bright, was heading straight for the peaches.

"Hap," she screamed, "turn her!"

His mouth fell open when he saw what was happening, but realization came too late. The sow barrelled straight between two of the drying racks, knocking both over, sending hundreds of peach halves tumbling into the dust. A minute later Hap pulled his horse up in front of her.

"Miss Annie, I didn't mean to—"

"What did you think you were doing?" she demanded.

"Them pigs, Miss Annie. I caught 'em headin' toward the herd."

"I don't believe it," said Anne.

"We warned you that one hog could cause a stampede. Why, if a whole slew of 'em got in with the cattle—"

"You did this for spite!" Anne accused him.

"No, ma'am, I—"

"Look at my peaches! They're all over the ground. Filthy. Hours of work."

"But, Miss Annie—"

"You dolt! You did this because you don't like pigs. Well, you get down off that horse, and you wash every one of those peaches, you hear me? You set up my racks again and wash the dirt off every single peach."

"Listen, Miss Annie," said Hap, flushed bright red, "I didn't hire on to be no peach washer, no more'n I hired on to be no pig herder."

"Wash!" said Anne, cutting him off, and she leveled her rifle straight at him.

"You wouldn't shoot me," said Hap confidently. "Would you?"

"What the hell's goin' on here?" demanded Last, pulling his horse up beside them.

"He drove the pigs through my peaches, and now he won't wash the peaches off," Anne said, bursting into tears.

Last gave Hap a disgusted look. Then he turned back to Anne. "Now, Miss Annie, no need to cry. I think what you better do is get on back in the house an' have yourself a nice nap."

"I don't have time for a nap," said Anne, her sobs subsiding into sniffles. "I have too much to do."

"Ain't nuthin' you got to do won't wait till tomorrow. You're all wore out. That's your problem."

"I am not."

"Course you are. Hell, you're carryin' the biggest baby ever known to man."

"That's a terrible thing to say, Last." She peered down at her stomach. "Do I really look that bad?"

"You look fine, Miss Annie, but big. Real big."

She started to cry again.

Last dismounted hurriedly, put a dusty arm around her shoulders and began to urge her toward the porch. "You're gonna have yourself a nice nap, Miss Annie, while me an' stupid here look after your peaches."

"What about supper?"

"As soon as Hap finishes with the peaches, he'll fix it."

"I don't know how to cook," said Hap. "An' I ain't gonna learn. I'm quittin'."

"You quit if you wanna, but you do it after you've taken care of Miss Annie's peaches an' after supper."

"What about them pigs?" asked Hap sullenly.

"I'll take care of the pigs," said Last. "That ought to make you happy. Now come along, Miss Annie. You're gonna have a long nap." He escorted her gently to the house, leaving behind a loudly grumbling Hap.

"I guess I never apologized for runnin' them pigs in among your peaches," said Hap, his face white with shock and pain.

"That's very gracious of you, Hap," murmured Anne, "but I still have to remove this bullet."

"Yes, ma'am. Is it gonna hurt much?"

"You want to have someone knock you out first?"

"I'll knock him out," offered Jocko.

"Hell you will," cried Hap. "I'll just bear it, ma'am."

"Fine, and you needn't worry, Hap. I'm not holding a grudge. In fact, I'm sorry for being so hard on you yesterday. I guess the hot weather and—and everything got to me."

"Yes, ma'am," said Hap, trying not to stare at the 'everything' that swelled her black dress as she leaned over him, examining the wound where a bullet had lodged in his thigh. "I just wish I coulda shot that feller afore he got the bull, steada after."

"I do too," said Annie, sighing for the loss of her one blooded bull. "Now you boys will have to hold Hap down while I probe for this bullet. Want a drink of whiskey before we get at it, Hap?"

"That'd go down good."

So they fed Hap a long drink, and Anne went to work. Much faster than she had expected, she managed to dig the bullet from Hap's thigh with an instrument from her surgical kit. Hap was pale and shaking, but he hadn't made a sound, and Anne, smiling at him, murmured to Jocko, "Now I'll take that whiskey."

"You gonna have a drink?" asked Jocko, surprised. "I 'member the last time you done that, Miss Annie. You didn't feel too good the next day."

"It's not for me," she replied, and she tipped the bottle right into the wound. Hap howled and shot up into a sitting position. "That's to keep down the infection," she explained and put the bottle into his shaking hand. "Have another sip, Hap."

"Yes, ma'am." Trembling, he lay back down with the bottle clutched against his chest. "I wouldn'a yelled. It just took me by surprise."

Anne nodded, feeling exceedingly discouraged. They hadn't had any trouble at all in July until this. She packed up her surgical kit, said, "I'll be down to see you later in the evening, Hap," and walked back to the house.

"Good heavens," said Henry Barnett, his eyes widening at the sight of her girth. Anne flushed. "Forgive me. That was neither tactful nor gentlemanly," added the lawyer, his poise shaken for the only time Anne could remember. "It's just that I hadn't realized you were with child."

Anne wondered if he believed the story about a secret wedding in December to Pancho Tighe. How she hated the lying! "Sit down, won't you, Henry. I'm surprised to see you here."

"I had a number of matters to take up with you and as I had business in Weatherford . . ." He tapped his fingers together and stared at them fixedly.

Anne sank gratefully into her rocker, taking up a palm fan she kept close by. "I'll swear it's hotter every day. August is worse than July was. Can I get you a drink?"

"Anne, why don't you let me do it?"

She laughed. "I must look even more cumbersome than I feel."

"Well, perhaps, but you're a lovely woman all the same. Being with child enhances a woman's beauty, in my opinion."

"Aren't you a flatterer," she replied dryly.

"No, I remember, as if it were yesterday, when my wife . . ." He stopped, his eyes bleak. "Well, her beauty did her no good. Our child was stillborn." He fetched them both cool water, then settled down beside her again.

"First, Mr. Tighe's will has gone through the courts, and I've brought you the deed to the Rocking T. Then I have this draft on Van Zandt and Tidball, several as a matter of fact. This particular one represents the remainder of Mr. Tighe's estate."

He passed the paper over, and Anne drew in a surprised breath. "My goodness, is this all from playing poker?"

Henry chuckled. "No, I believe that much of it's the proceeds from a herd that was sent up the trail, commissioned to Harte Brothers."

"I didn't realize that Pancho did business with Justin."

"Actually, your foreman signed the contract with David Harte. Now these two drafts"—he handed them to Anne—"represent the proceeds from Bar M cattle, which Harte Brothers bought outright. One is your share from your half of the Bar M. The other represents your half from Colonel Morehead's share."

Anne stared at the third draft. "That doesn't leave them much to live on."

"I hardly think you need feel sorry for the colonel."

"It wasn't the colonel I was worrying about. It's my sister. Have you heard anything of her?"

"No, I haven't."

Anne sighed. "I wish he'd let her come to visit, but I suppose that's too much to hope for."

At her invitation Henry stayed for the midday meal and joined her on the porch afterwards when she'd expected him to start home.

After a long silence, he said quietly, "I'd always thought I'd never marry again. In fact, I believe I said that to you once."

Anne looked at him questioningly.

"However, I find that I'm lonely, and I wonder if you'd consider . . ." He hesitated.

Anne felt nothing but astonishment at what she suspected might be coming.

"I wonder if you'd consider marrying me, Anne. I realize our acquaintance is not of long duration, but I must say I have a great admiration for you, and I think we'd do well together as husband and wife."

"Henry," said Anne, "I'm—I'm about to have a child. My goodness . . ."

"A child needs a father," he said quietly.

She sighed and wondered when life was going to stop presenting her with surprises and problems to solve. "Henry, I'm very touched and very honored—"

"But not favorable to the idea," he finished for her.

"No, I guess I'm not, although I'm probably a foolish woman to say no. I'm sure you'd be a fine husband and a good father, but I just couldn't marry you."

"Perhaps you're in love with someone else," he suggested.

Anne swallowed. Henry was too smart by far. Had he guessed how she felt about Justin? Had he been testing her with that proposal? "I've lost two husbands. That's enough," she replied, hoping to end the conversation.

"It's all right, Anne," said Henry. "You're under no obligation to explain yourself to me. It was perhaps a foolish idea on my part anyway. I know that I am too old for you, and that I can't, in truth, offer you a great romance." He sighed, and Anne realized that, through her and her child, he had hoped to reclaim a little of what he had lost with the deaths of his own wife and child.

"I suppose I thought that we had both had our time of romantic love and could live together comfortably on affection and respect," he explained wryly, "but you're much younger than I and can hope for more than that."

"I don't know that I have such hopes anymore, Henry, but again, I do thank you." His proposal brought home to her all that she would never have again, and a great sadness replaced the measure of content, hard won, that had settled over her as the birth of her baby approached.

"I'll bid you good-bye then, Anne, but let me say one more thing."

She stiffened. Was he going to tell her he knew she had refused him because of Justin?

"I think you should make every effort to avoid your stepfather."

The colonel? She almost gasped with relief.

"The man makes me uneasy."

"But I never see him," Anne replied, bewildered. Nor did she expect to.

"I'm relieved to hear it. Don't let anything, even your love for your sister, convince you to approach him. I'm a good judge of character, and Colonel Morehead, in my opinion, is a man without compunction when his own interests are at stake."

Anne was rather surprised at Henry's strong statement.

Anne had awakened the last three mornings feeling full of energy. Although Last insisted that she was too far along for such activities, she had dragged a reluctant Bobby with her two days in a row to scavange for berries, grapes, and plums. Today she had sent him back to cowboying while she set huge pots of fruit to bubbling on the stove and readied glass jars to receive the results.

The baby, according to her calculations, was due any day, any minute. Not that she was in a hurry. The later it came, the more likely it was to be accepted as Pancho's, so she couldn't very well let Last know how close to term she was. Consequently, when he'd gone on and on at breakfast about the dangers of leaving her alone, she'd shooed him and the men off to their work, reminding him that when she went into labor, she had only to fire three shots. They'd hear and could come back. Finally, he'd grunted, given in again, and off they'd gone.

Anne rather liked having the place to herself, and she hummed and sang as she stirred sugar into the fruit and daydreamed about having her own baby. How wonderful that would be. After their mother died, she'd raised Sissie and loved it, just as she'd love bringing up this child. And this one she'd have all to herself when it was tiny as well as when it was older. Would it be a boy or a girl? Pancho had wanted a boy. She imagined Justin would too if he knew he was about to be a father. And the way the baby kicked—She chuckled and glanced down. She could even see that little foot stirring the black fabric of her gown through the wall of her womb.

"Just turn around real slow, and don't reach for your gun," said a voice behind her.

Anne froze. How had he gotten in without her hearing him? She hadn't been listening. That's how! She'd been singing and daydreaming like a thoughtless fool.

"Hands over your head and turn around real slow."

She did as she was told, turning away from the stove, saying, "If it's money you're after, I—" Then she stopped in horror. "Colonel?" For beside the shaggy man in her doorway stood her stepfather.

"You stay out in the yard and keep watch till we're through here, Haynes," called the stranger. There was an answer from outside.

Three of them, she thought. She no longer wore her pistol; she couldn't get the belt around her middle. And the rifle was over by the table. "Colonel, it's been awhile since I've seen you," she said, trying to put a brave face on fear, which was hard to do when that rough-looking man with his dirty, unkempt hair was holding a large bore pistol on her.

"This ain't what you'd call a social visit, little lady," he said, "but since you mentioned money, maybe you better tell me where it is."

Anne gulped. "There's a little in a locked box in my bedroom. It's under the bed." It was hard to keep her voice from trembling. Why was her stepfather here with that gunman? Well, as the man had said, it wasn't a friendly visit. She only had to look at the colonel to see that. Henry had been right in warning her to stay away from him. How she wished that she could.

"You best take care of your business," said the man. "We don't want to stick around too long, no longer than it takes to shoot her an' take whatever money she's got."

Shoot her? Anne's heart began to pound. "That wouldn't be a very good idea," she said, trying to sound calm and reasonable. "People would guess who did it."

The man who was rifling through her desk laughed. "Why, they'd just think it was the rustlers, right, Colonel?"

"I'm afraid you brought this on yourself, Anne," said the colonel. "If you'd just stayed at the Bar M—"

"You made that impossible."

"Not impossible at all. I only disciplined you as you deserved. Even after that if you hadn't got nosy about David's money, things would have been all right."

"In other words, I should have allowed you to take the inheritance without protest?"

The colonel shrugged. "I had need of the money; you had none. After all, you were married to the gunfighter. You could have stayed with him."

"That still doesn't give you the right to steal from me."

"No matter," said the colonel. "Now I'll have it all."

"By the look of her, you're not a day too soon neither," said the other man. "If she'd a dropped that baby afore you killed her, you'da had to kill the young 'un too, an' that really would look suspicious. Now you kin inherit both ranches with one bullet."

"You're no blood kin of mine," cried Anne, beginning to panic. "You won't inherit anything."

"Sissie will," said the colonel, "and I can handle Sissie."

Anne tried to shake off the nightmare horror of her situation. She couldn't just stand here and let them kill her.

"I'm goin' in to look fer that strongbox. Now you quit talkin' an' shoot her, Colonel. Course, I know you'd rather I did it, but you're the one gettin' the money, not me."

He walked into Anne's bedroom, and her mind began to work frantically. Could she dive for the rifle? No, the colonel would shoot her first. She had to distract him, and fast. "If you shoot, my crew will hear you and come back."

"Oh, I doubt it," said the colonel. "But what if they do? We'll be gone."

He was coming toward her even now, to make sure, presumably, that he didn't miss his shot. Like Pancho, he must know that a pistol was better within eight feet. Realizing that she had but a second or two left, Anne leapt sideways, even as his shot rang out, grasped the pot of bubbling preserves, and flung them at his head. His scream cut the air, high-pitched and agonized, as she dove toward the table and caught up the rifle before she fell. *Oh Lord*, she thought, when her body hit the floor, *the baby*. She had forgotten the baby. The colonel continued to scream as boiling plums, which had hit his face and chest, now began to run down his body. And her hands! She had to blink back tears, for she'd burned her hands when she grasped the pot of preserves, and holding the rifle, her only protection, was painful.

"What the hell?" cried the man in her bedroom.

She already had her sights on the door and pulled the trigger when he came into view. It was a good shot. She saw the blood spread on his chest.

"Jesus, Colonel," cried the man outside, "can't you put another shot into her and stop that screamin'?"

Anne edged herself around the table. She still had

one more to deal with, no two. The colonel had
dropped his gun and was feeling for it on the floor
where he had fallen. She snapped a shot toward him
and hit his arm. Now the man outside. Would he come
in? Or would she have to go after him? The colonel's
screams had dribbled off into moans, and Anne, who
before had had only the condition of her hands to
contend with, now had a huge pain blossoming in her
back, so overwhelming a sensation that she could
hardly think.

Concentrating with difficulty, she tried to evaluate
her situation. The first one was dead, as far as she could
tell. The colonel seemed to be disabled, but she
couldn't afford to ignore him lest he try for that gun
again. And the man outside. God, she wished he'd
come in. She could hit him in the doorway if only he
would. Because she was going into labor, and if he
caught her during a contraction, he'd have the advantage instead of the other way around.

"Zeb?" called the voice from outside.

She couldn't answer for Zeb.

"Colonel?"

She heard the man's footsteps, hesitant across the
porch.

"Zeb?"

Agonizingly, she raised the rifle and sighted at the
doorway. Then she saw his head in the window and
snapped off a shot. There was silence. Had she hit him
or not? The pain in her back was coming again. She
caught her lower lip in her teeth to keep from groaning.
One right after the other as if she were about to deliver.
In falling, had she hurt the baby? Something was
wrong. And her water had broken. She could hear
nothing from outside, no sound, no movement, but the
colonel was still moaning. If the other one was sneaking
up on her, maybe she couldn't hear because of the
colonel.

Should she use another bullet to stop him? How

many had she used already? Zeb, the colonel, the one
outside. Three. The pain hit her again, and she gasped.
Three bullets. If she'd been able to laugh, she would
have. That was the signal to Last that she was in labor.
Three shots. *Hurry up*, she thought desperately and
edged herself into a more comfortable position, her
back propped against the table leg. *Hurry up, Last,
Bobby, someone.*

It seemed hours to her, hours and hours before she
heard hoofbeats pounding toward the house. And what
if it wasn't Last? What if the colonel's men had hit the
herd at the same time? As they'd done before? What if
these were rustlers coming into the yard, and she with
only three bullets left and the agony blooming again in
her back and belly? She panted for breath against it,
just as she'd always told the women she delivered to do.

"Miss Annie. Miss Annie, are you all right?"

She couldn't even answer, not from the throes of the
contraction.

"Who the hell is that?" She heard Last's voice.

"Never seen him before, but he's shot bad," said
Jocko. Their boots were on the porch.

"Miss Annie?"

"I'm here," she said, allowing her painful grasp on
the rifle to loosen even as the contraction receded so
that she could speak.

"God help us!" said Last. "What happened to him?"
He was looking at the colonel, who was curled up on the
floor, moaning.

"I threw the plums at him."

"So you did." Last had to turn his head away from
the sight of his former employer. "And the other one?"

"Shot him," said Anne. "Get the doctor."

Last used the toe of his boot to roll over the one
named Zeb. "Good shot," he said. "Fella's dead."

"Last," she cried desperately, "the baby's coming.
Get help."

Last looked startled, but only for a second. "Jocko,

catch Hap. Send him to the Bannermans' for Miss
Florence and Miss Sarah. You head on into town for
Dr. Waller. Tell Bobby to scour 'round to see if there's
anyone else out there gunnin' for us."

"What about Miss Anne?" asked Jocko.

"I'll take care of Miss Anne till you all get back with
help."

"Yes, sah." The black man holstered his gun, and
almost immediately the hoofbeats of his horse
drummed away from the ranch yard.

"Now, Miss Anne," said Last gently, "I'm gonna
carry you on into your bed."

"I'm too heavy, Last. What if you throw your back
out?"

"Well, maybe you're right. I ain't as young as I used
to be." He bent and lifted her to her feet. "Can you
walk?" She nodded. "Just skirt on around here," he
directed, leading her past the colonel's twitching body.

"Maybe you ought to do something about him."

"I'll worry about him once I've took care of you.
What started all this anyways?"

"He was here to kill me." She nodded toward the
colonel. "He figured on inheriting my land."

"By God, if that's the case," said Last, leading her
slowly toward the bedroom, "I think I'll leave him just
the way he is. I was thinkin' of puttin' him out of his
misery, but he don't deserve it. Here now, can you step
across this one?"

Anne nodded but then tripped over Zeb's crumpled
body and through the bedroom door. Last caught her.
"Here it comes again," she mumbled.

"All right, just a few more steps now. Here you go,
just lie down. That's a girl."

Anne could feel the sweat starting on her forehead.

"How close are they together?" he asked.

"Close," said Anne. "My water's broken."

"Lord, does that mean you're about to—to—"

"Don't worry," she gasped. "I'll tell you . . . what to

do. I've delivered . . . lots of babies."

"And so have I, Miss Anne, but they been baby cows. Still, I reckon it's pretty much the same, so don't you fret. I ain't gonna go off an' leave you, an' maybe if we're lucky, help will get here afore your baby does."

"I don't know," she gasped. "It's not the same . . . having one . . . as it is delivering one. I think I'd like to . . . get it over . . . as quickly as possible."

"Sure nuff, Miss Annie. Whatever you want. Now if you're gonna give me some instructions on human baby delivery, I'm listenin'."

CHAPTER

Twenty-Four

"I take your point, Mr. Cauley," said Florence Bannerman stiffly. "I was not implying that Mrs. Tighe and her husband had—ah—anticipated their wedding. Although the dates *were* questionable, I don't doubt the twins are premature. And such a dreadful thing to happen to poor Mrs. Tighe. You yourself did a creditable job under trying circumstances."

"You can say that again," grunted Last. "Miss Annie talked me through the first one, but then when we seen it wasn't over yet, we didn't know what the hell to think. She hadn't never delivered twins herself, an' cows don't generally drop no more than—"

"Really, Mr. Cauley, I do not consider the birth of a calf comparable to the birth of a human child."

"Well, there ain't that much difference," said Last.

"Mr. Cauley!"

"Reckon I better get back out to the herd if I ain't needed here. You're sure Miss Annie's all right?"

"If you won't take my word, you might at least take

Dr. Waller's. He said she was doing very well before he left to take Colonel Morehead and that other miscreant back to Weatherford with the sheriff's deputies. He even thought the babies were doing well, although I must say their size worries me."

"Well, if you got two, I guess you gotta split what space there is. Still, if anything happened to them babies, I reckon it would break Miss Annie's heart."

Sarah came in from Anne's bedroom and cried, "Hello there, Mr. Cauley. Would you like to step in to see the new mother? She's awake."

Suddenly all Last's impatience and anger with Florence Bannerman disappeared, and he smiled broadly. "Don't mind if I do, Miss Sarah."

"This way," said Sarah.

Florence gave a loud "Humph—ph!" and went over to the wood stove to tend dinner.

Last stepped hesitantly into Anne's bedroom as if he hadn't been there just the day before delivering her twin sons. "Well, Miss Annie," he said, hat in hand, shifting from foot to foot, "you're lookin'—ah—a heap thinner."

Anne laughed delightedly. "I imagine I am, Last, and I do owe you the most heartfelt thanks for taking such good care of me—of us. Won't you come look at the babies?"

Last edged over and peered down at the sleeping boys, one in the cradle Anne had had ready and one tucked up in a drawer from her bureau.

"Aren't they beautiful?" she asked, an ecstatic smile lighting her face. "Did you ever see such perfect children?"

"Well," said Last, staring at them, "they look a little red and wrinkled to me, same as they did yesterday."

"Last Cauley, shame on you! They're gorgeous. Sarah, if you'd just pass me one."

"Now, Anne," said Sarah, "let them sleep. You're forever wanting to cuddle them."

"Well, of course I am. Last, would you like to hold one?"

"Oh, no, ma'am," said Last, backing away. "I already held both of 'em. Once was enough."

Anne giggled. "You told me yourself there wasn't that much difference between a calf and a baby. If I handed you a calf, you wouldn't back up, would you?"

"Probably would," said Last. "Well, I'd best get back out to the herd. Glad to see you lookin' so good, Miss Annie."

"Come visit again after dinner," she called after him. "Maybe the babies will be awake then." She heard him mumble as he left and asked Sarah what he'd said.

"I think he said, 'That's what I'm afraid of.'"

"Oh, he just likes to act gruff. He's really embarrassed about having to deliver them himself, but I surely thank God he was here. I might have managed one on my own, but when the second one started coming, I just panicked. I didn't know what to do."

"Oh, Anne," said Sarah, "I don't know anyone who's had more terrible things happen to her and borne up under them more bravely. I still can't believe that the colonel came over here to—to—"

Anne frowned. "What happened to him?"

"The doctor took him back into town and says if he lives, he's going to be horribly disfigured, which serves him right. Anyway, he's going to hang."

Anne shuddered. "Sarah," she said, looking worried, "has anyone told Sissie?"

"I don't know," Sarah replied. "I hadn't even thought about Sissie. We'd best send a messenger to the Bar M."

"Tell her she must come and live with me now. She can't stay there by herself."

"I'll take care of it, Anne. Now just lie back. You need your rest."

"I don't have time to rest," said Anne. "I have things to do."

"You don't have to do a thing but stay right there in bed. Everything's being taken care of. Here." Sarah picked up one of the babies and shoved him into Anne's arms. "Maybe that one, whichever one he is, will keep you quiet."

"Oh, isn't he beautiful? This is David."

"I don't know how you can tell them apart. They look exactly the same to me."

"No, they don't," said Anne, running a bandaged finger gently over the one curl on young David's head. "Edward has a little birthmark on his shoulder, and his hair's different, and there's a slightly different shape to his eyes. Why it's as clear as anything which one is which."

"You're the only woman I've ever heard of who named her children after both of her husbands and did it at the same time."

Anne laughed happily. "Well, men always want sons. Somewhere they're probably happy to know they have namesakes. Look at his little fingers. Aren't they beautiful? And so tiny. The doctor did say they'd be all right, didn't he?"

"Yes, Anne. He said they seemed very healthy."

"Oh, thank God. Two babies. I'm so lucky. Now if I could just take these bandages off my hands so I could really touch them."

Sarah smiled. "All in good time, Anne. Dr. Waller said even your poor hands will be as good as new in a week or less."

"Anne," said Justin. His eyes were slow to adjust from the bright sunlight of the ranch yard to the dimness inside, but then he saw her in the rocking chair by the cold hearth, one child at her breast, the other asleep in the cradle beside her. She looked up, startled, when he said her name, then flushed and tried to detach the nursing baby and cover herself.

"Don't disturb him on my account," said Justin

softly as he strode across the room. "I've never seen a sight more beautiful." He smiled down at her. "Nor a woman more beautiful." He reached out his hand, touching her breast with one long finger and the infant's cheek with another. "Lucky baby," he murmured, and leaned over to press his lips gently against hers.

Her heart melted with love, and she tipped her head back, the better to receive his kiss, which deepened immediately. The tug of the child's mouth at her breast, the gentle penetration of Justin's kiss turned her whole body liquid with yearning, but then she must have tightened her arms around the baby because he released her nipple and whimpered. Anne sighed and turned her head away.

Justin, straightening, said, "I was in Weatherford when they brought the colonel in, and I couldn't believe it when I heard what had happened, what he tried to do." He laid his Stetson on the table and turned back to her, frowning. "I came straight out to see if you were all right, you and the babies."

"We're fine."

"I hope he hangs," said Justin roughly.

"After what I did to him"—Anne shivered—"he may welcome hanging."

"Nothing that happened to that man could be as bad as he deserves. Henry warned me that he was completely without conscience. I should have paid more attention."

"He told me the same thing in July," Anne agreed.

"How did you happen to see Henry that recently?" asked Justin, his eyes narrowed.

"He's my lawyer, too!" Anne snapped. "He was bringing me deeds and bank drafts." How like Justin. He couldn't say four words to her without taking offense because some man had tried to do her a good turn. The baby at Anne's breast had gone back to nursing, but the baby in the crib had begun to stir. She forgot her pique and said, with a slight smile, "I hope you don't mind a bit of hungry crying."

Justin too relented and glanced into the cradle. "May I hold him?"

"Of course," she replied, surprised, as she watched Justin lift her tiny son and cradle the baby against his chest. *How strange*, she thought. No other man at the Rocking T wanted to hold one of the babies. They all turned pale and backed off if she even suggested it, and yet Justin strode in and picked little Edward up as if he knew it was his own son he held, and the baby nestled right into his father's arms and stopped fussing. When Justin offered the child a finger, Edward grasped it and held on, and Justin smiled.

"He's a tiny thing, but he's got a grip on him." He glanced down at Anne. "Little, but very lucky to have you for his mother. I won't mention this to you again, Anne, because the memory of the whole thing must seem like a nightmare, but I did want to say that I've never known a woman more brave or resourceful than you, even my own mother. I'm not sure she could have got the best of three men bent on killing her."

"I guess God was looking out for me that day." David had stopped nursing, so she put him against her shoulder and patted him, then laid him in the cradle and held out her arms for Edward. "I say a prayer of thanks every night that we all survived."

"I reckon we gave that man the benefit of the doubt one too many times."

Anne nodded and cuddled little Edward who was suckling happily.

"I wish I could have been here for you," said Justin. "I wish I could stay longer now, but I've got to get back. The Cattlemen's Association is very interested in this trial, needless to say." He leaned against the table and studied her. "Are you all right now? It's only been— what?—three or four days since you gave birth? Shouldn't you be in bed?"

"I don't have time for that, not with twins." She

beamed. "I still can't get over it. Last and I—we didn't even know what was happening. For David, I told him what to do, but after that . . ." She shook her head. "I was scared to death. So was he, but it was worth it."

Justin nodded. "You have two beautiful sons."

"Ah, Justin, you know what to say to a new mother. That silly Last said they were red and wrinkled. Can you imagine?"

Justin smiled, then laughed. "How could he say such a thing when they're obviously the handsomest two baby boys ever born in Parker County."

"Just Parker County? I'm sure they're the handsomest two boys ever born anywhere. And so will yours be, Justin." Her heart was overflowing with warmth, even for the child Penelope was expecting. "Must be soon now, isn't it?"

Justin's face darkened. "It can't hold off long enough to suit Penelope. With just a month to go she's frantic, and driving everyone else frantic as well."

Anne frowned. "Shouldn't you be home with her then?"

"When I am, she spends most of her time screaming at me. I'll be there for the birth, but I've business to attend to, and there's no use delaying it for a woman who'd prefer anybody's company to mine."

"I'm sorry, Justin," said Anne, embarrassed that she felt a pinprick of uncharitable satisfaction.

"It's my own damn fault," Justin muttered, "for ever marrying her." He turned away. "Shouldn't you have another woman here with you? You're just out of child bed with two children and a ranch to run, and the only help you have is that cowboy out in the yard."

"I'm hoping Sissie will come now that the colonel's in jail."

"Much good she'd be!" Justin snapped.

"Sissie's changed. I don't know how you could fail to notice that. I'm not sure I'd ever have gotten through those last few days before the ball if Sissie hadn't been there to help me. Penelope certainly never did anything but make demands on me."

"She was pregnant," mumbled Justin.

"So was I, Justin," said Anne bitterly.

He flushed and rubbed a hand into his hair. "Of course you were. I just didn't know it."

"I wonder if it would have made any difference."

"Anne, I don't want to fight with you."

"Then don't criticize my sister. She's in a terrible situation now, and I want her here. I want to take care of her."

"Forget her. Who's going to take care of you?"

"Well, obviously there's no one to do that, is there? Pancho tried, but he's dead. You tried, but you were usually too angry to stick with it." Suddenly Anne thought miserably, *Why am I doing this? Ruining what little time I have with him*? "I'm sorry, Justin," she murmured wearily. "I don't want to quarrel with you either. You did as much as you could for me. Maybe you're even the reason Pancho married me."

"He sure hadn't offered before I went to see him," Justin muttered. "Well, I'd best be getting back to Weatherford. I just had to see for myself that you were all right."

He was already moving toward the door, and Anne's eyes followed him wistfully. For a few minutes there, they'd almost been a family, even if Justin hadn't known it.

The sheriff had stepped out into the street so that Justin could talk privately with Sissie, not that it was doing him any good. "You can't see him," said Sissie stubbornly. "He's in terrible pain, and the sheriff says he doesn't have to talk to anyone he doesn't want to."

Justin scowled. "Do you know what he planned to do to your sister?"

"Of course I do," said Sissie. "He went over there to ask her not to take so much of our profits from the ranch. Why, we didn't have any money at all. I haven't had a new dress in months."

"By God, you haven't changed a bit!" snapped Justin.

"Well, you never liked me," Sissie snapped back, "so why should I care what you think? Anyway, she got angry about the money and threw the plums at him. That was a terrible thing to do. He's in agony, and he'll be horribly disfigured, and she did that after he'd saved her life."

"Saved her life? He went there to kill her."

"That's a lie!" cried Sissie. "He found those two outlaws there, and he shot them, and then—"

"Your sister shot the two outlaws. One of them was stealing from her; the other was supposed to keep watch while the colonel killed her so that you could inherit the Rocking T and her half of the Bar M."

"I don't want her land, and Papa would never hurt Anne."

Justin gave her dry look. "He already had."

"Well, that was different," mumbled Sissie. "But to say he'd kill her . . . Anne just misunderstood."

"He stole her inheritance from David. Do you deny that?"

"Papa's had hard times. If he used her money, he would have paid her back."

"You're a fool, Sissie, if you believe what he says. You should get out of here and go to Anne."

"He's my father," cried Sissie, tears filling her eyes, "and I have to stay and take care of him. You can't see him, so go away."

Justin scowled at the weeping girl and turned on his heel. So that was going to be the colonel's defense. Well, he hoped to hell that the other rustler lived to contradict the colonel's testimony in court. Justin strode rapidly down the sidewalk toward his hotel, his thoughts entangled with Anne and her sons. She could have died in childbirth, even when the colonel hadn't managed to shoot her. She could have lost the babies. He hoped they hung the man.

"Justin!"

"David. By God, David." Taken by surprise, Justin embraced his brother. "You're back earlier than I expected. How did the drive go? Did you get a good price?"

"None better," said David. "I heard Sissie Morehead's in town."

"That's right." Justin scowled. "The little fool is over at the jail, nursing her father."

"What's he doing at the jail?"

David looked stunned when he'd heard the whole story. "Poor Sissie," he murmured. "She's a loyal little thing to stick by him, and you, brother mine, can be a sanctimonious prig when you put your mind to it." David was already walking away.

"Where are you going?" Justin demanded.

"To see Sissie, of course."

Justin's arm shot out, and he detained his brother forcibly. "Stay away from that girl, David. She's nothing but trouble."

David's eyebrows rose. "Justin, I'm of age. I reckon I can take a fancy to whomever I want."

"You're a fool if you settle on Sissie Morehead."

"Well, maybe that kind of foolishness runs in the family." He turned back toward the jail, leaving Justin to think about his own wife who no doubt awaited him at home with the usual store of hysterical recriminations.

"She's a beauty, Mr. Harte," said Calliope, handing the newborn to Justin.

His heart melted as he looked into the face of his daughter. She was indeed a lovely child, completely unmarked by the ravings of her mother. As Penelope's labor advanced, she had fought it every step of the way. He and the whole household had endured language worse than anything Justin had heard from drunken sailors on the Galveston docks, and all the abuse was directed at him. His wife hated him, almost to the point of madness. Then, when the baby was finally born, she wouldn't even look at it. She'd demanded that Calliope take it away.

Justin touched his daughter's cheek tenderly and watched the little mouth turn, seeking, toward his finger.

"She wants the breast," said the black woman, sighing.

"Best wake Penelope then," said Justin.

"Ah don' know, Mistah Justin. She already said she wouldn't. Feeling the way she does might turn her milk sour, might do the chile more harm than good."

Justin gritted his teeth.

"Now don't you fret," soothed Calliope. "Ah got me a goat, jus' 'cause Ah figgered this might happen. We won't let the little one go hungry."

"You're a good woman," Justin muttered. "God knows what I'd have done without you these last months. I keep asking myself why the hell I ever married Penelope."

"Oh, well, Miss Penelope, she can be as sweet as sugar cane if she sets her mind to it, but her daddy, he jus' spoiled her plumb rotten. Like to ruined her, he did. Wasn't never nuthin' she wanted she didn't git from the time she was old enough to want things, an' Ah swear that girl was born wantin' the world."

"Well, I can't give it to her," said Justin coldly, "and I don't intend to try."

"'Fraid you ain't never gonna convince her of that. You want me to take the baby now?"

"No, I'll hold her a minute."

"Now don't you make the same mistake with your little one her daddy made with Miss Penelope. I can see that same look in your eye."

Justin glanced up from the tiny face. "I may love

her," said Justin, "but I'm not fool enough to ruin her with ill-conceived indulgence. Poor child, she'll have a hard enough time with a mother like Penelope."

"Maybe not," said the maid. "Ah wouldn't be surprised if Miss Penelope don't just ignore her."

Justin scowled. "Not if I can help it."

"That attitude, Mistah Justin, that might be a mistake. What are you gonna call her?"

The name that appeared immediately in his mind was Anne, and he had to laugh at himself. He could hardly do that. "Jessica," he said. "I had a sister I loved dearly, died in childhood. Her name was Jessica."

"All right, little Miss Jessie," said Calliope, taking the child from her father, "let's see how you like goat's milk."

"We'll just build another wing, Last," said Anne. "All the new bedrooms can open out on the veranda for coolness in the summer."

"But four, Miss Anne!"

"We've got the whole winter. Surely we can build on four more rooms."

"Don't see why you need so many."

"One for David. One for Edward."

"They sleep with you."

"Well, they're not going to sleep with me forever. They'll grow up; they'll need space of their own."

"Not this year, an' hell, they're twins. They can share."

"If they want to do that, we'll have a guest room. And one room for Sissie."

"You don't know Miss Sissie's coming here. From what I hear, she believes everything the colonel says."

"What could he say?" asked Anne, surprised. "Anyway, it will all come out at the trial, and then Sissie will be home with us, poor thing."

"She should be takin' your part."

"She should be doing just what she's doing. She's

showing a good deal more maturity than she ever has before. The colonel's her father, and she's bound to stand by him as long as he needs her."

"You're a heap more tolerant than I'd be," muttered Last. "All right, so we want a room for Miss Sissie, if she ever shows up to use it. That don't explain the fourth one."

"That's for guests."

"You'll have a guest room, 'cause them two boys will wanna stay together."

"Then we'll have two guest rooms. One for ladies; one for men. I've been thinking maybe we should have a Christmas party. Wouldn't that be nice? You like to dance, don't you, Last?"

"Not particular, but I wouldn't mind a party."

"Well, you see, we definitely need four rooms."

"I don't know why I ever bother to argue with you, Miss Anne."

"Tighter," said Penelope to the dressmaker. "I had a nineteen-inch waist before, and I intend to have one again."

"Miss Penelope, you're going to make yourself sick," Mrs. Bailey, the dressmaker, said.

"Nonsense. I want all these dresses made with nineteen-inch waists. Now pull those strings."

"Maybe you should try eating less," said Justin dryly from the doorway.

Penelope rounded on him, face flushed with anger. "Don't you tell me what to do!" she screamed. "My figure wouldn't be ruined if it weren't for you!"

"Don't you think you should save those complaints for a more private arena?" asked Justin coldly, thinking of the guest in the parlor who must be overhearing all this. "And why aren't you with the baby?"

"Why should I be?" retorted Penelope sullenly. "Calliope's feeding her."

Penelope's refusal to nurse the child had caused her a

good deal of pain when her milk came in, and she had blamed that on Justin as well. "Let me see what you've got done so far on the green merino," Penelope demanded of the dressmaker. The woman sighed and moved toward her sewing machine, held up the half-finished dress. "Look at that!" exclaimed Penelope angrily. "Sloppy work. You'll have to do it all over again."

The dressmaker's lips compressed. She tossed the gown onto a chair and began to pack up her equipment.

"What are you doing?"

"I'm leaving. You owe me for a week's work, Mr. Harte. Considering what I've had to put up with, I think you owe me a bonus."

"You can't leave. You've not finished my wardrobe."

"And I don't intend to, Mrs. Harte. I'd rather work in a New York sweat shop than work for you."

"You'll have your money," said Justin quietly.

"You're supporting her? She has no right—"

"Of course, she does, Penelope. Mrs. Bailey has her own business. She doesn't have to work for people who ill-treat her."

"All right then, I'm going into Fort Worth to have my wardrobe done. I should have insisted on that in the first place. In fact, maybe I'll take a steamboat to Galveston and go on to Paris. Reeva Lee Merriweather did that last year, and I've always wanted to go."

"Not on my money," said Justin. "You'll stay right here and take care of your child. You'll not have a penny from me to go flying off on irresponsible, self-indulgent trips, not to Fort Worth, and certainly not to—"

"I hate you!" screamed Penelope.

"You've made that perfectly clear. I'll be gone to Weatherford for a week. See if you can learn something about mothering in the meantime."

"You're leaving again? You're always gone. I'm surprised you got back in time for my confinement."

"Considering your behavior, I wish I hadn't. However, I have a rustler trial to attend in Weatherford. I'll be back next week."

"You can just stay away forever for all I care," shrieked Penelope. "You're a selfish, unfeeling husband. You never show me the love or consideration you owe me." She ran weeping from the room.

"My apologies, Mrs. Bailey. What do I owe you?" asked Justin wearily.

"Five dollars and twenty-five cents," said the seamstress. He handed her a ten-dollar gold piece. "Why thank you, sir," she said, surprised, then hesitating, murmured, "new mothers, they're sometimes hard to get along with."

Justin's lips curled in a cynical smile. He was sure that Penelope's ill-humor would dissipate miraculously when she discovered what he had actually come in to tell her, that an old beau of hers, Hugh Gresham, was in the house, ostensibly to discuss a banking scheme he and Justin were involved in, but more likely to moon over Penelope. The man had been badly smitten and very disappointed when Penelope decided that Justin's cattle interests offered her more prestige and money than Gresham's mercantile and banking ventures in Fort Worth. And how much of Penelope's latest tirade had Gresham heard from his chair in the parlor? Probably enough to take some of the glow off his continuing infatuation. Well, Calliope would have to deliver the news of the guest. Justin himself had had enough of his wife's shrewish tongue for the moment.

Sissie looked so white and weary that David's heart went out to her. "Come out to dinner with me, Miss Sissie."

"Oh, I can't leave, David."

"You've fed him, haven't you, and given him his nightly dose of laudanum?"

"Yes, but—"

"He'll sleep. If he needs you, the sheriff can send a man. Come along now. You're thin with sleeplessness and worry."

"But, David, Papa's worse. I know something's wrong. I think he's feverish."

"What does the doctor say?"

"He just says not to worry, but I know . . ."

He took her arm and urged her from the jail. "Dr. Waller's the best in town. If he says your father's no worse, he's probably right, and in the meantime, at least I can give you a good meal."

Sissie brushed surreptitiously at the tears gathering in her eyes. "I don't know why you're so kind to me. Goodness knows, no one else is, and I'm surprised your brother allows you to see me."

David laughed. "Sissie, I'm my own man. Now what will you have for dinner?" he asked as he held the door to an eating place close by the jail. "How about a big steak?"

"I couldn't eat a big steak," said Sissie. "The truth is I don't feel very hungry."

"The truth is if you don't eat more, you're going to disappear entirely, taking my poor heart with you."

Sissie giggled halfheartedly and said, "You're such a flirt, David."

"I know you think that, and your sister's certainly told me I was often enough, but I'm not flirting, Sissie."

He looked at her seriously, and she looked back, her eyes wide, thoughts diverted momentarily from her worries. Did David Harte mean . . . She didn't let herself think it. His brother would never allow him to express any honorable intentions toward her. Confused and saddened, she looked down at her menu. "Have you seen Annie? How is she?"

"I haven't seen her, Sissie, but Justin says she's fine, and so are the babies, although they were born early and not under the best circumstances."

"But it just can't be true that Papa—that he—"

"I'm afraid it is, Sissie. Much as I admire your loyalty to your father—"

"But why won't anyone believe what he says? He's explained it all."

"The truth will come out at the trial, Sissie. Don't worry about it till then. How about chicken and dumplings if you don't want steak?"

"Oh, I don't care. You order for me."

"All right," said David enthusiastically. "The lady will have . . ." and he began to detail an enormous list of food that had the waiter gaping and Sissie trying to interrupt him before he was done.

"I'll just have the chicken and dumplings," Sissie finally managed to say.

"Yes, miss," said the waiter, relieved. "And you, sir?"

"Oh, well, if she won't have that order, I will," said David.

"David," cried Sissie, "you can't eat all that."

"Of course, I can," said David. "Love gives me an appetite."

Sissie blushed and, her hands trembling, returned the menu to the grinning waiter.

CHAPTER

Twenty-Five

Justin smiled as he watched her flying about, cleaning the table, humming to herself, light of step and graceful. The firelight made her red hair glow, and as always it was escaping in curls and waves from its pins. Yet he shouldn't be smiling; he should be lecturing her, for she was quite unaware of an intruder at her door, and he was an intruder. He shouldn't be here, not when he had a meeting to attend in Weatherford. He, Hugh Gresham, and various other businessmen, farmers, and ranchers from the three county area, had been talking for a year about the formation of a farmers' and ranchers' bank. Their first meeting, ironically enough, had been at Hannah McDivot's the beginning of the year, a meeting that he had left to rescue Anne from the clutches of young Sam Junior. The bank was now about to come to fruition, and it was a project in which he had a large stake. He had no excuse for making this side trip to see Anne, and yet here he was, demonstrating yet again his inability to overcome the temptation of her.

Anne came around the table to clear the far side and noticed Justin. As her mouth opened and her brown eyes widened in surprise, he took an involuntary step toward her. Oh, how he wanted to kiss that open mouth. Instead, he closed the door quietly behind him and said, "I've brought you news of Sissie."

"Is she coming here?" asked Anne eagerly. "We're building her a room. Actually, we're building five rooms." Her face shone with excitement and delight. "One for me, one for each of the boys, one for Sissie, one for guests." She counted them off on her fingers. "And a roofed passageway to separate them from the kitchen and the sitting room, which is just my old bedroom. The passageway, that's to separate the bedrooms in case of fire."

Justin nodded solemnly, then started to grin. "The babies must be growing fast if they need their own rooms."

"Well, they don't yet," said Anne indignantly, "but it's best to look to the future I always say." Then she started to giggle. "I might never be able to talk Last into building again. You can't imagine all the arguing I had to do. He didn't even want to build four rooms without a connecting passageway, but, Justin . . ." She halted her enthusiastic description of her building plans and frowned. "What about your own baby?"

"I have a girl," said Justin. "A little beauty."

"I'm sure she is," said Anne, smiling warmly. "How could she not be with such a handsome father, and—ah —of course, Penelope."

"Penelope won't even nurse her." Justin scowled.

"Oh."

"Well, that's not what I'm here for. I gather no one's said anything to you about Sissie."

Anne shook her head. "I keep expecting her, but . . ."

"She's in Weatherford taking care of the colonel, and Anne, he's told her a pack of lies."

"What lies could he tell?" asked Anne, amazed.

"He said that he shot the two outlaws to save your life and that he'd come here to ask you to relent, for Sissie's sake, about taking half of the profits from his part of the Bar M."

"But surely no one would believe that."

"Let's hope not," said Justin. "For one thing, I doubt the other outlaw, Haynes, will be willing to take the blame for the threat on your life."

"He could say there wasn't any threat," Anne mused. "They could make it look as if I attacked the colonel over money instead of—instead of—I could be the one going to trial." Her eyes had become huge and frightened. "What if Haynes doesn't live, or lies about what happened?"

"Don't panic, Anne," said Justin forcefully. "The sheriff doesn't believe any of this hogwash."

"But a jury might."

"The one you killed, Zeb, he's a known renegade, wanted for murder and horse theft in the New Mexico territory and in Oklahoma. The other one's wanted too, and has only about a fifty-fifty chance of surviving anyway."

"If Haynes should die, it's my word against the colonel. If he lives, it's my word against both of them. Even if he tells the truth, he's still an outlaw and might not be believed." She nibbled her thumb anxiously. "I could end up in jail, and who would take care of my babies?"

"Anne, calm down. I'm not going to let anything happen to you. Have you forgotten that we can prove the colonel cheated you out of David's money, that his actions in relation to rustling have always been suspect?" He laid a calming hand on her shoulder. "I didn't come here to frighten you. I just thought you should know that Sissie's not taking your part. She's standing by Morehead, nursing him at the jail."

"Well, that's as it should be," said Anne, trying to get

her breath, to halt the wild flight of her heart.

"Why the hell is it?" Justin demanded.

"He's her father," said Anne simply. "Even if she didn't believe a word he said, she owes him a daughter's care." Her mouth trembled. "Well, I'll just have to trust that things will turn out right," she murmured, but the glow he had seen on her face when he first arrived was gone, and she looked weary, disheartened, and afraid.

"My love," he said, coming close to her, "I'm sorry to be the bearer of bad news."

"None of this is your doing, Justin. Now tell me about your daughter," she urged, trying to put on a brave face. "What have you named her?"

"Jessica."

"After your sister."

"Right. How did you know about Jessie?"

"I think David told me."

Justin scowled. "Even if the colonel's convicted, your sister might never come here. My thrice-foolish brother seems to be staying in town to court her."

"And what's wrong with that?"

"I could think of a better wife for him than Sissie."

"You're hardly one to judge," said Anne coldly.

They stood a minute, scowling at one another; then Justin sighed and slid both arms around her waist. "Anne, I've missed you so badly."

Anne's eyes flickered with surprise and alarm. He was aroused already, and he'd barely touched her. She could feel his hardness and the quick melting within her, for she reacted as she always had to his desire. "Justin, you'd best let me go," she whispered. "This is not a good idea."

"It never takes more than the sight of you to stir me," he muttered, and his mouth descended hungrily on hers in a kiss that he would not relinquish and that she yearned to continue until it swept them both past sense and sanity.

When finally he released her mouth, she said dazedly the only thing that came to mind, "I must see to the babies."

She tried to pull away, but he had looked over her shoulder. "They're fast asleep, Anne," he said, noting that there were other changes at the Rocking T. The second boy was no longer in a dresser drawer; he had his own cradle. Justin wondered who had made it. New rooms, new cradle, new children. Anne was building her own life without him, and it made him feel desperate. "The babies are sleeping soundly," he said in a low, rough voice and swept her up in his arms, heading for the bedroom.

"The men must still be awake," she protested weakly.

"They won't come here after dinner."

"Justin—"

He lowered her to the bed. "Don't say no to me again, Annie. I've ached for you so long." He held her body captive with the weight of his own, her head motionless with his hands cupped around her face, his fingers entangled in her shining hair. "You can't imagine how often I think of you, how much I want to be with you. No matter what I'm doing, you're always in the back of my mind, and all too often in the forefront, driving out the things I should be concentrating on."

He had eased his thighs between hers, spreading her beneath him so that he could press against her, almost as if there were no layers of clothing between them to thwart his desire for her. He moved slowly in the promise of ecstasy, and Anne began to lose her grip on practicality as her body flowered with yearning. He was the father of her children, and she wanted him, wanted his nakedness on her own, his power within her. She moaned softly and gave him kiss for kiss in the lamplit bedroom.

By the time he had stripped away her clothing and begun on his own, her whole body throbbed in an agony of desire. It had been so long, and she loved him so desperately that she could no longer deny him, or herself, and so she watched him as he discarded his clothes beside her bed. He was the epitome of male power, all muscle, his shaft erect and demanding as he came to her, an instrument to satisfy a woman beyond all expectation, to give her pleasure, and satisfaction— she shuddered at the power of his entry—and children. Her eyes flew open. "Justin," she gasped. "You'll get me with child."

He drew back, almost out of her, making her think that he had heeded her plea, and her body, with a will of its own, clenched on him. "Would that I could," he groaned, and reentered her, deeper than before. "It seems," he murmured into her ear, "that only Tighe can give you children, but I, at least, can give you pleasure."

And he did, drawing out the loving, never quite letting her passion come to fruition until she stopped thinking of consequences and thought only of the culmination she so desired, until she was whispering, "Oh, Justin, please, please." Only then did he take her over the edge into an exploding ecstasy.

"I love you," he said. "If I never have anything else to offer you, I do love you."

If he never had anything else to offer. And he didn't, Anne thought. Released from the bonds of her desire, she focussed again on her boys. He should offer them the security of a father, but he didn't. This night he might well have given her another child, and what would that do to her sons? To have a mother branded as a slut? And no father?

Justin eased off her and tried to curl her into his arms, to press her face down against his chest. "Don't be sad, Annie. As long as we're both alive, we can at least see each other from time to time."

"It's not enough," said Anne.

"Anne, it's all we can have."

"No, it isn't all," she countered with a desperate determination. "You say you love me. You come here and take me when you know you shouldn't, when you know that you're committing adultery, endangering my name, and now the well-being of my children."

"No one's going to know about this."

"You can't be sure there'll be no consequences."

Justin flushed, a bitter line to his mouth. "That's not likely, is it?"

"Why isn't it likely? I'm not barren; you're not sterile." She was skirting the edge of safety. Unless he agreed to her terms, she could never tell him the twins were his, but he had a responsibility, and she had decided that she would not let him escape it, nor would she let herself back off from the decision she had made. "You say you love me. Prove it. Come to live with me."

"What?"

"Live here with me. At the Rocking T. Spend the rest of your life with me."

"Anne, I can't."

"It's been done before. In time, people would even get used to it."

"But I have a wife and child," said Justin.

"And I have children," Anne countered. "You don't love Penelope; you say you love me. If it's so, then we should be together, even if we can't marry."

"What am I supposed to do about the Crossed Heart?"

"You told Penelope once that David could run it. Well, let him. Send Penelope back to her father. She'd probably be happier there anyway."

"Anne, the scandal would be terrible."

"If you keep coming here, the scandal *will* be terrible, and it's I and my children who will bear the brunt of it. At least, if you're with me, I'll have something. I'll have your love and support where it can do me some good."

"But my daughter . . ."

"Bring Jessica with you. I'd be a better mother to her than Penelope ever could."

Justin was sitting up, his face tight in lines of anxiety. "Anne, I—we can't do this."

"Justin you can't keep your wife and your respectability and expect to have me, too. I've two sons to consider now. What kind of life are they going to have when it gets around that their mother is Justin Harte's whore? My hands may already know that you've bedded me tonight."

"That's nonsense."

"And if they know, they'll talk." She brushed the tumbled curls away from her face. "And what if I'm with child?"

Justin's eyes softened. "Oh, Anne, how I'd love to see you carrying my child."

"Stop it, Justin. That's pure selfishness. You wouldn't be the one to bear the stigma; I would. You have to choose. Live here with me or leave me alone."

His face hardened, and she realized that he was going to refuse. "You're not offering me a choice I can make, Anne."

"I'm offering you a choice you have to make," she countered. "Part of love is responsibility. Neither of us has shown much of that."

"I've always done what I could to help."

"It was never enough to balance what you took."

"You sound like Penelope!" he snapped.

"Get your clothes on, Justin," said Anne wearily. "And try to be discreet when you leave." She turned away from him and closed her eyes hard against her tears. She could hear him as he dressed, and as he walked out of her bedroom. She had offered to expose herself to the world for him, live openly with him; he had offered nothing. A minute later, the sound of his horse's hoofs drummed and receded. Only then did she let the tears flow. If he really loved her, if he were really a man of honor, he would have come to live with her.

He would have shared the stigma he obviously thought should be hers alone.

Anne had come for his trial but attended his funeral instead. Infection, according to Dr. Waller. She had killed her own stepfather in self-defense, driven by desperation, but still she had killed him, and in the most horrible way. Sissie, pale and dazed, had turned away from her at the funeral, then had testified at the inquest that the colonel had gone to Anne's house to beg her to let them keep more of the profits from the Bar M, which they needed badly. According to Sissie, he had shot the two outlaws to protect Anne. Anne wondered, as she testified herself, whether anyone would believe the truth after her sister's tear-stained story. It was as she had predicted to Justin: Anne herself was on trial, and he had said he'd take care of her. Her eyes drifted over the crowded courtroom. She had many friends here to support her. Henry Barnett sat at her side, but Justin was absent. He had made his choice—Penelope and the Crossed Heart. Bitterly, Anne turned to the judge who had just called the sheriff to testify.

"I didn't take no one's word for anything," said the sheriff. "I got the cartridges the doctor dug outa all of 'em—Zeb, Haynes, the colonel. .44/.40s—all three from Miz Tighe's Winchester. The colonel was carryin' a .45 Army revolver like you'd expect. One cartridge missin'. We found it in the wall behind the cook stove where Miz Tighe musta been standin' when she threw them preserves, so he sure didn't shoot them two outlaws."

Did Sissie understand the significance of that testimony? Anne wondered. Her sister wasn't even looking up any longer.

The outlaw, Haynes, who had to be carried into the courtroom, testified next. "Until the woman got half his ranch, Zeb had men on the colonel's crew, an' we could git information about other outfits an' hide out on his land. Zeb paid the colonel good. I tole Zeb killin' the woman was dumb, gonna cause trouble, but they didn't never listen to me. Zeb said she'd been trouble ever since she got here."

So the colonel had been in league with them all along. How stupid she'd been about him. She could feel the waves of anger in the room. Too many people had lost stock to the gang. She wondered what would happen to Haynes when he came to trial. Surely, at least, she would be cleared of her stepfather's death. Anne felt cold and frightened. She had killed him; they might still try her. She felt Henry's hand on her shoulder again, firm and steady. Too bad she couldn't love Henry. Maybe he was right. Respect and affection might stand her in better stead than her hopeless passion for Justin.

"I find that Mrs. Tighe acted in self-defense," said the judge.

Anne started to tremble, couldn't seem to stop. People were crowding around her, wishing her well. She handed little David to Florence Bannerman and pushed through the crowd to fall on her knees beside her sister. "Come home now," she said. Sissie, weeping, didn't seem to understand. "Come home," said Anne. "Your room's waiting."

Hope springing from despair in her eyes, Sissie whispered, "Oh, Annie, can you forgive me? Again?"

Anne stood, pulling her sister into her arms. Over Sissie's shoulder she saw, turning away at the back of the thronged courtroom, Justin's somber blue eyes. He'd come after all.

Justin rode on through the town of Palo Pinto. Friends and acquaintances hailed him from a saloon, a blacksmith's shop, several of the dry-goods stores, but he continued into the cedar-covered hills that surrounded the valley. To the north, the dark thunderheads built cloud on cloud. There was a norther com-

ing, and it matched his mood, grim and cold. He had no
desire to pass the time of day with friend or stranger.
He wanted to get back to his own home range, not that
he expected any warm welcome there. Likely as not,
Penelope would be as shrewish as ever, and heaven
knew, the trip to Weatherford had done him little good.
He'd gone to meet Hugh Gresham, and the man hadn't
been there. In fact, an associate had said he'd thought
Hugh was on his way to Palo Pinto to meet Justin. But
that hadn't been their agreement at all.

The temperature was dropping fast now, the wind
picking up, and Justin buttoned his heavy jacket and
pulled his hat down low over his eyes. Surely Anne
realized he couldn't live openly with her. It would be a
disaster for both of them, and yet by refusing, he'd cut
himself off from her. Well, one of them had to be
sensible for all their sakes. He hunched his shoulders
against the wind and urged the blood bay into a canter.
Best get home to the Crossed Heart where he belonged.

"Must have got our signals crossed somehow or
other," said Hugh Gresham, who was comfortably
ensconced in Justin's parlor with Penelope when finally, long after the dinner hour, Justin arrived home.

Justin shrugged out of his heavy coat, scowling at his
future banking partner. "The plan was to meet in
Weatherford five days ago."

Hugh flushed. "I thought it was to be here."

"Well, what difference does it make?" trilled Penelope. "Hugh and I have had a lovely visit while you were
pursuing some silly rustler business."

"Every cow they steal," said Justin dryly, "is one
petticoat less for you."

"Oh, don't be silly," she snapped. "You'll make a lot
more money banking with Hugh than you'll ever make
on a bunch of smelly cows, and bankers at least live in
nice houses in cities instead of out on cold, nasty

ranches. Hugh's been telling me all about his new house in Fort Worth. Why, it has chandeliers from Europe just like Papa's."

"Bully for Hugh," muttered Justin. "If you'd married him, all those chandeliers would have been yours."

Gresham shifted uncomfortably, and Penelope gave Justin a furious look. "Well, at least if I'd married Hugh, I wouldn't have had to listen to ungentlemanly remarks like that." She turned her back on her husband, murmured sweetly, "Would you care for another brandy, Hugh? You'll have to ignore Justin. He's obviously in another of his ugly moods."

"Obviously," said Justin to the back of her head. "In which case, I'll relieve you of my unpleasant company."

He turned sharply and strode from the room to go in search of something to eat, which his wife hadn't thought to offer. Penelope's tinkling laughter followed him down the hall, grating on his nerves as it always did.

"He came to see you?" Sissie's mouth trembled.

"Yes, he did," said Anne, "but—"

"Well, of course," said Sissie. "Why wouldn't he? Everyone knows you'd make a wonderful wife."

"Wife?" Anne looked at her sister, puzzled.

"I'm going to my room," said Sissie.

"But I want to tell you what David wanted. I thought you liked him."

"Of course, I do. He'll be a wonderful brother-in-law."

"Brother-in-law!" Anne shoved an impatient hand into her hair. Had Sissie taken a fancy to some other Harte, one Anne didn't know? "Well, I wish you'd told me, Sissie," said Anne irritably. "Considering how nice David was to you while you were in Weatherford, you might at least have given him serious consideration. Here he dropped by to ask my permission to court you, and I said yes in all good faith. I had no idea you were interested in someone else."

"What?" Sissie tears turned off as quickly as they'd begun. "I thought David had come to court you."

"Me? Why would he court me? Twice widowed, two children, older than he is. For heaven's sake, Sissie, be sensible. He's been pursuing you for months."

"You told me he was just flirting."

"Well, I was mistaken. He wants to pay court, and as your only relative, he's asked my permission. If you're not interested, you'll have to tell him yourself." Anne slapped down her knitting and stamped out of the room.

"David wants to marry me?" Sissie whispered. "Me? Anne," she cried. "Anne, wait! What did he say? Why did he leave before I got back? Did he really say he wants to marry me? When will I see him?"

"In about two minutes," replied Anne dryly. She had picked up one of the babies and was looking out the window. "He and Last went off to look at the new bull, and they're riding into the yard right now."

A beatific smile lit Sissie's face.

"I want to go home for Thanksgiving," said Penelope, tossing golden curls back over her shoulders.

Justin stared at her sourly. He had made up his mind to try to ease the bad feeling between them, but it was hard work when she was always coming up with some new idea, more foolish and selfish than the last.

"I missed Papa's Thanksgiving feast last year and I don't intend to do it again."

"Penelope, have you looked outside? It's bitter cold. I wouldn't be surprised if it snowed by nightfall, and you want to ride all the way into Fort Worth? You know how far it is, how bad the weather can be this time of year."

"I'm going," said Penelope, a full pink lip pouting

out. "If it snows, we'll just stop at some ranch along the way until it stops."

"I haven't time for a social trip to Fort Worth."

"Then don't go!" she snapped.

"And although I realize your father would probably like to see the baby," Justin continued with hard-won control, "the weather's much too bad to travel with her."

"Fine. She can stay here, too."

His eyes narrowed. "In fact, maybe you never planned to take her. Well, give it up, Penelope. You're staying here with Jessie."

"Papa will expect me," she wailed.

"As you said, you didn't go last year, and he survived. I reckon he can wait till spring."

"I need to shop. I haven't anything decent to wear. That stupid dressmaker—"

"Oh, I see. It's not your filial duty you're worried about. It's your clothes."

"Papa always buys me a new wardrobe for Christmas."

"Well, he can save his money till spring. As long as the weather's too poor for the baby to travel, you'll stay here and do your duty." Justin noted her white-mouthed fury, the wild anger in her eyes.

"You'll be sorry," she muttered.

"I'm sure I will," he replied. "You're not very pleasant company under the best of circumstances, and when you don't get your own way, you act like a spoiled child. However, you needn't waste your time on a tantrum, Penelope. I've made up my mind. And now, I've work to do, so—"

"You'll be sorry," she whispered again, whirling to leave. "You'll be sorry."

Justin sighed and went back to his books. He could almost feel sympathy for her. Oliver Duplessis had spoiled his beautiful daughter so thoroughly that she had come to marriage without the ability even to imagine that anyone would thwart her wishes. Well, she had to adjust somehow. The patience he'd shown her in the early months after their wedding was gone. He was stuck with her, and she'd have to learn to be a wife and mother. She had no choice.

CHAPTER

Twenty-Six

Several hours after the argument Justin closed his ledgers and stretched wearily. The house was quiet now, Calliope and the baby napping, and Penelope. . . . Well, she was probably sulking in her room. He didn't understand how she could show so little interest in her own daughter. Jessica, at two months, was a pretty, well-behaved baby, if somewhat thin and quiet. He was worrying about his daughter when he heard the first screams and hurled himself from the chair.

At the door of the nursery he found Calliope, her face twisted with emotion, Jessica clutched protectively in her arms. White-faced and trembling, his wife stood across the room near the lace-draped cradle, a ruffled pillow in her hands. "Be quiet," she had just hissed to the black woman.

"What's happened?" The terrible foreboding that had overcome him when he first heard Calliope's screams intensified. "The baby—"

"She's fine!" snapped Penelope.

Justin turned to the black woman. He had never seen Calliope afraid, but now her eyes glistened with fear and horror. "Calliope, what is it?"

"It's nothing," Penelope interposed. "Why are you asking a foolish, superstitious servant?"

"Calliope?"

"Ah . . . found her by the cradle."

"Well, of course!" Penelope snapped. "I heard the baby whimper."

"She—she had the—" Calliope clutched the silent child more closely to her breast.

"What is it?" asked Justin. "Is Jessica all right?"

"She's fine," said Penelope. "She just needs her nap. Everyone's always babying her. You'll spoil her to death. She'll—"

"The pilla—" said Calliope.

"I was putting the pillow under her head," cried Penelope desperately. "She was restless, and I thought she'd be more comfortable, so I—"

Justin frowned. "You don't put pillows in a cradle."

"Nonsense!" snapped Penelope. "What would you know about it?"

He turned back to the black woman.

"She was holdin' it—the pilla."

"I just said I was. Give me that child."

"She had—she had the pilla over—over the lil one's face."

"I didn't!" screamed Penelope.

Justin felt the blood drain from his heart.

"She was pressin' the pilla over the lil one's face."

"I wasn't!"

Justin reached for his daughter. "When you got to her, was she breathing?"

Tears trickled down Calliope's cheeks as she released the child. "Mistah Justin, Ah don' know. Ah's so skeered. Ah couldn't b'lieve Miss Penelope—"

"You're lying!" screamed Penelope.

"That's what you meant?" Justin demanded. "That's

how you were going to get even?"

"You're all against me."

"You never come in here. You've never willingly done a thing for the baby. Why would you start now?"

"I told you. I heard her—"

"If she make a sound, Ah hear it," said Calliope.

"You were asleep. I looked in, and you were asleep. If anything's happened to her, it's your fault."

"So you thought Calliope was asleep, and no one would know."

"No, I went in because I heard the baby—"

"You were going to kill her."

"No," whispered Penelope, looking frightened.

"And we'd all have thought she died in her sleep."

"Calliope's lying. I want her whipped. You whip her. I won't have a servant lying about me. I want her whipped and thrown off this place. You hear me, Calliope? I never want to see you again."

Justin looked at the baby. She seemed to be asleep, but how could she be sleeping through all this? He leaned his face down close to hers. Did he feel the whisper of her breath? She was so pale and quiet in his arms. "Is she dead?" he asked Calliope, his voice breaking.

The black woman stepped hesitantly toward them. "Ah shoulda stayed in the room," said the maid. "I should never left the baby alone. I knew Miss Penelope din' love her."

"There's nothing wrong with the baby." Penelope was edging toward the door. "She's just sleeping."

Calliope raised a black hand and stroked the baby's cheek, and the small face turned weakly toward the gentle finger. The rosebud lips pursed.

"If she's dead, it's your fault," said Penelope.

"She alive. Thank the Lord, she alive."

"How long was the pillow over her face?" asked Justin.

"Ah don' know, Mistah Justin. When Ah come in,

Ah see it, but Ah don' know how long."

"How long, Penelope?" Justin put the baby into Calliope's arms and headed for his wife, who tried to run from the room. She wasn't quick enough. Justin grabbed her by the shoulders and shook her.

"Mistah Justin, don' kill her. Make her answa. We gotta know."

"How long?" asked Justin, his voice deadly. "Answer me." He lifted one hand from his wife's shoulder and slapped her hard across the face.

Penelope, who had been screaming at him, started to whimper. "You hurt me," she gasped, her eyes wide and filled with accusing tears.

"You tried to kill your own child. Now answer my question. How long was the pillow over her face?"

"I hate you," said Penelope.

"That's nothing to the way I feel about you. What kind of woman would suffocate her own baby to free herself so that she could go buy another closet full of clothes?"

"I'm going to tell my father you hit me."

"You'll be lucky if that's all I do to you." He glanced at Calliope, who had dropped into the rocker, crooning to the baby.

"She taken the bottle, Mistah Justin. Maybe she be all right."

Justin turned back to his wife. "If anything, anything turns out to be wrong with that baby, you'll pay."

Penelope cowered away from him, but Justin tightened his hands cruelly over her arms.

"What are you going to do?" she quavered.

"I'm going to lock you in your room. You aren't fit to be among decent people." He took the key from the doors and flung her inside.

"You can't keep me in here!" she screamed.

"Just watch me," he replied in a harsh, grating voice, and he swung the double doors closed, then ordered his foreman, who had just come down the hall, to nail the shutters on Penelope's windows shut. Finally, having pocketed the key, he turned back toward the nursery where Calliope still sat crooning to the baby. "Do you think she's all right?"

"Lord, Ah don' know. How kin Ah tell? I ain't no doctah."

Justin stared broodingly at his little daughter. "We've got to take her to one."

"Miss Penelope, she gets to her papa, she might want the baby back jus' to spite you. An' lawyers an' such, they jus' nacherly give babies to they mamas. You gotta get this baby away. Gotta hide her somewhere safe."

"If only I could take her to my own mother."

"Tha's a good idea. Ain't nobody gonna take a baby away from yo mama."

"But she goes visiting this time of year. We could trek all over hell and back looking for her."

"Take her to Miss Anne then," said Calliope.

Justin's heart twisted. "No, I can't."

"Miss Anne loves babies, an' Miss Anne loves you. She ain't gonna let no one hurt yo baby."

Miserably, Justin turned to stare out into the cold darkness. "Anne has no reason to do me any favors," he said, his voice harsh with regret.

"Maybe not," said Calliope, "but she take yo baby. She wouldn't let nuthin' happen to lil Miss Jessica."

"Anne has two of her own now," said Justin.

"Tha's all right. She got room in her heart fo one more. An' Ah go along wid Miss Jessica. Miss Anne, she'd take the two of us in, no mattah what you done to her. We bettah go right now. Wha's dat sound?"

"Rollo's having the shutters nailed shut on Penelope's room."

"Best you nail the doors shut too. That one, she's got a devil in her. You lock her up, an' we'll git away."

Rollo stuck his head into the room. "I did what you said, boss, but she's pounding on the doors."

"Set a guard," said Justin. "She's not to leave that

room. I want the closed buggy and the best team we've got, blankets and food, everything for a two- or three-day trip for Calliope and me and the baby."

"Boss, the weather's bad. You sure don't—"

"Just do what you're told, Rollo."

The foreman, shaking his head, left again. Justin went to pack while Calliope wrapped the baby. How could he take his child to Anne? How could he ask anything of her after he'd failed her so utterly and so often? But then he thought of Jessica's safety, and he knew he had to try. At least, Anne would know a doctor he could trust.

In minutes they were leaving the house. "My wife's not to leave her room. I'll be back as soon as I can to deal with her," Justin said to Rollo. "No matter what she says, keep her in there. You understand?"

"I don't understand none of this," said Rollo.

"Nor do I," muttered Justin as he settled Calliope and the baby into the buggy and flicked the whip at the horses. Beside him, Calliope was again crooning to the child who had disappeared into a bundle of blankets and shawls.

Stunned, Anne looked up into Justin's haggard face. Behind him stood Calliope, and behind them both, the cold November wind howled around the corners of the buildings, whipped the dead leaves and dust across the yard. Anne shivered and hugged her shawl closer around her shoulders, her eyes still fastened, uncomprehending, on Justin's face. Had he come to accept her offer? To live with her?

"I know I've no right to be here, Anne."

What did that mean? she wondered.

"Miss Anne," broke in Calliope impatiently, "kin us come in outta the cold?"

Anne nodded and backed up to allow their entrance. Where was Sissie? she wondered desperately. She needed a barrier between herself and Justin, between her love and his pain, which radiated from him.

"What Mistah Justin cain't seem to say," said Calliope, shrugging out of a rough shawl, "is he's brung you his chile."

Anne looked from one to the other, confused, noticing for the first time the bundle in Calliope's arms.

"Miss Penelope tried to kill her," said the black woman bluntly.

"The baby? Penelope—"

"Ah found her pressin' a pilla down over the baby's face. We don' know how long. I tole Mistah Justin. Ah said you'd know a doctah who could look to her, who'd know not to tell no one what happened. Ah tole Mistah Justin you was a good woman who loved babies, an' you'd take our lil baby in so no one would ever hurt her."

The look that passed between Anne and Justin then was long and fraught with a thousand tangled emotions, his shame and fear, her astonished reproach. He wanted her to take in his daughter? He wouldn't come to her himself, wouldn't leave his wife, but he wanted her to take the child and to keep his wife's secrets? Then Anne, whose anger and disbelief had been growing, creeping from her heart into her eyes as the irony of what he was asking overwhelmed her, suddenly found Jessica thrust from Calliope's arms to her own, and she looked down into the tiny face. The child opened her eyes, and Anne's breath stopped. They were the blue of Justin's eyes, the deep, deep blue she saw every day in the faces of her own baby boys. This child might have been hers, she thought, gazing into the pale little face. The baby turned and nestled against Anne's breast, and Anne's heart turned over. Her arms tightened around the baby.

"You don' have to worry, Miss Anne," said Calliope, "'bout havin' too many babies to take care of, 'cause Ah'm stayin."

Anne looked up in surprise. She knew that Calliope

had been with her mistress many years, since Penelope's childhood; in fact, Calliope must have been a slave in the Duplessis household before the war. Calliope shook her head as if she could read Anne's mind. "You mah mistress now."

Anne turned questioningly to Justin.

"You'll take her?" he asked.

"She's welcome," Anne replied quietly. All the resentment was gone, washed away by the child's wide eyes, by the trusting curl of her tiny hand against Anne's breast.

"I couldn't risk keeping her at the Crossed Heart," he said, "and I don't know where my mother is. She goes visiting this time of year. I won't make it any longer than—"

"As long as need be, Justin. She's welcome. So is Calliope."

"Of course, I'll pay Calliope's wages."

"No need," said Anne proudly. "I'm quite capable of that myself." Then her eyes narrowed. "And what will you do about Penelope?" she asked.

His hands clenched, and a cold rage grew in his eyes.

"Think about it before you act," she said, forestalling his answer. "Anything you do will affect your daughter for the rest of her life. Scandal, for instance. You don't want that." She gave him a straight, hard look, and he flushed. "Well, Calliope," said Anne, "you're in luck. We've built onto the house, so there's plenty of room."

"The Lord provides," said Calliope complacently. "Ah knew you was the one we should come to."

"And you, Justin. What will you do now? You're welcome to a place in the bunkhouse until you leave."

"I'd best get back," he mumbled.

"As you wish," said Anne coldly. "She's your wife." Anne turned away, his child in her arms. "And you, little love," she murmured to the baby, "are you hungry?"

"She that," said Calliope.

Justin watched the two women move toward the hearth, reflecting sadly that once Anne had offered him a home, both him and his daughter. Now she'd accepted his daughter out of charity, but for him, she didn't even offer a meal. He pulled his hat low, muttered, "I'll be back when I can," and stepped out again into the cold. Anne didn't turn.

He heard her say to Calliope, as he closed the door, "We'll send for Dr. Waller. He's discreet and knowledgeable." Calliope murmured something, and then the howling wind filled Justin's ears, and he stared morosely at the buggy that would carry him back to the Crossed Heart and Penelope. He was about to climb in when he saw two riders approaching the ranch house, one of them David, the other Sissie Morehead.

"What are you doing here, David?" Justin asked sharply. His brother only frowned. "Sissie, would you mind leaving us alone to talk?" Justin's voice was commanding and unfriendly.

"There's nothing you have to say to me that Sissie can't hear," said David.

"In this case you're wrong," said Justin. "Do me the favor of taking my word for it."

David looked closely at his brother, then murmured to Sissie, "I'll only be a minute, love."

She nodded and climbed the steps to the veranda, looking as if she might burst into tears.

David began in an angry undertone as soon as the door closed behind her, "If you've come to tell me to stay away from Sissie—"

"That's not what I'm here for, although you know what I think about her."

"I know, and I'm not interested. Well, if you're not here to interfere in my life, what are you doing here?"

Justin closed his eyes. How could he tell his brother what had happened?

"What is it?" asked David, alarmed, noticing for the first time the anguish on Justin's face. "Is it Mama?"

"I don't know where Mother is. If I had, I wouldn't be here." In as few words as possible, Justin told the story, and finished by saying, "I brought Jessica to Anne for safekeeping."

"Damn it, Justin. Do you think that's fair? Anne loves you, and you're using her." Justin's face went white under his brother's scathing glance. "I knew she was in love with you the first time I ever saw the two of you together, and what have you ever done but exploit her? First, you let her act as a maid to your wife, and when Penelope was through with her, you shipped her off to Fort Worth so she could make money for you in some damned boarding house."

"For God's sake, David, it wasn't like that."

"No? How was it then? Don't you know people were talking? It may not have hurt you, but it sure as hell must have hurt Anne. And now that she's finally got her life straightened out, look who comes riding in with his child. I can hardly believe you had the nerve."

"Was I supposed to keep the baby at the Crossed Heart and chance Penelope trying to hurt Jessica again?"

"What are you going to do about her?" David demanded. "She belongs in jail."

"I have to think of the baby, try to keep this quiet, so I'm going to send Penelope back to Fort Worth. I may be tied to her for the rest of my life, but I'll be damned if I'll live with her."

"You separate from her, and she'll try to take every penny you've got," David predicted.

"Well, if I have to, I can always have her arrested."

"Oh, I see. Your concern for Jessica only holds as far as it doesn't cost you anything."

"God damn it, David, I need your support, not your condemnation."

David's hand came down heavily on Justin's shoulder. "Oh, I'll stand by you, but a lot of your troubles you bring on yourself, Justin. You're always so damned sure you know what's right. Well, I'm going to marry Sissie, and I don't want you interfering."

"How can you expect me to approve a marriage when it looks like you're making the same damn mistake I did?"

"Because I'm not," said David. "There's a world of difference between Sissie and Penelope, and if you hadn't already made up your mind, you'd know it," snapped David disgustedly. "Well, you'd best get back to the Crossed Heart. You've got a problem to deal with."

Justin's lips compressed, and he climbed into the buggy.

"What do you mean she's gone?" demanded Justin.

"We done what you said, boss. Kept her locked in that room no matter how she screamed. I ain't never heard such language from a woman in my life, but we only ever opened the door to pass in the food an' take out the chamber pot, an' half the time she done flung it at our heads. Then this fella came along—Gresham. You had him here before."

With great relish, the foreman told an impatient Justin every detail. Hugh Gresham had insisted on seeing Penelope, even to the point of entering the house uninvited, where he discovered a cowboy standing guard at Penelope's door and Penelope shrieking to be let out. When Rollo and Baker refused him the key, Gresham had shot the lock off the door.

"Hell, Justin," said Rollo, "I din know what to do, an' neither did Baker. He's jus' standin' there with his mouth open, an' this here Gresham, he waltzes right into Miz Harte's room, an' she tells him you beat her up an' locked her in an' he's gotta, for God's sake, take her on into Fort Worth to her daddy, an' she's cryin' an' carryin' on like lil Miss Never-Done-a-Mean-Thing-to-Anyone-in-Her-Whole-Life, an' the-whole-world's-pickin'-on-her, an' a course this Gresham, he says to me, 'What's the meanin' of this?' an' all like that. Hell, I din' know what to do."

"And then?" prodded Justin impatiently.

"An' then they packed up her jewelry and that fur cloak you give her. Din' take her clothes 'cause she said they wasn't worth takin', an' off they go, him holdin' the gun on me all the time, an' it ain't that I probably couldn't a killed him, but I din' know as how I should. Looked to me like things was pretty bad anyways, an' killin' him might jus' make 'em worse."

Justin listened to the whole recital, then swore long and viciously. "All right, Rollo. We're going after her."

"Whatever you say, Justin, only maybe this time you'll tell me what's goin' on, an' where is it we're goin'."

"Fort Worth. Isn't that where she told him to take her?"

"Yep. You figger she's runnin' off with him, like in elopin'?"

Justin looked at him in surprise and shook his head. "If you mean is she in love with him and running off, Penelope's not in love with anyone but herself. She's trying to run away from the consequences of her own actions, just the way she always does. Let's get going."

"Whatever you say, boss, but I'll tell you, we're gonna freeze our asses off. It's gittin' colder by the minute. How far you plannin' to ride afore nightfall?"

"I'm not planning to stop at all. I need to get to that woman before she makes any more trouble than she already has."

"Go to sleep, Calliope. Take the room at the end of the hall. I'll rock her by the fire," Anne said.

Calliope nodded and trudged off. The two women had been up all night trying to get cow's milk into the baby, who couldn't seem to keep anything down. Calliope thought it was because Jessica was used to goat's milk.

Wearily, Anne dropped into her chair. For the moment Jessica stopped whimpering and lay weakly against Anne's breast. In another two hours it would be dawn, and her own sons would awaken, ready to nurse. What would happen if she. . . . She stared down at the baby, mesmerized at her own thought. The child's eyes opened, long dark lashes over deep blue eyes. Jessica might have been her own. She felt the bond. Could she nurse all three of them? she wondered. Her milk seemed more than sufficient for the boys.

Not allowing herself to think any further than the need of the baby in her arms, her fingers went to the buttons of her dress, and in a second she nudged her own nipple into the baby's mouth. At first the child didn't seem to know what to do, and Anne remembered sadly that she'd never been put to the breast. Was it that? Or was Jessica too weak to nurse, too far gone? Anne cradled the child against her, rocked her, sang softly to her, and felt the first tentative suckling. *Let this be the right thing, Lord,* she prayed.

Two hours later Jessica was peacefully asleep in her nest of blankets. She hadn't been sick. She had nursed, not too long, then fallen asleep in Anne's arms. As she put the baby down, Anne thought fiercely, *Now she's mine.*

"We'll stop in Weatherford, put up in a hotel for a few hours, sleep, then ride on."

"Sounds good to me. I could use a meal, too. Beef jerky an' cold coffee in the saddle ain't my idea of anything to warm a man's gut when there's a winter wind blowin' down outta the Indian Territories."

"It's a bitter day," agreed Justin, and his words reflected more than the weather. He could imagine that his wife was spreading vicious tales about him everywhere she went. She'd blacken his name, and his only defense would be the truth, which would hurt his daughter and cause a scandal worse than anything stupid, thoughtless Penelope dreamed of.

By the time he and Rollo had turned in their horses at a livery stable in Weatherford and walked into the Bates Hotel, Justin was too tired and cold to care where she was or what she was saying. He leaned wearily against the desk and asked the clerk for a room.

"Why, Mr. Harte, Mrs. Harte checked in not an hour ago. I wouldn't be surprised if she's not fast asleep. Looked mighty tired she did, didn't even mention that you'd be along, but I reckon you'll want to—"

"Of course," said Justin, his exhaustion falling away. "What room?"

"Twenty-six. Think I've got another key here."

"What about Hugh Gresham?" asked Justin. "I need to see him, too."

"Let's see. Mr. Gresham's in—ah—twenty-nine. Right down the hall." He handed Justin a key.

"Thanks, Tate." Justin and Rollo exchanged a long look, for the foreman had been told the whole story.

"Think maybe I better come along," Rollo suggested. "Just in case you git an itch to throttle her."

"Maybe you better at that. God knows I'd like to get my hands around her throat."

"Maybe we oughta have a drink before we go up there."

"Maybe we'd better not," said Justin. "Probably wouldn't take more than one to drop me in my tracks. Except for what I had in the saddle, I haven't slept for—hell, it must be three days."

They'd reached the top of the stairs and turned. It occurred to Justin that he was going to the very room into which he'd pulled Anne the night she'd discovered he was married, the night Brother Foley had seen her leave and accused her of an act of adultery, which, ironically enough, she had refused to commit. He stood staring at the door, thinking not of the confrontation ahead of him, but of Anne, who, in the end, had been willing to compromise her beliefs, to sacrifice everything to make a life with him, who had wanted both him and his daughter. If he'd done what she asked, if he'd had the courage she had, none of this would have happened. Instead, his daughter was with Anne anyway, and he had neither of them.

"Well, you gonna knock?" asked Rollo.

Justin dragged himself back to the present. "No," he said. "Better take her by surprise."

He fitted the key into the lock and opened the door quietly. There were no lights in the room, but enough daylight filtered through the drawn draperies and in from the hall to reveal that in the bed was not one person, but two. Beside him, Justin heard Rollo's horrified gasp, but Justin felt no horror, only an overwhelming, cynical sense of the fitness of things. Hugh Gresham, whom he'd thought of as a good man to be his partner, had evidently seen himself as an even better partner for Justin's wife, between whose legs he lay, spending himself in the most fruitless of passions.

Justin went inside, closed the door quietly behind himself and his foreman, leaned against it, and began to laugh. The two figures on the bed froze.

Then Penelope was pushing Hugh aside, sitting up with her gown awry, her eyes and hair wild. "I told you I'd get even," she cried. "It's what you deserve. You hit me. You—"

"Shut up," said Justin.

Hugh, flushed bright red, was trying to scramble into his clothes and some sense of dignity.

Justin watched him with sardonic amusement. "Did you enjoy that?" he asked.

"You don't deserve her," said Hugh defensively.

"I couldn't agree with you more," said Justin. "There are very few men so worthless they deserve a greedy, faithless bitch like Penelope."

"I won't let you talk about her that way," said Hugh, looking around wildly.

"If you're looking for your gun, forget it. There's no

way you could ever shoot me before I got you, and if you're dead, who'll be left to take care of Penelope?" He glanced contemptuously at his wife. "Although I find it hard to imagine her as anyone's lover. Now get your clothes on, Hugh. I need to have a few words with my wife."

"Don't leave me alone, Hugh," cried Penelope. "He's always mistreated me. I told you how he—"

"Penelope, you'd better stop and think a minute. You've just been caught in an act of adultery, and in front of a witness other than your husband, and you're guilty of other things, worse things."

"What are you talking about?" Hugh demanded.

"Things that were witnessed as well." Justin stared hard at his wife. "Are you going to tell Hugh about that?"

Penelope was beginning to look panic-stricken.

"Our marriage is through anyway. I'm returning you to your father. Beyond that, well, I'll have to see what my options are, but I'd advise you, Penelope, to keep your mouth shut. I'm not particularly anxious to involve us all in a flaming scandal, but by God I'll do it if I have to. If you want to salvage anything out of this, you'll keep your mouth shut and cooperate."

"You can't insult her like that, not after the way you've treated her," cried Hugh, who was looking more confused and distraught than ever.

"Hugh, you don't know what you're talking about. I'd be quite within my rights to shoot you down for seducing my wife, and no jury in Texas would fault me. In fact, I could kill you both." Justin had casually drawn his revolver. He hadn't even bothered to raise it, but the two of them turned deathly pale.

"You wouldn't," said Hugh.

Justin shrugged. "Not unless she provokes me. I intend to see her safely to Fort Worth. Then, as I said, I'll explore my options."

"I'm your wife," said Penelope. "You have no options."

"I rather imagine you're wrong about that," said Justin. He stepped toward her and added in a very low voice, "One of them is to send you to jail for attempted murder." Penelope's eyes widened with fright. "So keep that in mind next time you get some vicious little idea about taking revenge on me." He stepped back. "Rollo, I'll have to share your room. I'm sure as hell not going to sleep with this slut."

"Look, Harte, don't talk to her—"

"Get out of here." Justin did raise the gun then, and Hugh backed away. "Out." The man fled. "Now, Penelope, listen real good. I'm going to get about four hours sleep. Be in this room when I come back for you." Justin turned on his heel and left, Rollo close behind him.

In the minute before Justin dropped into exhausted sleep, the voices of Calliope and David sounded in his mind. After silencing Brother Foley, Justin had thought his secret and Anne's was safe, but he had been wrong. Both his servant and his brother had said, as if it were common knowledge, that Anne loved him. "No mattah what you done to her," those were Calliope's words. "What have you ever done but exploit her?" David had asked. Had he really treated Anne so badly? Even loving her as he did? And Penelope. How could he condemn her when others saw his own guilt so clearly? He had told Hugh Gresham that few men were so worthless as to deserve a woman like Penelope. Maybe he was. Maybe Penelope was his punishment. Justin fell into an uneasy sleep and had dark dreams.

CHAPTER

Twenty-Seven

Anne stood by anxiously as Dr. Waller examined the baby. He had approved of her nursing Jessica but advised the purchase of a goat in case her milk failed. As for damage from the attempt on Jessica's life, he saw none so far. "Watch to see if she shows signs of bein' slow," he advised, turning from the baby to concentrate on Anne. "I don't suppose you're going to tell me who put the pillow to her." Anne shook her head. "Seems wrong to keep quiet about such a thing," he muttered. Anne agreed, with great bitterness, but she kept her word to Justin and said nothing.

Cassandra Harte dismounted from her buggy, staring at her son's elaborate frame house. Not for the first time she clucked disapprovingly. Penelope was a beauty but a fool as well, and in this weather the girl would be freezing in that house she'd insisted Justin build, and Justin—well, Justin in most ways was the smartest and most sensible of her boys, except where his wife was concerned. Cassandra had a sad feeling that some day her son's head would rule his loins again, and then he'd come to think that marriage a poor bargain indeed. Still, children had to make their own mistakes.

Sighing, she glanced around the ranch yard. This was a cold welcome indeed. She'd sent a messenger ahead to say she was coming, and yet no one had ventured out to greet her. Likely Penelope was still abed, but Cassandra had expected her son to be on hand. The only person in sight was Rollo Tandy, now hurrying toward her from the stable. A worrying man if ever there was one, Rollo looked more harried than usual.

"Don't tell me Justin's off gallivanting, Rollo," Cassandra said, after greeting him.

The foreman flushed. "'Fraid so, Miz Harte. Fact is I just got back myself, not more'n an hour ago."

"And what took you away this time of year? I thought I was the only fool traveling in weather like this."

"Me an' Justin—ah—we had an errand to do, Miz Harte."

My Lord, thought Cassandra, *Rollo acts like he's stolen my horse and fears I'm about to accuse him.* "Well, I'd best get on in. These old bones have taken enough cold and jouncing for one day."

"'Fraid there ain't no one at home, Miz Harte."

"They've taken a new babe out in weather like this? No, she'll be inside with Calliope, and 'twas the little one I came to see. What'd they name her?"

"Jessica, ma'am, for your girl that died."

"Did they?" Cassandra looked pleased. "That was my mother's name, too. Well, I'll just go in and see young Miss Jessica."

"She ain't here neither, Miz Harte," said Rollo.

"That foolish daughter-in-law of mine took her into Fort Worth, did she?"

"No, ma'am," said Rollo, who was squirming in his boots. What was he supposed to say? "The fact is, ah—"

"Spit it out, man," said Cassandra, a frown deepening the wrinkles in her weathered face. "The child's not sick is she? Lord, she hasn't died, surely?"

"No, ma'am. Well, not that I know of."

"Not that you know of?"

"She an' Calliope, they're at the Rockin' T. Miz Anne McAuliffe—she took 'em in."

Cassandra Harte gave her Stetson a hard shove and glared at the foreman. "You're telling me, Rollo Tandy, that my granddaughter is off somewhere with a servant and a strange white woman?"

"Now, Miz Harte, there's no use for you to fret. Little Miss Jessica, she couldn't be in better hands. Miz Anne's got two new baby boys of her own. Why, she saved my life at spring roundup in '76, an' when we had the big party here last spring, 'twas Miz McAuliffe that did all the work an' made it such a success."

"All right, so this Anne McAuliffe—"

"Actually it's Miz Tighe. She married this here gunfighter that won Homer Teasdale's Rockin' T—"

"All right, all right, Rollo. I don't need to hear every bit of gossip you know. What's my granddaughter doing at this woman's house?"

"Mr. Justin, he took her there."

"Why? Where's Penelope?"

"Well—ah—listen, Miz Harte, I reckon Miz Penelope, she's in Fort Worth by now." Rollo remembered how Justin had awakened at the hotel to find that his wife had fled with Hugh Gresham a second time. "An' Justin, he's probably gone after her."

"Had a spat, did they?"

"You could say that," mumbled Rollo uneasily and earned himself another sharp look from Justin's mother.

"Well, that doesn't excuse their abandoning their baby with some strange woman. That all you're going to tell me?"

"Yes, ma'am. Fact is, it ain't my business, is it?"

"Don't know why," muttered Cassandra. "Seems to me you know everybody's business this side of the Indian Territories. Well, first off, I guess I'll drive on to Parker County since I came to see my granddaughter, though I didn't think I'd have to go that far to do it."

"Oh, now surely, Miz Harte, you want to light an'—"

"Not unless you plan to tell me what's going on."

"Well, ma'am, I cain't rightly."

"That's what I thought. In that case, I'm on my way to Parker County. The Rocking T you said? Poor Homer. He always was a weak-kneed fool. Losing his ranch in a poker game!"

"Yes, ma'am. Well, I heard he's resettled up in Colorado, an'—"

"Enough, Rollo. You're worse than an old woman gossiping at a church social." She climbed smartly into her buggy, flicked her whip, and she was gone.

"My darling girl," cried Oliver Duplessis, "more beautiful than ever."

The tight lines in Penelope's face relaxed, and she beamed at her father.

"Come in, come in. How we missed you last Thanksgiving, child, but of course, newlyweds . . . I understand. And where's Justin? Stabling the horses, I presume."

Penelope's smile disappeared. "I've left him."

"What!" Oliver Duplessis looked quite astounded, then he chuckled. "Trouble in paradise? Well, he'll be after you in no time." Penelope looked more alarmed than reassured, but her father continued with bluff good humor, "What man could bear to be away from so beautiful a wife?"

"I never want to see him again."

"Well, well. Many a bride has said so I'm sure. A few afternoons with the modiste will improve your humor I doubt not. The ladies tell me we have a French dressmaker who would do credit to Paris itself. It will be my pleasure, my darling daughter, to present you with a whole new wardrobe as my Christmas gift to you."

Penelope's face lit with delight. "Oh, Papa, you always know how to make me happy."

"Yes, yes, and Justin will be along by then, and—"

"No," said Penelope, her mouth settling in sullen lines. "He beat me. I'll never forgive him."

"What?" Duplessis' high-domed, bald head fell into thunderous furrows. "He laid a hand on my little girl?"

"Yes, he struck me. In the face," said Penelope.

Her father looked at her closely. "I see no bruise."

"Are you calling me a liar? He not only struck me, he locked me in my room."

"Why?" asked her father, continuing to frown. "I got you a good husband, a wealthy one with power and respect. What's gone awry?"

Alarm flashed through Penelope's eyes, and she said quickly, "He didn't want me to come home for the holidays, and I missed you so, Papa."

"Ah, well, darling girl, that's understandable, but perhaps Justin couldn't take the time away from his ranch. You could have postponed your—"

"He's always away. He leaves me home, and it's boring and horrible. I hate it."

"Well, Penelope, you would have a rancher. What did you expect?" snapped her father. "You could have married any number of wealthy men, Hugh Gresham, for instance."

"It was Hugh who rescued me," said Penelope.

"What does that mean?"

"Justin locked me in my room and made his men stand guard so I couldn't leave. They hardly fed me anything. If Hugh hadn't come, I'd probably have starved to death."

"You rode all the way back into Fort Worth with Hugh?"

"He saved my life."

"No chaperone?"

"What was I supposed to do? Justin's a violent man."

"He never seemed so to me."

"Don't you believe me?" cried Penelope hysterically, tears beginning to slide down her cheeks.

"Of course, of course," muttered Oliver. "I'll have to have a talk with Justin."

"He'll tell you all sorts of lies. He'll try to make something of it that Hugh rescued me. He's always been jealous of my suitors."

"He has?" Oliver looked skeptical.

"Of course. Everyone's jealous of me. Well, I'm never going back to him."

"Don't be ridiculous! And where's the baby?"

"What?"

"The baby. Where's my granddaughter? If you've left your husband, surely—"

"She's . . ." Penelope was momentarily befuddled, having forgotten about her daughter. "She's—he took her away from me to punish me."

"What did he do with her?"

"She's . . . back at the Crossed Heart." Penelope had no idea where the child was. "She's back at the ranch. I didn't dare try to bring her. The weather. And everything."

"Who's taking care of her?"

"Calliope."

"Ah." Oliver looked relieved. "Well, we'll work it out, dear child. Don't fret. You'll have your baby back. And your husband as well."

"And the Christmas wardrobe?" prompted Penelope.

"And the Christmas wardrobe," promised Oliver indulgently.

How to begin? Justin warmed his hands at the fireplace in Henry Barnett's office. It was a bitter day outside, and he had a bitter tale to tell. He drew a long breath and announced bluntly, "Henry, I want to divorce my wife."

The lawyer carefully placed the tips of his fingers together and stared at them. "On what grounds, Justin?"

"What grounds are there?"

Henry frowned and took down a law book. "If your wife was, as the law says, 'taken in adultery' or if she leaves your house and stays away three years. Those are grounds that come to mind."

"I don't want to wait three years," snapped Justin.

"She's abandoned you then?"

"Well, she ran away from home." His mouth turned hard as he debated how much he wanted to tell his lawyer. Still, he'd be a fool not to tell Henry everything. "And she was, as you said, 'taken in adultery.'" He noted with grim amusement that Henry looked nonplused.

"Is this just gossip or hearsay?"

"I found her in bed at the Bates Hotel in Weatherford with Hugh Gresham."

"Good Lord," muttered Henry. "I don't suppose there were any witnesses beside yourself."

"Rollo Tandy."

Henry looked even more astounded as Justin explained the circumstances. "Well, you've certainly got cause then," muttered the lawyer. "Hugh Gresham, you said? There goes the bank."

Justin almost laughed. How like practical Henry to look at it that way.

"I must warn you of one thing, Justin. If you should bring suit for divorce on grounds of adultery, and she could prove that you're guilty of the same thing, then there'd be no divorce." At Justin's look of surprise, Henry shrugged. "That's the law." He glanced down and read, "If in any suit for divorce for the cause of adultery it shall be proved that the complainant has been guilty of the like crime or has admitted the defendant into conjugal society or embraces after he or she knew the criminal fact—that means you can't sleep with Penelope again."

"No fear of that," Justin muttered. "As for the other . . ."

"Yes, well, I'm not asking you, Justin, if you've been a faithful husband. I don't want to know, but I'm warning you, you'll need to be very careful about your, shall we say, reputation."

Justin scowled. "If I have to divorce her for adultery, it's going to cause a damned scandal. Isn't there anything else?"

"Well—" Henry read further. "If there was to be a felony judgement against her and she stayed in state prison for a year without pardon, and she hadn't been convicted on your testimony"—he chuckled—"but I don't suppose—"

"Much you know about it!" snapped Justin. Henry frowned at him. "Anything else?" Justin demanded.

"Hmm. If either of you are guilty of 'excesses, cruel treatment, or outrages against the other and if such ill treatment is of such nature as to render your being together insupportable' —"

"God knows, life with Penelope is insupportable."

"You have any particular excesses, cruel treatment, or outrages, other than the adultery, in mind?"

"Does spending me out of house and home count?"

"Well, it might help you retain more of your property if we get to the settlement. What did you mean when you reacted to the section on felony conviction?" asked Henry, who always managed to pick up on the salient points.

"Calliope caught her trying to suffocate the baby," said Justin bluntly.

"My God!" exclaimed Henry.

"Which is why I not only want the divorce, I want the child, but I'd just as soon not have the attempt on

Jessica's life come up in court either."

Henry shook his head. "Justin, this is going to be a very ugly mess. Where is Jessica now?"

"I left her and Calliope with Anne Tighe."

"You involved Anne in this?"

"You needn't worry that Penelope's going to demand the baby. She never wanted it in the first place."

"And you don't think she'd use Jessica to get at you?"

Justin frowned. "If she tries, she's going to jail. That's all there is to it. If I have to take the baby and—" He just barely stopped himself from saying "the baby and Anne." "And move so far out on the frontier that no one's ever heard of us, I'll do it. But I'll never let Penelope near Jessica again, and I won't stay married either."

"Now I know you're angry about the business with Hugh Gresham—"

"I don't give a damn if the bitch goes to bed with everyone in Tarrant County!" snapped Justin. "I just want to be rid of her."

"Still, I hate to see you dragging Anne Tighe into this. Couldn't you have found someone else to leave the baby with, your mother for instance?"

"I didn't know where my mother was."

"What's between you and Anne?" Henry asked suspiciously.

Justin's mouth set in a stubborn line.

"I ask because she's a fine woman, and I don't want to see her hurt. In fact, I'd have married her myself if she'd have had me."

"You proposed to Anne?" Justin asked, his outrage blatantly obvious.

"I did," snapped Henry, "and though she didn't accept me, that doesn't mean I'm willing to see her name dragged through the mud because of your troubles with Penelope."

"It was Calliope who insisted we take the baby to Anne," Justin muttered. "We couldn't let her stay in the house with her mother."

"And it was Calliope who saw your wife try to suffocate the child. If it comes to court, do you think a black woman's going to believed over Oliver Duplessis' daughter?"

"It's the truth."

"It may be. I'm not disputing it, but you're stirring up a hornet's nest. Can't you just separate from Penelope?"

"I am separated from Penelope. It's not enough."

"Do you realize how much she could ask for and get in a divorce settlement?"

"No, you tell me," said Justin, glowering.

"Well, according to the law, anything either of you had before the marriage stays with you, although the courts don't always stick to that if the wife's ill-used."

"My wife's hardly ill-used."

"You're sure? What's she going to say about you?"

"What can she say? That I wouldn't let her go to Fort Worth because it was too cold to take the baby? That I slapped her when she wouldn't tell me how long she kept the pillow over Jessica's face?"

"She could accuse *you* of adultery."

"With whom?" asked Justin belligerently.

"I have no idea. Even if you're innocent, she could lie. Can you count on her to be truthful under oath?"

Justin sighed. "You can't count on Penelope for truth under any circumstances, but at least I've got witnesses."

"Witnesses, yes, but one's your foreman and one's a maid, both your employees."

"Whose side are you on anyway?"

"I'm on your side, Justin, and because I am, I have to point out the problems. Anyway, your witnesses can only testify to things you don't want brought up in open court. And what if Penelope decides to accuse you of adultery?" He propped his chin on tented fingers and stared at his client. "Her most likely choice would be

Anne Tighe, whom you brought to your house just last year, and whom you've done much to help since then. Now Anne has Penelope's baby. Your wife might have no evidence, but she could—"

"God damn it, Henry!"

"The safest thing would be to make some sort of amicable arrangement with Penelope before you go to court."

"For instance," said Justin, now dreading the very divorce he had so desired.

"Well, if you don't want to send her to jail and you don't want to accuse her of adultery, the divorce has to be on the grounds of excesses, cruel treatment, or outrages, and you'll have to agree between yourselves on something that's not too outrageous. It's been done before, but it takes cooperation."

"Not much hope of that," said Justin morosely.

"What about Gresham? He won't want it known that he committed adultery with a friend's wife. Could he be induced to put pressure on her, and do you think she cares enough about him to make her susceptible to persuasion?"

"God, Henry, I don't know."

"Well, these are the avenues we'll have to explore, and if you'll take my advice, you'll send that child to your mother."

"I would," said Justin, "if I knew where she was."

"Find her," Barnett insisted. "And stay away from Anne. At least, you can protect her, even if the rest of you have to wallow in your own scandals."

Justin glared at Henry, not because he didn't want to protect Anne, but because he hated the thought that she might have married the lawyer, might marry him still since Henry seemed determined to act as her champion. Lord, thought Justin anxiously, she might marry anyone before he could get himself cut free of Penelope, and he couldn't even tell Anne what he was doing. Could he? If he did and Penelope managed to fend off the divorce action, Anne would never trust him again. Of course, she didn't trust him now. How could she? Maybe he should ride straight out there, tell her his plans, and stake his claim. No, he had an overwhelming fear that, if he told her, told anyone, Penelope would destroy all his hopes—again.

When the knock came, Anne glanced around in surprise, picked up Jessica who had been awakened, and tramped over to the door where she found on her threshold a woman of middle years, tall and strong of body with a pleasant weathered face, graying blond hair, and sharp blue eyes. Anne shifted the baby to her hip, trying to remember who the woman might be. She thought she knew all her neighbors, but this one she couldn't seem to place.

"Mrs. Tighe," said the woman. "Anne Tighe?"

"Yes," said Anne. "Step in, won't you?" Edward set up a wail as the cold air invaded the warm room.

"Oh dear, there goes another one," said Anne. "Make yourself at home."

The woman was watching her curiously. Anne rushed over to placate Ned. "Have we met before?"

David, realizing that his brother was getting attention, started to howl as well, and Anne shrugged helplessly at the stranger, the corners of whose mouth were beginning to quirk.

"In answer to your question," said the woman above the clamor, "my name is Cassandra Harte, Justin's mother. Since you seem to have more than enough babies on your hands, perhaps you'd like to hand my granddaughter to me."

Anne swallowed. Cassandra Harte? Had she come to take the baby away? Anne glanced down at little Jessica, who was trying to grasp a button on the front of Anne's dress.

"This one," said Anne, stammering, "is Jessica." She nodded her head toward the baby on her hip.

"May I?" asked Cassandra.

Anne nodded reluctantly and released the little girl to her grandmother, who took one look and exclaimed, "Lord help us, the child looks just like the daughter I lost."

"Justin named her for his sister," Anne murmured.

"Of course he did," said Mrs. Harte. "He loved that child. It about broke his heart when she died. Mine too. She was the only girl I had."

"I'm so sorry," said Anne. "The loss of a child—I can't even imagine how terrible it would be."

"Well, you've two fine boys yourself from the looks of it," said Mrs. Harte, glancing from the baby Anne had picked up to the other in his cradle. "Perhaps you can tell me why my granddaughter's here."

"Penelope—I believe Penelope's in Fort Worth."

"So I hear, but why isn't her child with her?"

"Mrs. Harte . . ." Anne couldn't meet the eyes of Justin's mother. "Mrs. Harte, I think you'd best talk to your son about this. It's not my story to tell."

"You come into it somewhere, obviously, since he left the child with you."

"That was Calliope's idea."

"Ah. Then I'm to ask Calliope, am I? Where is she?"

"She's across the county, delivering a baby. I couldn't go, not with three here nursing."

Cassandra Harte's heavy eyebrows went up. "Three?"

Anne flushed and explained, "The doctor—he said it would be all right, that—"

"You've no need to defend yourself," said Cassandra. "Your conduct appears to be uncommonly generous in this whole curious affair. And, at least, I've got a lovely grandchild." She smiled down at little Jessica, who was clutching at the strings of her cloak. "Lively too."

"I'm afraid I've been remiss. I haven't asked you to come to the fire or offered you refreshment."

"And I accept both," said Mrs. Harte. She shifted the

baby to one arm, shrugged out of her cloak and took a seat in one of Anne's rockers. "It's a fine thing to hold a baby in front of a warm fire on a cold day. Makes me feel young again. Though how you're managing with three babies, I can't imagine."

Anne smiled at her, a special radiance glowing in her eyes and surprising the older woman. "It's no burden," said Anne. "I give thanks every night for the babies."

"Do you indeed? Well, I can see that you mean it. Obviously my daughter-in-law didn't feel that way."

"Well, I . . ." Anne flushed. "I don't know. Will you have tea or coffee? There's stew left from the noonday meal." Anne had put down a sleeping Ned.

"I could do with a bite," said Cassandra. "Little Jessica seems to have nodded off as well. Is this her cradle?" She tucked the child in. "Here, give me the one who's awake."

Anne handed her David. "This is . . ." Anne halted the introduction because Mrs. Harte was staring into the child's face, her expression shocked. "David," Anne finished uneasily. "Is something wrong?"

"No. No. What a lovely child. You named him David?"

"Yes, my first husband, Major McAuliffe, was named David. The other baby's Edward for my second husband, Edward Tighe."

"The gunfighter."

"Yes," said Anne.

"Well. David and Edward." Cassandra looked back at the baby, a strange expression on her face, and then, to Anne's astonishment, she bent down and kissed him. "A lovely boy," she said. "I'll look forward to holding Edward as well."

"Yes, of course," said Anne, puzzled and worried.

"Does he look like his father?"

Anne's heart lurched with alarm. Surely, surely Justin's mother didn't realize that she was holding her own grandchild. Anne knew the eyes of all three babies were like Justin's. "Why, yes. Pancho was blue-eyed."

"Aye, blue-eyed." The older woman's glance went back to the baby in her arms. "And dark-haired? Was Mr. Tighe dark-haired?"

"No," said Anne uneasily, "blond, but my mother had very dark hair."

"I see. Well, well." Mrs. Harte leaned her head back against the rocker and closed her eyes.

"I'll get you a plate," said Anne.

"My thanks, young woman. I'm hungry and tired, I must admit. I came straight here from the Crossed Heart when Rollo told me where the baby was."

Anne smiled slightly. "That's a long trip. I can see that you're every bit as persevering as Justin said."

"Justin's spoken of me, has he?"

"Oh, yes." Anne dipped stew from the pot and cut bread. "He loves and admires you above all women, but you know that I'm sure. Here you are." Anne exchanged the plate for the baby. "You won't mind if I nurse him? When they're awake and close to the time, I go ahead, what with three and all."

"I don't know how you do it, girl."

"Mrs. Harte," said Anne tentatively, "do you know about David, your son David?"

Cassandra broke her bread and, frowning, dipped it into the meat gravy. "You make a fine stew, young woman. I doubt not you'll find yourself a third husband soon enough and a father for your boys."

Anne could have wept to hear her say that.

Cassandra sighed when she saw that anguished expression. "Well, tell me of David, if you must."

"He's—well, likely you'll see him today."

"Indeed. He's here?" The woman actually scowled.

"David and my sister, they've just become engaged."

"Your sister?" Mrs. Harte looked astounded.

"The engagement party's three days hence," said

Anne anxiously. "David wanted to get word to you."

"And couldn't wait, I'll warrant," said Mrs. Harte dryly.

"Well, it wasn't exactly that. It's just that I was planning a Christmas party anyway, so we combined the two. They're very happy. I—I hope they'll have your blessing." Anne looked at her, the worry on her face obvious.

"And why should you think they wouldn't? I've no reputation as an interfering mother. If I were one, I'd have tried to come between Justin and Penelope." Anne gaped at her. "Is there something I'll find to dislike about your sister?"

"No," said Anne sharply. "Sissie's a lovely girl."

"Sissie? Sissie Morehead?"

"Yes, ma'am."

"Ah-ha. By God, I heard that story. Your stepfather, her father."

Anne nodded miserably.

"Well, I've never thought the sins of the fathers should be visited on the children, nor vice versa. You poor girl. The man tried to kill you, isn't that what I heard?"

"Yes, ma'am," said Anne.

"He must have been an evil person indeed. And your sister? How did she take all this?"

"She stood by him," said Anne. "As she should."

"Well, I don't quarrel with that. And so now David's engaged to her, and you think it's love, do you, not sympathy on David's part?"

"He was taken with her last year. You see, I stayed at the Crossed Heart a while after—after I had to leave my stepfather's house."

"Did you?" said Cassandra sharply.

"Yes, and Sissie met David there when she came to visit, and then they met again this fall, after my stepfather—after he—"

"When do they plan to marry?"

"January or February."

"Well, they're giving themselves a bit of time."

"I hope you like Sissie."

"I reckon I will. Why should you think I wouldn't?"

"Because—because Justin doesn't."

"Justin doesn't! Why not?"

"He thinks she's flighty and selfish."

Cassandra laid down her spoon and laughed heartily. "Justin objects to a woman who's flighty and selfish! Well, there's an irony for you. And your sister, *is* she flighty and selfish?"

"She may have been at one time. Now, she's a good girl, and kind, and loving, and she's learning to cook and keep house. I'd started to teach her before I married and left home, and I've taken up where I left off now that she's come to live with me again."

"So you raised your sister, did you?"

"For a time after our mother died. I'm a good deal older than she."

"She must be a babe in arms then," said Cassandra dryly.

"She's eighteen."

"Old enough to marry, certainly, and David, for all he seems a scamp, has a fair head on his shoulders. I doubt he'll make the same mistake Justin did." She finished her stew and set the bowl aside. "So Justin wants to come between them? Well, of course, I'll have to judge your sister for myself, but if she's what David wants, I've no doubt she's what he'll have, and it's none of Justin's business. Even as a boy, he seemed to feel he knew what was right for everyone. You'd think age and trouble would have knocked a bit of that out of him, but it didn't happen with his father either. Mule-headed, both of them."

"Would you care for a piece of pie?" asked Anne, taking David from her breast and putting him in the cradle, lifting Jessica, who was stirring. With the child in one arm, she cut Justin's mother a piece of pie and passed it to her.

"It's a strange thing to see you nursing my granddaughter."

"If you object . . ."

"I don't object. It's just strange. This is a fine pie. I like a woman who can bake. I doubt my daughter-in-law could if her life depended on it. What happened between her and Justin?"

Anne, caught off guard, mumbled inadequately that Justin would have to explain that, and Cassandra eyed her sharply. "I was telling you about the engagement party," Anne rushed on. "I hope you'll stay for it. I know it would make Sissie and David very happy."

"It appears to me that you've got a full house now—three babies, Calliope, your sister, David."

"But David can move into the bunkhouse. Calliope and Jessica share a room. Sissie has her own, and the boys can stay with me."

"Well, you're very hospitable, and I think I will stay the night, but then I'm driving into Fort Worth. I've a mind to find out just what's going on."

"Some things are best left alone," murmured Anne.

"You're wrong there, girl. I set great store by the truth, and I intend to find it, so I'll be off tomorrow morning."

"But Sissie and David—"

"I presume I'll meet the engaged couple tonight, and I'll be back in time to give them my blessing when you have the party. Your Edward's awakening. Shall I hold him while you finish with Jessica?"

Anne couldn't very well object, and she told herself it was ridiculous to fear that Cassandra Harte would recognize the twins as her own kin. Many children had blue eyes. Mrs. Harte had no way of knowing that Pancho's had been a light, light blue, but there was the woman studying young Edward as intently as she had studied his brother, and Edward was staring right back.

It was almost as if the two recognized one another. Anne shivered. What would Justin say to her if he ever found out? He didn't want her; he'd made that clear. Would he try to take back not only the daughter she'd come to love, but her sons as well? Oh God, was there never an end to trouble?

CHAPTER

Twenty-Eight

"Well, Justin, lad," said Oliver Duplessis expansively, "this is a family matter. No need for lawyers." He looked at Henry Barnett, and his forehead fell into bulldog folds. "So Mr. Barnett, why don't you just—"

"Oliver," Justin cut in, "I don't know what Penelope's told you, but our situation has gone way beyond anything that can be settled within the family. I'm afraid the best we can hope for is to contain the scandal. Whatever happens, the marriage is over."

"You want a separation?" asked the man, surprised.

"I want a divorce."

"Divorce is out of the question!" snapped Duplessis.

"In this situation, divorce is the only answer. I want Penelope out of my life."

"I don't think you know who you're dealing with," said the older man ominously. "Why, I could ruin you, boy."

"I seriously doubt it," Justin replied, "but I guess you can try. However, be warned, Oliver. The more trouble you make, the deeper the hole you dig for Penelope."

"What kind of threat is that?"

"A very serious one, Mr. Duplessis," said Henry Barnett, entering the exchange for the first time.

"All the girl wanted was to come home and visit her papa for the holidays. That's hardly—"

"She tried to suffocate Jessica."

There was a minute of stunned silence. "That's nonsense," gasped Penelope's father, a dangerous flush suffusing his face. "That's slander. Don't you dare accuse my daughter of such a monstrous deed!"

"There was a witness. If there hadn't been, she'd have succeeded. Ask yourself why she came here without the baby."

"The child's at the Crossed Heart with Calliope, a perfectly responsible woman. I wouldn't have had her in my house all these years if she weren't. Who's this witness?"

"Calliope," said Justin, "the woman you just described as a responsible member of your household."

Duplessis swallowed hard. "There's some mistake here. Penelope wouldn't do such a thing."

"Penelope wanted to go to Fort Worth. I told her she couldn't because the weather was too harsh for the baby, so she decided to get rid of the baby."

"The devil she—"

"And that's not the end of it, Oliver. While I was taking Jessica to a safe place, it seems Hugh Gresham came to the house and rescued my wife." Justin's voice dripped venom at the work "rescued."

"Well, nothing wrong with that," Oliver stammered defensively. "You had her locked up. You'd hit her."

"Oh, yes, she told Hugh all about it. She just omitted to tell him why. Rollo Tandy and I followed them and found your daughter and Hugh Gresham in bed together at the Bates Hotel in Weatherford."

"You're going to charge her with adultery?" gasped Duplessis.

"I don't want to. I'll never let her see Jessica again, but I can't wipe out the fact that Penelope's her mother, and therefore I have no desire to blacken Penelope's name. I want a nice quiet divorce, but unless you cooperate, I seriously doubt that Penelope's smart enough to realize that it's in her interest as well."

"You say Tandy was with you?"

"He was, and if he has to, he'll testify, graphically, to what he saw, which isn't going to please anyone, including Hugh Gresham. Not that I give a damn about him, but I doubt Hugh'll want to marry Penelope if all this comes out in court."

Oliver sank into the chair behind his desk and stared morosely at an engraved letter holder that had been given him by his late wife. "What happened, Justin? It should have been a good marriage."

"Penelope married me thinking she was going to live in Fort Worth, spending my money and being the queen bee. When she found out being a rancher's wife meant living on a ranch, having babies, and not getting her way all the time, she lost any sense she might ever have had. Now do you want to hear what Henry's worked out, or do you want me to charge her with attempted murder and adultery?"

Oliver sighed. "Let's hear it."

"What I propose, Mr. Duplessis," said Henry, calmly producing his meticulously detailed notes, "is to tell the court that on your daughter's side, the isolation and hardships of ranch life are affecting her health and her happiness to such an extent that the marriage has become insupportable to her. On Justin's side, that she is not temperamentally suited to function as a ranch wife since she neither keeps house nor cooks nor fulfills the usual duties expected of a country woman, and that she has no great fondness for her child."

"Here now, I won't have you say that."

"It's indisputable," snapped Justin. "She tried to kill the baby."

"That she is not suited to motherhood," continued Henry, "and has refused to have further children or, in fact–er–submit to the duties of the—ah—marriage bed, and therefore the marriage is insupportable to Mr. Harte as well as to Mrs. Harte and they wish to dissolve it."

"I might agree if you leave out that business about the children and—"

"She never wanted children. After the first few months she didn't even want to share my bed."

Oliver looked at Justin with great dislike. "What did you do to her?"

"Nothing untoward, I assure you," said Justin coldly. "When I married her, I loved her and took a great deal of trouble with her. Her problem was that she didn't love me. She evidently didn't think anything should be expected of her except that she look good in public."

"I'll agree to Barnett's proposal as long as the business about children and the marriage bed isn't included."

"It has to be," said Justin. "There must be no question that the child stays with me. Penelope is to retain no rights whatever, not even the right to see Jessica."

"As far as the financial arrangements are concerned," said Henry, "Mr. Harte does not wish to continue supporting Mrs. Harte, either during the period of the divorce or afterward. Everything that Mrs. Harte brought to the marriage will remain with her. Any gifts Mr. Harte gave her—clothing, jewels, household furnishings—will be hers, but nothing more."

Oliver scowled. "You're being very cheap about this, Harte."

"Your daughter has spent me blind for two years. She's had her last penny from me. If she makes the mistake of trying to get her hands on my land or cattle or anything that belongs to me except the things I bought for her, I'll crucify her in the courts."

Henry cleared his throat. "I think Mr. Duplessis understands the situation, Justin. You may wish to discuss this with a lawyer, sir. Someone will, of course, have to represent your daughter. I would advise you to choose a person who is extremely discreet and then be brutally frank with him about the reasons for the divorce."

"I don't need your advice, Barnett."

"Indeed not. I'm representing Mr. Harte's interests, which is why I mention these things."

"What Henry's trying to tell you, Oliver, is when you get her a lawyer, don't let her lie to him."

"You're calling my daughter a liar?"

"She's already told both you and Hugh Gresham a pack of lies. She's lied to me endlessly. Maybe you'd like me to tell the court how, when I said I wanted a child, she claimed to have the opinion of a doctor in Weatherford that it was too dangerous for her. That was a lie, and she admitted it when I insisted that we go in to see this doctor. You'd better watch her, or we'll all end up besmirched, and you'll never be able to marry her off."

Henry cleared his throat again. "I do think, gentlemen, that the more amicably this matter can be handled, the better for all concerned. Do you have any questions, Mr. Duplessis? Would you, for instance, care to have sworn statements as to your daughter's adultery and attempted child murder?"

Oliver Duplessis, his scowl in place, his many chins lapping belligerently over his cravat, said, "I'll be in touch with you."

"Without delay," Justin warned. "I want this divorce action instituted within the week."

Oliver glared at him. "You wouldn't have a woman on the side, would you?"

"No, I wouldn't!" snapped Justin.

"Because if you do, Harte, I'll find out about it, and I'll make you wish you never—"

"Now, now, gentlemen, none of that," interposed Henry, who had given Justin a sharp nudge as soon as he demanded a quick divorce. "An acrimonious debate can only hurt all parties concerned, including the child. You might keep in mind, sir, that Jessica Harte is your granddaughter and an innocent party in all this."

"I've never even seen her," muttered Oliver. "What does she look like?"

"Blond-haired, blue-eyed," said Justin. "She's a little beauty, or will be if she survives."

"What does that mean?"

"Have you forgotten? Penelope tried to suffocate her. And she refused to tell us how long she had the pillow on the baby's face. It will be months, maybe years before we know how much damage Penelope did."

Oliver's scowl disappeared, and he looked sick. "Dear God, you think she won't be all right?"

Justin shrugged. "She could die in infancy; she could live to maturity, beautiful but mindless, perhaps not able to do the simplest things for herself."

"I had no idea, Justin," said Henry, aghast.

The three men stared at one another in somber dismay.

"Well, son," said Cassandra Harte, "I've come a long way to find you."

Justin had opened the door to his hotel room expecting to find Henry; his mother's appearance took him by surprise.

"Aren't you going to invite me in?" she asked, kissing him on the cheek.

"Of course." He ushered her to a chair and dropped wearily into another. Now he'd have to turn Jessica over to his mother, and he didn't want to. The baby gave him a tie to Anne that he didn't want to sever.

"I've just come from the Rocking T, Justin, and you needn't look so surprised. I went to see my granddaughter, although neither Rollo nor Mrs. Tighe seem willing to tell me why she is there."

"I—I left her with Anne Tighe because I didn't know where you were. Mrs. Tighe was with us for a few months last year, and Calliope thought that she'd take good care of Jessica until I could find you."

"Have you been looking for me?"

"Well, I had other business first, but I'd have—"

"Which months did Mrs. Tighe stay with you?"

"February and March," Justin replied, wondering why his mother wanted that information.

Cassandra Harte scowled. "That doesn't explain anything. How long have you known her?"

"Why, I—I met her at spring roundup in '76." ·

"Perhaps I should ask how *well* you know her?"

"What are you getting at, Mother?"

"I take it your wife has left you, and evidently with good reason."

"The reasons were all on my side," said Justin harshly, "but then you don't know anything about the situation between Penelope and me."

"I can certainly guess," Cassandra retorted, "since Mrs. Tighe has borne you two sons, about a month, I'd guess, before Penelope had Jessica."

"Mother, who gave you an idea like that? Those children are Pancho Tighe's sons."

"The devil they are! Do you take me for a fool, Justin? You think I wouldn't recognize my own grandsons? Oh, for a time, I suspected that they might be David's, but his relationship to Sissie scotches that idea."

Justin's face had gone deadly pale.

"Those two boys look exactly the way you looked when you were a baby," Cassandra continued. "When I took the first one in my arms, I thought I'd somehow jumped back thirty years in time and was holding you again."

"Mother, you're—you're mistaken." His mind reeled. Could it be true?

"I am *not* mistaken. They were born in August. That means they were conceived in November, which was before she married Mr. Tighe—if she married him. Did you or did you not have relations with Anne Tighe in November?" Cassandra studied her son, who was obviously in shock. "Well, I see you didn't realize you were the father, though how you could be so blind I can't imagine. You can be sure their mother knows who sired them."

"But she never—"

"Told you?" Cassandra snorted. "Carried the burden all by herself, did she? Well, that makes her a remarkable woman, not that I approve of adultery."

"She didn't know I was married," Justin mumbled. "And the idea that they were Tighe's, that was mine." How must Anne have felt when he laid the blame—his blame—for her pregnancy on Pancho Tighe? "My God, the things I said to her." And she'd let him. Why?

"Indeed. Well, evidently Penelope knew. Otherwise, why would she have left you?"

"Penelope knew nothing about it."

"Then why did she run off with Hugh Gresham?"

He dropped his head into his hands. "Dear God, this is a nightmare. Anne's sons—"

"We've straightened that out. I want to know about Penelope."

"I'm divorcing her."

"I see. You're discarding your wife because you've been unfaithful to her. I seriously doubt that the courts will allow you to do that, Justin. A man can divorce a woman for adultery, but as far as I know a woman does not have the same privilege."

"Penelope *has* been unfaithful to me. I found her in

bed with Hugh Gresham, a week ago I guess it was. After I'd left the baby at Anne's."

"I see. Well, I don't approve of what your wife did either, but your actions are worse. Do you really feel justified in divorcing Penelope for the very sin you committed?"

"No, it's the baby. You don't understand about the baby."

"Indeed I don't. I find it very hard to imagine why you would take the child away from her mother and give her to your mistress, for all Mrs. Tighe's very good to her."

"Penelope tried to kill her."

"Penelope tried to kill Anne Tighe? I thought you said she didn't—"

"No, Penelope tried to kill Jessica."

Cassandra Harte stared at him incredulously. "Justin, that's a terrible thing to say, no matter how much you want to discard your wife."

"It has nothing to do with what I want." He explained and added, "Calliope caught her and stopped it, but, Mother, we don't know how much damage she did to the baby."

"Jessica seems all right to me, Justin. Are you sure of this?"

"I'm sure. If you don't believe me, ask Calliope."

"Dear God in heaven, I never liked Penelope, but I never dreamed she was capable of something like this."

"She's selfish to the bone. There's nothing she wouldn't do to get her way. You can be sure, for instance, that she didn't sleep with Hugh out of love. She's providing herself with a second husband, a richer one."

"Perhaps you're right," mused Cassandra, "but I must say, Justin, that you have made a distasteful shambles of your life."

"I'll set it straight," said Justin, "all but poor Jessica. There's nothing I can do for her except wait."

"Aye," said Cassandra. "Well, we must pray for the child. But this divorce? Is it possible? The scandal's going to be terrible."

"Maybe not. Oliver doesn't want to see the whole story come out; I don't; Hugh won't either. Between the three of us, we may be able to control Penelope. Henry's got it all figured out, if we can just make her toe the line long enough to get us through it."

"And then what will you do?"

"I'll marry Anne if she'll have me. Dear God, I can't believe it. She never told me—"

"That she was carrying your child? She must love you a great deal to protect you when she needed protection herself."

"Not long ago she asked me to live with her," said Justin miserably, "and to bring Jessica. She'd have spent the rest of her life with me, without marriage, raised our three children, and I, like a fool, said no. If I hadn't done that, Jessica would be all right."

"She may still be," said his mother, "and perhaps things will work out for the best, but I think, Justin, you should sit down and give your actions some careful scrutiny. Had you been a little less set on having your own way, you might have avoided so much unhappiness. Which brings me to another reason for my visit. Your brother is now engaged to Sissie Morehead."

"The devil!" snapped Justin. "I told him he was a fool if he—"

"That's enough. You leave those two children alone. They're deeply in love, and their engagement will be announced in just a few days. I don't want you interfering. In fact, don't attend the party. It's bad enough that you've left the child with Anne Tighe. If Penelope takes it into her head to resent it, you'll bring more grief on the woman you claim to love, so stay away."

"You approve of this engagement?" Justin asked.

"I do."

"Sissie Morehead is as selfish as Penelope."

"Sissie's young, but she's in no way as self-centered as your wife, and the really great difference, Justin, is that Sissie loves David. Penelope, I doubt, has ever loved anyone, which is something you might have realized had you not been ruled by your senses instead of your brains. Be that as it may, don't try to ruin your brother's life because you've mismanaged your own so badly."

Then because her son looked so disheartened, she added, "It's not that I don't wish you well, Justin. I do, and I love you dearly, but a modicum of humility on your part wouldn't be amiss. Now get on with your divorce, and for God's sake, try to do it as discreetly as possible. There are a number of people who can be hurt by your actions as well as yourself and Penelope. Give a little if you have to," she advised.

"Give? She's had enough from me. I'll give her nothing."

Cassandra sighed. "How like you. Maybe what drew you to Penelope in the first place was a common streak of vindictiveness." She rose and pulled on her gloves. "Well, I'm going back to celebrate the engagement of my younger son and enjoy my three grandchildren. If you ever plan to do the same, you'll have to start showing a good deal more sense and a good deal less arrogance."

Anne's heart lifted. It was a wonderful party, and David and Sissie radiated happiness. Their wedding was set for late January, and her house was full of friends and neighbors come to celebrate their joy. Mrs. Harte had returned and made the announcement herself, giving them her blessing. Justin had not come. Anne sighed. Well, what could she expect? He didn't approve of the engagement, and he had turned away from her entirely since she had asked him to forsake Penelope and come to live with her. Anne swallowed hard and gave a bright smile to Major Bannerman who had complimented her roast antelope.

"Anne, I wonder if I might have a minute with you?"

She glanced away from the dancers to Henry Barnett, who had appeared at her side. "Why, Henry," she said, laughing, "do you want to dance?"

"No, I'm afraid that wasn't my intention."

"Then you must think me forward indeed."

"Not at all. I'd be most flattered if you asked me to dance, Anne."

"Well, I suppose it's some legal business you have in mind. Come along and let me get you some refreshment. We'll slip off into a corner, and you can tell me about deeds and profit splits and such." She presented him with a cup of hot mulled cider and led him to a chair. "Is the colonel's will all settled? I'd hoped to have Sissie's inheritance straightened out before she and David marry."

"No fear there. Another week should do it," he murmured, "but that wasn't why I wanted to talk to you."

"Oh, what then?" asked Anne curiously.

"Is Justin Harte's daughter still with you?"

"Why, yes," she said, surprised. "She is."

"Anne," said Henry, "I've noticed that Mrs. Harte is here as well. I think you should let her take the child."

"Why?" asked Anne, bristling. "Little Jessica's happy."

"You don't know the circumstances in which her mother and father find themselves."

Anne looked into Henry's eyes anxiously. "No, I don't suppose I do, not entirely, but the baby's welcome here. In fact, I love her dearly."

"Even so, Anne, it would be better for you if Mrs. Harte took her away."

"How can that be?"

"Because . . ." He frowned. "I shouldn't be telling you this since I'm Justin's lawyer, but as he hasn't seen fit to protect you, I feel that I must."

"Protect me from what?" asked Anne, fear beginning to rise in her heart.

"You must not repeat this."

"Very well, you can trust me."

"I know I can. They are now . . ." Henry considered how much, in good conscience, he could say. "They are formally separated at present."

Anne's lips parted in a gasp, and her eyes shone with hope. If Justin was not going back to his wife, maybe there was yet a chance for her and Justin.

"And though I hope it will not be so, it could become a very ugly situation indeed."

"He's going to use what she did to the baby?"

"You know about that?"

Anne nodded.

"They have other problems as well."

"But what has that to do with me?"

"He's left her child with you. What if Penelope decides she wants Jessica back? She might well turn on you. What if, say, she decided to accuse you and Justin of adultery?"

Anne's eyes closed.

"You can see that the baby being here might add credence to such an accusation."

"No, I can't. The baby's here because Justin feared for her life."

"All the same, the baby would be just as safe with Mrs. Harte, and then you too would be safe."

"But I love her," cried Anne.

"Ah, Anne," Henry sighed, "I was afraid of that. And do you love Justin as well?"

Anne turned her face away. "What possible difference could that make?"

"You know it could make a difference. Penelope is an unscrupulous and vindictive woman."

"There's no reason that I should be brought into their marital quarrels. I knew nothing about their separation until you told me." Why hadn't Justin told her? Anne's heart plummeted because she knew the answer. "If Justin were in love with me, I'd be the first one to know, wouldn't I?"

"Still, if Penelope decides that it's you who's a threat to her—"

"Oh, she dislikes me, if that's what you mean. She kicked me out of her house last spring, but not because she thought I was a danger to her marriage," said Anne bitterly.

"Who can tell what a woman like that thinks? I hope you'll give some thought to what I've told you. It truly would be best if you gave the baby to her grandmother."

Anne felt as if her heart would break. Justin had left Penelope, and he hadn't even mentioned it, and now Henry thought she should give up Jessica as well.

"Anne, don't look like that," said Henry.

"How am I supposed to look?" she asked sharply. "I've lost two husbands; my stepfather tried to kill me; my sister's about to leave my home, not that I begrudge her her happiness; I've just been warned that I may be publicly accused of adultery; and now I'm asked to give up a baby I've come to love."

"You still have your sons, Anne."

"Yes, my sons." Justin's sons, she thought, but even when he was free, it looked as if he would never claim them or her. Well, she wasn't going to give up Jessica without a fight. If Cassandra Harte suggested taking the child away, Anne would argue—beg—do whatever it took to keep Justin's daughter.

CHAPTER

Twenty-Nine

"I'll have tea and some of those little iced cakes," Penelope said to the waitress.

When the girl queried Justin, he replied brusquely, "Nothing. I won't be here that long."

Then he turned back to his wife, who was looking more beautiful, if possible, than when he'd married her. She had on a lilac gown that complimented her blond hair and blue eyes. He noticed wryly that it had the long, fitted lines from shoulder to hip that had once caused a tantrum when the dressmaker told her a pregnant woman couldn't wear a gown of that cut. "Why is it you wanted to see me, Penelope?" he asked. "I'd have thought any remaining questions between us could be handled by the lawyers."

"Oh, I'm sure you thought that, Justin." She gave him a sweet smile, a smile which he now realized covered a world of malice. "The problem, you see, is that I didn't agree to this arrangement you and Papa came up with."

"What are your objections? I find it hard to believe that you'd want to stop the divorce."

"I don't. What I do want is my share."

"Ah."

"Half at least," said Penelope.

"Half of what? The ranch? The cattle? You've never shown any interest in them before."

"Well, I'll take those if I have to, but I'd really prefer money, and I'm sure you have lots of it. Although that could change, couldn't it? I'm told that you can't dispose of any holdings until the divorce is final, which must put a crimp in your business affairs. For instance, how will you finance the cattle drives next spring?"

"Very astute, Penelope, although there isn't and never has been as much hard cash as you may have thought. Most of my personal assets are in what we call real property, and I don't intend to give you any of it—not a cow, not an inch of land. Surely, that was made clear to you. What you'll come away with in this divorce is what you came in with and what I gave you in the interim, nothing else."

"Well, you're wrong, Justin, because you see you're either going to give me half of everything, or I'm going to make you very sorry, and then I'm still going to get half."

"How? Since most of my dealings are in concert with my brothers, the threat to tie up my assets is empty. They can act for me, so our legal troubles, yours and mine, won't have any significant effect on me."

"Maybe, but, Justin, I'm also going to demand custody of your darling little Jessica, and everyone knows that mothers get the children, especially girl children, and very especially babies."

"Not mothers who tried to kill those children," said Justin dryly.

"No one will take that accusation seriously," she cried, her voice shrill. "Who's going to believe Calliope!"

"Everyone who saw the way you acted while you were carrying the baby and after she was born. All the hands, and they're not black," he hissed. "Truth to tell, Penelope, your maid probably commands more respect and affection in the community than you do."

His wife flushed, and the hate leapt into her eyes, but she took a deep breath, smiled again, and said, "If you really believe what Calliope said, you can't afford to take the chance that I might get charge of Jessica. My goodness, what sort of father would refuse a little money in exchange for the safety of his daughter?"

"It won't work, Penelope. I'll see you in jail before I'll let you squeeze one more thing out of me, including my daughter. And once you've been in jail for a year, the law says I can get the divorce anyway."

Penelope's musical laugh rang out. "You're living in a fool's paradise, Justin. Do you really think any jury of men would send *me* to jail? Good afternoon, Mrs. Appleby."

"Penelope dear, you're looking lovely," said the older woman, who was passing their table. "Justin." She nodded to him as well.

"You see. Even censorious old witches like Mrs. Appleby think I'm a lovely girl."

"She won't for very long if all this comes out in court," said Justin.

Penelope frowned at him. "And then there's one other thing. I found out what you did with Jessica. You took her to that slut Anne McAuliffe, so I'll tell you what else I'm going to do, Justin. I'm going to bring suit against you for adultery. How do you like that? Naming Anne McAuliffe. I'll say those two babies are yours, not Pancho Tighe's, that you were friendly with her for ever so long."

Penelope looked very pleased with herself. "I remember how shocked she was when she met me at the wedding. Of course, I know she was just jealous because my gown was so much prettier than hers, but I'll *say* she was your mistress, and you hadn't bothered to tell her you were married. It could have happened that way, not that it matters. All I have to do is say it did in court."

She bit delicately into a tea cake and smiled at him. "Think how terrible it will sound when I tell them you brought your mistress out to the ranch when I was with child and she was too, but trying to keep it a secret. That whole business about being secretly married to Pancho Tighe—nobody's going to believe that after I testify." Penelope's laughter was absolutely gleeful. "I'll ruin her reputation and yours, and then I'll get my divorce and everything else I want."

Justin controlled his expression with difficulty. How ironic that Penelope should have hit upon the truth, and God knows, it did sound damning, even though she didn't believe the story herself and was proposing to tell, under oath, what she considered to be a pack of lies.

"So you see, Justin, you either agree to my terms, or you'll lose your daughter, and you'll ruin your own reputation and the reputation of the estimable Mrs. Tighe."

"I'm afraid you've beaten me," said Justin.

Triumph flashed across her face.

"I'll have to take you back."

"What are you talking about?" she demanded, setting down her tea cup so abruptly that the hot liquid splashed into the saucer. "I'm not going back to you. I might marry Hugh Gresham though," she added calculatingly. "He's ever so rich now. With your money and his, I'll—"

"You'll have no choice, Penelope. Your plans insure that there'll be no divorce."

"What does that mean?"

"I don't know what lawyer you went to, but obviously you didn't bother to tell him about yourself and Hugh. If you had, he'd have told you that if both parties are guilty of infidelity, the state will not give them a divorce. That being the case, Penelope, you and I will be tied to one another for the rest of our lives."

Justin eyed her vindictively. "So, of course, I'll have to pack you up and move you out to the frontier. You, my dear Penelope, will never see another city or dressmaker or store or ball or afternoon tea with iced cakes of the sort you're now eating for the rest of your life. Do you remember when I told you I'd take you to Mitchell County and install you in a dugout? Well, that, my dear, is where we're going if I have to live with you."

His eyes were narrow and triumphant. "How will you like that? A baby every year. Of course, I realize I can't let you bring them up, but my brothers will marry. They can raise my children, and I can visit them while you're carrying the next one out there on the frontier. And this time, Penelope," he promised, leaning forward threateningly, "you'll learn to be a good wife to me, or I'll damn well beat you."

As he talked in a low, harsh voice, Penelope's face turned whiter and whiter. "I'll never agree to this."

"You'll have no choice. Now you go to your lawyer, or whoever told you you could hold me up for money, and tell him what I said. And this time you'd better tell him the truth about yourself, lady, because if we go to court on anything but the polite things that were agreed upon earlier, all this is going to come out. You'll either end up in jail or in Mitchell County." He clenched both fists on the table. "Given your disposition, I think you might prefer jail. Oh, and, Penelope, I'll want an answer from you by the end of the week. Don't think you can put off unpleasantness this time. My earlier offer expires in three days."

As he rose, the waiter came hurrying over. "Sir, did you want the bill?"

"I had nothing to eat or drink. Present the bill to Mrs. Harte."

He strode out and down the street, heading for Hell's Half Acre and as much whiskey as he could pour into himself in the next hour or two. Was she fool enough to think she could get away with what she threatened? he wondered. Stupid and greedy, that was his wife. She just might try, and if she persisted, he'd have to give in or at least compromise. He couldn't let Anne and his sons be dragged into this, and he couldn't risk his daughter's life.

Justin stalked through the swinging doors and leaned against the bar, weak with anger and worry. How pleased Penelope would be if she knew how badly she'd shaken him, how close she'd come to the truth when she wasn't even looking for it.

"Whiskey," he said to the bartender, and took a long drink when he got the glass. It burned down his throat into his gut, and his fists uncurled. In truth, he should go see Henry, but for once in his life, he didn't want to do the sensible thing. He wanted to get so drunk that he drowned it all, washed it away in whiskey.

David found him there several hours later well on his way to the oblivion he craved. David too signalled for a drink and then turned to Justin and said, "You couldn't even come to my engagement party, could you? Couldn't even wish me well."

Justin turned blank eyes on his brother, and David stared in astonishment. "How long have you been drinking, Justin?"

Justin shrugged and looked back into his glass. "Not long enough," he muttered.

"What's happened?"

"You don't want to hear about it, and as for your engagement, I do wish you well, David. I can't say that I recommend marriage, but I pray God that yours works out better than mine. Maybe there's something in Sissie I haven't seen." His words were slurred and hardly audible. "God knows, I'm no judge of women. I've only loved one, and she's too good for me." He pushed the glass away and dropped his head into his hands.

"Justin, where are you staying?" asked David. "I'll take you back."

"No, let's have another drink," said Justin.

"All right. We'll get a bottle and tie one on together, but not in public."

"Good idea," muttered Justin and heaved himself straight, his face weary, his eyes blurred.

David walked him back to the hotel, then pushed him into bed, thinking that whatever had happened to Justin must be unimaginably bad, and he intended to find out what it was.

Justin slept twelve hours and awoke with what David took to be an excruciating headache. In that weakened condition, David got the whole story out of him, everything except the fact that Penelope's accusations against Justin and Anne were true rather than the lies she herself thought them to be.

"Dear God," muttered David when he'd heard it all, "that woman's a first-class bitch."

"No argument there," Justin agreed. His face looked gray, and David urged more toast and coffee on him.

"There's another problem that you may not even be aware of."

"What's that? I don't know whether I can face another one."

"It's Anne."

Justin straightened, instantly alert. "Is she ill?"

"No, no, but why the hell did you ever take your daughter to her?"

"I know," groaned Justin. "By taking Jessica there, I've exposed Anne to Penelope's viciousness."

"I wasn't thinking of that," said David. "The problem is that Anne loves her. Did you know she's nursing Jessica?"

Justin felt his heart turn over.

"It's going to break her heart when you take that baby away. I don't mean to add to your burdens, brother, but it worries me. Anne's had so much heartbreak, and then this too."

He stopped because he couldn't interpret the look on his brother's face, but what Justin felt was hope, because no matter what happened, he and Anne and their children were going to be a family. Whatever he had to do, he'd accomplish it. Maybe he couldn't promise her anything today, but tomorrow or sometime soon, he'd free himself of Penelope, and he and Anne would be together. He took her attachment to Jessica as a sign that it was meant to be.

"David," he said, "I'm not going to let Anne get hurt."

"I don't see how you can help it."

"Trust me. I won't. And as for Sissie, I wish you both happiness, and I'll go out myself to tell her."

All through the long ride from Fort Worth to the Rocking T, Justin thought about Anne and the children. For the first time he could hold those boys and know that they were his own. He could hold his daughter again, knowing that Anne loved her. The only thing he couldn't do was hold Anne and tell her that if all went well, they could be together. He would have to keep silent. If he were to admit what was actually happening in Fort Worth, he'd also have to reveal Penelope's threats, and he didn't want to cause Anne more anxiety. He wanted to come to her, a free man, and offer her marriage. So he'd keep silent and pretend that the only reason he was at the Rocking T was to make his peace with Sissie.

Well, he could offer to pay for the wedding. Yes, that would be a good thing to do. If Sissie wanted to, she could have the most beautiful gown she could find and invite everyone in the state of Texas, and he'd pay for it. He did want David and Sissie to be happy, and maybe

David was right. Maybe Sissie would make him a good wife.

The sight of Justin in her doorway threw Anne into confusion. Hopes and fears chased through her mind one after another. Had he come to stop Sissie's wedding? Or to take Jessica away? Or to tell her that he was trying to separate once and for all from Penelope and that there might be a future for them? No, it couldn't be that, she decided. He didn't look joyous. He looked serious, thinner, harassed. Well, Penelope was probably giving him a hard time. She always had, probably always would as long as she had a hold on him. And Anne had to resign herself to the painful conclusion that basically what Justin had felt for her was lust, and when he spoke of love, he had spoken of what his body felt, not his heart.

She dropped her eyes from his and turned back toward the hearth, asking softly, trying to keep the resentment from her voice, "What have you come for, Justin?"

"I . . ." He looked hungrily at her slim figure, her bright hair, the child in her arms. "I came to see Sissie," he said reluctantly, "to tell her she and David have my blessing."

"Well, that's a change. And it will make her very happy," she added hastily, not wanting to hurt Sissie's chances of a good relationship with David's family just because she was still pining for Justin.

"Could I hold the baby," he asked, "while you get Sissie?"

"This isn't Jessica," she replied.

"I know. It's Edward, isn't it?"

He held out his arms, and she, surprised, passed the child to him. "We call him Ned now, but how did you know which one—"

"The eyes. They're shaped a little different from David's."

Anne felt almost dizzy with shock. She had thought she was the only one who could tell the boys apart, and yet Justin could too. The two of them stared at one another and she thought, *Oh, please, Justin, tell me that you're leaving Penelope and that you want me.*

Justin looked away, leaned down to kiss the child's cheek, and her heart contracted painfully. It was almost as if he knew Ned was his son.

"I'll get Sissie," Anne said and hurried off before he noticed the tears welling in her eyes. She had to throw on a cloak and go out to the wash house to find her sister who was working there beside Calliope. With three babies in the house, the washing was endless; the fires seldom went out under the pots.

"Come along, Sissie," she said. "Justin's here to make his peace with you. I'll stay and finish up while you talk to him."

"Oh, no, Miss Anne. You go on back, too," Calliope insisted. "Mistah Justin, he'll wanna hear all about Miss Jessica, an' who bettah to tell him than you."

Anne felt a stab of fear. "Do you think he's come to take her?"

"Be a fool if he did," said Calliope, "an' Ah'll tell him so. Don't you fear. That lil one's thrivin' here, like she nevah did at home. In fact, Ah'll go tell him right now."

Calliope dried her hands on her apron and stamped out of the wash house, leaving the two sisters staring at one another in astonishment. They hurried after her in time to hear her say, "Now, Mistah Justin, if you thinkin' a takin' Miss Jessica away, Ah'd think twice. Miss Anne's doin' real good with her. You ain't gonna find no one in the whole wide world who do bettah by that baby than Miss Anne."

"Calliope, I wasn't—"

"Feedin' her on her own milk, Miss Anne is." Anne turned bright red. "An' the child's thrivin'. All you has to do is look."

"Calliope, I'm not—"

"See heah." Calliope lifted the little girl from her cradle. "Looks bettah, don't she? Looks two, three times bettah. Looks happier too. Heah she gits love an' cuddlin', so Mishah Justin, you just bettah think agin—"

"Calliope, I'm not here to—"

"Before you go takin' her away. This heah's where this child belongs. We even beginnin' to hope Miss Penelope din' do her no damage, tryin' to kill her like she done."

Sissie, who had never heard the story, gasped.

"Seems like she comin' along the way she should. Wouldn't you say, Miss Anne?" Anne nodded. "Heah, you hold her." Calliope thrust the baby at Anne. "She loves you the best."

Anne saw the hurt flash across Justin's face as Jessica wiggled and cooed in her arms. "Wouldn't you like to hold her?" She offered the baby to him, and he, confused, looked down at Edward in his arms. "Sissie, take Ned," said Anne.

Hesitantly, looking as if she were afraid he might attack her, Sissie approached Justin and took the little boy, who immediately plunged a tiny fist into her hair and pulled it down around her shoulders. Sissie started to giggle. "Why does he always do that, Anne?"

"Why, because it makes you giggle, Sissie, and then he giggles, and—well, you know how it goes."

Justin watched the two sisters smiling at one another and wondered how he could have thought Sissie like his wife. Anne had turned to pick up David, who had been chewing his fist and kicking his feet in a little fenced-off affair they had for the babies.

"It looks to me," said Justin softly, "as if someone's always holding one of these babies."

"It's good for them," said Anne defensively. "They need to know they're loved."

"That's right," said Calliope. "Only have to look at

yo own girl to see that. When Miss Penelope din' wan'
no one pickin' her up, she was always a sad, skinny lil
thing. Now she's fat an' happy, gittin' lots a love an'
good mothah's milk." Anne gave Calliope a quelling
look, and the woman stopped talking.

"Anne," said Justin softly, "I owe you a debt I can
never repay."

Anne turned her head, thinking bitterly that the only
repayment she wanted from him was love, and she
obviously wasn't going to get it. He didn't even want
her to know he was separated from Penelope. He
probably thought if she knew, she'd pressure him to
come and live with her. "Well," said Anne coldly, "you
wanted to talk to Sissie."

"Yes," said Justin. "Sissie, I've come to wish you and
David every happiness."

Sissie smiled shyly.

"I'm going to stand up for David at the wedding,
which he tells me is the end of January."

Sissie nodded.

"And I wanted to offer . . . well, I'd like to buy your
wedding dress and pay for the wedding."

"I'm taking care of the wedding, Justin," said Anne.
"That's the responsibility of the bride's family, as you
well know, and we're quite able to afford it."

"Anne, I didn't mean to insult you. I just thought—"

"I know what you thought. You probably imagine
Sissie wants some elaborate gown and a ceremony like
you and Penelope had." Her eyes narrowed on him
accusingly. "Well, I'm making Sissie's wedding dress.
Do you want Justin to buy you one instead, Sissie?" she
asked, willing her sister to refuse his largess, to prove
that she was not as greedy and vain as his wife.

"Goodness no," said Sissie. "It's very kind of you to
offer, Justin, but Anne's designed my dress herself. It's
going to be so beautiful, and I can always treasure it
because she made it. And in years to come if David and
I have a daughter of our own, she can wear it, too, and

she'll know that it was Anne's work." Sissie's face was glowing. "I do thank you, of course, but we're making all our own preparations—Anne and Calliope and me," she continued proudly. "It's going to be a lovely wedding. Not big or anything like that, just family and close friends, and I'm so glad that you're going to stand up for David. Anne's going to stand up for me and . . ."

Anne's heart sank when she pictured that. She'd have to listen to the wedding ceremony in the company of the man she could never marry. She blinked hard to hold back tears. "So you see, Justin," she said, interrupting Sissie's happy chatter, "we've everything well in hand, though, of course, we thank you for your offer."

"Yes, well . . ."

"Now maybe you'd like to spend time alone with your daughter before you head back to Fort Worth or wherever you're going. Come along, Sissie, we'll take the boys with us to the wash house." They bundled the babies up and left.

Justin watched them go with an aching heart. She had not forgiven him. He looked down into the face of his daughter, who was indeed a chubby, cheerful baby now, happily investigating his beard and then his ear. Bending to kiss her, he wished that Anne had let him hold David, too, had stayed herself to talk and to share their sons with him. God, what if he never won her back?

"Justin," said Hugh Gresham, looking decidedly nervous as Justin entered his office. "About Penelope. I guess you know I've always loved her, and I—well, I shouldn't have done what I did, but after she told me the way you treated her, my God, I couldn't just leave her there."

"Are you planning to marry her after the divorce?"

"Of course. I told you I loved her, and look, I appreciate your willingness to—to keep this discreet."

"I may be willing, but Penelope's not."

"What do you mean?" asked Hugh.

"I mean Penelope's decided that she wants half of my assets. The original agreement was that she keep everything she brought to the marriage and everything I gave her and that I keep my land, cattle, businesses, and so forth."

Hugh nodded. "Sounds fair to me."

"But not to Penelope, so we're back where we started. I'll file on grounds of adultery, naming you as corespondent. Oh, and the longer this drags on, the less chance we have of that bank being established."

"You committed yourself."

"The court won't let me spend a penny of my own until this is all settled."

"Damn," Hugh said. "That's an important deal."

"Tell your future wife," Justin snapped and turned to leave.

He knew his mother would chastise him for this bluff he was running, but he couldn't bring himself to let Penelope win. He had to hope his threats and pressure from Hugh would force her to back down, but she was always so damned sure she'd get her way. He and Penelope might end up convincing a judge they were both adulterers, which they were, and then they'd be stuck with each other. Was he bringing some kind of malign justice down on his own head?

CHAPTER
Thirty

The house was silent. The music and dancing were over, the bride and groom were gone to the Bar M to begin married life, and the guests had finally departed for home. Even Calliope was asleep. Anne looked down into the faces of the babies who were all down for the night now. Soon she'd have to begin weaning them. She knew she hadn't enough milk for three growing children. Already she and Calliope were supplementing their feedings with goat's milk and mashed solids. But they were all strong, plump, and happy, and, somehow, she'd given them what they needed, so the weaning shouldn't be difficult, except for her. She hated to think of losing that closeness when there was so little else in her life now.

Oh, it had been a beautiful wedding, and Sissie the prettiest and happiest of brides, and David the proudest of bridegrooms. And she knew they'd have a good life, and they weren't far away. She was happy for them, but so sad for herself because they had what she'd never have. Justin had been there, of course, standing beside David, so handsome, and radiating a sort of barely leashed impatience. She supposed he was anxious to be gone. She'd felt his eyes on her time and time again, but he'd said nothing. Penelope wasn't with him, so she assumed that they were still separated, but still he'd had no word for Anne, and he had gone with the other guests, leaving his daughter behind, but for how long? Once she'd weaned the baby, Justin would probably take her.

She'd lose Jessica just as she'd lost so many—her father, then her mother, David and Pancho, Justin and Sissie. All of them gone. And the boys, they'd grow up and go away too. Anne swallowed hard and brushed her hand across her eyes. What a terrible thing, to be crying on Sissie's wedding day, and she wouldn't. She had more courage than that. Even if she lost Jessica, she'd have the boys. There were years yet before they'd leave her, years of growing up, growing to be as handsome as their father, growing to be fine men. Maybe they'd want to stay and take over the ranch. She bent to kiss each of the children in turn, softly, so as not to wake them, and then rose and moved silently to the door, her fine black silk skirts whispering across the floor.

Perhaps she'd stop wearing black soon. It seemed to her as if she'd been in mourning forever. People would be surprised, shocked even, but perhaps she'd put away the black clothes, make herself something bright and cheerful, try to face life on her own with a smile. She owed that to her children. She owed it to herself.

Closing the door quietly, she raised her chin and headed across to the other section of the house. There was cleaning to do, all the debris from the wedding feast and party, and she'd sent Calliope to bed because she knew she wouldn't sleep anyway. Well, she'd work. Work was good for the soul. That's what Mama had always said. Poor Mama. If only she'd lived to see Sissie married to such a fine man.

Anne surveyed the room. There hadn't been that many guests really, but, Lord, what a mess! She swept an apron of Sissie's off the peg. It was white and ruffled and pretty. Well, that was a beginning. Anne pulled the neck piece over her head, tied the sash around her waist, although why she should protect this black dress she didn't know since she might never wear it again, not in her new life.

She unbuttoned the cuffs, rolled the sleeves up to her elbows, and started toward the long table with its piles of dishes, and then suddenly she stopped, for Justin had risen from the rocking chair beside the fire. Because it was so high-backed and because she had been so taken up in self-pity and in New Year's resolutions, she hadn't seen him, couldn't imagine what he was doing here now. Anne shivered with apprehension. It must be Jessica. He'd come back to take his daughter away with him. So soon. Anne had thought she'd have the child at least a little longer.

"Justin," she said, her voice trembling.

"Anne, I'm free."

Free? What did he mean? Free? *He'd* always been free. She was the one who'd been tied to him with bonds of love and passion so powerful they'd almost destroyed her life.

"God help me, Anne," he said, "is it too late?"

"Too late for what?" she asked, confused.

"Too late for us."

"Us?" Her eyes went wide; her heart contracted in fear and hope. "You mean you've changed your mind? You're going to live here after all?" He was shaking his head. "Justin, what *do* you mean?" she cried desperately.

"I mean I'm really free, Anne. Penelope and I are divorced."

"Divorced?" Anne couldn't believe it. Oh, such things were possible; she knew that. But if he had managed it, what did it mean to her? That he was free to take his daughter and go home to the Crossed Heart?

"Anne, if you'll have me," said Justin, "I want to marry you."

"Marry." It was only a whisper. Maybe she hadn't said it aloud. Maybe it was a whisper in her mind, that word that she'd never, never thought to hear from Justin, not since Gretchen Bannerman's wedding and her first sight of Penelope. "You want to marry me?" she said, finding her voice at last.

"Of course I do. I've always loved you, and now I can offer you a real life with me, if you'll take it, for you and me and our children."

Anne looked up sharply. He'd said "our children!"

"Anne, I know the boys are mine."

She felt dazed. "How could you know that?"

"My mother only needed one look." He almost smiled. "You can't imagine what she had to say about my intelligence because I didn't figure it out for myself. All this time I've been wondering why I never guessed, because, God knows, I loved them as soon as I saw them. I wanted them to be mine before you ever bore them. Maybe I wouldn't let myself understand how deeply, terribly responsible I was for everything that happened to you."

"Oh, Justin, you can't think that I regret the boys. They're the most wonderful thing in my life, except for you and Jessica. I love her too, you know, as if she were my own."

"I know that, Anne. Now can you love her father?"

"I've always done that. Almost from the first moment I saw you. But Henry said you were separated from Penelope, and when you never told me yourself, I thought—"

"You thought I was deliberately keeping it from you?" She nodded. "That damn Henry. He should have kept his mouth shut until I could tell you myself, until I was free to propose. It was only last week I was sure I wouldn't end up stuck with her or involved in some huge scandal. She wanted to drag you into it, Anne."

"Henry was afraid of that. How did you manage to stop her?"

"I'm not sure I'm the one who did. All of a sudden she gave in. Maybe her father insisted, maybe Hugh Gresham—"

"Hugh Gresham?"

"It's a long ugly story, but it has a happy ending or it will, if you'll have me. Will you marry me, Anne? Let me adopt my sons?" He seemed hesitant until the radiance of her smile showered him with joy.

"Justin, how can you ask? I've already told you I'd live with you openly when we couldn't marry. I'm not likely to refuse an honorable proposal, especially from my sons' father."

Laughing, he swept her into his arms. "Then you will?"

"Anytime you want, anywhere. I'd even move to Mitchell County with you." The two of them began to laugh. Then Anne sobered. "Actually, I wouldn't mind that. Or if you wanted to take up trail driving again, I think that would be wonderful."

"You'd go up the trail to Kansas with me? And three thousand cattle? And three babies?"

"Why not? They'd have a wonderful time. So would I."

"Oh, my love," groaned Justin, "what a life we'll have."

Anne reached up to kiss him, then whispered in his ear, "We're a match, you and I. We'll make more beautiful children and enjoy every minute of the rest of our lives."

Justin threaded his fingers into her glowing curls and tipped her face up to his. "Will you do one more thing for me?"

"Anything," said Anne.

"When we're married, I'd like to choose your wedding gown."

Anne's eyebrows rose. "I wouldn't have thought, after your years with Penelope, that you'd ever want to consider female clothing again."

"Just promise me."

"All right, Justin," she agreed, mystified. "I promise."

"Good. I don't know exactly what it will look like yet, but by God, it won't be black. I'm sick to death of seeing you in mourning for other men."

"Why, Justin," said Anne, "I was just thinking that I might give up my widow's weeds, so we're of the same mind. What color had you thought of for my wedding dress? Red to match my hair?" She gave him a mischievous smile.

"My love, I think you're fiery enough without a red gown. In fact, if I could marry you in just your beautiful skin, I'd do it."

Anne laughed softly. "You did say your divorce is final? Nothing we do now can change it?"

"Nothing," said Justin.

"Then come to bed, love. I'll wear my beautiful skin for you tonight."